JASMINE'S

In Memory
The American Jesuit of Iraq,
Father Merrick SJ

JASMINE'S TORTOISE

A MODERN HISTORY NOVEL OF INTRIGUE
AND ESPIONAGE SET IN BAGHDAD
AND LONDON

✥ ✤ ✥

Corinne Souza

PICNIC

First published in Great Britain 2007 by Picnic Publishing
PO Box 5222
Hove BN52 9LP

Copyright © Corinne Souza

The right of Corinne Souza to be identified as the author of this work has been asserted by her in accordance with the Copyright, Designs & Patents Act, 1988.

A catalogue record for this book is available from the British Library.

ISBN: 9780955610509

Printed and bound in Great Britain by Biddles
Designed by John Schwartz, john@thefrontline.net

All rights reserved. No part of this publication may be reproduced or transmitted in any form or by any means, electronic or mechanical including photocopying, recording or information storage or retrieval system, without the prior permission in writing of the publishers.

This book is sold subject to the condition that it shall not by way of trade or otherwise be lent, resold, hired out, or otherwise circulated without the publishers' prior consent in writing in any form of binding or cover other than that in which it is published and without a similar condition being imposed on the subsequent purchaser.

ACKNOWLEDGEMENTS

My thanks to: AM for her kindness when I first drafted this book; Peter Voss and his wife Antoinette Goodman-Voss when I typed it up; GL and Jane Crossley, for the hours reading it; the Sussex Authors Society for editorial assistance; the Society of Authors for publishing guidance; and John Simmons and Iain Dale for putting me back in touch with John Schwartz who typeset and designed the striking cover.

Special thanks are due to: John Booth who 'bullied' my former boss Arthur Butler into correcting textual political/historical errors – some are deliberate(!); the aforementioned Arthur Butler to whom I owe much more, over nearly thirty years, than I can ever say; Caroline Doornbos and her partner Iain Bailey for determination throughout the publishing process; Josette Sollberger-Heche & her husband Pierre Heche – the former for reading several drafts, the latter for putting up with this, and both for their hospitality in France; AM – again – for her generosity and painstaking care; and Rena Valeh for hour upon hour of assistance – on one occasion working through the night.

Finally, my thanks to Julia de Souza who first visited Iraq in 1949 and shared some of her memories which have found their way into this book, and Richard Moir whose international relations advice has been invaluable. As he says, 'every word is an argument'. My gratitude to him always for his overwhelming support and encouragement.

PROLOGUE

❋ ❋ ❋

General Nico Stollen's textbook *Children & Spies* went to the top of Amazon Books within days of publication. Published by Vivienne Solomon QC, director general of the international ngo the Concert of Rights, it was purchased by many on the basis of his name recognition. Known affectionately in the British press as 'James Bondski', he was one of Moscow's most decorated intelligence officers. He became a global celebrity following the Old Bailey trial of the British arms-dealer Ghazi El-Tarek.

Although Stollen did not attend the court, his heroism resulted in the collapse of the case against the Iraqi-born businessman. The minute reporting restrictions lifted, bemused CIA and MI6 old hands recalled the Muscovite's fabulous leaving party in London a decade earlier. The occasion had been blighted because Britain's then Secretary of State for Defence, Andrew Fitzwilliams, died 'suddenly' the same evening. The politician had been on his way to the American embassy in Grosvenor Square at the time. He left a distraught young widow Jasmine – née Palmeira – a beautiful Anglo-Indian.

Written 40 years before, Nico Stollen's manual was a straightforward operative recruitment guide. What surprised was the image of a wooden tortoise on its dust-jacket. A brief biographical note stated he served in Iraq in the 1960s and in

Britain throughout the 1970s and early 80s. It gave no indication as to why the pretty ornament photographed was significant.

The charm of the tortoise fronting the general's book was in stark contrast to his writing-style. Observing British intelligence officers had similar expertise to the Soviets, he wrote: *Espionage is for adults. Its finest practitioners have a keen interest in grooming children for their work. Accordingly, a spy's relationship with parents – particularly mothers – is crucial. A spy is never sentimental about whom he uses.*

In a later section, under the heading 'The Grammar of Espionage', he explained chillingly: *To do his job, a spy requires an understanding of the 'grammar' of another person's community. Children can facilitate this goal. They are the 'hyphens' of the clandestine world.*

In summer 2002, his book seemed embarrassingly prescient. Its publication followed a claim made by the Defence Secretary's widow Jasmine that as a girl she had been little more than a ping pong ball between a Secret Intelligence Services diplomat called Sir Peter Ligne and General Stollen himself. (The Secret Intelligence Services was better known as MI6. From the mid 1960s to the early 1980s, Peter Ligne had been head of its Iraq desk.)

Pointing out that General Stollen had been based in Baghdad when Peter Ligne was first assigned, Mrs Fitzwilliams stressed the two men knew each other's working methods well. (Stollen had been a colonel in those days.) He and Ligne had been friends of Jasmine's late father Philippe Palmeira who, like herself, had been born in Baghdad.

As Jasmine explained in an interview with the distinguished *Times of India* London correspondent, her Indian grandfather Jiddu established the Mesopotamian branch of the Palmeira family business in the late nineteenth century. Although Jiddu Palmeira cherished his Indian identity, he considered Iraq his home. Like Jasmine's father, he knew Peter Ligne and Nico Stollen. He regarded only one – Stollen – to be his friend.

The *Times of India* was interested in Jasmine's story because its readers fretted for the plight of the Iraqi people, as well as the well-being of the many Indian trading families in the wider area. As importantly, her account added to a cumulative portrait of a historically cosmopolitan, multi-racial and multi-cultural outward-looking global nation: The Palmeiras had countless modern parallels.

Back in London, the cognoscenti inferred the appearance of General Stollen's manuscript apparently in Mrs Fitzwilliams' support, was an example of his colleagues' revenge on Britain for its publication of the *Mitrokhin Archive* three years earlier. (This was the view from Washington too.) Their reasoning rapidly evaporated. The Russian Federation swiftly pointed out that following the horrors of 11 September 2001, it worked with all reputable partners and would not confound one of America's principal allies at this unbearably difficult time.

As importantly, it was aghast at Mrs Fitzwilliams' assertion – as was the recently re-elected New Labour government – that General Stollen and Sir Peter Ligne 'groomed' her. It made clear it had nothing to do with the emergence of General Stollen's book. The preparation of children for espionage, however historical, was not something with which either administration wished their civil servants associated.

(Interestingly, although British officials disowned Sir Peter Ligne, the same could not be said of Nico Stollen's colleagues. His previous associates and their present successors stood by him. 'James Bondski' was a true Soviet patriot. Those with whom the general had served were proud of him.)

Initially thrilled with his unexpected endorsement, it took Jasmine Fitzwilliams a few days to realise she had in fact been outmanoeuvred. Her first intimation of this came when the media identified Stollen's editor as an aristocratic Irish-Bostonian, Father Anthony. The American Jesuit subsequently confirmed the general's manuscript had been passed to him some considerable time before by US Congresswoman Betsy Meredith. Like Nico Stollen and Peter Ligne, Father Anthony had close ties with Iraq – Jiddu Palmeira, a devout Roman Catholic, had been one of his closest associates.

Soon after, Jasmine discovered Stollen's publisher to be Vivienne Solomon. Prior to heading up the Concert of Rights, the eminent barrister had been Ghazi El-Tarek's defence counsel. In addition, her twenty-year old cousin Leah Solomon – along with Peri, the daughter of a Kurdish warlord – had been murdered in 1972 in Abu Ghraib, a filthy sinkhole of a prison outside Baghdad. Father Anthony and Stollen had known both girls and been inconsolable on their deaths.

Jasmine's suspicions were finally confirmed when her English mother Suzie offered the *Times of India* an interview independent of her daughter. Contacting its editor, Suzie Palmeira explained she believed herself to be one of the mothers upon whom Stollen based his manuscript. 'Jasmine is unforgiving because she does not understand what espionage does to people once it gets a hold on them,' she introduced herself.

The editor immediately despatched his best writer – the same one who interviewed Jasmine – to meet Suzie at a venue of her own choosing. To his astonishment she suggested Grand Lodge, the headquarters of Britain's worldwide Masonic fraternity. Recognising his stupefaction, Suzie explained a previous Grand Secretary, Sir Julian Lawrence, had been one of Jiddu Palmeira's oldest friends. At the meeting, she showed the journalist an ornamental wooden tortoise in Grand Lodge's care – the model for General Stollen's book jacket.

As if this was not betrayal of her daughter enough, Suzie invited him to her house the following day to view a series of photographs she was releasing to the media. These were of Jasmine enjoying herself at the races with Ghazi El-Tarek and family, and looking stylish at a 'society' wedding with the wife of the former French ambassador to Iraq, Laure de Chebran. Another set pictured Jasmine in a nightclub with several friends, including city analyst Bobby Lomax.

(Lomax was an acknowledged authority on Lloyd's of London, in particular contracts insured on behalf of the construction giant Fitzwilliams International. Jasmine's late husband Andrew Fitzwilliams inherited the private company when he was in his early twenties.)

The implication could not have been clearer. Suzie Palmeira was saying whatever happened to Jasmine as a child, she made a good recovery. The latter had been beside herself with rage. She had intended her assertion on children and espionage to lead to a wholly separate conclusion: The re-opening of the investigation into her husband's death.

Andrew Fitzwilliams had been the golden boy of British politics. Cut down shortly after the Falklands war, he had been forty-one years old when he died. Tall, blond, elegant, the Defence Secretary had been the delight of constituency stalwart and Tory grandee alike. The minister and his dazzling, much younger wife Jasmine added lustre to the political landscape.

The coroner described the politician's loss as a 'tragic accident'. Jasmine an 'assassination'. Overturning the decision had been her objective for twenty years.

Finally accepting she would be consistently thwarted, Jasmine, so she believed, short-circuited the status quo by seemingly changing her agenda and championing another. She had gone quiet about her husband's fate and approached a new generation of correspondents – who had little recollection of Andrew Fitzwilliams anyway – on a different issue which she declared to be in the public interest: The need for a public inquiry into Britain's involvement of children in espionage. She expected her new-found media exposure to re-ignite interest in herself and therefore in Fitzwilliams.

It was at precisely this moment Vivienne Solomon released General Stollen's textbook onto Amazon, and Suzie Palmeira gave her interview to the *Times of India*. Within a matter of hours, the British government announced an inquiry into *Children & Spies* – the title of General Stollen's book. The ambush of Jasmine Fitzwilliams was complete when the Prime Minister's office released the names of the members of its specially convened two-man Special Hearing: The Lord Miro and Jim Richards MP.

Miro was the founding chairman of Britain's powerful intelligence services oversight committee. (He was elevated to the peerage for this purpose, following the sale of his construction company Douglas Miro International.) Before this, he had been the first black president of the British Board of Infrastructure. Fitzwilliams International – Andrew Fitzwilliams' company – had been one of its member contractors.

At a joint press conference, Miro refused to answer questions, referring the media to Jim Richards MP. The latter, unlike Miro, was a career politician and media-savvy. As the present chair of the intelligence committee, he was happy to declare that General Stollen's former colleagues had given the Special Hearing their full backing. (The Russians had been invited to participate but declined, viewing matters arising as essentially for the British.)

Jim Richards, nearing his fifties, cerebral and fine featured, had a less obvious presence than Miro but was not disadvantaged by this. He handled questions deftly and ducked those he did not like. One of these, which he ignored, referred to his relationship with Mrs Fitzwilliams.

Reporting restrictions then came into operation. As a result, the media was unable to recount Jasmine's complaint that Lord Miro and Jim Richards MP were conflicted.

To nobody's great surprise – certainly not Jasmine's – the Special Hearing concluded the day after it opened. Downing Street issued a brief statement to the effect the government accepted Lord Miro and Jim Richards MP's recommendations.

These were that guidelines pertaining to intelligence officers and their possible influence on children be tightened. The Russian authorities were happy to concur with these findings.

The public was not advised Miro and Jim Richards MP conceded privately Andrew Fitzwilliams had indeed been murdered. Nor that British and Russian officials had agreed further investigation would serve no useful purpose.

It was informed that reporting restrictions would not be lifted.

1965

CHAPTER ONE
�֎ ✺ �֎

BAGHDAD, IRAQ: Night was falling as Jiddu Palmeira's party was driven from the racecourse. Father Anthony, the aristocratic American head of the Jesuit mission, watched them leave with a broad smile. On Sunday in church, he would call out the names of the race-goers from the pulpit. It never failed to boost the collection.

Jiddu – a Roman Catholic scion of an Indian merchant family long settled in what was once known as Mesopotamia – was habitually relieved of most of his winnings this way. It was some consolation Father Anthony was scrupulous in ensuring part of the church funds collected were ploughed back into racing the following week.

'Another successful day?'

Father Anthony started, hearing Colonel Nico Stollen's gently teasing voice. 'Not too bad,' he agreed. 'Although doubtless there will be complaints when I demand more than my tithe!'

He looked at Stollen with affection. It was a matter of deep regret the Russian's winnings were beyond the reach of the Roman Catholic church. Stollen could not be said to be in awe of the Almighty. Nor, come to that, of Father Anthony. For politeness sake, he was called a diplomat.

Jiddu's car had all but disappeared from view. Offering his cigarette case, the Russian remarked, 'The old man was on good form. Still complaining, mind, the Baghdad Races are nothing like as splendid as those he attended in India as a boy!'

The priest nodded, a slight breeze raising the fold of his robes. Declining a Sobranie – he had given up smoking the previous week – he responded, 'He told me he had joined the Communist party.'

'So I gather. He asked the other day whether it was still all the rage in Delhi.'

'And is it?'

Stollen grinned. In his late forties, he was a good-looking man, with heavy features and thick black wavy hair. Blowing a perfect smoke ring, he replied, 'How would I know? My colleagues specialise in India, not I.'

Father Anthony was surprised by the easy admission. Behind him, the race-club lights were switched on. The evening was cool. He was in no hurry to go indoors. Neither, it seemed, was Stollen.

They had taken Jiddu's new affiliation to Communism with a pinch of salt. It had been a sensible precaution now Communists in the Iraq army were running the central government.

Looking sideways at the priest, Stollen murmured, 'Given the old boy is a Roman Catholic, he cannot decide which in your view is worse. Him being a card-holding Communist or a freemason!'

'Being a freemason. Particularly as he is Worshipful Master!'

The freemasons were well-established in Iraq. Generous benefactors of countless charities, they were an acknowledged part of the country's status quo. Jiddu was Worshipful Master of the United Grand Lodge of England's sole branch in Baghdad. Additionally, he was a long-standing personal friend of the freemasons' powerful Grand Secretary in London, Sir Julian Lawrence. Father Anthony, while not liking the friendship, had accepted it with equanimity.

In front, a stable-lad led a string of ponies along the track. The animals were being taken to the north. Further up, parked on the right, were several horse-boxes.

'I hear Jiddu has been in touch with Sir Julian about the Kurdish water supply – and that, as a result, he has written to you?'

The suddenness of the American's question took Stollen by surprise. He raised one heavy black eyebrow. For all his companion's skill, Father Anthony would learn nothing from him he was not happy to disclose.

'You have been misinformed. The Grand Secretary would no doubt like to contact me. However, I have always made clear I am a Soviet first – not a freemason! I only became a Masonic Brother because it was useful to those I am privileged to serve. It is most unlikely therefore I will hear from him about the north of Iraq.'

Father Anthony frowned. 'That's a pity. Jiddu tells me he is relying on you. He is so concerned about the situation in the north, a sample of the water has been passed to a scientist attached to Britain's parliamentary science committee.'

'It probably has. The committee, so far as I can remember from my time in London, was the most prestigious of the Westminster groups. Useless, of course, but nonetheless prestigious.'

A mother and child cantered passed with a groom in attendance. The men guessed the trio were headed for the bedouin encampment, well beyond the race-course. It was a favourite ride. The youngster, on a leading-rein, waved.

'Jiddu and the Grand Secretary believe the British government are intent on betraying the Kurds, to win favours in Baghdad,' continued Father Anthony. 'I understand the senior freemason hopes he will be able to use the science committee's findings to embarrass it.'

Stollen sighed. Naiveté always annoyed him. He disliked being privy to that which he knew would fail. 'Government is never embarrassed. Julian Lawrence, who is not a fool, would be the first to know it.'

Disappointed, Father Anthony moved towards the clubhouse. Stollen followed behind. Now the heat of the day was over, the groundsmen had begun to water the trees. A couple of years younger than the Russian, the Jesuit was slimmer but much the same height. Their shadows on the baked earth complimented each other.

Patting down his fine hair – the sun had bleached it ash blond – Father Anthony asked, 'What sort of man is Julian Lawrence?'

'One of the finest,' came the unhesitating reply.

They heard shouts in the distance. Turning, they saw a tiny form on the ground. The child had fallen off his pony. Dismounting, the servant re-seated him.

Seeing all was well, Father Anthony and Stollen resumed their direction. They often had a drink at the end of the day. 'How did Sir Julian meet Jiddu Palmeira?' asked the Jesuit.

Stollen considered the matter. 'I am not certain. They are secretive, those two. A couple of years ago, Sir Julian saw through the formation of most of the English Lodges in India, into an independent Grand Lodge. I suspect Jiddu fought to keep Baghdad Lodge, which hitherto came under India, attached to London.'

Father Anthony absorbed the information without comment. A few moments later, he queried, 'Why did he initiate you into freemasonry?'

His companion shrugged. 'I never inquired. I assume it was because the Americans, anxious about Communist infiltration in Britain, were interfering too deeply in British affairs. Sir Julian seeks balance in his own way. Probably, he initiated me as a warning shot: When I became a freemason, I was given access to all of London society.'

Father Anthony gave a wry smile. 'I do not doubt it!' Changing the subject, he observed, 'The US political officer at the embassy here is a decent man. I understand he would be happy to discuss the situation in the north of Iraq, if you were willing. He is anxious to help the local people.'

Stollen chuckled. 'As you say, the American political officer is indeed a decent man. However, I am not willing.'

In the distance, the groundsmen switched off the water-sprays leaving the trees glistening, their damp leaves releasing a sweet smell of sap. Although nearly dark, the racetrack could still be seen clearly. Far to the left were the starting gates that some hours earlier had been the scene of such anticipation and excitement. Further on were the stables. Beyond these were Jiddu's collection of old automobiles.

Father Anthony looked at Stollen thoughtfully. They were both fond of Jiddu and the Palmeira family. The Russian had met the old man nearly eight years earlier when he had helped to deliver Jidda's only grand-child, Jasmine. Suzie, the girl's mother, had not made it to the maternity home in time and had gone into labour close to his embassy. As a result, she joked, she had Stollen to thank for the gift of a daughter.

'Tell me, Nico, did you come across Peter Ligne when you were in London?'

Peter Ligne had been identified in the *Iraq Times* as Britain's newly appointed Iraq intelligence head. In a long editorial, the newspaper had also reported the civil servant would visit the country shortly. As a result, local chaikhanas had been more alive than usual with talk of intrigues and conspiracies. The news had been the chatter on the racecourse too. Several had remarked the water problem in the north coincided with Peter Ligne's appointment.

Although surprised by the question, Stollen replied readily enough. 'Certainly, I knew him. And found him amusing company, I must say.'

'You liked him?'

'I was happy to spend time with him.'

'This is not the same thing and well you know it!' Protecting his eyes from a sudden swirl of dust rising off the desert floor, Father Anthony continued, 'Rumour has it, a certain Colonel Nico Stollen assisted the *Iraq Times* with their inquiries . . .'

Stollen smiled. It was fairly common knowledge the week before the article on Peter Ligne appeared in the newspaper, he had presented himself at the British embassy in Baghdad to congratulate Ligne on his new appointment. The British ambassador had not heard of him but, somewhat startled, had thanked Stollen and promised to pass the message to London.

A short while later, Whitehall had confirmed Ligne's status to the ambassador. The following day, the entire diplomatic community had read about it in the *Iraq Times*. 'How did you manage it?'

Stollen had the grace to blush. 'As a member of Royal Arch...'

– Royal Arch was the most prestigious British Masonic order –

Father Anthony groaned. 'The British ambassador is also a freemason?'

Stollen nodded. 'He is in a lesser Lodge than I. It made my task so much easier.'

The priest's eyes widened. 'You mean you pulled Masonic rank on Her Britannic Majesty's ambassador?'

He did not demur.

Father Anthony's joyous whoop could be heard at the far end of the racecourse. 'Nico, you are priceless. Absolutely priceless.'

Placing an arm around his shoulders, he steered him towards the clubhouse. Stollen made no objection. He cared for the Jesuit's friendship if not for his good opinion.

'Ligne, I assume, is also a mason?'

Stollen shook his head. 'Not that I am aware of, no. Apparently, freemasonry is too middle class for him. He probably meant it is run by aristocrats, which he is not. Besides, to be a mason, you have to believe in God. Ligne, so far as I can recall, was not a believer.'

'And you are, my friend?'

Stollen was not to be so easily caught out. 'I have always

thought it necessary to put as much distance as I can between myself and the Almighty. You, of all people, should know this.'

Once inside the clubhouse they made their way up the stairs into a cool timbered long room. At the bar, Father Anthony ordered whiskies, knowing Stollen would pick up the bill. The latter had assured him Soviet spies were keen on Bostonian priests and would be happy to pay for his tipple. He had ordered doubles ever since.

Stollen made his way over to the window and settled himself into a comfortable whicker chair. The clubhouse was almost empty at this time of day, although a couple of elderly patrons lingered over British newspapers up to three months out of date. These were shipped from Britain in bound volumes, along with heavy tomes of *Punch*.

As Father Anthony drew up a chair, the Russian mused, 'My ambassador's garden has been looted again. The lemon tree this time. It might, of course, be coincidence, but I understand Jiddu wrote to Grand Lodge in London about the care of such plants if uprooted. It is said the Grand Secretary wrote back with copious notes. You know how often he and Jiddu exchange gardening advice.'

A faint rosyness suffused Father Anthony's face. He was already aware that earlier in the day, Jasmine had painstakingly explained to Stollen how she had helped him and Jiddu plant a lemon tree in the shade of the mission church.

'What's more, I understand from the Americans their lemon tree has disappeared too. They are very upset,' continued Stollen.

'They would be.'

A little sheepish, the Jesuit moved his chair closer to the window. From where he was sitting, he could see the race-course, the sand now almost obliterating its markings. Beyond that, the desert. The boy brought their drinks a few moments later.

'Jiddu is worried, Nico,' he said when the youth had gone. 'He believes Peter Ligne will try to recruit his son Philippe. They were at Oxford together.'

'He probably will,' agreed Stollen. 'Philippe Palmeira is bound to interest Ligne given how well placed he is. In addition, Jasmine needs a passport. Philippe's Indian papers are not recognised by the British and Suzie cannot pass on her nationality. Every man has his price. Palmeira's could be a passport for his daughter.'

Father Anthony's eyes moistened. 'Jiddu believes Ligne's interest in his son will encourage you to involve the family in politics too. He begs you to leave them alone.'

Stollen made no attempt to avoid the priest's anxious gaze. His job was to involve others. And betray them if necessary. Even those to whom he was profoundly attached.

'I delivered Jasmine – I am bound to be concerned with the Palmeira family,' he murmured.

'And I baptised her!'

'Calm yourself, Father,' he tried to soothe. 'You have nothing to fear. I will not harm them.'

Draining his whisky, Father Anthony retorted, 'Your job, my friend, is to harm. You will destroy them,'

'You are mistaken. It is others who will destroy them – not I.'

CHAPTER TWO

※ ❀ ※

The night was bright with stars as Jiddu's driver Hussein pointed the car in the direction of the desert road. Hugging the race track for a quarter of a mile or so, the man expertly negotiated the rise and steered the car safely on to the tarmac.

He wore a long white Arab robe and traditional headgear. His employer, wearing western clothing, sat beside him, his grand-daughter Jasmine asleep in his lap.

'It's about time this road was fixed,' Jiddu complained.

Hussein saw no reason to respond. All were agreed the route needed considerable improvement. Behind them sat their racing companions, Abdullah El-Tarek and Samuel Solomon. Cuddled up between was Samuel's youngest daughter, Leah. At thirteen, five years older than Jasmine, she was a beautiful girl with dark eyes and black hair.

Abdullah El-Tarek, the jovial head of a large Sunni family, was the country's chief veterinarian. Samuel Solomon was a prominent member of what remained of the Baghdadi Jewish community, its brilliance decimated since the late 1940s.

Abdullah El-Tarek broke the silence. Addressing Jiddu, his voice erupting in the darkness, he said, 'Eh, Abu Philippe . . .'

– 'Abu' meant 'Father of' in Arabic –

'. . . Thank you for the lemon tree. Um Ghazi will be delighted. As you know, she is a passionate gardener.'

'Um' meant 'Mother of'. Ghazi was the couple's only son.

Jiddu grinned. He prided himself on pilfering only the best of plants for his friends. These were stolen exclusively from the embassies of the super powers. Hussein, who acted as getaway-driver, knew all the embassy gardeners. These habitually alerted him as to the quality of what was available.

They were on the main highway now. The lights of Baghdad city could be seen in the distance. It was a beautiful sight. 'What's the latest about your girls?' queried Jiddu, turning around.

Samuel, to whom the question was addressed, shrugged. The plight of the Iraqi Jews was dire. In view of the deteriorating political situation, he had hoped to send his children to his widowed sister-in-law in London. She had a daughter Vivienne, who was Leah's age.

'Bad news, I'm afraid,' he replied, fingering the yellow identity papers in his pocket the Iraq government forced him to carry. 'The girls are British Overseas Passport Holders. Regrettably, this gives them no right of abode in Britain. It is a terrible disappointment . . .'

Jiddu sighed. Jasmine was in a similar position to Samuel's daughters although for the moment she could travel on Suzie's passport. On this basis the child was to be sent to school in England in a few months time.

'. . . Now I have applied for visas so they can go to America. Henri Sale-Gonfleur says he has approached the appropriate authorities and is doing his best.'

Henri Sale-Gonfleur, plump and pop-eyed, was one of countless European delegates living in Baghdad. As everybody knew, his best would be expensive. The price of American travel documentation was going up all the time.

Abdullah El-Tarek listened to his friends despondently. He regarded all Iraq's people as his own and was embarrassed by their circumstances. Leaning across Leah, he patted her father with affection. 'The situation will improve. You'll see.'

Samuel sighed but made no response. Abdullah had little to fear because he was a well-connected Sunni with two cousins – one a Shia – in the government, as ministers for defence and protocol. However, they all knew conditions were getting worse.

The Jews were suffering the most. In the hope of ameliorating his position, Samuel had decided to follow Jiddu's lead and become a Communist. He was profoundly aware each day he delayed, his family's circumstances grew more precarious.

However, he could not join the Party until he had sent the girls to safety. The Americans would not consider youngsters with Communist fathers. This had been the reply from the British too – he had made the mistake of being honest in his application.

In front, Jiddu bit his lip. They all had problems with their children. Even Abdullah. Not that Abdullah had any inkling of what his son had been up to. Wishing it had not fallen to him to break the news, he shifted his sturdy frame and queried, 'How is Ghazi getting along?'

In the darkness, Samuel raised an eyebrow. He had wondered whether Jiddu was going to raise matters. The latter had told him earlier in the day, the Masonic Grand Secretary in London, Sir Julian Lawrence, had written about the young man.

Blissfully unaware of the reason behind the question, Abdullah turned his face heavenwards. 'Do you think Ghazi tells me? I am just his father. All I am required to do is send money. His mother is going to Paris again soon to take my horses to Chantilly when no doubt he will be on his best behaviour, but neither one nor the other will tell me about his studies.'

Jiddu laughed. 'Philippe was as bad. They're all the same. How old is Ghazi now?'

'Twenty-three, Allah be praised. Time he came home. What good is all this learning if it is for the benefit of others? This dear country of ours needs its educated young people.'

Abdullah's companions made no comment. Ghazi's return had been eagerly awaited by his parents for so long, they had all but given up. It was quietly understood he spent much of his time on a race-course.

'We are hoping Ghazi will marry one of his cousins,' his father continued. 'His mother will discuss it with him when she is in France. This will bring him back to Baghdad. It is good that he settles down, no? A wife will make a man of him.'

Despite himself, Jiddu chuckled. He had assumed his son would marry one of his cousins too. Instead, Philippe had brought home Suzie, his English bride.

He glanced down at his grand-daughter's face. Knowing the time he had left with her was limited, he coveted every minute she was with him. Even when sleep claimed her.

'Meantime,' Abdullah prattled on, 'I have stopped Ghazi's allowance. I made him too comfortable in France. That's why he's stayed overseas for so long. Of course, his mother is cross with me. She thinks the boy will starve! This is why he has asked her to visit him. I have told her to take a firm line. No money until he comes home!'

He folded his arms across his ample belly waiting for the others to speak. Their answering silence was almost deafening. In the dark of the car, his merry smile evaporated. Perplexed, he leaned forward, tapping Jiddu on the shoulder. 'What's this, my Brother? Something I should know?'

Jiddu made no immediate answer.

'Come effendi you are silent? What is the problem?' The surprise, bordering on hurt, in his voice was unmistakable. 'If the lad has done something wrong, I apologise. Let me put things right.'

Jiddu's face, illuminated by the headlights of an oncoming car, was taut. 'Yes,' he agreed, 'There is a bit of trouble. Two of our Kurdish Masonic Brothers saw Ghazi in London . . .'

'In London! What was he doing there?'

Jiddu ignored the question. It would become all too apparent soon enough. ' . . . He offered to supply them with handguns.'

Abdullah started. 'Handguns! What nonsense. Ghazi is a student. There must be some mistake.'

'No, my friend, there has been no mistake.'

Abdullah shook his head vigorously. 'Of course there has. Someone has been spreading lies about him. Handguns? Whatever next. He is doing post-doctoral studies in Paris . . .'

'For safety's sake, the Kurdish Brothers complained to the Grand Secretary, Sir Julian Lawrence.'

'Then they are liars! Which Kurdish Brothers?'

'The Warlord was one. He had taken Sir Julian a sample of the Kurdish water supply.'

Grief swept across Abdullah's face. The Warlord was one of his oldest friends. He had looked after his bloodstock ever since

[24]

he had qualified as a vet. It was the Warlord's ponies Father Anthony and Stollen had witnessed being loaded into horseboxes. The Warlord would never lie about Ghazi.

He slumped in his seat. If the Warlord had made a formal complaint, then matters were indeed serious. Particularly in view of other sensitivities.

The central government regarded all freemasons with suspicion. The Kurdish ones were deemed to be almost as suspect as the Jewish Brothers who were maliciously accused of spying for America or Israel.

He ran his hand over his face. If it became known Iraqi and Kurdish freemasons had been meeting outside the country to discuss weapons supply, all their lives would be in jeopardy. He closed his eyes, unable to bring himself to speak. How dare his son endanger them and shame his father?

Jiddu interrupted his thoughts. 'You will speak to Ghazi?' he asked without reproach.

Abdullah nodded. 'I am sorry for what my son has done. Please be assured I will write with a formal reprimand.'

The men lapsed into silence.

In front, Jiddu stared out of the window. The car headlights picked out the eyes of a startled pye-dog. If there were pye-dogs, then they must be passing the bedu now. Squinting, he could just detect the outline of their tents to the right of the desert road.

Twenty minutes later, they entered the city. It seemed deserted as they slipped into town. Increasing his speed, Hussein steered the motor through quiet roads and wide avenues – Baghdadis prided themselves on the safety of their streets – dropping off Abdullah first.

Next, it was Samuel and Leah's turn. Ten years before, Samuel had felt confident enough to move his family out of the Jewish Quarter and into the mixed middle class district where Abdullah lived. He had since transferred it back again. Merely a precaution, he had said.

Manoeuvring around winding, cobbled lanes, Hussein brought the vehicle to a halt outside the Solomon family's ornately decorated steel door. Set within a heavily fortified high wall, it had a shuttered eye-level slit-window. Stirring his daughter, Samuel bid Jiddu and his driver goodnight.

Confirming arrangements for the following week – Father Anthony had invited them to bring the children to the Baghdad observatory – he tugged at a heavy brass pull before disappearing inside with Leah.

Jiddu was glad it had been a beautiful day. It would soon be too hot to go to the races. He had wanted to take Jasmine one last time before a British boarding-school claimed her. More importantly, he had wished her to absorb the richness of Iraq's people, the colours of their dress, and the plethora of language and nationality.

In the early morning, before the racing had begun, he had taken her to look at his collection of motorcars parked permanently behind the race-course stables. The Russian, Nico Stollen, along with Leah and her father, had accompanied them. Parked in neat formation, old Rolls Royces, Bentleys and Morris Oxfords had glinted in the sunshine. Soon, Jiddu had informed his friends with glee, he would have a pre-war

Landrover too – a gift from one of Abdullah's ministerial cousins.

As he spoke, little boys had waited with as much eagerness as Jasmine and Leah for Hussein to raise the car-bonnets. Their patience rewarded, they had clustered around as he had explained the intricacies of car mechanics. Parents grateful to have their offspring entertained, had moved off to watch the horses being prepared.

Along the racetrack and in the club-house, Baghdadis mixed with Kurds, foreigners with locals. Shia and Sunni picnicked with Christian and Jewish neighbours. Diplomats placed their bets.

Laure, the French ambassador's wife, arrived in an arribana, an open carriage pulled by two fine horses. Wearing a splendid feathered hat, she carried a scented parasol. Twirling it to protect herself from the sun's rays, the scents of France had wafted across the track.

Propped up beside the motorcars: Young men courted their sweethearts; old men quarrelled about politics in the shade; women complained about the cost of bread and rice. Further along, Ibrahim the school-teacher protested to all who would listen about the British meddling in Iraq's affairs, before being hurried along by his heavily pregnant wife. They lived next door to Father Anthony's mission.

Tiring of the motorcars, Jasmine and Leah merged into the throng, their ponytails bobbing from the top of their heads. Catching sight of Nico Stollen now with a Kurdish friend, Leah shouted, 'Look Jasmine, Uncle Nico is with Peri! He has a camera!'

Hearing their voices, Stollen pointed the lens in their direction, capturing them running towards him holding hands.

His companion, seeing Jiddu and Father Anthony not far behind, beckoned.

Perisan – known as 'Peri' – was the Warlord's daughter, racing again following her return from America. Usually, her father was with her but on this occasion he had been detained in the north. She was betrothed to Lalo, who was doing postgraduate studies at a London teaching hospital. In keeping with the tenets of Islam, they would go chaste to their wedding-bed.

Rushing onwards, the children collided with Father Anthony and Jiddu. Soon caught up in the embrace of strong arms, their squeals brought Abdullah and Samuel to their side. In due course, the adults called for peace, demanding shade, sweet lemons and cool drinks.

They had soon been seated underneath the branches of the date trees, in a quiet corner of the race-club gardens. Revelling in the scene, Stollen photographed them until his film ran out. Moments later, citrus fruits and plates of water melon were served, along with orange ice made of fresh juice and wonderful thick cream.

As the sun rose higher in the sky, Jiddu escorted the party indoors for lunch. Stollen took charge of the children, racing them across the manicured lawns. Reaching the clubhouse, he collapsed in a heap on the top stair. Peri, having joined Jiddu and Father Anthony's more dignified progress, waved.

Tall and fair-skinned, her thick blond hair was caught in an elegant swirl on her neck. A civil engineer, she had completed her studies at the renowned engineering college in Baghdad. (Much to Father Anthony's delight, she had obtained further qualifications in Boston. Stollen had wanted the Warlord to send her to Moscow.)

Abdullah and Samuel walked in front. Turning around and speaking loudly so Peri could hear, Abdullah opined, 'It is good for a woman to be educated. That way she need never be at a man's mercy. How else can we hope to persuade pretty girls to marry our no-good sons. Even then, we're not always successful!'

Peri smiled. Ghazi, Abdullah's son, had once been suggested as a suitor for her. She had demurred. While she had the deepest affection for Ghazi, and he for her, they had not been suited. A short while later, she had met Lalo. Ghazi had stood aside immediately.

Gracefully picking up a corner of her brightly coloured skirt, she caught up with him. 'My father hopes you have picked him some good ponies!'

'Would I fleece your father?'

'He says you would!'

Up ahead, Jasmine and Leah tripped on the clubhouse steps in a flurry of legs and petticoats. Excusing himself, Abdullah ran after them, exclaiming, 'I had best go and rescue Stollen!'

Following behind, Samuel laughed, 'I cannot see our poor Nico volunteering for girl duty again! After four daughters, I am an expert!'

Peri, Jiddu and Father Anthony proceeded at a more dignified pace. The sun burned down relentless. The men mopped their brows with large handkerchiefs. At that time of day, the trees offered little in the way of shade. Peri dabbed at her wrists with rose water.

'Jasmine tells me she is going to school in England,' she remarked, slipping her arm through Jiddu's.

The latter shrugged. 'My son and daughter-in-law are spending the summer in England as usual. They will return in the autumn without the child. Her father, that damn fool son of mine, is insisting on it. He says she is "British" – when Britain will not even recognise his papers, let alone provide the girl with any. She is stateless!'

Grief had been written all over the old man's face. Like many Indians, he had once been proud to serve the Union flag. Following the untold horrors of Partition, countless memories tormented him, his only comfort being the same could never happen in Iraq. That the United Kingdom, the country he had served so loyally, refused to give his grand-daughter a nationality caused him further anguish.

'You consider Jasmine to be Iraqi now?'

'What does it matter? She is of this soil. This little country is the land of the many communities. I am an Indian but my heart beats for Iraq, as once it did for Britain. My beloved wife, God rest her soul, had a Kurdish father and an Iraqi mother. Our blood is equal to our grandchild's English stock. What will an education in Britain achieve for Jasmine, other than the eradication of her identity?'

His outburst over, he was soon contrite. 'You must forgive me,' he said squeezing Peri's hand. 'At eighty years of age, I sometimes forget my manners.'

He was rewarded by her dazzling smile.

'Now I feel forty once more!'

They arrived at the outer edge of the gardens. At the top was a thick hedge of white and pink rose bushes. He plucked Peri a flower.

Threading it into her hair, she reassured, 'Jasmine will not lose her identity – ask Father Anthony if you do not believe me.'

'Of course Jiddu believes you,' soothed the latter, in his beautifully modulated Irish-Bostonian voice. 'He knows the memories of childhood run deep. Why else do you think Stollen takes so much trouble with her? England, my friend, will not fade Jasmine's recollections. Rather, it will sharpen them.'

'You do not think she may become confused?'

'Of course not.'

In better heart, Jiddu allowed himself to be led indoors. Retaining Peri's hand as they mounted the stairs, he grumbled, 'Of course, the real problem is that Britain is Anglican. How can you run a country which is founded on divorce?'

A hungry Father Anthony raised an eyebrow. 'Rather well,' he murmured. 'Probably because its people are secular. Tolerance tends to thrive in such conditions.'

Jiddu grinned. 'A bit like you tolerating the freemasons, eh Father?'

Soon, they were all seated in the race-club restaurant. Leah insisted she sit next to Peri, Jasmine beside Father Anthony, opposite Abdullah, Stollen and Samuel at the far end. Jiddu on the right.

'Amu . . .' queried Jasmine a few moments later, addressing Abdullah with the Arabic word for 'Uncle'.

'Hm,' he smiled, anticipating what was to come.

'Did you remember my tortoise? You promised I would have one from the north for my birthday.'

'Did I?'

It had been Leah's turn to catch his eye. Checking to make sure her father was not listening, she asked with similar eagerness, 'Also, Amu, you haven't forgotten about the ballet shoes, have you? You said Ghazi would send two pairs – one for me and another for my cousin Vivienne in London.'

He hooked his chubby arms behind his head. Basking in their attention, he replied, 'You'll just have to wait and see, won't you, little madams!'

Jiddu smiled. It was no secret Abdullah had wanted a football team of daughters. The latter meanwhile assured him sotto voce he would bring Jasmine's tortoise to the next Masonic meeting.

Soon, lunch was served. Large bowls of rice and ladies fingers, accompanied by yoghurt served with garlic, were placed next to plates of steaming minted lamb. Samuel and Abdullah motioned Father Anthony to say Grace.

As the drinks arrived, Peri asked, 'Have you heard anything about the new roads?'

Jiddu nodded. 'The Masonic Lodge will pay for them and the central government has given the go-ahead. One will be built to the west, and another to the north. I have cabled Sir Julian Lawrence in London. He has passed on our wishes to the British Board of Infrastructure to ensure we are quoted a fair price.'

'Do you know which construction company will be involved?'

Draining the excellent local beer, a cool Farida, he replied, 'I understand it is to be the family-owned firm Fitzwilliams

International. A youngster, Andrew Fitzwilliams, recently inherited his father.'

Stollen hid his dismay. He had hoped the contract would go to the Soviets – one reason why his colleagues in Delhi had tried to prevent Jiddu from securing English patronage of the Baghdad Lodge. Masking his true feelings, he called for the waiter. 'This demands a toast,' he pronounced with apparent good humour.

Soon, Jasmine and Leah watched wide-eyed as champagne corks popped. The racing began at 16.00 hrs, after the heat of the day was over. 'Remember Jasmine,' said Stollen as the party left the club-house, 'It was your Uncle Nico who gave you your first glass of champagne.'

CHAPTER THREE

�֍ ✹ ✶

GRAND LODGE, LONDON: Grand Secretary Sir Julian Lawrence, the country's leading freemason, rolled his wheelchair along the seemingly never ending corridor of Grand Lodge's ornate London headquarters. It was a cumbersome vehicle. However, he was a nifty driver.

He had been Grand Secretary – which is to say, chief executive – of the United Grand Lodge of England for the past fifteen years. Before this, he had been a minister in Clem Atlee's Labour government. Born into an ecclesiastical family, its austere morality had suited him.

The Second World War had cost him the use of his legs. It had taken also his wife, who died in the London Blitz, and their only son, killed at Tobruk. 'The loss of my sweetheart and our child, destroyed my life,' he had once confided to his old friend Jiddu.

'I was left with two choices: To seek death for myself or devote whatever remaining years I was granted, to their memory. I chose the latter. Knowing war is a boys' club, I threw myself into a Brotherhood where womenfolk across the world could be assured their men had been provided with an alternative. This is what our fraternity means to me.'

From his office in English freemasonry's landmark building in central London, he had overseen the administration of lodges throughout England, Wales and the Commonwealth.

Now, he was preparing for the celebration of the 250th anniversary of Grand Lodge's formation in two years time.

His wheelchair creaked as he negotiated a tricky corner. Solemn paintings and sculptural portraits lined the walls. On his lap was a parcel wrapped in brown paper.

Blissfully ignoring Grand Secretary Sir Julian's high station, young Ghazi El-Tarek had turned him into a postman. *Dear Bro Julian*, his cheerful note had read, *Could you please forward the enclosed to Bro Samuel Solomon's niece? Her name is Vivienne and she lives in London. Her cousin Leah asked me to send. I have lost the address. Sorry for the bother.*

In a scrawled postscript, he had added, *My Dad's annoyed with me. I guess you know this.*

Grand Secretary Sir Julian most certainly did. Nevertheless, having satisfied himself as to the contents of the package, he addressed it by hand to Vivienne Solomon, care of her mother. (He prided himself on knowing all 'his' Masonic families.) Now in the process of taking it to the Masonic post-room, he frowned.

Wheeling over the black and white marble tiles, he decided the problem with Ghazi El-Tarek was that it was impossible to dislike the boy for long. Nevertheless, he had been horrified to learn the lad had become involved in selling French handguns. The Kurdish Warlord had told him. The weapons, they agreed, must have been surplus from the Algerian fiasco.

'Ghazi has been made to think himself a man. We must not be too hard on him,' the Warlord had remarked.

'And in this way, many a foolish youth has been seduced into an immoral trade!' the Grand Secretary had retorted.

He had been upset further when the Warlord informed him young El-Tarek's conduct was being actively encouraged by Britain's new head of Iraq intelligence, Peter Ligne. The latter had not returned the Grand Secretary's call when he telephoned to protest.

Having delivered Ghazi's parcel, he returned to his office and, still incensed by Ligne's rebuff, rang the man's superior. In addition, he spoke to the government chief whip. He knew both well. Long ago, they had served Britain in uniform. They continued to do so in city suits.

One hour later, the Grand Secretary's driver dropped him off outside Parliament. The amiable policemen at St Stephen's Entrance soon raised him in his wheelchair up the stairs. At the top, he sped off, rolling himself along the hall.

At the far end, another helpful duo lifted him into the central lobby. The domed antechamber was almost empty when he arrived. On his right, an elderly peer made his way through the swing-doors towards the stairs leading up to the committee corridor.

As Big Ben sounded the half-hour, he looked at his wristwatch. A stickler for correct time-keeping, he was pleased to find himself punctual as ever. The Chief Whip was similarly so and arrived as the Grand Secretary was greeting one of the Parliamentary ushers whom he hoped to interest in joining his 250th Anniversary Steering Committee.

Escorting the senior freemason to his untidy office, the politician listened attentively to his old friend's anxieties. Soon – which is to say, with the aid of three further policemen – the latter had parked himself beside the Chief Whip's large desk.

'Our system is informal. It relies on the honour of its participants. One bad apple . . .' the Grand Secretary was observing, as the Chief Whip shut the door.

'Would destroy it?'

'Exactly.'

'You are suggesting Peter Ligne is a bad apple?'

'How would I know? The man will not even return my calls!'

Not wishing to delay the Chief Whip any longer than was necessary, Sir Julian declined a drink.

'Nonsense, old boy. I wanted to see you anyway,' came his companion's surprising response.

Pouring them a decent malt whisky, the Chief Whip settled himself into a shabby leather chair. 'Apparently, M'lad, you have upset the Americans again. They're unhappy you are using Grand Lodge to fund the Concert of Rights . . .'

- a newly formed local group seeking to address miscarriages of justice in Britain –

' . . . They think it's a Communist front.'

Taking out his pipe, the Grand Secretary's lips twitched. 'Which – the Masonic Lodge or the Concert?'

The Chief Whip chuckled. 'Both, probably. Ruddy Yanks. They are sensitive about most things at the moment. They have still not got over the fact you welcomed a Soviet – the Russian, Nico Stollen – into the Brotherhood.'

'A case of two and two making five, eh?'

The Chief Whip nodded. Swirling his drink, he commented wryly, 'I should say the Prime Minister is delighted with your involvement in the Concert . . .'

The Grand Secretary raised an eyebrow.

'... He says that now the Americans have "found" a real high ranking member of the British establishment who is undoubtedly a traitor and Stalinist – you, mon vieux! – the heat has been taken off his lads at Westminster! It's worth a peerage at least.'

The Grand Secretary laughed. He had heard about the Concert of Rights through his fellow freemason, Samuel Solomon in Iraq. The Concert was assisting Samuel's sister-in-law, Beth Solomon, in her campaign to bring her nieces to Britain.

Packing his meerschaum with precise care, he responded, 'Hang the peerage. Tell the PM, I want visas for the Solomon girls. It is nothing short of scandalous what we are doing merely because, in order to survive, their father is considering membership of the Communist party. Have we forgotten the Holocaust already? Those children have British papers.

'If we had not wanted to honour the peoples of the Commonwealth and empire, we should not have given them passports in the first place. The Worshipful Master of the Baghdad Lodge, Jiddu Palmeira, has similar worries about his son and grand-daughter.'

Unable to hide his regret, his colleague shook his head. 'The PM's hands are tied, I'm afraid, old man. The Home Office will not budge. Thirty years from now, we will have the same problem with Hong Kong.'

He refreshed the Grand Secretary's glass and topped up his own. Replacing the exquisite cut glass decanter on a rickety table, he continued, 'However, we do have some good news ...'

Searching among his papers and finding what he was looking for, he glanced at his companion with affection. 'I have heard from my friends on the science committee. They recommend a chap called Miro for your road project in Iraq. The chap has a distinguished background.'

Wanting to be assured Iraq's development was in safe hands, the Grand Secretary queried, 'Is he a member of the British Board of Infrastructure? I cannot pull in all the required insurances unless he is.'

The Chief Whip chortled. Handing over a typed-up note, he responded obliquely, 'He is now! Although I fear the BBI consider he was bounced on them.'

The Grand Secretary scanned the paper with interest. *Dr Douglas Miro*, it read, *joined the Ministry of Supply at Harwell after graduating with a first in chemical engineering. Specialising in water-cooled nuclear reactor systems, Dr Miro has written extensively on health and safety issues. He left the industry following the death of his father, whose small civil engineering company he inherited. Today, aged thirty-eight, he is a broadly-based engineer operating principally in the road construction field.*

A widower with a teenage daughter, Miro is the son of a Ghanaian princess and Scottish irrigation specialist. Brought up in the Highlands, he is fiercely proud of his ancestry – a wonderful union of Highlander and African aristocrat – and is known locally as the 'Black Scot'.

His original application to join the British Board of Infrastructure was rejected. Following the general election, members of the science committee – in particular its hereditary peers in the Upper House – were able to take the matter up with the new Labour Prime Minister. The latter has been happy to pressurise the BBI into opening up its membership. (You will be aware the Prime Minister is an outspoken critic of the construction cartel in which the BBI has been complicit.) In consequence, Miro is to attend his first BBI council meeting this week.

Pleased with what he had read, the Grand Secretary queried, 'Miro is one of us?'

The Chief Whip nodded. 'Certainly. Initiated into one of the Edinburgh Lodges by his proud father not long after you saw through the separate Irish and Scottish constitutions.'

'Is his company large enough to take on the road programme?'

'Probably not, but the science committee will sort something out with the BBI. As its note makes clear, its members are determined Miro get the tender. The country needs modern skills and new blood. Organisations like the BBI are a closed shop and holding it back.'

'Perhaps it would help if you made it known to the BBI's member contractors I support Miro?'

The Chief Whip beamed. The BBI depended on Masonic goodwill to facilitate the award of construction tenders. In addition, most recommendations for honours and decorations were passed to Grand Lodge for approval.

The Grand Secretary's suggestion would be just the trick, he responded.

Vivienne Solomon clutched her mother's hand as they made their way briskly from Hampstead tube station. The weekend traffic flowed passed them. 'Leah says Ghazi will send me a pair of ballet shoes just like hers. So I drew around my foot and sent the drawing to him in Paris so he would know what big feet I have!'

Beth Solomon looked at her daughter aghast. 'Who on earth is Ghazi and, more to the point, why should he be buying you ballet shoes?'

'He's Leah's friend,' responded Vivienne, as if this said it all. 'He says her cousin is his cousin. His daddy is a vet. Leah wants to be a vet too. Ghazi's father has told her if she cannot come to school in England, he'll teach her himself.'

'That's as may be. But it does not mean you should have asked his son for ballet shoes!'

Vivienne bit her lip. 'I'm sorry, Mum. I didn't think, that's all. Leah said Ghazi liked buying presents.'

Squeezing her daughter's hand, Beth Solomon crossed the road. With their beautiful chestnut red hair and delicate colouring their relationship was unmistakable. Mother and child were returning from a surprise visit to the Home Office civil servant responsible for visas. The Concert of Rights had come up with the man's private address.

To Beth Solomon's regret, the meeting had not been a great success. A boy of about fifteen had answered the door. 'Is Mr Richards in?' she had asked politely.

The teenager had disappeared to fetch his father. Finding out who they were, the latter had sent them away. Mustering her remaining energies, Mrs Solomon had pleaded, 'Please help, Mr Richards. The authorities in Baghdad have now closed the Jewish school. My nieces are not even allowed an education . . .'

He had shut the door.

'What did they want, Pa?' Jimmy Richards had asked his parent when they had gone.

'Nothing.'

The boy had watched his father for the rest of the day hoping he would say something but the subject had been closed. Later, he had heard his parents talking quietly in the kitchen.

'I cannot assist the Solomon girls because their father is a suspected Communist sympathiser,' his father had said forlornly. 'It does not help their aunt is connected with the Concert of Rights which is also believed to be a Communist front.'

'And is it?' Jimmy had heard his mother ask.

Through the crack in the door, he had seen his father bow his head. 'I have no idea. In the present climate, even a suspicion of Communism counts against them. People think officials do not care. We do. We try our best to help. When we fail – as I have – we are heartbroken.'

Anxious about being discovered, Jimmy had tiptoed upstairs to his bedroom. He had thought about the woman and her daughter who visited his father for days afterwards. 'Vivienne', he remembered, had been the red-haired girl's name.

Running ahead of her mother, Vivienne swung open the gate to their house. Neat borders of spring daffodils bobbed each side of its gravel path. Turning around, she called with excitement, 'There's a parcel on the doorstep, Mum. It must have been too large for the postman to put through the letter-box! It's addressed to me!'

Unwrapping the package quickly, she found two pairs of ballet shoes. A scrawled note read: *One for now and one to grow into. With love from Ghazi.*

CHAPTER FOUR

MI6 HEADQUARTERS: Peter Ligne's eye swept the disordered room. It looked like the den of a particularly untidy academic. 'The Chief' – the head of MI6 – was on the phone but waved him in. Out of politeness, he remained standing.

Disconnecting a few minutes later, his superior urged, 'Sit down, M'boy, sit down.' He was a long, thin man with mousy, nondescript coloured hair. 'That was the Masonic Grand Secretary, Sir Julian Lawrence. He is not best pleased with you – all but accusing you of poisoning the water supply in the north of Iraq, while exploiting some young chap's stupidity and greed by involving him in the sale of hand-guns.'

Peter Ligne grinned. Selecting a straight-back chair, he responded, 'Heavy sins, sir!'

The Chief laughed. 'And are you? Encouraging an innocent to sell handguns, that is?'

Ligne's wide open face and clear blue eyes held his. 'Yes and no, sir. The French are moving in on Iraq's lucrative armaments trade. They are using a well-connected middleman to assist them. A young fellow called Ghazi El-Tarek who, when he is not on a race-track, is studying in France.'

The Chief heard him out in silence.

'My worry is two-fold. First, we have nailed our interests too closely to the Kurds. Second, HMG will lose out if we do not beat the French at their own game – at this very moment the Iraq government is offering a not inconsiderable weapons contract!

'... With this in mind, I saw no reason not to get alongside this Ghazi chap too. Not that I think he's driven by greed. His debts permitting, he's probably in it for the fun.'

The Chief sat back in his chair, his brow furrowed. After some reflection, he declared, 'We do not involve innocents in our work, Peter, greedy or otherwise. You are to drop all contact with Ghazi El-Tarek at once. The Grand Secretary's call was an embarrassment. Our reputation is at stake.'

Ligne apologised.

The Chief raised his hand, signalling he had more to say on the matter. 'I served with The Grand Secretary in the last war – we were in the same regiment. His son was too. The man lost everything. Hate could have filled his heart. Instead, he personifies the best of public service ...'

Fixing his eye on Ligne, he continued, '... Our way of doing things is based on trust. As The Grand Secretary says, it would take one villain to ruin what we have allowed to evolve. The good name of all is at stake.'

Satisfied his meaning could not be misunderstood, his usual pragmatism was soon restored. 'Now then. Any suggestions about how this weapons contract can be steered in HMG's direction?'

'As it happens, sir, yes ...'

Ligne gave a brief summary of his plan. Three minutes later, he concluded, '... The chairman of Lloyd's of London told me the family owned construction company Fitzwilliams

International could be ideal for our purposes. He suggested we set up a subsidiary that could handle sensitive engineering projects as well as act as a conduit for weapons supply.

'It would need a holding address outside the UK – West Germany springs to mind. The chairman assures me Lloyd's would be happy to organise the necessary insurances.'

The Chief considered the plan carefully. 'As I recall, Andrew Fitzwilliams inherited Fitzwilliams International from his late father last year. He cannot be much more than a boy.'

'Andrew Fitzwilliams is twenty-four, sir. He is going into Parliament like his pater – Fitzwilliams père was the Home Office minister when the POUKI was set up.'

The POUKI – Points of Understanding in UK Industry – was funded by private business ostensibly to promote free enterprise. In reality, it performed several jobs on behalf of the business and intelligence community which they were not permitted to do. The Concert of Rights was one of its most recent targets.

'Ah yes!' observed the Chief, 'There is always a Fitzwilliams in politics. Fitzwilliams International has been run by the British Board of Infrastructure for as long as anyone can remember. While the family looks after the BBI's interests in Parliament, it keeps the company going commercially – a sensible arrangement in my opinion.'

Ligne inclined his head. It was common knowledge construction contracts were offered in rotation. 'The BBI expect the present Fitzwilliams to be in government before too long. Once, of course, the Tories are back in office! The BBI "grows" a minister – Roman Catholic, needless to say – every ten years. It is understood by all concerned that as a Catholic, Cabinet rank is possible but not Downing Street.

'In view of this, and so as not to compromise young Fitzwilliams' future ministerial career, the chairman of Lloyd's suggested we bring in an outside contractor to run the subsidiary. The type who could be dropped quietly were things to go wrong.'

The Chief winced. He was not a man who found it easy to behave badly. Preferring silence to further discussion, Ligne made no attempt to persuade his employer one way or the other. Two minutes later it was a done deal. The outside contractor selected was Douglas Miro.

The Chief gave a broad smile. 'I don't think you should mention to the BBI you have been discussing its affairs with the chairman of Lloyd's! The old boy who runs it might be dazzled by the City but his members as a whole are not. Typical Roman v English Catholic stuff!'

Ligne chortled. What the Chief actually meant was that the contractors were, for the most part, of Irish or Scottish descent. Pragmatists, the former – unlike the Scots – tended to eschew the Roman Catholic Lodges for the English ones answerable to Grand Lodge. They seldom offered fraternal greetings to their Anglican Brothers in the City of London. It took a general election to bring them together.

Miro and the British Board of Infrastructure's other newest member, Andrew Fitzwilliams, attended their first BBI Council meeting together. There the similarities ended.

Andrew Fitzwilliams was swept away on a plume of friendly cigar smoke having been at school with the sons or grandsons of most of those present. Miro was kept at a distance. For the most part, the contractors had never shared a table with a black man before.

Unruffled, he sipped his coffee and looked about him, admiring the beautiful Art Deco building, with its polished marble floors, mosaics, stained glass, dark woods and heavy bronze door-handles.

'More Grand Lodge than Grand Lodge!' his patron, the Labour government's Chief Whip, had remarked when he telephoned to inform Miro he had been accepted into BBI membership.

A well-built, imposing man, Miro gazed at the portraits of past presidents lining the wall. It had already been agreed he would head a Fitzwilliams International subsidiary to build Iraq's roads. In addition, he had been informed by the BBI Chairman that he and Andrew Fitzwilliams, accompanied by a civil servant called Peter Ligne, would visit the country the following week.

The Chairman called the meeting to order. The first item on the agenda was the Conservative party. The mood in the room was sombre. The Chairman reported that ever since the Conservatives lost office, the POUKI's work had increased tenfold. Here, looking around the large mahogany table where the contractors were seated, he paid tribute to 'our American friends'. These, he said, continued to be both generous and helpful, although he acknowledged there were some moves afoot to minimise their input until the next general election.

'We have, of course, written officially to thank the Americans for their assistance, especially the aid they gave to the POUKI. I am only sorry that despite our best endeavours, the Labour party still scraped in with a ludicrous overall majority of only four seats!'

Miro listened in fascinated horror. Coughing, he caught the Chairman's eye. The latter gave way with icy politeness. New boys were meant to be seen and not heard. African ones in particular.

'I am familiar, gentlemen, with the POUKI from my days at Harwell . . .'

Plumes of cigar smoke wafted to the back of the room as, one by one, heads turned to where he was sitting.

Ignoring the obvious disapproval of his companions, Miro continued, '. . . When the POUKI was set up, its brief was to keep a check on subversives. Such remit never included soliciting America's help in an attempted overthrow of an elected British government.'

Aware of the chill blowing his way, Miro pressed on. 'Officials at Harwell were scrupulous in knowing the difference between a member of the Labour party and a subversive. It behoves us to follow their good example. Harwell's public servants maintained a tight rein on the POUKI's brief. So should we.'

Without missing a beat, the Chairman ignored the intervention. Moving swiftly on to the next item on the agenda – Conservative Central Office – he commented, 'CCO are very grateful. Moneys are flowing in for the next general election. The treasurer feels another £100,000 should do it . . .'

As if in slow motion, the cigar smoke headed to the top of the room again.

' . . . In addition, thanks to POUKI – and our American allies . . .'

- In cold rebuttal of Miro, the Chairman allowed his voice to linger over the word 'American' -

'. . . Anti-subversive research is going well. In Parliament, our MPs and peers are watching the Labour party like hawks.'

The contractors were appreciative of the efforts of all concerned. Soon a joke was cracked at the Labour Prime Minister's expense. Laughter rumbled around the council chamber.

Coffee was served a few moments later. As the Chairman smiled in genial good humour and helped himself to a heaped spoonful of sugar, a report on Miro's extremist views was passed to the POUKI. Filed under 'Known Subversives', the name 'Douglas Miro' was cross-referenced with 'Africans', 'Negroes' and 'Stalinists'.

Peter Ligne and the two contractors left for Iraq on a chilly May morning. Sharing a taxi with Andrew Fitzwilliams to Heathrow airport's Oceanic Building, the civil servant kept up an unending stream of anecdotes. Miro travelled separately and a short while later joined them in the VIP departure lounge.

Here he found Ligne comfortably struggling with the *Daily Telegraph* crossword, while Fitzwilliams talked to a striking young woman. Seeing Miro, Ligne rose. A few moments later, he introduced Fitzwilliams' companion as the Warlord's daughter, Peri. Having visited her fiancé in London, she was returning to Iraq on the same flight as the Britons.

Always comfortable in female company, Miro sat down beside her. Initiating a light-hearted conversation with immediate ease, he teased, 'Did you discover the sites of London or . . . the shops?'

'The shops! I was looking for skis but was unsuccessful.'

'Skis?'

Peri nodded. 'We have problems with our water supply at the moment. Once these are sorted, my father is hoping to develop a ski resort in Kurdistan. Geography may be against us . . . but the snow is not! The Persians have already shown what can be achieved across the border. We are hoping Kurdish oil revenues will, in due course, finance the project.'

The last remark was directed with a straightforward glance at Peter Ligne. 'I believe my father made you aware of his plans when he visited London, Mr Ligne?'

The latter avoided her eye. He had no wish to discuss things with the Warlord's daughter. And certainly not with Miro present.

'Why bother, when the skiing in St Moritz is so much better than anywhere else?' interrupted a boyish Andrew Fitzwilliams.

'Perhaps because St Moritz is not in Kurdistan,' replied the Warlord's daughter.

CHAPTER FIVE

❊ ❈ ❊

BAGHDAD: Jasmine was asleep in her grandfather's lap. She had had an exhilarating evening. Father Anthony had shown off his observatory's new telescope. She and Leah had watched the heavens in amazement as, one by one, the stars had appeared.

Now, they were on their way home. Hussein steered the car along empty streets. As always, he had dropped off Leah and her father first.

Jiddu stared out of the window. Across the river, the palace stood stark against the sky. The building, home to the Boy King before his murder in 1958, seemed to stand in silent reproach. Jasmine had been born the year before the Iraqi monarch's life had been extinguished.

It was long passed midnight. Soon, they turned on to the Bund along the Tigris. The Flit lorry, late again, sprayed mosquito killer.

Returned at last, the car swung into the parking area, the house-lights gleaming along its silvery flank. Bidding Hussein goodnight, Jiddu carried Jasmine to bed. Afterwards, he stood for a while on her balcony.

Below were the gardens he had planted for her grandmother. These sloped down to the Tigris beyond the orange grove. Directly underneath was the high veranda. Beneath was Suzie's delight – the aviary, full of beautiful singing birds with stunningly coloured feathers.

He smiled as he heard the low murmur of his son and daughter-in-law's voices below. Craning his neck, he could just see their shadows as Suzie's tinkling laugh filled the night air. He loved to hear her.

She had won his heart the day his only son had brought home his bride. 'A family is always lucky if there is a daughter in the house,' he had said in welcome.

Suzie, in her mid-twenties at the time, had gazed at him out of clear blue eyes. The British, Jiddu had been heard to remark soon after, still had some good points – and Suzie was one of them. Her own parents had disowned her on her marriage.

It had been plain to everyone she and Philippe were deeply in love. When Jasmine arrived a year after their marriage, their little family had been complete. 'It is as if her beloved grandmother has sent me another flower to cherish until the Almighty calls me to her side once more,' Jiddu had murmured as he rocked the infant in his arms.

He sighed. Nearly eight years on, their peaceful, joyous existence was crumbling before his eyes. His son was increasingly drawn towards politics.

Flickering lanterns lit by families cooking Musguf – large trout roasted and eaten with flat bread baked in mud ovens – sparkled along the riverbank. Caught in the moonlight, Jiddu saw a couple dancing. They could just as easily have been Philippe and Suzie.

He heard Hussein checking the heavy iron gates below. Soon the servant would make his way to the jetty and share a cigarette with the watchman. The man had hardly left Jiddu's side since the women had taken away the body of Jasmine's grandmother for washing before burial.

After the ceremony, they had stood waist high in the Tigris as one of the dead woman's favourite dresses had been released into the waters and infinity. It was a Hindu custom – Iraqis were promiscuous when it came to other people's faiths.

Leaving the balcony, Jiddu made his way noiselessly through the house. Philippe and Suzie were listening to the BBC World Service when he joined them. Harold Wilson was in government in England and Willy Brandt had entered into discussions with the Eastern bloc as his people lost heart with American promises Berlin would be re-united.

Hearing his father, Philippe put out his cigarette. Although thirty-five, two years older than Suzie, he did not smoke in front of him. He wore a long white shirt that touched the floor. It contrasted with the darkness of his skin and the thick black hair of his arms.

Suzie wore a silk dress that held her scent every time she moved. She and Philippe had flown down to the Shatt and spent the day where the two rivers meet. It was a favourite haunt of lovers. Afterwards, they had gone riding. Suzie was a fine horsewoman.

'You should not have kept Jasmine out so late,' she chided her father-in-law.

Kissing her, he put his arm around her slim shoulders. 'Is it my fault we had four punctures?' he asked playfully.

Philippe poured his father a glass of port.

'Anything on the news?' queried the old man.

His son shook his head. 'Nothing much. It seems the French have withdrawn from a minor arm of NATO. Our Russian friend Nico Stollen says it's because they are suspicious of

American and Soviet talks to control further nuclear developments. They're redoubling their efforts to sell arms to the Arabs.'

'That way, at least we will have some independence from the super-powers,' replied Jiddu.

Immediate anger swept across Philippe's face. 'Independence, Father? This would mean nothing more than isolation and abandonment. Iraq does not want independence. It wants to belong – to the British Crown – like it used to.'

Jiddu looked at him in despair. They seemed to rehearse their respective hostilities every evening. 'How can you be such a fool? The British are patriots – and rightly so. They are fighting for their own survival. They cannot serve Iraq's interests as well as their own. We must be like them and protect Iraq . . .'

'You sound like an Iraqi nationalist, Father.'

'And why not? Grow up, boy! Britain has no interest in us. I do not expect it too. All it wants are our antiquities and oil.' His temper rising, the old man continued, 'If you do not believe me, will you consider what Stollen says? His source at Lloyd's of London has informed him the British are setting up a company to export weapons to Iraq. They want us to fight each other. Brother against brother. This is why they make secret deals with the Kurds . . .'

This was too much even for Suzie. 'Really, Father, I love Nico Stollen dearly but he is nothing but a trouble-maker. What can you expect from a Communist? The British would never behave badly. We are just not like that.'

The old man's eyes moistened. It seemed all they did was quarrel these days. He and Philippe had exchanged furious words only the night before – his son had informed him that, if asked, he would consider it an honour to assist the Briton, Peter Ligne. Suzie had not witnessed the row nor had Philippe told her of it afterwards.

'Did my son tell you of our argument last night?'

Mystified, she shook her head.

'In which case, my dear, you do not know he wants to be a spy?'

Suzie laughed. 'For Queen and Country, I hope! You do speak a lot of nonsense sometimes, Father. What a notion! It is far too dangerous. It is not as if we are at war or anything.'

Enjoying Philippe's discomfiture, Jiddu hid his smile. 'You had better tell her, my son. I had no secrets from your mother. Nor should you from your wife.'

He retired a short while later. Kissing his daughter-in-law goodnight, he said softly to Philippe, 'If you bring espionage into this house, my child, you will destroy us.'

Abdullah El-Tarek replaced the receiver. He had been speaking to his wife in Paris. Their son Ghazi had also come on the line. He wished he was with them. He loved Paris: The pretty girls and rich French meals, entrées blanketed with sauces and the puddings smothered with cream.

Missing his family, he made his way thoughtfully across the marble floor of his home to his guests. The two contractors, Miro and Fitzwilliams, were staying with him rather than at the British embassy because their visit had been at the invitation of the Baghdad Masonic Lodge. (Peter Ligne – who was not part of the official party – had also eschewed the embassy.

Valuing his independence, he had checked into the Semiramis hotel.)

Stopping in front of a large silver and brass mirror, Abdullah straightened his tie. He was never at his best when his wife was not with him. And tonight, of all nights, he would have liked her by his side.

She had laughed when he told her he missed her. 'But darling, now you have time to see your mistress! You can fly her in from the Lebanon.'

Her comment had upset him. There was no point seeing a mistress, as she well knew, if she was not around to get jealous. Not that he actually had a mistress. Merely that he kept an apartment in the Lebanon to pretend he did because this was the manly thing to do. His wife had understood.

Mind, there had been occasion some years before when she had been less than forgiving. He grinned at the memory. It made him feel closer to her some how.

It was the touring cabaret girl that had done it. She had sung at the night-club to which he had taken his wife on her birthday. On finding out he was the country's leading veterinary surgeon, the singer had asked to see him 'professionally', as she put it, the following day.

Abdullah had assumed all he would be doing was looking at the girl's canaries. These, apparently, had stopped singing. 'Stopped singing?' his wife had shouted, 'I'll give you her canaries have "stopped singing".'

It was only then Abdullah had found out the cabaret star had meant she was the canary. It was funny how wives intuitively knew these things.

Outside in the garden, Miro and Fitzwilliams relaxed under a brilliantly star-studded sky. Lying on a table were several copies of a typed-up note outlining the hospitality arranged over the coming weeks. Miro had read through the details with pleasure. Feeling himself respected in Iraq, he was at ease. As a rule, the civil engineer was not held in similar esteem in Britain.

Seeing his host return, he nudged Andrew Fitzwilliams to his feet. The latter shot him a grateful look. Knocked out by the journey, he had nodded off.

'My sons, what must you think of me for leaving you for so long?' spluttered Abdullah. 'I hope the programme for your visit is to your liking.'

Having taken no interest in the agenda, Fitzwilliams looked to Miro for help. The latter assured their host all was well and they were grateful for the trouble taken. The younger man smiled his concurrence.

The situation he found himself in was so foreign, he was touchingly beholden to Miro. He had not wanted to visit Iraq – with Miro running the Fitzwilliams International subsidiary, he had not seen the need. However, the elders of the British Board of Infrastructure had obliged him to fall in with their wishes and, as always, he had done so.

'Tonight we will have champagne. We have much to celebrate,' Abdullah was saying. 'My wife telephoned to tell me our only child Ghazi, is to marry a beautiful English girl.'

Miro and Fitzwilliams were quick to congratulate him. Correctly interpreting the situation, Miro remarked soon after, 'The engagement has come as something of a surprise?'

Embarrassed he had been so easily read, Abdullah replied, 'A little. Ghazi's mother and I expected him to marry one of his cousins. My heart aches because he has always liked Europe, finding Baghdad too small for him. Now he has an even better reason not to come home!'

Miro smiled. The child of a mixed marriage himself, he was testament to the happiness of many such union. 'I am sure Ghazi and your future daughter-in-law will visit you soon.'

Abdullah nodded with vigour. 'My wife is returning with the young couple in a few weeks.'

Happier, he seated himself on one of the wrought iron benches made comfortable by thick velvet cushions. 'I am glad Ghazi is to wed, even though I was not permitted to chose his bride,' he declared. 'It is the way of society that all men be defined by women, otherwise what identity do we have? How can a young man learn his father's responsibilities unless he has a wife?'

He looked searchingly at his guests. 'You are married?' he asked Miro.

The latter shook his head. 'My wife passed away when our daughter was a baby.'

Abdullah was quick to apologise for being so tactless. 'Allow me, my son, to take a father's liberty. You must marry again. You could pay no truer compliment to the mother of your child. A man is nothing without a woman. What is the point of establishing our dominion if there is no-one around to see it?'

Next, he turned the kind spotlight of his attention onto Andrew Fitzwilliams. 'You are courting too? You have found a bride like my Ghazi?'

[59]

Andrew Fitzwilliams was at a loss. His mother had died while he was at prep-school. About all he could remember of family life was that his parents expected good manners of each other, as well as of their son. Out of his depth but wanting to please, he replied, 'No, sir. However, I have been advised to marry before the next election. Voters prefer it.'

Abdullah looked perplexed. 'You require a vote if you wish to marry in England?'

Inadvertently catching Miro's eye, Fitzwilliams stifled a giggle.

'What Andrew means, is a parliamentary candidate can be regarded as being more credible if he is married,' intervened Miro.

A broad smile enveloped Fitzwilliams' face. 'Bravo, old boy!'

Wagging an admonishing finger at him, Miro helped himself to a ripe, juicy peach. Perhaps even to his own surprise, he found he liked the younger man. The light from the garden lamps illuminated his high cheek bones. 'Your future daughter-in-law will convert to Islam?' he asked Abdullah.

'I did not inquire. It is for her and Ghazi to decide. Their children will respect both faiths.'

'You are not a religious man?'

Abdullah laughed. 'I drink alcohol. All Iraqis do. This does not mean I do not apologise to the Holy Prophet when I pour whisky out of a tea-pot and call it chai!'

Their easy banter was interrupted by a servant pouring sparkling champagne into exquisite glasses. Taking a long sip, Abdullah proposed a toast.

'My son is to be married,' he said with pride. 'Ghazi and his beautiful bride will merge two races and cultures. And Allah, in his kindness, has willed on this beautiful night, two Englishmen share my joy.'

Miro grinned and shook his head. 'Only one, my friend. I'm a Scot.'

His host clapped his hands with mirth. 'I understand! I understand! The Scots are like the Kurds. Independent. Separate. But part of the whole.'

CHAPTER SIX

❊ ❊ ❊

The reception held by the Baghdad Masonic Lodge for the visiting contractors two days after their arrival was a spectacular affair. Peter Ligne was also included in the entertainments. Hussein, Jiddu's driver, fetched him from his hotel.

The Russian, Nico Stollen, drove Jiddu but declined to attend. Throughout the short journey they avoided discussion. Jiddu had a great deal on his mind: Abdullah El-Tarek's ministerial cousins had informed him the central government had advised its ministers it wanted the Lodge shut. The men did not know which of the super-powers was agitating against it. Jiddu suspected it to be the Soviets.

Once arrived at their destination, he turned to face his companion. 'Julian Lawrence, the Grand Secretary in London, asked me to convey his deepest affection for you, Nico. He tells me you are a most unusual man. He hopes you will not disappoint him.'

Stollen's reply did little to reassure him. Conscious of Jiddu's suspicions, he responded coldly, 'Emotional blackmail does not suit you, my friend – you know the Lodge is finished! As for Julian Lawrence, he is well aware other people's tragedies mean nothing to me. I do not give in to sentimentalities.'

'I ask for honour, not sentiment!'

Peter Ligne arrived as Stollen drove off. He and Jiddu

walked into the Lodge together. The night before, he had strolled comfortably around the souks of old Baghdad.

Passing one chaikhana, he had been amazed to find himself greeted by its owner like a long lost relative with two kisses on either cheek. 'Come in, Mr Ligne, come in,' the man had beamed. 'You must be the British spy, Colonel Stollen told us about. I read the article in the *Iraq Times* last month. My brother the airport driver told me you had arrived.'

Torn between exasperation and amusement, Ligne had accepted sticky sweets with pistachio before returning to his hotel. He had slept well, disturbed only once by the telephone. It had been the Warlord.

They had made arrangements to meet clandestinely during the Lodge's Festive Board – the informal amusements that follow the formal Masonic rituals. The Lodge, the Warlord had informed him, had lost several prominent members recently – including Abdullah El-Tarek's relations – because of the problems with the northern water supply. Now, the Warlord was leaving too.

The news had delighted Ligne. If the Kurds abandoned the Baghdad Lodge, it could no longer claim to represent the whole country, on which basis rested much of its legitimacy. He had long recognised he could not wrestle the Iraqi freemasons into submission. Instead, he hoped for their Lodge's collapse. This circumstance now looked increasingly likely. Falling asleep, it had pleased him to know the Soviets were being blamed for its uncertain situation.

Once inside the Lodge, Jiddu introduced Ligne to one of the stewards and hurried to change into his Masonic regalia. Now mingling with the freemasons, the civil servant was careful not to catch the Warlord's eye. About fifty men were gathered.

Photographers from the *Iraq Times* circulated. All were freemasons. To protect their Jewish Brothers – bearing the brunt of the central government's suspicions – they made sure none were photographed.

Several young men were to be initiated into freemasonry that evening by proud fathers. They stood in corners rehearsing words memorised over long months. Christians, Jews, Muslims, Iraqis and Kurds, Sunnis and Shia chatted. On all sides, Brothers issued invitations to each other which spring naturally from such relaxed and happy gatherings.

Welcoming the three Britons, Jiddu's address was wide-ranging. In due course, he announced with regret the Warlord was leaving their fraternity. He looked at the Kurd with special pleading in his eyes, in the hope, even at this late hour, the latter would change his mind.

The Warlord shook his head. He and Jiddu knew in their hearts their trusted world had already collapsed. Bowing respectfully, he withdrew. Jiddu stuck to his agenda with dogged determination.

The suggestion a Garden of Lemon Trees be created was well received. It was agreed planting would begin as soon as possible. Next came general condemnation of the practice of selling visas. Jiddu was pleased to announce that Father Anthony, with the kind assistance of the American political officer, had managed to secure US visas for the Solomon girls.

Samuel accepted his Brothers' good wishes. He did not tell them that in order to protect the Lodge, he too would not be attending another meeting. Nor had he mentioned it to Jiddu.

Oblivious to his friend's decision, Jiddu continued with good cheer, 'I have further to say on the subject of Father Anthony! He has asked me to remind the Lodge his mission could do with a new vehicle.'

A gale of laughter rippled around the room. The American Jesuit, a somewhat precarious driver, had knocked over Baghdad's first set of traffic lights. For a while he had become something of a hero until it had been discovered he had not done it on purpose.

Father Anthony got his mission car. It was an appropriate gesture given he had been responsible for a large donation arriving from His Holiness the Pope in Rome for Iraq's education fund.

'I believe the Father omitted to mention to His Holiness we were freemasons. You will appreciate, Brothers, His Holiness takes a dim view of American priests involved in freemasonry,' reported Jiddu without so much as a flicker of a smile.

The room applauded, the noise reaching a crescendo when he informed the assembled men that all the widows in the city would receive free meat and cooking oil.

Taking advantage of the clamour, Ligne slipped out of the room. Once outside, he made his way to the Warlord waiting in the dark behind the tall iron gates. A thousand stars brightened the sky. The leaves of the date palms rustled. Neither was aware of Jiddu's driver Hussein and Father Anthony watching from the shadows.

'Our arrangement is sound?' queried the Warlord.

The civil servant nodded.

'If I seem anxious, please forgive me,' continued the former. 'I said goodbye to my Brothers tonight and this has made me sad. I hope one day I will be able to return. Meantime, I must secure my country's future behind their backs. My deceit burdens me.'

Ligne made no comment.

'You will encourage the Iraq government to give the Kurds autonomy?' the Warlord persisted. 'In return, the Kurds will guarantee the oil from Kirkuk. You must pay a fair price for it.'

'I have arranged to speak to the oil companies. Things will take time to organise,' responded the Briton.

'Do not take too much time, my friend. How can I develop the north without the funding the oil provides?'

Ligne acknowledged the urgency.

The Warlord pressed on. 'Meanwhile, I have raised sufficient funds for weapons purchase, in case the time comes when I have to defend my people against the Iraq army. Because of my treaty with the British, I am prevented from buying from the French although they offer better prices. I hope you will honour our agreement, as I honour it now.'

'Her Majesty's Government,' assured Ligne, 'Have authorised me to confirm our commitment to the Kurds and our readiness to supply weapons to your side. You may place your order via Fitzwilliams International's subsidiary in West Germany. The paperwork should talk in terms of the Iraq road contracts. All communications should be addressed to Douglas Miro.'

'The black man?'

'He knows nothing.'

The Warlord smiled without amusement. So. The black man was a pawn too. The only difference being he did not know it.

Looking pointedly at Ligne, he emphasised, 'Nothing must endanger the members of the Masonic Lodge. They are only old men and boys. Innocents.' His voice faltered. 'They are my friends.'

Ligne slipped back into the building a few moments later. The Warlord made his way into the night. Inside the Lodge, the meeting continued. Above the heads of the crowd, Jiddu noticed Ligne's return, just as he had noted his absence.

'Ah! Mr Ligne, I was beginning to think the rumours I hear about you are true. Where have you been? A secret rendezvous? All you spies are the same!' Abdullah El-Tarek's jovial voice hailed him.

Before he could reply, an affectionate voice chuckled from behind, 'Welcome to Baghdad, Peter . . .'

Turning around, he found Philippe Palmeira beside him. They had last met some fifteen years before. Palmeira looked much the same: Jet black hair, trim physique. Ligne was the taller of the two.

Abdullah El-Tarek excused himself. The two men scarcely noticed him go.

'My father thinks you will be a bad influence on me!' continued Philippe.

'I hope so! Point me in the direction of the best nightclub in town and let's be off!'

Philippe gave a mock grimace. 'My night-clubbing days are over, I'm afraid, Peter. I am a married man now. The best I can offer is a night-cap at home.'

'You mean your father will allow it?'

Philippe smiled. 'He makes one condition. No politics! For my part, you can make yourself useful and smuggle in my daughter's tortoise. She knows Abdullah is bringing it to the Lodge tonight and is bound to wait up. Jasmine is eight years old tomorrow.'

Ligne was delighted to oblige. He was good with children, taking infinite pains to amuse them. They, in turn, responded as flowers turn towards the sun.

While Ligne and Philippe Palmeira chatted, Abdullah El-Tarek and Samuel Solomon made their way to the back of the chamber. There they found Jiddu sampling the specially prepared sweetmeats.

'I'm not allowed these. They are too heavy for my digestion,' he confided.

'You'll be sorry tomorrow,' responded Samuel, tucking in himself.

'I know. But today I am happy.'

Abdullah raised an eyebrow. 'Happy? When that awful man Peter Ligne is creeping around and making troubles already. I am sure he followed the Warlord outside. The fellow is a horror – and will damage the esteem in which other Britons are held.'

'Yes, happy,' replied Jiddu, helping himself to one more nibble. 'I stationed Father Anthony and Hussein by the Lodge gates. They will tell me what passed between Ligne and our Brother. Meantime, I do not feel so bad accepting the British ambassador's whisky – a gift because I allowed him to hunt on my land. He sent two bottles. I gave one to Father Anthony.'

'I thought you were not allowed whisky?'

'I am not. But the ambassador does not know this.'

As Abdullah steadied him, Samuel queried, 'How much whisky have you had already, Worshipful Master?'

Jiddu hiccoughed. 'Not nearly enough,' he replied, offering Samuel the bottle.

Half an hour later, Abdullah, Jiddu and Samuel slumped against each other, giggling their way to sleep.

At the mission, a tiddly Father Anthony raised his glass to Hussein. 'To the British ambassador's excellent whisky.'

Jiddu's driver, who was drinking Fanta, held up his bottle in amiable salute.

Looking slightly fuzzy-eyed, the priest continued, 'You should become a Roman Catholic, my friend. Then you'd be allowed alcohol.'

'I know, Father. This is why I prefer to be Muslim. Who would look after us, if we were all drunk?'

CHAPTER SEVEN
❊ ❊ ❊

PALMEIRA VILLA, BAGHDAD: Peter Ligne talked with Philippe Palmeira long into the night. They were on the veranda overlooking the river. Ligne wanted to appraise his host, although he had known even before he left London he would not leave Iraq without having first recruited him.

For his part, Philippe Palmeira was overwhelmed with the pleasure of seeing his old friend again. He wished Suzie had been more welcoming but shrugged it off. He had no doubt his father had filled her head with nonsense.

Mind, even he conceded Ligne had not 'played the game' about Jasmine's tortoise. Still, he had apologised and this was the main thing. Not having children himself, he could be forgiven for getting too caught up in the excitement of it all.

The water slapped the walls beneath. Suzie and Jiddu had long gone to bed. 'Your father keeps his age well,' commented the civil servant lighting a cigarette.

'Despite coming home drunk, you mean?'

Ligne chuckled. 'Sorry about giving Jasmine her tortoise. I couldn't resist it. Will Suzie and your father ever forgive me? It seemed a shame to disappoint the little thing since she had waited up.'

'I expect so. Although my father might take a bit of time accepting she has called the beast "HMG"!'

Ligne beamed. Joyfully unrepentant, he replied, 'This was a master-stroke, wasn't it? So naughty of me, I know.'

He leaned forward and helped himself to a handful of grapes from the fruit bowl on the table in front. 'I can't help but think your old pater deserved it in a way. He really was a bit strong after the Lodge meeting. All I did was slip out for some fresh air. How was I to know the Warlord would be waiting outside – let alone Father Anthony and Hussein?

'That's why I told Jasmine her tortoise came all the way from England in my briefcase and was called "HMG". I shouldn't have aggravated the old boy, I know. But it was irresistible. Jasmine, by the way, is a delightful child.'

Philippe Palmeira smiled. No real harm had been done. 'To be frank, Peter, I think it was your views on freemasonry that most upset my father. You should not have described it as the soft underbelly of British society.'

'Why? Because he considers me the soft underbelly?'

The smoke from his cigarette burning in the ashtray spiralled in the air.

'No,' responded Philippe, his voice surprisingly crisp. 'Because my father is fond of the Masonic Grand Secretary, Sir Julian Lawrence, in London.'

'I'm sorry. Me and my tactless tongue. I shall telephone to apologise in the morning. And to Suzie too. I could tell she was furious when I gave Jasmine her tortoise.'

'At least you have a fan in my daughter. She thinks you are wonderful!'

Ligne stubbed out his cigarette. This had been his intention.

His good humour restored, Philippe continued, 'In any case,

freemasonry is not that bad. Because of it, Grand Lodge reaches everywhere. As a result, Britain needs no marketing policy. It could not have picked up the Iraq road tender – which would have gone to the Soviets via India otherwise – without the freemasons.'

Ligne gave a mock shudder. 'Marketing policy? Good God, I should think not. Whatever next. You sound like an American!'

Philippe chortled. No worse insult could be hurled at his head.

'. . . It must be the influence of that priest, Father Anthony. I was surprised he was outside the Lodge.'

Philippe grinned. 'The American Father is everywhere! His commitment to Iraq goes deep. The Jesuits are, if you like, the front-line troops against Stalinism.'

Ligne raised an eyebrow. 'Except in Rome, old boy! As we speak, HMG is conducting an inquiry into the links a few of its cardinals have with the Soviets! At the request of the Vatican, I might add.'

'Ah!' responded Philippe. 'This is why the Italians thought they might pick up part of the road project too.'

Ligne nodded. 'The West Germans believed they were also in with a chance. The Soviets made promises they could not keep.'

'Surely you mean East Germans?'

'Them as well.'

Philippe sighed. 'What you say, ties in with my father's worries. He suspects the Soviets are trying to sabotage the Lodge.'

His companion considered the matter. 'I'd be more inclined to blame the Americans. They would knock us out if it was torpedoed. The Soviets have other means of influence. The local trades unions come to mind.'

Philippe looked at him in admiration. Ligne had only been in the country a few days and already had its measure. A slight breeze came off the river. On the far bank, the flame of the Dhoura oil refinery splashed orange against the sky. In the distance, a dog barked as the guards patrolled the grounds.

In another part of the house, the lights went down. Jiddu was obviously ready for sleep. A shadow moved across the wall by the side of the aviary.

'It is only Hussein,' Philippe reassured. 'He does not rest until my father has retired. Now Jiddu has gone to bed, he will drop you to your hotel whenever you wish.'

Ligne was in no hurry to leave. Instead, first offering his cigarette case to Philippe who declined, he lit up again. 'Do you still get up to the north much, yourself?'

Philippe shook his head. 'Not since toxins were dumped on the melting ice. My father was hoping to teach Jasmine to ski there – the snow can be good – but it is too dangerous now. It is even difficult transporting goods across the mountains into Turkey although the poor roads do not help.'

'Do you still trade all over the world?'

Philippe nodded.

'The old Indian Mafia, eh?'

Ligne considered his host. Philippe Palmeira was just what he wanted. He was certain of that.

'Tell me . . .'

Uncertain as to what was coming, Philippe looked at his guest inquiringly.

' . . . Can I consider you a Friend? Are you still pro-British?'

'Of course. It is not Iraq that has abandoned Britain, but the reverse.'

Ligne nodded. 'HMG has made terrible mistakes,' he admitted. 'I am endeavouring to put things right. I even told the Warlord this evening I would have a word with the oil companies – although they are mired in trades union problems. It seems every oil-worker in Iraq believes . . .'

Philippe put a warning finger to his lips. 'I am sorry, Peter. I gave my father my word I would not discuss politics under his roof. May I suggest a stroll along the river? It is a pleasant walk at this time of night.'

Ligne was quick to agree. The two men made their way through the gardens to the jetty. Hussein greeted them. Quietening the dogs, he commented in faultless English, 'It is a beautiful evening.'

Ligne responded in equally faultless Arabic. They conversed in each other's language as a matter of principle. 'What time will you want me later?' queried the old retainer.

'Go to bed, effendi. I will drive our friend,' responded Philippe.

Hussein shook his head. 'I promised Jiddu I would return our visitor to his hotel whenever he wished to leave. Take your time, gentlemen. A walk along the river clears the head.'

Recognising it was pointless to argue, Philippe and Ligne moved off. 'He doesn't like me. Mind, I can't blame him. I'd think he was up to no good if I caught him on a dark night talking to the Warlord!'

'Not here, Peter,' Philippe warned. 'Hussein can still hear you. I love him with all my heart but he reports everything to my father.' Further off, he asked abruptly, 'You do not deny, Peter, you saw the Warlord in London?'

'Of course not. The Warlord is anxious about Iraq's central government. In exchange for HMG granting the north autonomy, he says he can guarantee the oil supply from Kirkuk – along with the workforce! HMG had to see him.'

Philippe frowned. Close to anger, he responded, 'I was not aware HMG was in a position to make such an offer.'

Giving him a sidelong glance, Ligne sighed. 'Of course we're not. HMG saw the Warlord to try and calm things.'

'I hope so,' replied Philippe. 'The only civilian ministers in the Iraq government are well known at the Lodge. They are Abdullah El-Tarek's cousins and excellent men. They wish to see the whole country develop – including the oil industry's trades unions. It would be wrong for the Warlord to move in the shadows when so much good is possible.'

'An exact mirror of my own thoughts – with the exception of the unions! No more than a dastardly Communist front, dear boy.'

'Rubbish! Individual unionists in Britain may be Communist, Peter. This does not mean you condemn trades unionism.'

Ligne gave way immediately. 'Quite so,' he relied with a grin.

They had come to a stop by a low wall. The view was breathtaking. 'I asked you earlier whether you were still a Friend. You did not appear to understand what I meant,' he continued.

Philippe stared over the water, the stillness broken by the noise of a skimming bird sliding across its surface. 'Do not take me for a fool, Peter. I understood what you meant. Once upon a time I believed in Britain and everything for which it stood. As the son of an Indian, I had British papers I was prepared to honour. It is not I who changed but your country: The people of your former empire mean nothing to you. In this respect, my father is correct.'

Ligne shook his head. 'It may seem this way but appearances are deceptive. Countries belong to their own citizens – not to Britain! We had to let the empire go. Nevertheless, Iraq remains central to our plans.'

Philippe gave a wry smile. 'I do not doubt it.'

His companion flushed. 'If you insist on being cynical . . .'

Philippe stilled him. 'Do not let us argue, Peter, and waste this opportunity to renew our friendship.'

Happy to agree, Ligne pleaded, 'Please accept HMG wants the best for Iraq . . .' Correctly surmising his host, after some initial resistance, wished to be persuaded of his good intentions, he continued, ' . . . We need someone we can trust, Philippe, who has the vision to recognise in serving Britain, they serve Iraq. A man of honour. Surely this is you? You cannot refuse, old friend. We are both patriots.'

A few minutes later Philippe Palmeira was recruited into the service of the Crown.

'The salary won't be much, I'm afraid,' commented Ligne, audible delight in his voice.

Philippe shook his head. 'I do not expect, nor want, money, Peter. I am a rich man. I require no salary.'

Ligne laughed. 'You will have to have a salary, otherwise HMG will really think you're a spy. For the other lot!'

Philippe smiled. The logic was typically British. 'Let them think what they like. I will not accept money to do my duty.'

Seeing him obstinate, Ligne turned his back on him. 'You insult the Crown.'

Philippe was stung into silence. When he recovered, he responded, 'Let us not trade insults. The Crown gave me British papers which it does not recognise because I am an Indian, and in consequence my daughter has no passport. And you talk of insults?'

Turning around, Ligne apologised. 'If you will not take financial reward, may I suggest you accept Jasmine's passport as a token of HMG's esteem?'

Philippe bowed his head. He asked for nothing else. As if signalling their new arrangement, he volunteered, 'There is a Russian called Nico Stollen in Baghdad. He says he knew you in London . . .'

Ligne nodded. 'Certainly, I knew the colonel,' he acknowledged.

'He tried to recruit me. He had the cheek to tell my wife he would be particularly interested if you did as well!'

Shaking his head with amusement, Ligne responded, 'He is the very devil, that man. He always was. If he asks again – accept. A double agent will put HMG well ahead of the Americans which should annoy them no end!'

'We are not playing games, Peter.'

Ligne accepted the rebuke with good grace. 'Forgive me. Our goal must be to protect the oil supply. Unless we do so, this beautiful land will be turned into a football kicked between the Russians and Americans. If I seem flippant, it is only because I fear being overwhelmed by the enormity of our responsibilities.'

As they walked back to Hussein, he made his wishes clear. 'Please do whatever Stollen asks. In addition, become a Communist cardholder.'

Philippe refused. 'Absolutely not! My business would not survive. Nor would my family be able to travel freely in Europe or America.'

His companion did not mask his disappointment. 'HMG would send you other business and, moreover, organise all necessary travel documents.'

Philippe was intransigent. 'Stollen has already invited me to become a cardholder. I declined. What reason could I give for changing my mind?'

Ligne gave a sardonic snort. 'All men have their price. Let Stollen believe HMG's was too small to tempt you.'

'This would mean Stollen would feel obliged to offer me a salary too!'

'Naturally. I will arrange for HMG to open a Swiss bank account to receive it.'

They could see Hussein in the distance. He had settled down to a game of trik-trak with the guard, their play illuminated by a flickering candle. Catching sight of them, the man waved, his silhouette outlined in the moonlight.

Acknowledging him, Philippe flicked his worry beads. Made of amber, their aroma scented the air. A few moments later, he and his guest were within hearing range of the servant. Seeing him stand, Philippe motioned he sit down again. 'Please finish your amusement. Mr Ligne and I will have a brandy, so do not hurry.'

Soon, he and Ligne were settled on the veranda once more. They stared out across the Tigris. A graceful dhow, lit across the sails, slid past. Opening his cigarette case, Ligne offered it to his host. This time, Philippe accepted.

'What do you wish to know?'

'Everything, old chap. Who is working for whom in this infernal city. HMG needs introductions.'

Philippe grinned. 'In which case, let me throw a party for you.'

Ligne choked. 'As a rule, we spies tend to keep a low profile!'

'Nonsense. Everybody knows you are here anyway. I will hold a "Spies Party" for you. Baghdad will love the joke.'

Finishing their drinks, he led his guest through the silent house. It was 03.00 hrs. Leaving by the main door, they waited patiently for Hussein to bring the car around.

'What school have you put Jasmine down for?' asked Ligne conversationally.

'We haven't. We intend looking at a few over the summer.'

As Hussein started the motor, the driveway was flooded with welcoming light.

'No need, old thing. We have good links with an excellent one.'

Philippe thanked him. As they waited, Ligne held his eye. 'I must emphasise the need for secrecy. Tell no-one, not even your wife . . .'

Philippe looked at him in surprise. 'I tell Suzie everything. Even that to which I know she is opposed. I learned that lesson from my father.'

'Whatever for? We tell our wives nothing. It is for their own protection,' added Ligne lamely.

'And that, Peter, is why you haven't got a wife!'

Ligne acknowledged the comment with good humour. 'Speaking of married women, do you see anything of the French ambassador's good lady? I used to know her – and her husband, of course – in London. She's quite a good-looking woman.'

Philippe laughed. 'You mean Laure de Chebran.'

'Princesse Laure de Chebran,' murmured Ligne.

'We don't pay much attention to titles here, Peter. But yes, we know Laure and Freddie well. They are a delightful couple. My father says all the men in Baghdad are in love with your princess.'

'London was rather in love with her too! She and Freddie were there prior to their posting to Iraq.'

'London, Peter? Or you were in love with her.'

Looking sheepish, Ligne made no reply. The car glided to a stop by his feet. Hussein got out to open the door for him.

Extending his hand in farewell, the civil servant said under his breath, 'I am serious, my friend. It is imperative Suzie is not made aware of your work.'

'I, too, am serious. If I lie to my wife, how can I expect her to honour me?'

Ligne telephoned the MI6 Chief in London from the British embassy later that morning. Within minutes, Jasmine Palmeira's schooling had been organised, as had her British passport.

'Doesn't Palmeira have an elderly father?' asked Ligne's superior. 'Perhaps we ought to offer him and Palmeira, British papers too. Just to show willing. Your new recruit was probably too proud to ask.'

Ligne was delighted. This, he guessed, had certainly been the case. 'As for the rest, sir, Palmeira struck a hard bargain. He wants cash, paid into a Swiss bank account. The Russians have also recruited him and are likely to prove generous. I have agreed this money can similarly be paid into Switzerland. I hope I have not exceeded my authority.'

'Far from it. I always feel more comfortable when a man has been bought several times over.'

CHAPTER EIGHT

✳ ✺ ✳

FRENCH EMBASSY, BAGHDAD: The day after the Masonic reception, Peter Ligne was delighted but unsurprised to learn the French ambassador and his wife, Freddie and Laure de Chebran, were serving cocktails at their embassy at 16.00 hrs. Arriving promptly at a grand, imposing looking building, he took the steps two by two. As he did so, the lady herself bore down on him in a cloud of glorious scent.

'Cher ami, What a wonderful surprise. I do hope you have brought me a present!'

Ligne grinned. Laure de Chebran was shameless. Absolutely shameless. Stooping over her hand, he replied, 'I am your present, Princesse. Surely this is enough.'

'Bof!' replied Laure. 'You Englishmen are all the same. So mean. I want you, dear Peter, as well as a present! Still, it is wonderful you should find the time to come to my party.'

Everybody found the time to come to Laure's parties.

'What are we celebrating?'

'Do we need an excuse? I told Freddie if he must invent one, the twentieth anniversary of the ENA – Ecole Nationale d'Administration – would do. Alternatively, of course, I said we could celebrate Francois' first attempt at the Presidency.'

'Francois?'

'Mitterand. He is a very old friend. Hélas, Freddie said "non". Presumably because Francois is not an enarque!'

Ligne laughed. Freddie de Chebran was a distinguished alumni of the ENA. 'Does he still boast ENA placements will one day dominate France's top jobs even more comprehensibly than Oxbridge does in Britain?'

'Ask him yourself!' replied Laure, motioning to an antique chaise longue behind.

Turning around, Ligne discovered the French ambassador, as distinguished as his wife was charming, settled in comfort. Happy to be caught in the act of studying his guests, the diplomat rose and queried with good humour, 'Ask me what?'

Ligne looked at the piece of furniture with a half-smile. It had been at the French embassy in London too. He had once made rather a fool of himself on it. He hoped Laure had forgotten the incident.

'What brings you to Baghdad, Peter?' continued her husband. He was a spruce man, both sartorially and in his manner.

'The weapons contract, of course!' responded Laure, the embodiment of aristocratic nonsense. She did not add this was the real reason she had given her party.

Moving on and happy to show off his impeccable command of languages, Ligne was soon deep in conversation with the Italian and West German military attachés.

The de Chebrans surveyed their guests. Taking his wife's hand, and entwining her fingers through his, smiling this way and that, Freddie asked in his quiet way, 'Have you found out, ma cocotte, what that bastard is really up to?'

'No, cheri, but doubtless someone will tell me in due course.

Meanwhile, I cannot stand the way he calls me "princesse". I am not Grace Kelly.'

'What are you two conspiring about?

The couple started, embarrassed they had been caught so deep in conversation. Seeing Father Anthony, Laure went up on tiptoe to kiss him. 'We are not conspiring, mon père. Merely discussing the British.'

'Then perhaps I can be excused from participating until I have been fortified by one of your excellent Dubonnets!'

As if by magic, a waiter bearing a large silver tray appeared at his elbow. Father Anthony took two glasses on the basis he had some catching up to do. Downing one, he pronounced, 'My dear, these really are excellent!'

'I am glad you think so, mon père. It was the Queen Mother in London who taught me how to mix a Dubonnet cocktail. Enough Dubonnet to give colour. The rest – gin!'

Father Anthony chuckled. 'You were saying about the British,' he prompted.

Making things up as she went along, Laure declared, 'That they have never forgiven France for not regretting it beheaded its Royal Family. This is why, deep down, the British love the Russians. They cherish the fiction they do!'

Father Anthony smiled his disapproval.

Unabashed, she continued, 'Have you heard Nico Stollen's latest?'

He shook his head.

Her eyes sparkling, she informed him, 'Nico was so cross Peter Ligne named little Jasmine Palmeira's tortoise "HMG", he went out and got her another one called "KGB", so now the child has two! Jiddu gave his approval on the basis they are ideally suited.'

Amused, Father Anthony took her arm. 'Is Jiddu not joining us?'

She shook her head. 'He sent his apologies. He says the "KGB" and "HMG" are keeping him far too busy! He sent you a message, by the way – if the pair mate and have a baby, he will name it "CIA"!'

Laughing as they made their way into the embassy's main salon, Father Anthony remarked, 'Things could be worse: He could have called it "Vatican"!'

'He considered this – but proclaimed its agents too worldly! You may take the matter up with Philippe and Suzie. They have been delayed because of the arrangements for their "Spies Party". Suzie tells me Philippe is so cross with his father at the moment, they are not speaking!'

At her house on the Tigris, Suzie Palmeira answered the telephone. Her voice was brusque. Several diplomats had already rung to find out why their invitation to her assembly had not arrived and she was irritated at being interrupted further. In addition, she was faced with the prospect of her husband and father-in-law continuing at loggerheads.

'Is it senior spies only, or can I bring the Russian ambassador?' she heard Stollen's laconic voice asking.

Despite herself, Suzie giggled. 'Bring him by all means, Nico. After all, the British ambassador has been invited. And he's not a senior spy!'

'So true, my dear. Are you aware that at the last count, the British had forty-eight spies in Beirut, Amman and Baghdad? Forty-nine if I include your husband.'

'You do talk a lot of rubbish, old thing.'

Laughing, Stollen asked for Jiddu.

She emitted a theatrical sigh. 'He is causing a great deal of trouble "potting" a flower-bed for Jasmine's tortoises on her late grandmother's balcony. There is earth and mess everywhere – just as we need things neat as a pin! Apparently, the beasts keep getting lost in the garden. He says he prefers to have the KGB and HMG where he can see them!'

A gleeful Stollen rang off. A few moments later, she found her daughter beside her. Tugging at her sleeve, the little girl cried, 'Mummy! Mummy! Listen to the new song Jiddu's taught me. It goes like this:

HMG! KGB!
What a busy bee I'll be,
When they come round for tea!'

'He says it's for Daddy.'

Philippe Palmeira was with Iraq's Minister of Protocol. The latter was more than happy for the 'Spies Party' to proceed – all social events required ministerial approval. He said it proved Iraq's independence from the super powers.

Thanking him, Philippe remarked, 'Naturally, Minister, you will meet Peter Ligne.'

'I have already met him. He tried to influence the weapons contract. The two-faced bastard – to prove his bone fide credentials – even told me about the guns he is supplying the Warlord.'

Philippe's face was a mask.

The minister continued, 'The Russian, Nico Stollen, believes Ligne intends to recruit you. If he does – and has not already – tell him to stop meddling with the Kurds. In the old days we fought the real enemy – the British. Now we fight ourselves.'

Philippe laughed. 'Ligne has not recruited me, Minister. He said it would be far too obvious!'

The falsehood came so easily, it was as if he had been lying all his days.

CHAPTER NINE

�֍ ✲ ✶

PALMEIRA VILLA, BAGHDAD: The night of the 'Spies Party' came all too soon. It was a beautiful evening. Philippe and Suzie's home and private beach along the Tigris were lit with fairy lights. The Masonic orchestra played all the modern tunes. Everybody looked their tip-top best. Many of the guests arrived by boat, landing at the little jetty beyond the gardens which sloped down to the river.

Suzie, in lilac chiffon, stood beside her father-in-law as the guards, in white and gold, their rifles slung across their backs, assisted the wives of the ambassadors of France, West Germany and the United States. Their vessels jostled as they landed at the same time. Philippe greeted those arriving by motor car at the front of the house. He and his family liked a bit of a 'do'.

Stepping out in white tails, Ligne shook Philippe's hand, noticing the Masonic ring he was wearing. 'Good grief, effendi, you make me feel guilty – Grand Secretary Sir Julian Lawrence in London made me promise not to involve the Worshipful Master's son in politics!'

'It is not deliberate, Peter, I assure you,' smiled Philippe. 'I am wearing it to please my father. He is battling to save the Lodge from closure. He believes it can hold the country together and wishes to emphasise this to our guests.'

Ligne lingered a few moments longer before making his way inside. As he left, Philippe commented, 'The Minister of

Protocol tells me you informed him of HMG's secret agreement with the Kurds . . .'

Apparently puzzled, Ligne replied, 'Certainly I did. Did you not think I should? I thought it the best way to protect the Warlord. Have I done wrong?'

Philippe motioned him away with good humour. Ligne had made a mistake but it had no malicious intent.

Following the hub-bub, the civil servant found a vast crowd at the centre of the house, his eyes dazzled by fabulous jewels sparkling on pretty necks and slim wrists. In a far corner, a cabaret girl sang *I Wanna Hold Your Hand*, followed by *I Get A Kick Out Of You*, staring pointedly at Abdullah El-Tarek.

The latter watched with a silly expression on his face until his wife, recently returned from France, got hold of him. 'I promise, angel, I did not even look at the singer,' he protested loudly. 'Me? Flirt? Of course not. The girl merely asked me earlier to adjust the strap of her dress.'

Sensing the beginning of a quarrel, Jiddu joined the performer in The Beatles song *Love Me Do*, before they gave way to Laure, radiant to the eye, singing *All You Need Is Love*. Abdullah's wife, quickly reconciled with her husband, clapped her hands in delight. Next, Suzie emerged, her gown drifting and submerging in the crush, to dance with Father Anthony. She excused herself as *Tell Me What Is Love* rang out in a brilliantly fast tempo.

Philippe, knowing he was missing the fun, looked at his watch with impatience wondering whether he could yet go indoors. Seeing his wife come to join him, he kissed her. The photographer caught them laughing into the camera.

Two minutes later, the couple greeted the Hungarians. Next the British ambassador's Rolls wound its way up the drive. Behind came the Minister of Protocol in his old Landrover.

The Rolls came to a stop. The guards stood to attention as the diplomat and his wife alighted. 'Not the last to arrive, I hope,' he greeted his hosts, meaning the opposite.

'No,' responded Suzie. 'The Minister of Protocol is behind in his old Jeep.'

In the large room leading on to the veranda, Miro talked to the Warlord and Peri. They were soon joined by Abdullah and his wife, as elegant as her husband was not. Ligne watched them from the far corner of the room.

Further on, he could see Father Anthony and Stollen falling over themselves to light Laure's cigarette. He moved closer. 'On my daughter's honour, we are not poisoning our own water,' the Warlord was saying.

Abdullah nodded. 'My Brother, it is one of the super-powers trying to cause problems.'

'I am told the gossip on the race-course is that Peter Ligne is responsible.'

Abdullah giggled. 'I said one of the super-powers!'

'The Americans?'

'Possibly. Although it is more likely to be the Soviets in the hope you will blame the USA. Do not play into their hands, whoever it is. Speak with my dear cousin, the Minister of Protocol, who will be here tonight. I know he is anxious to talk to you about Ligne. He believes him innocent of any connection with the poisoned water. Nonetheless, he wants to warn you Ligne is duplicitous.'

Unperturbed, Ligne helped himself to another glass of champagne and a scoop of caviar, wondering to which group he could most profitably attach himself. A few moments later, he noticed Stollen, his arm around Laure, join the Warlord.

The Frenchwoman's hair was swept high above her neck and held within the circlet of a diamond tiara. Matching diamonds sparkled at her wrist and throat. Having first greeted Abdullah's wife in French – the latter having been educated in Paris – she fixed Miro with her alluring green eyes and held out her hand.

'We have not met before, Dr Miro, but I have heard much about you. I do hope you can attend a small reception I am holding next week. I regret no-one told you of our Open House the other day.'

Miro, in the full dress kilt of his father's clan, was overwhelmed. The room, it seemed, shone. Ligne continued to inspect the group from his discreet vantage point.

Even all these years later, he still admired Laure. Rising forty, she cast her spell effortlessly. He had once confessed to her husband, she was the only woman with whom he would have considered marriage. 'A career move?' Freddie had inquired.

Despite the noise, he could hear her husky laugh. She had everything that mattered to him. Looks, birth, charm and keen intelligence.

Stollen, he noticed, was up to his old tricks, paying her particular attention while talking to the Warlord at the same time. 'I don't blame the British for renewing their secret alliance with you,' he was saying.

The Warlord frowned. His daughter Peri had heard the comment.

'What secret agreement?' she demanded.

Her father was unable to meet her eye. Seeing his discomfort, Stollen laughed. 'Pay no attention, my dear. I am merely seeking to make trouble between you and your parent.'

'If that is your intention, Nico, you shall not succeed,' interrupted Laure, her gloved hand gently cuffing his ears. Stollen captured her fingers.

'We are lucky in Madame la Princesse. She is the only one who can shame you,' remarked Peri.

Laure shook her head. 'Remember always, Nico is without shame.'

Stollen made no attempt to disabuse her of Laure's opinion. Shrugging, he saw Ligne across the room. Seeing his eyes fixed upon Laure, he held her closer. The Briton's evident annoyance was a pleasure, even from a distance.

'Penny for them.'

Ligne started, finding Freddie de Chebran at his side. Following the civil servant's gaze, the latter chuckled. 'Uh-huh, as you will remember, Laure and Stollen are childhood friends. Stollen's father was ambassador to Paris some years before the Second World War.'

'The man's a bloody Communist!'

'So's Laure. This, I must admit, is something of an embarrassment to her old admirer Francois Mitterand, since he is no longer!'

Ligne raised an eyebrow. 'I understand Mitterand is making an assault on the presidency. I assume he will not get in.'

The French ambassador nodded. 'Not this time, no. But Mitterand will succeed one day. Why else do you think Stollen takes such care to court him? Mind, their liking for each other is genuine. And, of course, they have Laure in common.'

Ligne frowned. 'And this does not compromise you?'

Freddie looked mystified. 'Why should it? The French Communists have a valiant history. It was only when they became an embarrassment to de Gaulle that they were marginalised. Besides, Laure only fancies me!'

Despite himself, Ligne laughed.

Freddie held his eye. 'I expect you have been told there are worries about the water supply in the north, Peter. In view of this, perhaps I could point out my government worries a great deal about the Kurds in the area. Grace a Dieu we are lucky in Father Anthony . . .'

'I was not aware France was that keen on Americans, even if they are Jesuits.'

Untroubled by the barb, the ambassador waved his hand in the air. 'We have nothing against Americans at all. It is just they have no idea how to run a republic!'

Ligne grinned. 'I have never quite got to grips with republican competition.'

'Touché!'

A few moments later, his voice now serious, the ambassador observed, 'America is out of its depth in Iraq.'

'But France is not, Eh, mon vieux?'

'Of course not. Only the Germans know it as well. It is the Ottoman connection. The French continue to have the advantage because Germany is split in two.'

'You appear not to rate the British.'

'No-one can rate HMG more highly than it does itself.'

Before Ligne could respond, the Minister of Protocol joined them.

'Perfect timing, Minister,' remarked Freddie de Chebran.

'Indeed? In which case, I must have missed a choice insult!'

'An insult, certainly. But not that choice,' laughed Ligne.

The men bantered good-naturedly. A few moments later, raising an eyebrow at Ligne in mock provocation, the minister opined, 'I am informed by Andrew Fitzwilliams he is to be a politician like myself. He says he will pick up what he calls a "safe seat". He confirms what I have always suspected . . . Britain's democracy is "by appointment" only!'

Refusing to rise to the bait, Ligne replied, 'You have taken Fitzwilliams out of context, Minister.'

The latter chuckled. 'I think not, Mr Ligne. We have the same system here. I am a Shia, my cousin a Sunni. We are both freemasons. Our other relatives are Ba'thi and Communists. We represent them all.'

'Hardly democracy, Minister – you have no Parliament.'

A huge smile pervaded the man's face. 'We tried this system out, Mr Ligne, but found it unsophisticated. It suits the British. You herd all your senior tribesmen into the House of Lords to give them something to do. This keeps Britain together. In our case, we found it fractured Iraq.'

Changing the subject, he turned to Freddie de Chebran. 'I understand anti-Semitism is rising again in France, Mr Ambassador. Learn from my country's wickedness. Once, Baghdad had a glorious symphony orchestra. Today it does not. Why? Its finest musicians were Jewish – and they were thrown out of the country because of this. It will take years to rebuild our musical traditions: Iraqis adore music.'

'You are right, Minister. French anti-Semitism is indeed rampant and shames the Republic. Do you not agree, Peter?'

'If you say so, old boy.'

They ignored his obvious anti-Semitism. Accepting a drink, the minister continued, 'Jiddu, Samuel and I are agreed co-operation among the People of the Book, free of Western interference, is the only way forward for our little country.'

The ambassador looked unhappy. 'However noble your intentions, you will be thwarted, sir.'

'You are saying Iraq is doomed to be the pawn of the super powers indefinitely?'

The Frenchman nodded.

It was time for the Iraqi to move on. There were countless foreign officials present with whom it would be courteous to exchange a few words. On the point of leaving, he remarked, 'Ah yes. I almost forgot, my dear Freddie. My cousin the Defence Minister looks forward to meeting you tomorrow, if this is convenient . . .'

Freddie de Chebran bowed. He was well aware of the significance of such an invitation. The Minister of Protocol refused to accept his thanks.

'Mr Ligne, here, delivered your contract. He sells arms to my Brother the Warlord, and, to cover himself, tells me about this – as well as the latter's promise to deliver Britain the northern oil-fields, along with the workforce and its unions. It is a true democrat trick. I prefer the French way of business. They negotiate with any who pay the price and tell no-one. For this reason, the weapons deal belongs to France.'

Bringing his heels together, he made his farewells. As he

departed, he said to the Briton, 'Please convey my regards to your ambassador's good lady. It was nice of her to ask whether I liked my beef "rare or well done".'

When he had gone, a furious Peter Ligne turned his back on the French ambassador and made his way to Stollen. The Russian was still flirting with Laure. 'Do all aristocrats know each other?' he enthused as the civil servant kissed her hand.

Despite himself, Ligne felt absurdly pleased with the compliment as Stollen had intended him to be. When the dinner was announced, he went out of his way to walk beside Miro.

'Glad Laure has invited you to her next bash. It makes it so much easier for our chaps . . .'

Puzzled, Miro queried, 'What do you mean?'

'Oh. Did you not know? Negroes are not allowed at the British embassy.'

Miro swayed. Apparently oblivious to the humiliation he had caused, Ligne sauntered ahead. Samuel Solomon, who had heard the comment, took the contractor's arm.

'Prejudice, my friend, is wicked. Doubly so, when it is unexpected. Rise above it.'

'But I am a Scot, as my father was, and his father before him,' responded Miro in bitter disbelief.

'And I was born in Iraq. This does not mean my beautiful girls can call it home.'

Putting his arm around Miro's shoulders, he continued, 'Learn, my friend, to glory in those without prejudice. There are more of them than there are of the others.'

CHAPTER TEN

❋ ❋ ❋

'SPIES PARTY', BAGHDAD: Philippe and Suzie officially opened the dancing after the banquet. Peri, at the instigation of Samuel, insisted Miro lead her on to the floor.

A short while later, as the sound of the *Dashing White Sergeant* filled the air, he abandoned himself to the gaiety of those who welcomed him. The beautiful Tigris river gleamed in the moonlight. Within minutes, the room was filled with whoops and whirls.

Arabs and Kurds swirled to the sound of bagpipes more usually heard on Burns Night. Samuel's daughters danced with scarlet ribbons in their hair. Miro spun Peri, his red tartan swaying.

As a lively Military Two-Step came on, Ligne escorted Suzie. He surrendered her to Jiddu for the Twist, joining Philippe for a cool drink. Soon after, following an energetic Charleston, an exhausted Laure and Andrew Fitzwilliams collapsed at the foot of the staircase. Glancing up, they saw Jasmine in her night-gown.

'Come down, chérie. I will make sure you do not get into trouble with your mother,' called out Laure.

Requiring little encouragement, the child was beside her in seconds. 'This is Mr Fitzwilliams. He is a friend of Dr Miro and Mr Ligne.'

Jasmine curtsied. Peeping up, she asked Andrew Fitzwilliams coyly, 'Mr Ligne said "HMG" came all the way from England in his briefcase. But Uncle Nico told me Amu Abdullah brought it from the mountains of Kurdistan. Is one of them lying?'

Fitzwilliams did his best not to give the game away. 'A little white lie, perhaps. Although I must say, I am sure I saw Peter Ligne give "HMG" a lettuce leaf when we were on the aeroplane together.'

Against all the odds, he was enjoying himself. Earlier, he had partnered Samuel's daughters, followed by Suzie and Peri. He had led Laure several times.

On an impulse, he stood up and excused himself from the French ambassador's wife. Guessing his intentions, she blew him a kiss. Next, with a graceful bow, he asked Jasmine to dance.

The latter was beside herself with joy. Accepting his hand like a true grande dame and confident of her steps, she was on the floor within seconds. As the music got faster and faster, her beau lifted her high off the ground in an ever more energetic Quickstep.

Seeing them, Stollen, dancing with Suzie, commented, 'Your daughter is stealing an Englishman's heart!'

'So long as it is that way around. Otherwise, Jiddu will most likely shoot him!'

The latter, they noticed, was standing at the perimeter flicking his worry beads. Jasmine waved to her grandfather. He smiled. Philippe claimed his wife soon after.

Leaving the couple, Stollen joined Ligne by the large window over-looking the garden. Like Jiddu, the Briton was watching Andrew Fitzwilliams and Jasmine with a bemused look on his face.

Acknowledging the Russian, he queried, 'Do you know anything about the Minister of Protocol, Nico?'

Stollen shook his head. 'Very little. He gives me as wide a berth as possible – he disapproves of Communists – and leaves me to his cousin, the Minister of Defence, who does not. Why?'

'HMG lost the weapons contract. I imagine the French are paying the cousins a cut.'

Stollen laughed. 'Make up such comforts if you must, Peter. However, be assured, neither of them take bribes.'

'You knew about the contract?'

Stollen inclined his head. Finding no comfort in his companion, Ligne looked around for Laure. Guessing his intention, Stollen gestured towards the moonlight. 'She has, I believe, led Freddie into the aviary.'

'You sound jealous, Nico.'

Stollen's jaw hardened. 'Why should it bother you?'

Surprised to find him so sensitive, Ligne raised an eyebrow but let the matter drop.

'Miro says the problems in the water supply are coming from Turkey,' he ventured a few moments later.

His companion nodded. 'Which, as we all know, means the Americans.'

Ligne grinned. 'Good try, Nico!' Mouthing good-night to Jasmine, now being led upstairs to bed by her mother, he continued, 'My government does not like getting the blame for poisoning a water supply when it is innocent of such wrongdoing.'

'I'm sure it does not, mon cher.'

'We could make trouble. After all, we could commission

Miro to do a full study – he is sufficiently honourable to count as an independent witness.'

'Indeed he is.'

'Or, I could blame the French.'

Stollen laughed. 'If you wish.'

'How about Iraq's trades unionists?'

'Contrary to what you believe, Moscow is indifferent to them.'

'Unlikely, old boy, but very well, the French it is. And in return? I really do not think I can let you have something for nothing.'

Stollen's good humour evaporated. Looking at his companion with something approaching disdain, he replied, 'I never expect anything for nothing, Peter. I offer to discredit the American political officer for you. He is an excellent man. It should make your task in Iraq so much easier if I damage him.'

Ligne nodded at Stollen in appreciation. He was glad they understood each other. 'I wouldn't mind seeing the back of that American Jesuit too. Father wot-not.'

He was surprised to see Stollen stiffen. 'I am offering only the American political officer. I do not interfere with priests.'

'You must be the only KGB man who does not!'

Casting a languid eye over his companion, Ligne continued, 'Your only anxiety about the water supply, Nico, is for us to deflect attention from the Russians?'

'Correct.'

'Then we are agreed.'

He whisked two glasses of champagne off the serving boy. Passing one to Stollen, he remarked, 'There is another small matter with which you can help – I'd like you to invite Miro and Fitzwilliams to Moscow.'

'Why?'

'Because they would be the first representatives of a western employers union to visit the country. If I were able to organise such a trip, I would petrify Mr Wilson, the Labour Prime Minister. He would wonder what the intelligence services were playing at!'

They made their way to the veranda where tables and chairs had been arranged. Once settled, Stollen considered the matter. 'Given Dr Miro's nuclear background, the Americans will think the British are trying to screw up their talks with my government,' he mused. 'The French, however, will be delighted since they will assume the talks have been screwed up!'

Grinning, he concluded, 'Yes, my friend. I am happy to invite Miro and Fitzwilliams to Moscow.'

Ligne raised his glass. The sound of music and laughter drifted outside. Along the river, the boatmen lit a fire.

'What are you paying Philippe Palmeira by the way?'

'A fortune. Attractive wives come expensive.'

The Russian smiled. Lighting a cigarette – Ligne declined – he remarked, 'I understand you have persuaded Philippe to send Jasmine to school in Kent. Isn't that Fitzwilliams' future constituency?'

'What of it?'

Exhaling, Stollen replied, 'It is reassuring to know while controlling the father, you will be incubating the child.'

'Merely pre-emptive. Girls can make useful marriages.'

Chuckling, Stollen agreed. 'I shall be very disappointed if Jasmine does not grow up to marry, at the very least, a British cabinet minister for me!'

'Boo! Guess who?' Laure's voice squealed in Ligne's ear as her gloved hands covered his eyes.

Laughing, he kissed her fingers. 'What have you done with Freddie?'

'Abandoned him in the aviary. He fell over and is covered in goodness knows what.'

Turning to Stollen, she wagged her finger. 'You! You wretch. How dare you poison the water supply in the north.'

'You would do better to blame the Americans.'

'Nonsense,' spluttered Laure. 'Do you think me a fool? The American political officer is a good person. It is you!

'You are probably using the Turks to make trouble between the Iraq government, the Iranians and the Americans – in the process setting every Kurd against each other, along with the freemasons and Jews in the Lodge. Meantime, the whole of Baghdad thinks Peter here is responsible!'

Stollen did not deny it. 'Do not put that theory to Ligne too boldly, my dear,' he said with affection. 'You will undo all my good work. We have just agreed to blame you. It was either this or the trades unions!'

Laure smiled her sweetest smile. 'It must be such a comfort to the Soviets, the Allies work against each other so well.'

A few moments later, she and Ligne stepped inside. 'And where are you going after Iraq?' she asked as he led her on to the floor.

'The Italian Lakes. Coming with me, Princesse?'

Suzie scanned her husband's face. He seemed strangely elated. 'Darling, what is it?' she asked with a sense of foreboding.

Philippe held her closer. As he spun her around, he whispered Peter Ligne had arranged for him to sign the Official Secrets Act and swear the Oath of Allegiance at the British embassy the following day. Suzie was aghast. She did not like Ligne.

It might have been because of the way he spoiled Jiddu's pleasure by giving Jasmine her tortoise, when it had not been his pleasure to spoil. Or it might have been because of the influence he had so quickly established over her husband. Either way, she did not like him.

'Darling, it is too dangerous . . .'

Philippe twirled her around, her beautiful dress following behind like a sea of lilac froth. 'I have British passports for Jasmine and my father – and one for myself,' he murmured, drawing her closer again.

'But Father does not want a British passport! He was only worried about yours and Jasmine's!'

The *Iraq Times* devoted a full page and pictorial record to the Palmeira party the following day. Flying back to Britain on the BOAC aeroplane that evening, Ligne reflected on the photographs. One in particular caught his attention. Laure and Miro were pictured standing next to Stollen and the Russian ambassador. He snipped it carefully, cutting out Laure.

By the time it had been filed in MI6 records back in London, the caption read: *Dr Miro held secret discussions with the Soviets in Baghdad.* A copy was also passed to the POUKI.

Miro and Fitzwilliams left the country at the end of the

week. Driven to the airport in one of Jiddu's finest motorcars, they arrived to hear the Masonic band playing *Give My Love To London*.

The American political officer was the next to go. Compromised – as Stollen had said he would be – he returned to Washington in disgrace. Innocent of all wrong-doing, it took him years to clear his name. Henri Sale-Gonfleur's evil visa trade was back in business the minute he had gone.

Finally, Philippe and Suzie left with Jasmine. Jiddu declined to accompany them. He continued to decry the fact his granddaughter was to be educated in Britain. However, he was quiet about his disapproval in front of the girl.

At the airport, he pulled her to him. 'Do not forget us, will you my pet, when you go to school?'

She shook her head.

Suzie kissed her father-in-law. 'Thank you for making things easier for us, Baba,' she murmured, using the Arabic word for 'Daddy'.

The old man shrugged. 'What hope is there for old men if they do not accept their children's world?'

Catching Philippe's eye, he held out his hand. 'Have a good journey, my son. And know all the jewels in the universe are as nothing to those you can hold in your arms.'

Soon after, their flight was called. It was time to go. Jiddu pulled Jasmine to him one last time. 'The tortoise came from Kurdistan, not from England. Always remember Peter Ligne did not tell the truth.'

Obedient, she repeated, 'I'll remember, Grandfather. Peter Ligne did not tell the truth.'

1970

CHAPTER ELEVEN

✳ ✤ ✳

ROME: Father Anthony was escorted across the Vatican's cobbled courtyard by two Swiss guards in plumed helmets. He was apprehensive. Relations between himself and the Pontiff had been strained ever since, a couple of years before, he had refused to return to America to handle widespread dissent following publication of the Papal encyclical on birth control, *Humanae Vitae*. In his diary, Father Anthony had written: *Phew!*

Walking at a brisk pace, he was soon shown to the Pope's quarters and offices of his household and secretariat. Led into a smallish function room – which seemed at odds with the exotic procession of his arrival – he was offered tea or coffee before being left alone. A few moments later, a soft voice said from behind, 'Thank you for coming to see me, my son.'

Turning, he saw a wiry man with restless, energetic eyes. Smiling, the Pontiff extended his hand. He had entered the room via a hitherto unnoticed side door.

Father Anthony sank to his knees. For all his church's faults, and he acknowledged there were many, at that instant he had no doubt of his vocation. Raising him to his feet, His Holiness asked searchingly, 'Do the Chaldeans of Iraq think I have forgotten them?'

Father Anthony shook his head. Not so long ago, he had celebrated mass at St Joseph's in Baghdad, where the women and children had sung a hymn to the Virgin. It had been a hundred verses long and the Chaldes had known every word.

The two men considered each other in their own time. Shutting the connecting door so they could be quite private, the Pontiff motioned his guest to a large easy chair. 'When you return to Iraq, say you have seen Me. Tell them the Christians of Iraq beat in Our hearts forever and Il Papa never forgets them.'

Father Anthony's response could not have been more straight-forward. 'I hope so, Holy Father. At present, the Soviets are in the ascendant in Baghdad. As a result, my ministrations continue because one of their Russian diplomats, Nico Stollen, has ensured all the churches and synagogues remain open. Nevertheless, the plight of the Christians is almost as precarious as that of the Jews. In addition, anxieties remain that Iraq could go Communist.'

The Pope nodded. Seating himself opposite his guest, he picked up a pen and writing board. 'You have a letter for me, I believe, from a Kurd known as the Warlord?'

Nodding, Father Anthony pulled it from one of the deep side pockets of his clerical gown. Handing it over, he remarked, 'The Warlord hopes you will have some sway with the White House.'

The Pontiff sighed. He would have found it easier if his priest had not been so blunt. 'I am sorry to reproach you, my son. You are St Peter's emissary and must not concern yourself with . . .'

'Do you wish to be briefed on Iraq, Holy Father, or do I waste my time?'

Accepting the rebuke, a gentle smile illuminated the Pontiff's face. 'I see you are determined to speak, my son. Please do so. St Peter can wait.'

Father Anthony did not dissemble. 'Saddam Hussein – who is Iraq's leader in all but name – is the new strong man in the Middle East. He rattles the White House by challenging the Shah of Iran and threatening to invade Kuwait. Britain obstructed a fair settlement of Iraq-Kuwait issues and now we see the result.

'Simultaneously, having lost their foothold in Egypt, the Russians dig themselves deeper into the country. In response, the Americans unleash Muslim fundamentalism. This devours the tolerant nature and people of Islam, denying them secular or political voice.'

His Holiness lay down his pen. 'But I understood Saddam Hussein believes Moscow to have outlived its usefulness. The Americans therefore are in the ascendant. They are not even threatened by Britain, the traditional player in the Middle East.'

Father Anthony was pleased to find his Pontiff so well informed. 'This is correct, Holy Father. However, to hasten the departure of the Soviets, the Americans intend to give Saddam Hussein what he wants.'

The Pope looked at him with mild inquiry in his eyes. 'Which is?'

'Saddam Hussein is on the trail of his own nuclear bomb.'

'How do we know this?' came the pragmatic reply.

'Saddam Hussein's desire Iraq become a nuclear country has been known for some time. He asked the French to assist first.

They were honourable and refused. He was so angry he expelled the ambassador and his wife. Freddie and Laure de Chebran are packing as we speak. It is Laure de Chebran who told me.'

The Pontiff's gaze never left his face. 'You are saying the Americans have given the go-ahead for an Iraqi nuclear missile programme?'

'Yes. Stollen, who has a source in Lloyd's of London says Lloyd's will provide the insurance.'

'Lloyd's does not insure war related issues.'

'Lloyd's, Holy Father, is a cynical institution. A British public servant, Peter Ligne, has arranged with the Americans that construction will be under the auspices of a civil engineering company called Fitzwilliams International. It has a phoney office in West Germany. The contract has civilian use – such dual purpose enables Lloyd's to insure the project.'

Deeply shocked, the Pope queried, 'Do you believe it possible Lloyd's and the British civil servant are America's dupe?'

'No. Peter Ligne's information is supplied by a man called Philippe Palmeira. Due to Palmeira's close friendship with Nico Stollen, he succeeded in worming his way into Saddam Hussein's dreadful satrapy to bring back vital knowledge. Despite this excellent intelligence, Peter Ligne turns a blind eye. Palmeira is devastated. He risks his life for nothing. It is a personal tragedy. He trusted Ligne.'

'Why was Philippe Palmeira so naive?'

Father Anthony took his time before replying. 'It is not naive to trust a friend. It is good faith.'

'And his friendship with Ligne . . .'

'Continues. Ligne has told Palmeira he is powerless against the Americans. He has blamed the US for everything.'

'And Palmeira believes him?'

'He is in too deep not to.'

The Pontiff sighed. All about him were those 'in too deep': The collapse of the Prague Spring two years before when he tried to convince the Soviets the uprising had not been an American plot; democracy in Chile undermined by the Americans despite the best efforts of the Vatican; problems in Northern Ireland, not least because of IRA funding raised in America. There was nowhere to turn. Not even to the British whose once moral integrity shaped the world.

He read the Warlord's letter twice to make sure he was certain of its every nuance. Father Anthony was already aware of its contents. Having understood the concerns expressed, the Pope queried, 'What does the Warlord want Us to do?'

'Exert pressure on the American government. The Warlord accepts you cannot ask the British since, following their inquiry into the cardinals' links with the Soviets, the Holy See is in their debt.'

'Ah yes. A mistake. It gave them leverage. Has the Warlord written to anyone else?'

A flicker of hesitation crossed Father Anthony's face. Setting his doubts aside, he replied, 'Yes, Holy Father. Someone in London who is very close to the British establishment. The Warlord's letter will be delivered by Ghazi El-Tarek, the son of a prominent Iraqi. His father is the country's chief veterinarian.'

The Pope chuckled. 'And I am not allowed to know who this "someone" is, but you are nevertheless going to London to meet him?'

Father Anthony looked embarrassed.

Smiling, His Holiness confided, 'I am already aware you are meeting the Masonic Grand Secretary, Sir Julian Lawrence.'

Father Anthony looked at him in amazement.

'... When you see Sir Julian, tell him We admire his courage and what he is trying to do. But warn him. He has made many enemies by sweeping out so many of his fraternity's sagging old guard.'

Accepting the commission, Father Anthony asked how the Pontiff was so well informed. His Holiness was happy to explain his nuncio in London kept him abreast of such matters. 'Three years ago, Our nuncio worried he might not be invited to Grand Lodge's 250th anniversary. A spectacular affair, by all accounts. He thought the Grand Chaplain might veto his invitation . . .'

- The position of Grand Chaplain was one of the highest offices in English Protestant freemasonry –

'... As a result, Our nuncio – who is quite a one for a party – thought it best to keep an eye on Britain's Masonic Brothers!'

Hoping to maintain the liveliness of their conversation, Father Anthony teased, 'I am also going to London to see a thirteen year old school-girl!'

'Jasmine Palmeira?'

He was again dumbfounded. Pleased with his little joke, the Pope explained, 'She writes to Us from time to time. The Russian, Nico Stollen, put her up to it. In view of his seniority, her letters are brought to my attention.'

Father Anthony flushed with anger. 'I have always believed Stollen's influence on the child to be dangerous. Now I have the proof. He puffs her up so she thinks she can do no wrong. It is reprehensible. What exactly does Jasmine say in her letters?'

'She talks about the observatory in Baghdad. Stollen is playing a dangerous game.'

'Does she write about anything else?'

His Holiness beamed. 'Certainly, my son. She says you still yearn for nicotine and that Stollen keeps trying to tempt you to take up smoking again! So far, she reports, you have not succumbed.'

Father Anthony flew out of Rome early the following morning. Shortly before lunch, Ghazi El-Tarek greeted him warmly at Heathrow airport's Terminal 2. Kissing him, the American Jesuit complained, 'I preferred this place when it was called Europa Building. A terminal has no identity.'

Ghazi grinned. 'Heathrow is the junction of the world. What greater identity does it need?'

Snorting his disagreement – in his opinion, a numbering system was no more than a ruse to add even further anonymous buildings in due course – Father Anthony stood back so he could get a good look at the young man. Now aged twenty-eight, Ghazi was tall and fine-featured, with an engaging smile.

'Your parents are missing you,' he continued. 'They long for the day you make Iraq your home again. Maybe your wife . . .'

Ghazi was quick to interrupt him. 'No-one must blame her,

Father, for my reluctance to return to the Middle East. Like countless Britons, she adores the area. I am the guilty one ...'

'But what have you got against the place?'

Ghazi looked embarrassed. He knew his parents ached for his company and that of their daughter-in-law, of whom they were particularly fond. In addition, he felt guilty about abandoning Iraq.

Picking his words with care, he replied, 'I accept that one of these days, Baghdad will be one of the most advanced cities in the world. In the meantime, I do not like it. Every time I am there, I find neighbours forever informing on each other. It is no way to live. And not a single Arab journalist tells the truth!'

Father Anthony swung his airline bag over his shoulder. He did not disagree. Moving the subject on, he expressed his gratitude for the arrangements Ghazi had made for his visit.

Making genuine light of the inconvenience, the latter informed him, 'Your dinner with Grand Secretary Sir Julian Lawrence is fixed for tomorrow night. Meantime, my wife has spoken to Jasmine's headmistress and you will see the little minx that afternoon. Vivienne Solomon, Samuel's beautiful flame-haired niece, is also joining us. You will adore her.'

Following the younger man towards the exit, Father Anthony took long strides in an effort to keep up. For his part, Ghazi craned his neck so he would not lose him in the crowd. As the crush of people swelled, he waited until the priest was beside him before taking charge and steering him through the airport throng.

Side-stepping a luggage trolley, he remarked, 'We see

Jasmine as often as we can. She came to the races with us over half-term and put on a couple of wagers for Jiddu.'

Father Anthony laughed. 'So I gather. Jiddu reported she was refusing to put her shilling in the Sunday collection box because he told her there was no point wasting good money on the Almighty! As a result, she was banned from tuck-shop all week.'

Ghazi laughed. His dark eyes alight with mischief, he replied, 'She told my wife you were busy blessing Jiddu's horses and socking in a bill afterwards whether they won or lost! Hélas such pleasures are now denied me – my wife has banned me from gambling! I am only allowed on a race-course for social reasons. In Britain, I find it is a good place to do business.'

On reaching the exit, the men joined the queue for taxis. Soon clambering into one, Father Anthony declared, 'Jiddu tells me Jasmine's latest letter said she was canvassing for Andrew Fitzwilliams in the village near her school. She claims he is likely to be an MP soon.'

Ghazi nodded. 'Indeed he is. As for Jasmine campaigning for him, I think this has more to do with the Upper Sixth thinking he is a dish and using Jasmine to get to him! Some of them will be first time voters – the political parties in Britain regard this group as important. Half the girls in Jasmine's school got into trouble last week when they were caught flogging off the headmistress' prize rose-bushes for Fitzwilliams' constituency party funds!'

'I presume Jasmine is in love with him too?' queried an amused Father Anthony.

'Besotted, absolutely besotted.'

'What is Fitzwilliams like? He was such a spoilt young man when I met him in Iraq. Your father, I remember, found him charming.'

'I am not acquainted with him. However, the Grand Secretary may know something – Julian Lawrence is worried about Fitzwilliams' company, Fitzwilliams International. Nico filled him in . . .'

'Nico?' interrupted Father Anthony. 'Nico Stollen is in London?'

'Not now, no. But he was last week. The Grand Secretary summoned him. Dear Nico. He spends half his life winding people up, and the other half sorting things out for them.'

Ghazi El-Tarek did not add, the Russian had offered to insert him into Fitzwilliams International. He had said their respective interests could coincide. Ghazi's job was to lobby for large corporations in the pursuit of contracts – mostly armaments – for which if the bids were successful he received a commission.

'What did the Grand Secretary want with Nico?'

Ghazi chortled. 'Money. Lovely Vivienne Solomon – she is eighteen now – and some of her university friends, are volunteers for the Concert of Rights . . .'

'The organisation that once tried to help Samuel's girls?'

'Uh-huh. The funny thing is, another of the Concert's volunteers is the son of the Home Office civil servant who, years ago, turned them down. My wife wishes Vivienne would go out with him. He's a lovely chap. A boy called Jimmy Richards. He remembers Vivienne as a school-girl!'

The taxi edged its way along. Father Anthony wound down his window. It seemed a long time since he had been in the fresh air. He immediately regretted it. London air was almost as bad as Rome's.

Winding it back up, he replied with a shrewd smile, 'I take it this means your wife does not like Vivienne's actual boyfriend!'

Ghazi nodded. 'A scamp called Bobby Lomax – another volunteer at the Concert. Not nearly good enough for Vivienne. At the girl's insistence, I invited the lad to Chantilly. He swanned off the minute he arrived as if he had been born on a race-course and did not come back until it was time to go! I cannot tell you how hurt Vivienne was. I was ready to box his ears! My wife says he is a chancer.'

As much as Father Anthony loved to hear about young people's lives, knowledge of Stollen's visit to London had upset him. 'You were saying the Concert needed money . . .'

Ghazi inclined his head. 'The Grand Secretary asked Nico to raise some funding and send it through via Grand Lodge. He said the Soviets would not notice since they were shelling out for everything else reasonably subversive all over Europe! The alternative would have been for Julian Lawrence to ask the Americans who are doing the same.'

'But the White House has no interest in Britain or Europe!'

Ghazi agreed. 'This is why the CIA can get away with so much and London is developing into such a battle ground. The POUKI is even laundering American money pouring into Lloyd's of London. The Grand Secretary believes calling in Nico balances things.'

'Surely this leaves Julian Lawrence exposed to all sorts of accusations?'

'Undoubtedly. At this very moment, the POUKI is petitioning freemasons in the House of Lords to trip him up. The fool running the CIA across the Atlantic is causing all sorts of problems for Britain. He sees Communists everywhere. This includes the Grand Secretary. It is beyond a joke.'

They were entering the tunnel that connected the airport to the slip-road leading onto the motorway.

'What I love about Julian Lawrence is his sense of humour,' Ghazi chattered on. 'The Grand Secretary is so British. He sees nothing wrong with, as he puts it, placing Stalinist money where it can do some good. Nico agrees. He had the cheek to say that as a Soviet, if he wanted to create chaos in Britain, it will be so much easier as a freemason!'

Father Anthony let out a huge boyish laugh. As much as he disapproved of Stollen, he always found him amusing. 'I am sure Nico will soon be offering you advice about how to get on here. Be careful!'

'He already is. When I told him I was applying for British citizenship, he suggested I ask the Grand Secretary whether I could buy a knighthood before my nationality came through, or had to wait until after. I am not convinced he was joking. His next posting is London again, by the way.'

Father Anthony smiled. 'Why do you wish to be British?'

'I like the way they do business here. Anything goes, as long as it is not in Britain!'

Father Anthony shuddered. 'Listen to yourself, my son. You are in danger of sounding like a crook.'

CHAPTER TWELVE

❄ ❈ ❄

GRAND LODGE, LONDON: Grand Secretary Sir Julian Lawrence rolled himself to the window. He was trying out a new wheelchair and was quite pleased with it. Design flaws, of course, remained. 'Customised' did not mean it came with a decent pipe stand.

Packing his favourite with the last of the loose-leaf Sobranie Stollen had sent for his birthday, he stared out across the road below. Miro was expected for tea. Later that evening, Father Anthony and Ghazi El-Tarek would join them for dinner.

Craning his neck, he saw the newspaper seller's billboard. *LATEST! Labour Win Predicted*, it read. Having done well in the May local elections, Harold Wilson had called a general election for June 18: The anniversary of the Battle of Waterloo. It would be a long dirty campaign.

The Grand Secretary sighed. So much American money was flooding into POUKI outlets in the unlikely hope the Tory candidate – Edward Heath – would win, some were making personal fortunes. In addition, the POUKI was seeking to undermine the Grand Secretary's own position at Grand Lodge. His declared anxieties about Fitzwilliams International's bogus West German subsidiary had seen to that.

His old friends in Parliament were retiring – the Chief Whip had died – and he no longer enjoyed the same level of support.

The new breed had not fought the Second World War with him and were a different type.

Reversing, he tidied a few books on his desk. He was tired. Nevertheless, his mind was clear.

He had decided he would bring Fitzwilliams International's clandestine office to the attention of Parliament once the new government was sworn in. To go to the police, let alone the press, would be unthinkable. Parliament was sovereign. In the meantime, dear Miro remained titular head of the Fitzwilliams International subsidiary which was causing the Grand Secretary so much worry.

Searching out the Warlord's letter, he read it again. He was aware a similar missive had been sent to the Pope in Rome. The man sounded confused, fraternal and frightened. The only good news the hand-written note contained was that the Warlord was now a grandfather.

Placing it in a folder, the senior freemason shuffled through the rest of his papers. These confirmed some of the largest defence contractors in the world were now involved in Fitzwilliams International. In effect, a British public servant – Peter Ligne – was running an armaments company. Such conduct was not without precedence. The East India Company once controlled Britain from Leadenhall Street in much the same way.

To protect Miro, the Grand Secretary had ensured the Miro Building Group remained on the Masonic 'list'. As a result, the company received its fair share of tenders awarded by town hall.

Sir Julian was proud of his 'list'. It guaranteed workplace health and safety – a role, it was rumoured, some in the unions failed to perform. It was the best he could do given that excellent construction industry foremen – most of them freemasons – had been marginalised.

As the Grand Secretary considered the industry's problems, Miro slipped passed Grand Lodge's huge bronze doors and into the side entrance. After exchanging the usual pleasantries with the Masonic doormen – former old soldiers – he made his way up to Sir Julian's office. Mounting the stairs two-by-two, he was a startlingly good-looking man: Lean and muscular, slightly greying.

Greeting the Grand Secretary with habitual warmth, he settled himself in a red leather chair. He knew tea would not be served until the appropriate hour – his host was a stickler for rituals.

'What news about Fitzwilliams International?' asked the latter.

'Going from bad to worse, I'm afraid,' responded Miro. 'Stollen is forever circling around Ghazi El-Tarek putting all sorts of nonsense in his head.'

'Fitzwilliams International is far too attractive to reckless young men like Ghazi El-Tarek, no matter how personable they may be,' agreed the Grand Secretary. 'Do you think Andrew Fitzwilliams is involved?'

Miro shook his head. 'No – or at least, not knowingly so. He was very young when he inherited Fitzwilliams International. I cannot claim to have much knowledge but the short time I spent with Fitzwilliams in Iraq, he seemed a nice youngster. Peter Ligne is our man. I hope he has not influenced Fitzwilliams too much – given Ligne's approaches to Ghazi when he was a student, he has a track record.'

The Grand Secretary nodded. 'According to Stollen, Ligne is a very rich chap these days having done a deal with the

Americans. The nuclear facility being built in Iraq through Fitzwilliams International is a huge project.'

'Can we trust what Stollen says?'

'I think so. He tells the truth when it is in his interest to do so. We must proceed with caution. The minute this election is decided we will, after all, be accusing a British public servant of corruption – and on the say-so of a Soviet intelligence officer!

'Given there are at least a hundred Russian spooks here who, by rights, ought to be chucked out of the country, supporting one not even resident in Britain is difficult.'

Miro grinned. If nothing else, the Grand Secretary was a master of understatement. It was 16.00 hrs. The tea trolley was rolled in. Laden with fruitcake and toasted crumpets, the two men did it immediate justice.

A few moments later, Sir Julian handed Miro the Warlord's letter. 'Ghazi El-Tarek dropped it off yesterday. You met the Kurd in Iraq, I believe.'

The Warlord's neat handwriting covered two pages of A4. He had been contacted, he wrote, by the Americans who informed him they had 'taken over' his agreement with Peter Ligne.

I beg you, he implored, *to put an end to such overtures by speaking with Sir Peter.* Here he had added a note to the effect he understood Peter Ligne had been knighted.

He continued, *I severed all dealings with the British government a short while after Philippe and Suzie Palmeira's 'Spies Party' five years ago. Other than the one arms shipment – of which I informed Grand Lodge so it could, in turn, warn my Brothers at the Baghdad Lodge, and dear Miro in London under whose unknowing signature the paperwork was conducted – I have had no dealings with Fitzwilliams International, the British, or any other foreign power. Today, Ghazi El-Tarek handles all my requirements.*

Nevertheless, and to my regret, it appears Sir Peter has passed over the original documents to the Americans. Why, I know not. He has left me open to blackmail! This, at a time when Saddam Hussein wants to make peace with the Kurds. Already, there is much evidence he will keep his promises.

Even under his dictatorship, Iraq is building an impressive education and health service, improving transport and supplying villages with electricity – Britain (which he admires) is his model! In the foothills of Kurdistan – no ski resort yet! – the most modern hospital in the region is almost complete: A gift from Saddam Hussein. My son-in-law Lalo delivered Peri of my first grandchild there, a boy.

Were the UK to take Saddam Hussein under its wing, much good could be achieved. However, all this is now jeopardised. Should Saddam Hussein find out I have been conspiring against him, he will be ruthless. I beseech you to speak with the Americans.

The Warlord concluded, *I am writing similarly to His Holiness in Rome. Father Anthony has kindly agreed to deliver my letter. Meanwhile, I am grateful to Bro Ghazi El-Tarek for delivering this to Grand Lodge. Frequently what he does is more honourable than what he says he does.*

Wearing formal clerical dress, Father Anthony and Ghazi El-Tarek, in black tie, arrived at Grand Lodge a few minutes after the agreed time. The staff having long gone home, Miro received them. He, too, had changed into evening clothes.

Escorting them through the sombre building, he explained the Grand Secretary would be with them shortly. Once in their host's private dining-room, they found a cold supper laid out and some claret left to breathe.

Sir Julian joined his guests as Miro was pouring the wine. 'Welcome,' he greeted them, looking at Father Anthony with undisguised interest.

Taking the lead, Ghazi apologised for being late. 'We dropped Jasmine Palmeira back to school and stayed far longer than we ever intended.'

'I am glad you did,' responded the Grand Secretary. Turning to Father Anthony, he continued, 'Jiddu said in his last letter that young Jasmine and the lemon trees are growing almost as fast as each other! Here, you have the advantage over me, Father. I have never seen Baghdad's beautiful Garden but understand you know it well?'

'Indeed I do. I walk there every Sunday after church.'

'And how did you find Jasmine?'

Father Anthony laughed. 'Complaining about socks, Sir Julian! Apparently, "at Vivienne Solomon's old school", the girls were allowed to wear stockings at eleven. Jasmine is disgusted to still be in long socks at thirteen.'

The Grand Secretary chuckled. 'How well I know it,' he replied with feeling. 'I have archived a similar letter of complaint. I kept it, on the basis our dusty old files could do with brightening up.'

'She writes to you too?' queried Father Anthony in surprise. 'It was not Nico Stollen, by any chance, who put her up to it?'

The Grand Secretary nodded. 'We have no proof. However, her letters have Stollen's stamp all over them. Her most recent requested I tell the Grand Chaplain that St Paul was a bully!'

'He was!'

Laughing, the Grand Secretary agreed. 'Please light up, gentlemen,' he entreated a few moments later, taking out his tobacco. 'I know Father Anthony likes a cigarette before a meal.'

The latter looked at him in amazement. 'Whatever gave you this idea, Sir Julian? I have not smoked in years.'

The Grand Secretary grinned. 'A ruse, dear Father! One of Stollen's better suggestions! He says he has been trying to lead you back into temptation for as long as he can remember. You see, I like my pipe before eating . . .'

Father Anthony raised his glass. 'To Nico – long may I resist his temptations,' he remarked with good humour.

'To Nico,' intoned the Grand Secretary, setting his tobacco ablaze. 'Long may I succumb to them!'

Puffing away with contentment, he motioned them to the dining-table. 'Will you say Grace, Father? We will not tell the Grand Chaplain!'

The short blessing over, he inquired, 'Who else has Jasmine been writing to?'

'The Holy Father.'

The Grand Secretary frowned. 'Ah! Much as I love Nico, if he is putting Jasmine up to this sort of behaviour, he is behaving very badly indeed. What does she write about?'

Grateful for his understanding, Father Anthony responded, 'Her most recent letter informed His Holiness of the researches

I have been carrying out at Baghdad's observatory. She went on to say: *Given the difficulties caused by modern city lights in Rome, why does the Vatican not relocate its starwatching to Baghdad?*

'It would be funny were it not for the fact the Vatican, aware of the problem she pointed out, have – in secret, or so we supposed – set up a new observatory at the pontifical summer residence at Castel Gandolfo outside Rome.

'Jasmine's letter was Stollen's way of telling the Vatican that Moscow is well aware of the move. As well as instructing the child in his own philosophy, he is using her to threaten us. We do not like it one bit.'

The Grand Secretary sighed. 'We have strange friends in common.'

Father Anthony shook his head. 'I am fond of Stollen, Sir Julian. However, he is no friend of mine. Our visit to Jasmine should have been a surprise. Except it was not. Nico had already told her to expect me. When I turned up, it confirmed that which she already knew – "Uncle Nico" knows everything.'

Accepting the criticism, the Grand Secretary asked for news of the rest of the Palmeira family. Father Anthony took his time before replying. He knew Sir Julian was fond of Jiddu and did not wish to upset him.

'The old man is frail now,' he observed. 'Like you, he has to use a wheelchair these days. Hussein, his driver, never leaves his side.' Accepting some more wine, he continued, 'Meantime, Suzie frets about Philippe's work, while worrying her daughter is becoming a stranger. Jiddu's little family is not all it used to be.'

The Grand Secretary put out his tobacco. Father Anthony's

news did not altogether surprise him. 'Jiddu wrote a while ago to say he is anxious about Suzie,' he admitted. 'He wants her to have a break in England but she refuses to go without him and Philippe.'

'She is frightened she will not be allowed back into Iraq,' explained Father Anthony, sipping his drink. 'These are dangerous times. Every time Philippe travels – he is often in Moscow – Suzie is apprehensive. Jiddu says she is worn and thin. As for Ligne, she detests the man and the influence he has on her husband.'

CHAPTER THIRTEEN

PALL MALL, LONDON: Sitting comfortably in his club's discreet well-upholstered drawing-room, Peter Ligne teased Andrew Fitzwilliams with good humour. 'I hear you have found yourself a wife, dear boy. Your own this time – not somebody else's!'

Andrew Fitzwilliams made a wry smile. 'That's about the sum of it, sir, yes. Shame Jasmine isn't any older. The little rascal would have suited me perfectly! I'll have to catch her second time around. Belinda will do in the meantime!'

Ligne laughed, wondering for how much longer the younger man would call him 'sir'. 'I thought you were a Roman Catholic, old chap, and did not believe in divorce!'

He was far too wise to take a spouse himself. Too frightened her charms would fade, he had once confided to the Chief.

Picking up a copy of a glossy magazine resting on the arm of his chair and flicking through it, he continued, 'Your engagement has caused quite a stir. I had no idea you were such a catch!'

Staring out at him was Andrew Fitzwilliams' future bride. A double rope of pearls around her slim neck, Belinda Eyre had the bland perfection of youth. She was twenty-one years old.

'Pretty little thing,' he commented scanning the article on the facing page.

Fitzwilliams nodded. He had met Belinda through a senior council member of the British Board of Infrastructure. Too immature to fight the goodwill on all sides, the couple's betrothal had been a done deal almost before they had had their first date.

'Conservative Central Office approves – and that is the main thing,' he replied. 'Belinda is certainly enjoying the general election – along with Jasmine! That child! Needless to say she has taken to the campaign like a duck to water . . .'

Ligne quickly surmised Fitzwilliams was talking about the schoolgirl.

'. . . My constituency chairman firmly believes I do not need to put in an appearance at all. He says Jasmine – and Belinda, of course – is a little stunner and will win the election for me, no matter what happens in the rest of the country!

'Do you know that Belinda – needless to say, at Jasmine's instigation – rang the British Board of Infrastructure. Then she, Jasmine, and a party of the naughty cat's school-friends, all turned up in Belgrave Square with collection boxes. Of course, the BBI members were bowled over and shelled out another fortune for party funds!'

Ligne smiled politely.

'. . . Apparently, the Russian chap, Nico wot-not, put Jasmine up to it. The last time she was in so much trouble with her headmistress was when she was caught placing her grandfather's bets for the Derby. I couldn't work out how he knew the names of the runners. It turned out Nico Wot-Not was supplying them off the Russian embassy's high frequency radio in Baghdad!'

'Very probably,' chuckled Ligne. 'At one time the old boy got Stollen to invite the American priest – Father Anthony – around to listen to the baseball game on it!'

Calling the waiter to freshen the pot, the civil servant clipped the end of an expensive-looking cigar. Lighting it, he asked with casual interest, 'Is Jasmine often in touch with Stollen?'

'Uh-huh,' replied Fitzwilliams, helping himself to a cucumber sandwich and plucking a stray piece of watercress on the way. 'She says "Uncle Nico" is not above a little flutter himself. Apparently, Stollen and her grandfather advise which horses she back through the personal columns of *The Times* . . .'

'Wouldn't it be cheaper to send her a telegram? At least the MI5 lads who have to check all incoming and outgoing cables could pick up a tip or two!'

'That is how she got caught the first time around!' responded Fitzwilliams with glee. 'Stollen sent her a telegram naming the horses, not realising the school would check its contents.'

'What else does Jasmine say about Stollen?'

Fitzwilliams' lower lip trembled. 'Only that he wants to lay odds on her marrying a British cabinet minister for him! Apparently, my engagement to Belinda has rather put a spanner in the works. Stollen actually said so in his letter of congratulation!'

Ligne looked at his companion in amazement. 'You don't mean the bloody man wrote to you as well?'

'Certainly. He sent his letter – unsealed – care of Jasmine. Needless to say, she read it. I understand he expects me to be Prime Minister one day! I told Jasmine to let him down gently – as a Roman Catholic I'd never get the top job. She was ever so disappointed – unlike Belinda who looked relieved . . .'

'What else did Stollen say,' interrupted Ligne, his voice dangerously quiet.

Oblivious to his companion's sudden change of tone, Fitzwilliams could scarcely conceal his merriment. 'He congratulated me on my engagement! And then, if you please, complained about HMG's underhand behaviour. Apparently British honeytraps are luring innocent Soviets all over the world. The Ruskie said he would seduce Belinda to even things up! He is an absolute scream that chap. Jasmine adores him.'

'Did you reply to Stollen?'

Fitzwilliams beamed. 'Of course. I assured him Belinda only had eyes for me and the knaves in a deck of cards when she's playing bridge at Queens.'

Ligne suppressed a frown. 'Try not to give too much information away, old chap. Even in jest.'

He stared at the magazine again. There were several photographs of Belinda. In one, she was poised by the fireplace of her parents light and airy drawing-room. In another she was outside their house which stood, bathed in sunshine, in spacious grounds.

He considered the pictures with care, instinctively aware the girl would not hold Fitzwilliams' interest for long, if she did at all. What worried him was Stollen would know this too.

Fingering his immaculately starched cuff, a gold link with a crest momentarily visible, he cautioned, 'Keep an eye on Belinda, old boy. Stollen is a dangerous man. In addition, always remember that sweet Jasmine is Stollen's creation. She will do anything he puts in her mind. Make sure Belinda has her full measure.'

Fitzwilliams looked at him in disbelief. 'Poppycock! If Jasmine is anyone's creature, she's mine! As for Belinda, she adores her.

She says Jasmine is the only one who knows how to manage me. My only worry is the little witch might lead Belinda astray. As she says, I wouldn't want a wife with an opinion, would I? Jasmine, of course, has one on everything...'

– Ligne ordered another round of buttered toast –

'... My future father-in-law, by the way, is complaining this election is costing him a fortune in new dresses. He says it'll be a relief when Belinda has a husband to take over and I have a wife!'

'That is one good reason lad, why I do not have one!'

'Mistresses, I hear, come expensive too!'

Ligne grinned but made no comment. He had recently returned from the Italian lakes. Stollen had informed Jasmine that Laure de Chebran, who liked what she called her 'petits intrigues', often went to Italy at this time of year.

Accepting Ligne would give nothing away, Fitzwilliams prompted, 'You wanted to see me about Fitzwilliams International...'

Ligne nodded. 'Yes indeed. We have problems. Nothing serious, but I thought you should know...'

Fitzwilliams raised an eyebrow.

'... Grand Secretary Sir Julian Lawrence has a bee in his bonnet about the West German subsidiary, including Miro's position. In addition, the Americans are being warned off its Iraq project by the Vatican. The Yanks are furious and suspect a leak. They blame us – ! – when in fact it was the Kurdish Warlord's doing. He wrote to the Grand Secretary – as well as the Pope – and had his letters delivered by trusted emissaries.'

Fitzwilliams frowned. He knew nothing about his company's

activities. Nor did he have any interest in them. Trying to keep the boredom out of his voice, he commented, 'I hope you have things in hand.'

'Of course. Don't worry about a thing, old boy. I merely wanted to bring you up to date.'

Changing the subject, Fitzwilliams remarked, 'Incidentally, I almost forgot. Jasmine says Stollen wants me to meet a chap called Ghazi El-Tarek.'

'What!' exclaimed Ligne, his voice loud enough to puncture the usual quiet. Several elderly gentlemen looked his way and coughed. 'Stollen is the very devil! Stay away from Ghazi El-Tarek, Andrew. He is one of Fitzwilliams International's principal customers. He deals with its subsidiary on weapons supply all the time.'

'I am glad to hear it. He sounds a good man. What's more, Jasmine, the little scamp, has got him to cough up a fortune for the Party.'

Annoyed, Ligne retorted, 'I would like to think Conservative Central Office is particular from whom it accepts money.'

'Indeed it is. But the POUKI is not. It is so desperate about how the election is going, as long as El-Tarek ain't a Commie, it does not mind how he makes his brass.'

Signalling for the waiter, Ligne replied, 'In which case, there is nothing more to be said.' Signing the bill, he continued, 'By the way, HMG's lawyers have drafted the enclosed . . .'

He took a large envelope from his briefcase and handed its contents to Fitzwilliams.

'. . . The Americans, I am afraid, insisted. As I said, the Kurdish Warlord has set the cat among the pigeons. As a result, the Yanks are anxious to ensure HMG's arrangement with Fitzwilliams International is watertight. All understandable.'

Surprised, Fitzwilliams skimmed the document. 'This is a will . . .'

Ligne laughed. 'Not really, more a document of ownership. A mere precaution. All it means is that were you to fall under the proverbial bus, Fitzwilliams International would revert to HMG for disposal. Naturally, as it makes clear, your heirs would be protected.'

Fitzwilliams looked at him in amazement. 'I'm telling you this is a will. Making you my heir.'

Ligne stood his ground. 'HMG is requesting you name a beneficiary who would not hinder . . .'

'I have no intention of dying just yet, old chap. Moreover, my present arrangements are bound to be acceptable to HMG. The BBI organised them.'

He strolled out of Ligne's club a few moments later. Following a cursory chat with Belinda – arrangements for their wedding were advancing – he spent the rest of the evening with a girlfriend. As Ligne had surmised, his future wife bored him already.

Jasmine carefully sealed her letter and placed it on the silver tray outside her school's wood panelled dining-room. It would be collected in the morning. Blowing an imaginary kiss, she hoped she had remembered everyone.

Mentally, she went through her checklist. Suzie, Philippe, Jiddu, Hussein, Leah, Peri, Amu Samuel, Amu Abdullah,

Uncle Nico and Father Anthony. Yes. She was certain. She had included everybody.

It was her longest letter yet. She was to be a bridesmaid at Andrew Fitzwilliams' wedding and wanted all to know it. Mounting the wide stone stairs, she turned left at the top and made her way to the school library.

She always checked the personal columns of the Saturday *Times* on Sunday afternoons, to check whether Jiddu or Uncle Nico had sent her a message. Passing the recreation room, and waving cheerfully to a couple of friends playing jacks on the floor while *Bridge Over Troubled Water* blared out on the radio, she entered the library and headed to where the newspapers were stacked.

Finding the Saturday *Times* in an untidy jumble, she ran her eye over it. Nothing this time. She was not disheartened. The pleasure was as much in the looking as in the finding. It made her feel closer to home.

Sitting on the window-seat, she drew the heavy drapes around her. The school's ancient rose garden was just below, beyond that the running track, the hurdles not yet collected. Sighing, she wondered what Leah Solomon was doing.

During the last school holidays, they had visited Jiddu's motorcars at the race-course again. Leah had started smoking. Jasmine and Hussein had stood guard while she crept into the back of one of the cars – the Minister of Protocol's old Landrover – and lit a cigarette. They could see Father Anthony in the distance, watching the horses being exercised.

Soon, Leah had stubbed out her Black Cat in the sand beneath the running board. 'English cigarettes aren't as nice as

Iraqi ones,' she had coughed. 'But they're lots prettier. Thanks for bringing them. I'll try another one if you don't mind, or do you want me to hurry up?'

They had assured her she could carry on. This was when Hussein had explained to Jasmine how the aviary at home had burned down. Drunken central government guards, searching for Christians, freemasons, Jews, Kurds, Shia and Turkomans, had set it on fire. Now, all that remained were black scars that screeched up the side of the building. Baghdad was not Baghdad any more.

Throughout the holiday, Jasmine mused, she and her mother had avoided important questions. For example, Jasmine had never asked Suzie why they were not allowed to go riding in the desert any more. Instead, they had to stay close to the race club.

Philippe, meanwhile, with forced jollity, had teased Jasmine about her grades in Maths and Latin, and Jiddu had insisted 'HMG' and 'KGB' needed to have their balcony repotted when they did not. Only Hussein and Father Anthony had been the same.

Jasmine bit her lip. She had behaved badly in front of them and knew it. Making her way to the stables at the race-course, she had ordered the stable-boy to saddle her favourite pony. He had refused because it had not been correctly shod. Pulling rank, she had got her way.

As she had cantered off, it had been immediately apparent the horse should not be ridden. When she returned, she discovered Father Anthony remonstrating with Hussein who had flogged the boy.

'I did not beat him too hard,' an unapologetic Hussein had assured.

'He should not have been beaten at all! It was not his fault – it was Jasmine's!'

Hussein had nodded. 'The lad will soon recover,' he had soothed. 'In the meantime, did you not see how he glowed with pride when I praised him for not crying and gave him the fils in my pocket because he had been so brave? Now he is double the hero: Once for being beaten when he was innocent; twice for taking the thrashing like a man.'

'But what lesson will Jasmine learn?'

Knowing she had been within earshot, Hussein had replied, 'The only one I can teach her . . .'

'You will make her say "sorry"?'

Hussein had shaken his head. 'What will this achieve? The child will only feel the flush of virtue. Instead, I shall prevent her from making amends. This way she will remember that an accident of birth gave her the power to behave badly. In addition, Leah will refuse to talk to her.'

On the day before Jasmine's return flight to London, her father had organised a visit to the Garden of Lemon Trees. It was a magical park now, with beautiful flowers and a plethora of fountains, the water levels of which were set at different heights so it seemed it hummed a tune.

'Just like the Al Hambra in Spain,' Jiddu had shouted over his shoulder as Philippe and Hussein had taken it in turns to push his wheelchair.

Arm-in-arm, Suzie and Jasmine had followed behind. Suzie had wanted to know something about her thirteen year old daughter's life in England. Casting the stable-boy's beating – and Leah's disapproval – aside, Jasmine had boasted, 'All the girls are jealous because they can't telephone Andrew like I can!'

Her mother had laughed. The perfectly polished product that had fallen off the aeroplane looking like a summer pudding in a straw boater a few weeks before, was as much Andrew Fitzwilliams' creation as anyone else's, and she had known it. Jasmine had picked up every trick of social jargon and behaviour from him.

'I do hope, darling, you're not making too much of a nuisance of yourself. Mr Fitzwilliams is a very busy man.'

Overhearing, Jiddu had exclaimed, 'Fitzwilliams? Bah! There's a young man who could do with one of Hussein's lessons.'

The comment had been Jasmine's only indication Jiddu had been made aware of her poor conduct at the race-course. Staring out into the darkness of an English night, she still felt guilty.

'Anyone here?'

Jasmine froze. It was the games mistress. Not wishing to reveal her hiding place, she remained still. Seconds later, she was plunged into darkness as the library's central light was switched off.

She looked at the luminous dial on her watch wondering if she had time to call Andrew on the school pay-phone. Deciding she did, she crept out from behind the curtain and felt her way along the chairs and tables. She usually telephoned him on a Sunday evening.

Not, of course, that Andrew Fitzwilliams was always in. This evening, however, Jasmine hoped he was. She had something on her mind.

CHAPTER FOURTEEN

✳ ✺ ✳

ALBANY, LONDON: As Andrew Fitzwilliams let himself into his apartment, he heard his telephone ring. It was 07.00 hrs. He wondered who could be calling at that ungodly hour of the morning.

'Yes,' he answered in a brusque manner.

'Andrew . . .' Jasmine's pretty voice inquired.

Fitzwilliams grinned.

'. . . Where have you been? I phoned all night. Matron was furious! Where were you?'

'Fornicating,' replied Fitzwilliams, his voice deliberately inaudible.

'Four what?' responded the school-girl.

Fitzwilliams laughed. 'Never mind, sweetheart. What do you want?'

Jasmine took her time before replying. 'Vivienne Solomon called me . . .'

'Remind me, sweetie, who Vivienne Solomon is,' interrupted Fitzwilliams, his voice softening.

'She's Leah's cousin. She says the Chief Rabbi in Baghdad has been imprisoned and the plight of the Jews is "diabolical".'

Running his hand over his unshaven face, Fitzwilliams yawned.

Without stopping for breath, Jasmine continued, 'Vivienne's worried about Uncle Samuel and the girls. The

Concert of Rights is trying to help them again but the POUKI want it shut down. Last week, the POUKI-men beat up Vivienne and some other students, including her boyfriend Bobby Lomax and another guy called Jimmy Richards. I have written to Uncle Nico but he hasn't replied. Neither has Father Anthony.'

Andrew Fitzwilliams sighed. Darling little thing. She was so impressionable. Longing for his bed, he soothed, 'Don't worry, petal. I'm sure Vivienne Solomon is exaggerating. Most students are up to no good – wasting taxpayers money – so she and her friends probably deserved a good hiding. If you want, once I'm elected, I'll write to the Home Office . . .'

Jasmine whooped with pleasure. 'Would you, Andrew? Oh, would you?' she cried in excitement.

"Course. Now then sweetheart. Before we ring off, what are you wearing for Ascot?'

'What???? Has Smelly-Boots said I can go?'

'Smelly Boots,' was Fitzwilliams' nickname for Jasmine's headmistress.

'No,' he replied – he adored teasing her – 'You're too young. The stewards will never let you in. However . . .'

– he paused, knowing she was tantalised –

'. . . This does not mean you cannot join Belinda and me for dinner afterwards.'

Jasmine's happiness was complete.

It was an important year for Ascot. The whole of British society was to be there to welcome the Queen's sister. A Scottish MP had claimed the select committee to review royal finances had been rigged. He had been particularly incensed by the suggestion that Princess Margaret gave value for money. The patrons of Ascot wished to show that she did.

As the Princess was greeted with wild enthusiasm, Andrew Fitzwilliams strolled into the Members Enclosure with his future wife on his arm. The latter, he found to his increasing irritation, had very little to say. And that which she did, only irritated him further. Luckily, the day was saved by thirteen year old Jasmine. She never failed to delight him.

Two weeks later, he took Belinda Eyre to be his wife. Much to his enjoyment, it was apparent to everyone the chief bridesmaid had an enormous crush on the groom.

To its relief, private polling by Conservative Central Office towards the end of the 1970 general election campaign, indicated a likely win for Mr Heath. On the night he became Prime Minister, the party at the British Board of Infrastructure went on until the following morning.

Throughout the rest of the week, newspaper headlines were dominated by the formation of the new government. For this reason, it was not reported the Masonic Grand Secretary Sir Julian Lawrence had died in a car crash, along with his driver, shortly after attending the celebration at the contractors' headquarters.

Unusually, no obituary of the country's old servant was published in *The Times* or *Daily Telegraph* – the provincial Grand Masters who complained were quickly silenced. In addition, the Grand Secretary was laid to rest without his regiment being informed. Prior to his funeral, a post mortem revealed his driver had been drinking. Only the driver's family knew he did not drink.

Sir Julian's loss anguished many – the Grand Lodge of India was one of dozens to pay its respects. In Baghdad, Jiddu Palmeira was inconsolable – the Iraqi freemasons sent a large donation to one of London's Masonic teaching hospitals in the Grand Secretary's memory. It was a brave gesture given the Baghdad Lodge had finally been shut down by the central authorities.

If Jiddu was beside himself with grief, Nico Stollen was outraged. Having consulted Father Anthony, he wrote a private letter to the colonel of the Grand Secretary's former regiment.

It concluded: . . . *Sir Julian Lawrence was a role model for many, irrespective of their nationality or political system they serve. He devoted his life to public and international service and set a standard by which others may measure themselves. We are all the poorer without him. I grieve for myself, as much as I do for his loss.*

To this day, the Russian's letter – his identity protected by the regiment – is one of its proudest documents.

If death silenced the Grand Secretary, Miro was quietened in a different way – indecent pictures of his daughter were taken. She had been one of the students helping Vivienne Solomon and the Concert of Rights. In addition, he was shown a copy of his own image with Stollen and the Russian ambassador in Baghdad. It had been taken at Philippe and Suzie Palmeira's 'Spies Party'.

The photograph, Miro was assured, if published, could be manipulated to suck his daughter, as well as Vivienne Solomon and her uncle's family in Iraq, into a conspiracy of which they had no knowledge and even less understanding. Miro had been Peter Ligne's pawn ever since.

Two years after the general election, thirty-two year old Andrew Fitzwilliams was an acknowledged rising star on the government backbenches. Seeing as little of his wife as possible – he drenched her idea she work for him in the House of Commons with ice cold contempt – he was every inch the political princeling. Belinda Fitzwilliams' diamond earrings sparkled on her pretty little earlobes in vain. A devout Roman Catholic, she wanted a child but Fitzwilliams refused, insisting she remain on the contraceptive pill which, always obedient, she did.

Her parents blamed her that their son-in-law spent so little time at home. They had assumed that upon their daughter's marriage, they would become involved in his political whirl. They reproached Belinda this was not their reality.

She did not tell them she felt unwell and had to consult the doctor used most frequently by other Conservative MPs' wives in London – nor about her lonely wait for the test results, or her tears as, shy, naive and unaccustomed to gynaecological complaint, she cried alone in bed at night.

'And the other men you have been sleeping with?' the doctor asked Belinda without looking up from his notes.

Her frightened eyes searched for his. She had slept only with her husband. 'What do you mean?'

He told her. She had a venereal infection.

When she recovered, and ever more isolated, she sometimes played bridge at Queens Club where she was welcomed with genteel, albeit nosy, indifference. Her doctor's wife played there too. Mentioning to the medic she had seen Belinda, he, like all good political animals, passed the information to the government whips.

One day, Belinda was surprised but filled with happy delight when her husband suggested they spend more time together. She did not know his sudden interest in her had been at the behest of the whips.

Although his sexual peccadilloes and the lies and betrayals these involved were not held against him, he was nonetheless confounded by Belinda's medical records. There was no anxiety about a man who consorted with prostitutes. There was if wind of such conduct ever came to the ears of the elderly patrons of Queens Club.

Fitzwilliams' attentions to his wife and attendant charm offensive succeeded. His calm self-confidence, patrician demeanour and refusal to be remotely embarrassed or ashamed won the day. He was rewarded with the unpaid job of parliamentary private secretary to the Defence Secretary, the Rt Hon George Hillary MP.

Conservative Central Office was delighted with the appointment. Despite the recession, the contractors of the British Board of Infrastructure were donating again and had to have their reward. Fitzwilliams' promotion came just at the right time.

At Grand Lodge, the new Masonic hierarchy cut themselves from a different cloth to the late Sir Julian. To exorcise the past, the latter's old friends, including Jiddu, were expunged.

'That filthy Indian in Mespot is even asking for advice on lemon trees,' the Grand Secretary's successor complained. 'I told him to contact the Royal Botanic Gardens at Kew.'

The rebuff broke Jiddu's heart. Freddie de Chebran, now the French ambassador to Prague, took over the gap Sir Julian Lawrence had left. Advice on beautiful flowers arrived all the time. It was the only event that still brightened Jiddu's life. The world he knew had gone.

He hardly saw his son or daughter-in-law. Philippe was frequently in Moscow. Increasingly, Suzie accompanied him.

Returning to Iraq, they spent most of their time huddled furtively in corners. Then, in the dead of night, Philippe would knock out his messages to HMG, briefing Ligne about the latest developments. Jiddu had come to dread the 'tap, tap, tap' of the transmitter.

As for Philippe, plagued by nightmare uncertainties, he worked feverishly avoiding his father's haunted eyes. Ligne promoted him but this was little consolation. The family met at mealtimes but ate in silence.

Ligne himself could almost be called ostentatious. Philippe Palmeira's higher rank, meant a higher salary. Accordingly, 'his' Swiss bank account grew.

The civil servant invested the money sensibly. First, he purchased properties under Philippe's title – not thinking it prudent to buy in his own name – and rented these back to the intelligence services as 'safe' houses. Maintenance, refurbishment, decoration and furniture were paid by 'supplies'.

In addition, Ligne became a Name at Lloyd's. Explaining the nature of his work made it impossible for him to use his own identity, he was able to enrol Philippe Palmeira's instead.

Ligne smiled to himself. All in all, everything had gone rather well. The only shadow on the horizon was Andrew Fitzwilliams' consistent refusal to sign-over Fitzwilliams International.

Seeing the politician briefly at the House of Commons before leaving for his annual holiday in the Italian lakes, Ligne thought it counter-productive to raise the issue again. In any event, Fitzwilliams had a different concern.

Leading the way to the Strangers' bar, the latter asked, 'Any idea where we can unload a stock of reconditioned weapons? They're being dumped. Scrap metal value only. It seems a shame to waste them.'

Ligne laughed. 'I am sure we can come up with something – albeit not before I return from Italy. I have seats for La Scala.'

'What's that? A restaurant?'

Ligne sighed. 'Bloody philistine. No, dear boy, an opera house. I'm off to listen to some music.'

Fitzwilliams looked at him with a sly expression on his face. 'Dirty dog. Who with?'

Accepting the comment with good humour, Ligne did not volunteer any information.

CHAPTER FIFTEEN

❋ ❉ ❋

MAYFAIR, LONDON: Ghazi El-Tarek was beside himself with excitement. His wife was expecting their first child. After the birth, they would spend a couple of months in Iraq. His parents' joy at the prospect of becoming grandparents almost overwhelmed them.

Ghazi was pleased about something else too. The Kurdish Warlord had been in touch to say he was arranging for his daughter Peri to visit London. She would bring with her Fitzwilliams International's original documentation detailing her father's agreement with Sir Peter Ligne and its subsidiary. This, among other matters, would strengthen Ghazi's hand when dealing with the company. In addition, it would prove Miro's ignorance of matters pertaining to it, setting him free.

He lost no time in telling his wife. Thrilled for Miro, pleasure flooded her face. 'This is marvellous news, darling. And now, perhaps, you can also stop using Fitzwilliams International and Stollen will leave you alone: That Russian is leading you into trouble.'

Ghazi looked embarrassed. Holding her eye, he replied, 'Stollen is not leading me anywhere I do not wish to go already. I am a businessman. I do not pronounce on right or wrong. As long as it is legal, I do it. I am sorry you disapprove.'

She looked at him tenderly. Father Anthony had once likened her desperate efforts to control Ghazi, to Suzie

Palmeira's attempts to restrain Philippe. Both women, the priest knew, would be unsuccessful. Just as he knew they would be there when their husbands' lives collapsed.

'I cannot accept our lifestyle, while pretending I object to what you do. That would be a terrible hypocrisy,' she responded.

A week later, Ghazi El-Tarek had dinner with Britain's Secretary of State for Defence, the Rt Hon George Hillary MP. They ate at one of the deluxe London hotels. Ghazi picked up the bill.

The Secretary of State was short and plump but not unattractive. He had met his host at the races and was aware he was a major donor to the Conservative party. Not, of course, that Conservative Central Office had been all that happy to accept Ghazi's donations but needs must.

Studying the menu, the politician remarked, 'My parliamentary private secretary Andrew Fitzwilliams has mentioned you on several occasions. He looked a bit rueful when I said we were having dinner, since he has not had the pleasure of meeting you himself!'

Ghazi grinned. 'My wife will not let me contact Fitzwilliams. She says it would be networking!'

'Is that so wrong?'

'Yes – when our connection is a school-girl. My wife would deeply oppose . . .'

Enlightenment flashed across the Secretary of State's face. 'You don't mean the delightful Jasmine, do you? She was in the office over half-term. Fitzwilliams had her scouring through the *Hansards* for something or other.

'He loves having her about. We all do – aged fifteen, she is as bright as a button! It is a shame Fitzwilliams' wife has no regard for politics. Fitzwilliams has asked Belinda again and again to take an interest in Westminster but she just won't.'

The waiter hovered around them.

'I understand you have made the Party another generous donation,' the Secretary of State continued, as the man opened his napkin for him. 'It is always a pleasure to meet someone who shares our beliefs.'

'Which would those be?' queried Ghazi. 'I only whacked in a donation because I wanted a knighthood!'

George Hillary chuckled. He had no idea the chap was such fun.

'. . . Now I understand I have to be a Brit first,' concluded his host with a mock toss of his head.

'It does help. Have your nationality papers gone in?'

Ghazi nodded, tasting the wine. Signalling his satisfaction, he replied, 'Years ago. I keep wondering whether another donation to the Conservative party might help things along.'

The Defence Secretary was scarcely able to conceal his delight. 'It certainly wouldn't do any harm. Although I have to make clear I have no influence on these matters. The Home Office are a law unto themselves . . .'

Ghazi took out his cheque-book.

The politician – his eyes as round as saucers – continued, 'The civil servants, you see, give us a bit of grief. Always coming out with some twaddle about corruption and how important it is not only to avoid it, but to be seen to be avoiding it! They are so old-fashioned.'

Signing a debit, Ghazi handed it over. Averting his eyes from the amount, the Defence Secretary thanked him profusely. 'Very good of you, old boy. Very good indeed. The Party will be most grateful. As for the civil servants, I thought it best not to tell them I was meeting you.'

Looking puzzled, Ghazi commented, 'As you wish. However, I do not understand why you cannot inform your officials we are in contact.'

'Just one of those things!'

A few moments later, their orders taken, the main business of the evening commenced. Getting the ball rolling, Ghazi ventured, 'I am deeply disappointed by your Department's defence procurement executive. It has taken six months to have confirmation Britain can supply missiles. By the time its response came through, I had given my order to the French.'

George Hillary apologised. He had heard the criticism many times before. Buttering his roll, he advised, 'Go direct to Andrew Fitzwilliams in future.'

Ghazi thanked him. 'It seemed improper to do so without your prior approval. I deal with his company Fitzwilliams International all the time.'

The politician looked at him in surprise. 'Fitzwilliams International? Fitzwilliams' family firm? You must be mistaken. It is a construction company. The BBI run it on his behalf. You cannot possibly deal with it on weapons supply. You must be confusing it with something else.'

Ghazi did not correct him. Throughout the rest of the meal, their conversation flowed as richly as the wine. When the evening broke up, it was clear George Hillary was well disposed towards him.

'If Fitzwilliams is not around, other Tories might be helpful. It could cost you, of course!'

Ghazi raised an eyebrow. 'I am quite happy to pay out to any politician you suggest and would have done so before now. I did not know it was allowed.'

George Hillary laughed. Winking, so his meaning could not possibly be misunderstood, he replied, 'Everything, dear boy, is allowed. Except sodomy, of course. Still get into a bit of trouble with that sort of thing . . .'

Something died for Ghazi that moment. He had always believed in the British Parliament. Now he knew parts of it were a sham. George Hillary appalled him.

' . . . Also, dear boy, if you telephone the office, don't forget to be discreet in front of the staff.'

Ghazi nodded. Disguising his feelings, he asked, 'Would you and your wife enjoy a day at the races?'

'Always, old chap. But not with my wife!'

'In Paris?'

'In which case, most definitely not with my wife!'

George Hillary accepted Ghazi El-Tarek's hospitality on a regular basis after that.

'Incidentally, make no mistake. Fitzwilliams International deals in arms,' said Ghazi as the Secretary of State climbed into his government car.

George Hillary shrugged. 'Oh well. So long as I don't know!'

Ghazi telephoned Andrew Fitzwilliams first thing the following morning. The latter could not believe his luck. The

Iraqis, apparently, required a large amount of hand-guns. These were exactly what he had in store. It was the old stock about which he had consulted Peter Ligne.

Before making any decisions, he took the precaution of speaking to George Hillary. The Defence Secretary was more than happy to be helpful. 'Course I don't mind if you flog it off, lad! It's no use to us.'

The deal was arranged that afternoon. Momentarily, Fitzwilliams wondered whether he ought to wait for Peter Ligne to return from Italy but decided against. There was, in fact, no need to tell Ligne about the deal at all.

He smiled. This contract he wanted for himself. For an instant, he wondered if he ought to warn Ghazi about the quality of the goods. In the end, he decided not.

As for Ghazi, he found the price Fitzwilliams quoted on the high side but did not demur. A relationship with the Defence Secretary's parliamentary private secretary was worth a great deal more. Nonetheless, he took the precaution of spot-checking the shipment. He was dismayed by what he discovered – the weapons were unusable.

He rang Andrew Fitzwilliams immediately. The latter was amused to find himself so quickly discovered. He did not offer to repay Ghazi and Ghazi did not ask.

They understood each other. In future, Ghazi would be more careful. The latter was philosophical about events. Fitzwilliams, after all, was in the bag.

Returning home, he was in good heart albeit reflective. Explaining to his wife how his discussions had gone, he commented, 'I miss Grand Secretary Sir Julian Lawrence more than I could ever have believed possible. Britain is not Britain any more. Sir Julian acted clearly and morally. Everybody knew where they stood with him. Now, I have no stone in my shoe.'

'Then let us hope our new baby becomes an enormous boulder in your boots!' responded his expectant spouse.

Hearing her reproof, Ghazi smiled. 'It is up to the British authorities to provide the necessary checks in their system. Unless they do so, things will be out of control within a decade.'

Before she could reply, the telephone rang. It was Laure de Chebran calling from Paris, asking after her health and wanting to speak to Ghazi. Following the pleasantries, the latter took the receiver.

'Having a break from Freddie?' Ghazi inquired with good humour. 'I thought you were due in Italy about now. Andrew Fitzwilliams tells me your admirer is already there!'

Laure laughed. Ignoring his comment, she queried, 'How did you find Fitzwilliams?'

'A double-crosser, but a good-humoured one.'

Explaining himself, Ghazi recounted what had happened with the weapons.

'Good grief, I am surprised Peter Ligne gave permission for the deal to go ahead.'

'Ligne, my dear, as I have just told you, is in Italy,' responded Ghazi wryly. 'I am surprised you have not joined him. He is always inviting you for a naughty week-end at the opera at this time of year!'

For a moment, Laure seemed embarrassed. Rallying, she replied in a serious voice, 'Make sure France's intelligence services do not find out about the guns, Ghazi. Luckily, our

President insists on carrying out his political work via his diplomats, otherwise my darling Freddie would have given in his notice years ago.'

'It wouldn't bother me if the French did find out. The weapons are no good to me.'

Half an hour after disconnecting, Ghazi received a strange telephone call. He was unsurprised to learn Laure's line had been tapped. It was almost a national pastime in France.

What did surprise him was that the French were prepared to take the entire stock of handguns off him at the price he had paid. 'But the weapons are unusable,' he protested.

This it seemed, did not matter. The more unusable the better. They took possession of the shipment the following day. To be on the safe side, Ghazi rang Andrew Fitzwilliams. 'Mind if I sell the guns on to France?'

Fitzwilliams laughed. 'Sell them where you like, old boy. I knew you'd get rid of the lot at some stage. That's why I didn't offer you your money back.'

French Security sorted through the equipment with glee. Within two days, the arms had been polished and repackaged as new. The documentation made clear they had come from the Ministry of Defence in London. They were then shipped from Dover to Iraq.

Lloyd's of London insured the load.

CHAPTER SIXTEEN
❊ ❊ ❊

LA SCALA, MILAN: Anticipating the night ahead, Peter Ligne looked at his companion out of the corner of his eye. His lover arrived late, having been detained in Paris. The opera touched their souls.

Its patrons turned out in force to pay homage to its diva. The famously demanding loggionisti, the subscribers occupying the theatre's cheapest seats, were in ecstasy. Sharing their rapture and almost weeping with emotion, Ligne reached out his hand to find his fingers lovingly entwined.

Always receptive to exotic scent and exquisite French clothes, he moved a little closer. He loved the danger of their position. They both did. In the interval, he searched his paramour's eyes. They did not need to talk.

As Ligne made love that night, the repackaged weapons arrived in the Port of Basra. The French plan worked to perfection. President Saddam Hussein, furious at being tricked by the British, cancelled the defence contracts he had already given them and began negotiations with the Russians. Ligne returned to London to find the British and American defence contractors up in arms.

'What the fuck happened?!' he shouted down the phone, calling George Hillary and Andrew Fitzwilliams into his office for an immediate meeting.

Instructing their civil servants to cancel their morning appointments, the politicians presented themselves within the hour. George Hillary motioned his subordinate to explain. Taking a deep breath, Fitzwilliams recounted the details. A few moments later, he concluded,'. . . And so Ghazi and I off-loaded the ruddy stuff.'

Trembling with rage, Ligne clenched and unclenched his fists. 'And the pair of you did not have the wit to know what the French would do with the guns? I TOLD you to steer clear of Ghazi El-Tarek.'

George Hillary scuttled out of Ligne's sight as soon as he could – it was Defence Questions in Parliament that afternoon and he had to prepare for them. Andrew Fitzwilliams studied his finger-nails. He was mortified by what had happened. Moreover, he would have to pay Ligne his cut.

'. . . We're a laughing stock. The Chief has ordered us to win back those Iraq contracts. He does not care how.'

Mute with embarrassment, Fitzwilliams eventually dared to look Ligne in the face. He was relieved to see the older man seemingly less agitated. Motioning him to read a report on his desk, Ligne mused, 'It is just possible we can turn matters around.'

Scanning the closely typed-up note, Fitzwilliams learned the central authorities in Baghdad were having trouble with the Kurds in the north again. In addition, workers in the oil-fields were agitating once more for trades union rights. Half an hour later – following Ligne's expert tuition – he telephoned the Iraqi ambassador, making an appointment to visit him at his embassy that afternoon.

'By the time we've told our story, Saddam Hussein will give

us any contract we want!' commented a beaming Ligne as Fitzwilliams set off.

Arriving punctually, the politician was let into the embassy in Queensgate with little ceremony. The ambassador kept him waiting. Ignoring the snub, Fitzwilliams greeted him unctuously when he arrived.

'Your Excellency, please accept Her Majesty's Government's sincere apologies about the quality of the weapons your country received.'

Well rehearsed by Ligne, he continued, 'Following HMG's internal inquiries, I regret to inform you the shipment was switched. We now know the real arms were transported to the north by the Warlord on behalf of the Kurds and trades unions. The guns that arrived in the Port of Basra were not ours . . .'

The Iraqi envoy was polite but sceptical. 'The Kurds and trades unions do not have the money to buy such quantities of weapons.'

'Agreed, sir. But the Iraqi freemasons could have raised the funding for them. They are all Jews . . .'

The diplomat's eyes widened. President Hussein had always said the freemasons were so rich they must be working for the Israelites.

' . . . Moreover, two former ministers – cousins of the veterinary surgeon and leading freemason Abdullah El-Tarek – are involved. Naturally, the British government does not wish to make trouble for the men, but it has to be said that as a vet, Mr El-Tarek has access to the entire country.

'If it is any help, HMG can supply you with the names of the trades unionists. We hope this information will prove to Your

Excellency, and His Excellency the President Saddam Hussein, HMG is to be trusted . . .'

The Jews and trades unionists of Iraq were rounded up that night. The freemasons of Baghdad, as well as the Kurds in the city, were hunted down the following day.

Jiddu, relieved Suzie and Philippe were with Stollen in Moscow, rolled his wheelchair away from him and, on faltering legs, headed for his car and the Garden of Lemon Trees. He wished to draw the central guards away from the others. His driver Hussein insisted on going with him.

The Warlord did the same. He was anxious about his daughter Peri, son-in-law Lalo and their son, who had accompanied him on his visit to the capital.

In the Garden, he came upon Abdullah El-Tarek. They were praying in the direction of Mecca when the guards surrounded them. As clubs rained down upon the Warlord's head, he confessed he had made a mistake doing business with the British all those years ago. He begged them to let Abdullah go.

Screaming in pain, he assured them Abdullah El-Tarek knew nothing about politics which was the truth. It had no effect. Both were taken away for questioning.

Jiddu and Hussein were caught as their car turned left by the city's main mosque. The beauty of the minaret towered above them. Shaking with fear, Jiddu was dragged from his vehicle.

'Where are you taking him?' shrieked Hussein.

The guards told him to mind his business, and that 'the Indian traitor' was theirs.

'He is no traitor. His heart belongs to Iraq. He is old. He is your father. He is my father. He is father to us all.'

Laughing, the guards made no reply. They bundled Jiddu into a truck and set off for the Palmeira villa on the river. Hussein followed in Jiddu's car, arriving seconds later.

As they dragged the old man upstairs, Hussein pleaded, again and again, for them to leave him alone. The guards grinned as, moving from room to room, they smashed glass and beautiful porcelain. Finally, they made their way to the women's quarters.

Helpless, Hussein watched in horror as the guards beat Jiddu in his beloved late wife's bedroom. Next, they threw the earth from the tortoises' balcony in his eyes. Jiddu cried as they hurled one of the small beasts and then another across the room.

Ridiculing him, the guards asked what the 'pets' were called. In his fear, Jiddu babbled, 'I am not sure which one is which. Maybe "HMG". Maybe "KGB".'

In response, the guards shouted, 'Spy, spy,' as, in vain, Hussein shouted the names were a joke.

A short while later, the soldiers led the servant away, throwing him down the staircase. They would not kill him, they said, because President Hussein saved all Iraqis enslaved to the imperialists. Tears pouring down his face, he put his hands over his ears as Jiddu's screams rent the air. The guards had defecated into the gown that had kept his wife warm as life had slipped away from her.

It was in her clothes they found his British passport.

Under torture, Jiddu agreed the names of the tortoises were a secret code, the motorcars glinting in the sunshine at the bottom of the race-course were dead-letter boxes, and the Masonic meetings of the Baghdad Lodge had been subversive. To 'teach' him a lesson, he was made to prise off the tortoises' shells. He failed.

Next, he was commanded to jump on the animals until they were flattened. When his old legs refused to work, the soldiers jumped on them themselves. Unable to dent their hard veneer, they vented their anger on Jiddu, hitting him again and again, their batons marked proudly *Made in Britain*.

Meanwhile, Samuel Solomon tried to save his family. He rushed all his relatives to the airport. He had been told that although PanAm had been grounded, the BOAC flight to London had been cleared for take-off.

The Solomons travelled in two cars. Samuel's three eldest daughters were married now. Two were mothers.

Arriving in time, his sons-in-law, their elderly parents and his grandchildren, were not allowed to board the aeroplane. Only the immediate Solomon family – Samuel, his wife and their four daughters – could leave. There was, apparently, a problem with the paperwork.

Samuel's wife collapsed as her married daughters refused to leave the country without their husbands and babies. Needless to say, their mother also declined to go. Swiftly accepting the situation, Samuel pushed his youngest up the aircraft steps. Leah's screams of protestation were the last thing he heard as airline staff slammed the door.

Trying to catch a glimpse of her father, Leah stared through the porthole window. It was useless. As the plane took off, she noticed the bundle of papers he had thrust into her hands.

Sorting through them, she discovered her American visa, as well as those of her parents and sisters. Samuel had given her everything he could to secure her protection.

Declining food and water throughout the long flight – even the boiled sweets offered to passengers to protect their ears – Leah determined her future without reference to her own well-being. Prior to landing at Heathrow, she destroyed the documents that would have allowed her safe passage to America. She was put on a return flight to Baghdad as she knew she would be. It was the last Iraqi Airways jet to leave London.

Arriving in the dead of night, there was no-one to meet her, for no-one expected her. Telephoning her father, she found the line cut. An Iraqi family – taking pity on her and asking no questions – drove her into town.

They left her a short distance from the Jewish Quarter. She arrived home on foot. Samuel had bolted his family inside and it took a while before he could be persuaded to open the door.

The guards came for the Solomon family in the early hours of the following morning. They were all slaughtered. All, that is, except Leah, who escaped into a neighbour's garden.

From there she slipped into the back streets. She ran blindly, eventually finding herself in the beautiful Garden of Lemon Trees. Here, she too was captured and imprisoned as a plaything.

The freemasons were interrogated over many days – the central authorities had found the Lodge's Masonic records. 'Why did you take money from the Vatican for the education fund?' screamed the guards. 'Did you not know there are only Israelites in the Vatican?'

The freemasons, including Abdullah El-Tarek's former ministerial cousins, cowered as the interrogators shrieked louder and louder. Why, they screamed, as blows crashed down upon their already broken bodies, had clandestine meetings been held by the motor-cars at the race-course and who was present?

'Nobody! Nobody!'

'Don't lie,' they shrieked. 'We know the motor-cars are dead-letter boxes. Tell the truth. It will be better for you if you tell the truth. We know you were with someone, we found the cigarette stubs by the old Landrover.'

'Children,' screamed the freemasons. 'Children. They have always smoked in the motor-cars. It was not us.'

'Children do not smoke British cigarettes.'

Meanwhile, the trades unionists and Jews were held in another part of the prison. The authorities pretended they were adults. Only in Iraq could a teenage Jewish boy with toffee in his pocket be regarded as a man. Horribly tortured, all were hanged in Baghdad's central square.

At their 'trial' the freemasons confessed to being spies. The 'evidence' against them was Leah Solomon's cigarettes which she had smoked as Jasmine and Hussein had stood watch over her.

Abdullah El-Tarek was next. His death and torture were broadcast nationally on Iraqi television. The cameraman focused on the old vet's face as his eyes saw their last. He never knew about the little grand-daughter born in London, nor that his English daughter-in-law, as a mark of respect, converted to Islam after his death.

At the Jesuit mission, Father Anthony gathered what belongings he could. Foreign nationals had been given twelve hours to leave the country. Shortly before setting off, he made his way to Ibrahim the school-teacher. The latter's ardent anti-western sentiments had never stopped him from offering the American Jesuit the warmest of hospitality.

Father Anthony was too late. Ibrahim's views had been deemed to be a cover for espionage. The priest found him and his family beaten to death in the sadab, the deep, cool cellar that runs underneath all Baghdadi houses. All, that is, except seven year old Anwar whom Father Anthony found bleeding in the air-conditioning.

The boy died in his arms a few minutes later. Having no other choice, he wrapped the child in one of the family's Persian carpets, rolled up to cool the house in summer. Then, tears coursing down his face, he fled in the mission car to St George's, the Anglican church. Here, Britons who had made their lives in Iraq for over fifty years, and who knew nothing of their own land, stood in silence as space was found for them in the embassy picnic bus.

Joining the convoy of vehicles heading for the border to Jordan, Father Anthony was flagged down by one of the many Europeans living in Baghdad: Henri Sale-Gonfleur. He stopped to pick him up. The car was already crowded – before fleeing, the priest had managed to save Peri, the Warlord's daughter, with her son and husband. They drove through the night, the great stretches of land passed over, frightening in their deathly silence.

In the mission car, Henri Sale-Gonfleur rocked backwards and forwards. He had lost his mind. The visas he had sold the freemasons, including Samuel Solomon's sons-in-law, had been forgeries. And he had known it.

Eventually, peace returned to Baghdad. People came out of their houses. Shops reopened. Traffic clogged the streets once more. Saddam Hussein had learned the freemasons were innocent.

He had been duped. Under torture, the freemasons had nothing to reveal. For they had known nothing.

In revenge, Saddam Hussein gave the weapons contracts to the Russians and their allies the Chinese. It was the largest deal ever recorded. The oil companies were nationalised the same day.

Philippe and Suzie Palmeira returned to Iraq under Stollen's protection. With the Soviets in the ascendancy, they were Very Important People. The Aeroflot jet bringing them from Moscow was met at Baghdad airport with a red carpet.

Stollen's chauffeur drove them to their beautiful villa. Stollen was with them. He handed Philippe two envelopes.

One contained a copy of a letter from the Indian government to the Iraqis protesting Jiddu's death. The other was a cable from Sir Peter Ligne – like the Indian government, he had sent it via the Russian embassy, the only foreign legation that remained open. It read: *I weep with you in the death of your father*.

Arriving home, Philippe and Suzie lingered outside for as long as they could. Stollen went on ahead through a side door. He found Hussein whimpering in the women's quarters. The latter had washed Jiddu's wife's clothes.

In due course, entering via the main entrance, Philippe and Suzie found a manila packet on the marble floor. It contained a polite notice from the prison authorities requesting Philippe collect a 'package'. They meant Jiddu's body. They said he had died 'in error' and, given the family's absence in Moscow, there would be no charge for having had to keep the corpse for so long.

Stollen accompanied Philippe when he took possession of the remains of his eighty-seven year old father. Abdullah El-Tarek's widow was also there as she collected the body of the beloved veterinary surgeon. So too were the daughters of Abdullah's cousins, the Ministers of Defence and Protocol. Their mothers had lost their minds.

Philippe bowed his head. The first lie he ever told had been to one of their fathers. 'No,' he had said. 'No. I am not a British spy.'

In England, a fifteen year old school-girl scanned the personal columns of *The Times*. One morning she found the codeword for which she was looking. The message was not from her grandfather.

It read: *TORTOISE: Jiddu is at peace in the Garden of Lemon Trees. Pass your exams. Uncle Nico.*

CHAPTER SEVENTEEN

❋ ❖ ❋

HOUSE OF COMMONS: A few months after the massacre of Iraq's freemasons, the Warlord's daughter Peri arrived in London. Her visit was organised under the auspices of the French embassy in Prague – Father Anthony had sent her and her family to Freddie and Laure de Chebran. Stollen had assisted but kept a low profile given the prevailing atmosphere between the Czechs and Moscow.

Now, Peri was to meet Miro in Parliament's central lobby after which she had a meeting with the Chief Whip. Fulfilling her late father's wishes, she hoped to discuss Fitzwilliams International with him. She had invited Miro to accompany her.

Despite the crowd and habitual hub-bub at Parliament's heart, Miro spotted the graceful young woman as she entered. Seeing him, she felt immediately at peace. He led her to one of the green leather seats that circled the ornate hall. Neither had any interest in platitudes.

'My husband and son are well,' she informed him. 'Lalo has found work at the medical college in Prague. We have applied to live in Britain until it is safe to return to our own country. Lalo hopes his experience in the National Health Service will help our case.

'In the meantime, the people of Prague are kindness itself. Because of their burdens, President de Gaulle sent them his best diplomat – Freddie. Despite their troubles, they help strangers in need.'

Miro made no reply. What words of comfort could he offer?

'As for Laure, she has made a little bed for my son on her chaise longue, to pretend he is on a great adventure. She has restored his childhood. Meantime, through diplomatic channels, Freddie has arranged for me to discuss Fitzwilliams International with the Chief Whip.

'I am staying with the El-Tareks and leave tomorrow. Despite Freddie's best efforts, the British authorities would only grant me a 24 hour permit. They are wary of those living in Communist countries. Dear Ghazi paid for my trip. In addition, if my family are allowed to live in England, he will assist us financially until we are on our feet. Meantime, I hope to honour my father's memory and release you from Fitzwilliams International's subsidiary.'

Miro was overwhelmed by her kindness. The last time he had seen her had been seven years previous, at Philippe and Suzie's 'Spies Party' on the banks of the Tigris. He remembered the majesty of her father, gaiety of Abdullah El-Tarek and delight of all those who whirred and leapt to the sound of the bagpipes.

He remembered too, Samuel Solomon's words – 'Rise above prejudice, my son. There are more good people than there are of the others' – just as he recalled the joy of Samuel's daughters as they danced around the room with scarlet ribbons in their hair.

Unable to trust himself to speak, he held Peri's hand. On her wrist was a bracelet of turquoise, lapis and diamonds set in red gold. Showing it off, she said with a sad smile, 'They are Kurdish diamonds. My father presented me with the circlet when I gave him his grandson.'

At her feet was a richly coloured umbrella, with an intricate design carved into its bone handle. Seeing it, Miro queried, 'Laure's?'

His companion gave a brittle laugh. 'Of course. Who else would have such a beautiful ridiculous thing? Darling Laure, she insisted I borrow it because of the rain here. She tries so hard to pretend things are normal . . .'

Miro's unhappy eyes held hers.

'. . . She has planted a lemon tree in Prague, in memory of . . . in memory of . . .'

She could not go on. A solitary tear spilled off her face. It was the first time she had alluded to the massacre of her father and his friends. 'There are lemon trees growing all over the world. Father Anthony in America . . .' she started again.

'In Scotland, too,' whispered Miro. 'I will plant lemon trees in the Highlands.'

They were interrupted by a parliamentary official wearing tails who conducted them to a discreetly sited office just off the lobby. The Chief Whip, he informed them, had been unavoidably detained and sent his apologies. Instead, one of his private secretaries would attend the appointment in his place.

It commenced at the agreed time. Entering a few minutes after Peri and Miro, the deputising Private Secretary offered an urbane welcome. 'It is not often I am lucky enough to have a meeting with such a pretty girl!'

Peri recoiled. She was a mother, wife and civil engineer. Not so long ago, she had been a daughter too. She had not come all this way for empty compliments. Radiating a consuming chill, she returned his smile.

The Private Secretary recognised his error. Subsequently, throughout the precisely allocated forty minutes, he was polite but formal. Peri handed him her father's records.

Accepting them, he remarked briskly, 'You are saying a subsidiary of Fitzwilliams International is a covert weapons supplier and you, Dr Miro, are its chief executive albeit under duress?'

It was as if the massacre of the freemasons had never been.

'This is correct,' replied Miro. 'The late Grand Secretary Sir Julian Lawrence was on his way to discuss the matter with the Chief Whip's predecessor when his accident occurred . . .'

'Let us confine ourselves to immediate issues.'

Refusing to take the hint, Miro continued, 'I hope you will honour the Grand Secretary's last wish that Fitzwilliams International's activities be raised on the floor of the Commons.'

The Private Secretary took his time before replying. 'I am sure I do not need to explain, Dr Miro, that some matters are outside Parliament's remit. I am certain you are familiar with the terms of the Official Secrets Act.'

The threat was implicit. Reaching for the telephone secured to the wall, he continued, 'You will wish me to have a word with Andrew Fitzwilliams. It is, after all, apparently his company you are not free to leave. Although why you cannot flummoxes me.'

Fitzwilliams arrived a short while later. He recognised Peri the instant he set eyes on her. 'This is a surprise,' he said with a pleasant smile. 'What brings you to London – shopping for skis again?'

'The death of my father.'

'I'm sorry to hear that. Ill health?'

'Murder.'

He did not flinch.

The Private Secretary coughed. He explained the nature of Peri's visit, by the end of which Fitzwilliams' face was ashen. Without a second glance, he signed the affidavit releasing Miro from Fitzwilliams International.

'As for criticism of my company,' he commented, his voice cold, 'This is a matter for HMG. It must be free to promote the country's interests in any way it deems appropriate.'

He strode from the room without a backward glance. Miro did not bother to go after him. The young man he had once liked so well was no more.

The following morning, Miro collected Peri from the El-Tareks and took her to the airport. Tears flowed as she kissed Ghazi's wife and rocked their infant daughter in her arms. The journey to Heathrow with Miro was a silent one. It was soon time for them to part. Lifting her hand, Miro tried to kiss it.

Peri refused. 'Dear Miro. Always so gallant,' she murmured, brushing his cheek. She had known he admired her ever since they had danced together at the Palmeiras' party and had been careful not to give him any false hope. 'Thank you, mon cher ami and, if Allah wills, à bientot.'

He watched her go through passport control with a heavy heart. She gave a final wave and was gone. He was not to know airport security were waiting for her on the other side.

Apparently, Andrew Fitzwilliams – having been given permission by Peter Ligne – wished to interview her. The police saluted as she was brought before him. Once on their own, the politician turned his back on her.

Surprised, but not yet alarmed, she expressed the wish he did not delay her too long. He made no reply. When her flight was called, she was not on the plane.

Oblivious to Peri's troubles, Miro walked around aimlessly. Distracted by loneliness, he missed his train up to Scotland. This inconvenienced no-one but himself since no-one awaited him. He made it to his beloved Highlands the following morning.

Arriving home, he collected his post from the doormat. Leafing through – mostly the usual household bills – one letter mystified him. Surprised to read his company had not made any of the tender lists, he telephoned the British Board of Infrastructure. An embarrassed junior told him the POUKI had instructed the BBI could no longer take his calls.

A few minutes after Peri's meeting with Andrew Fitzwilliams ended, airport security handed her to their colleagues in immigration. They noted she was holding her arm awkwardly but made no comment. They had apparently 'lost' her French papers giving her permission to travel to Prague. She was accused of over-staying her visit to Britain by several hours.

'I have instructions to return you to Iraq on the first available flight. I am sure the French will let you reapply from there,' an airport official informed her.

Leaving Parliament, Andrew Fitzwilliams strolled into the sunshine to catch a cab. He was lunching with Ghazi El-Tarek. He had not seen him for months.

Soon arriving at one of London's smartest restaurants, he found his host seated at his usual table. 'Good God, old man, you have been lying low. The new baby I expect.'

Ghazi's face was gaunt. Under his eyes were huge black grooves. 'Not the baby,' he muttered. 'The death of my father and some family friends.'

Fitzwilliams expressed his sincere condolences. Eating Ghazi's food and drinking his champagne, he commented, 'At least you have a child to console you, old man. Much to my regret, Belinda won't, or cannot, give me one.'

Ghazi hardly touched his plate or raised his glass.

Oblivious, Fitzwilliams continued brightly, 'In any case, I expect you want to know what's happening with Fitzwilliams International. We've had a nasty scare. Some bitch turned up from your part of the world last month, trying to fill the Chief Whip's ear with all sorts of stuff.

'Ligne managed to head her off with a member of the POUKI masquerading as a private secretary! We had her deported: On top of everything else, she was a thief – had the cheek to complain we hurt her arm when she was stripped of the jewellery she had stolen. Beyond that, I'm pleased to say it is business as usual.'

'I am glad to hear it,' responded Ghazi. Crumbling his bread roll between his fingers, he continued, 'Who exactly was deported?'

'Kurdish bint called "Perree" or however you pronounce her Christian name. Quite a looker actually.'

Feeling almost physically sick, Ghazi studied the floral decoration in the middle of the table. 'Her name is pronounced "Perih". It is the abbreviation of the Kurdish name "Perisan". And I do not believe she would have a Christian name.'

Surprised by his host's tone of voice, Fitzwilliams apologised. 'Sorry. Tactless of me. I always forget you are a Muslim. Everybody tells me I have an appalling memory.'

Ghazi smiled. 'Some would say having a poor memory is an asset. Those who do so sleep easy at night.'

Fitzwilliams looked at him with curiosity. What had got into the man? He made his excuses as soon as he could.

On his way out, he commented, 'Belinda and I are taking Jasmine off to tea tomorrow. Her grandfather died a while back and she is a bit subdued. Still, the old boy had a good innings. In his late eighties, she said.'

Ghazi bowed his head, his expression impossible to read.

Trying to lighten the mood, Fitzwilliams continued, 'Between the two of them, Belinda and Jasmine are costing me a fortune. I bought the little minx a glorious parasol, carved bone handle, the lot, for doing so well in her exams. And, do you know, Belinda complained!

'Had to go out and buy her a more expensive present! She wouldn't settle on anything less than a gold bracelet! Red gold, if you please, with turquoise, lapis and diamonds. It cost an absolute packet, I can tell you.'

Ghazi smiled without amusement. He did not even pretend Peri was alive. How could she be when the parasol she had borrowed from Laure was now twirled by an English schoolgirl and her father's gift graced the pretty wrist of a British politician's wife?

In Iraq, life remained tense. One month after Peri's deportation, Stollen and Jiddu's old driver Hussein drove Philippe and Suzie to the border so they could cross in secret into Iran. Unless Philippe became a Communist card-holder, Stollen explained, he could not protect them much longer.

Where once the desert at night had been an awesome experience, now it seemed only eerily devoid of life. The sad little group made their farewells a short distance from the Iran-Iraq frontier. Stollen's colleagues in Teheran had been in touch with the Iranian government and the Shah had passed explicit instructions the couple be received. The route was well tried: For all Mohammed Reza Pahlevi's many wrongs, he ensured the safe passage of thousands fleeing Iraq, including its Jews.

Bringing his heels together, Stollen bowed over Suzie's hand. The moonlight caught her pale face. 'Thank you, dearest Nico, for all you have done. You will always be in our prayers.'

Next, he embraced Philippe. Before parting, they exchanged Masonic rings. These had been Jiddu's gift.

Afterwards, Stollen stood aside so Hussein could say his farewells in private. He had refused to go to London with the couple. Stollen had assured them the Russian embassy would look after him, which it did.

'Allah will protect me,' Hussein had said when Suzie implored him to change his mind and accompany them. 'I have done my duty and escorted Jiddu's children to safety. What would I do in England, my dears?'

'But how will you survive?' choked Suzie. 'Even with dear Nico's help, the guards may still kill you. And if they do not, how will you live? Who will look after you?'

Hussein shrugged. 'The guards will not kill me, and Allah always provides. I shall work in the Garden of Lemon Trees. The soldiers will think I have always been the gardener there.'

He pulled Suzie and Philippe towards him. Suzie wept uncontrollably. 'Go with God, my dears,' he comforted. 'And take Jasmine this cutting from the Garden. Tell her Jiddu sleeps.'

He walked back to the car without turning around. Stollen watched the couple for a little while as they crossed hand-in-hand into Persia. They had no luggage.

The lights of the pick-up flashed twice. It was signal enough. Stollen turned his motor around and headed back to Baghdad.

'Philippe has instructed I return to the villa and empty the safe,' he informed Hussein. 'All its contents are yours. He has asked me to sell the jewels on your behalf . . .'

'Bah!' responded Hussein. 'Do you think I will accept from the son what I would not from the father? Save the jewels for Jasmine. What need do I have of them? Iraq has lost its children.'

He cried for much of the journey. Half way to the city, their vehicle got into trouble and they had to let the air out of its tyres to prevent the wheels sinking into the soft sands. Come the dawn, they were on their way again. They had told the authorities they would be outside the prison gates at 08.00 hrs.

Stollen had seen no reason to tell Philippe or Suzie he had distressing news about Leah Solomon, nor that Peri had been handed to the guards the minute she landed in Baghdad. What would have been the point? They could not have been saved. He had accepted responsibility for their bodies.

Peri had been abused and tortured for so many hours, her beautiful blond hair had torn from her scalp. Her arm, badly bruised by Andrew Fitzwilliams when he stole her bracelet, had been crushed in several places. Eventually tiring of her, the guards threw her into a small, filthy cell. Landing heavily in a corner, she fell on top of a small, soft bundle.

It was Leah Solomon.

Leah had been raped so many times, her back had broken. In addition, the seed of one of her abusers now grew inside her smashed body. As if in further mockery, Leah was in labour. She had been in Abu Ghraib for nine months.

Peri delivered Leah's child that night. After the birth, she smoothed the hair from Leah's eyes and kissed her, before placing her one good hand across her windpipe. Leah died instantly. Her baby perished the same way a few moments later.

The following morning, the guards went mad when they discovered what Peri had done. They had enjoyed raping the pregnant Leah. They kicked her brutally in revenge.

The Warlord's daughter succumbed to her injuries several hours later. As her life ended, there was an eclipse of the sun. It was as if the world was deprived of light as her soul went free.

Stollen and Hussein buried Leah and Peri side by side under the palm trees along the banks of the Tigris. As Hussein bowed in the direction of Mecca, Stollen walked away and lit a cigarette. Staring out across the river, silence was the way he refused to speak to God.

1973

CHAPTER EIGHTEEN

QUEENS CLUB: Stollen settled happily into the London scene again. Despite the expulsion of so many Russians two years before – or perhaps because of it – he made a most welcome addition to Society. The fact it was rumoured he too was a spy made him all the more attractive.

'Oh Nico, what is all this we have been hearing?' twilled a lady in her late fifties, over the card-table at Queens one day where he had become an habitué. 'My dear husband says he met you at the Lodge last night . . .'

Stollen bowed his head in mock despair. 'Are none of my secrets safe, Mrs Eyre?' he teased Andrew Fitzwilliams' mother-in-law. 'All I said was that I would find it interesting to attend a Labour party conference so I could see democracy in action and now I am accused of . . .'

'My dear, if it is democracy you wish to see, you must go to the Tory party conference. It is, after all, the Tories who have safeguarded democracy. Indeed, were it not for us, there would be no Labour party.'

Stollen allowed himself to be corrected. Raising the lady's fingers to his lips, he flirted, 'Then allow me, chère madame, to ask you to escort me to party conference. But warn your husband. I am not to be trusted in the company of such a charming companion!'

A pink flush suffused the woman's face. 'Oh my dear, how

you do talk. I was only telling him the other day what a seducer you are. He said, "seduce away!"'

She looked about her, hoping others would find her as amusing as herself. Stollen gave a mock sigh. Winking conspiratorially to the young woman to his right, he murmured, 'Would that it were so easy. Hélas, madame, it can never be. After all, everywhere I go, I am followed by British security men. We could never be private!'

At this, all the occupants in the room laughed. They chuckled even more when he sent the men from M15, waiting in the car park below, tea and scones. Eventually, the laughter subsided.

Mrs Eyre leaned forward. 'I believe my dear husband told you our son-in-law, Andrew Fitzwilliams, is a Member of Parliament,' she queried in a loud voice so everybody could hear. 'Andrew will invite you to party conference. Won't he, Belinda?'

Evidently surprised to be brought into the conversation, Belinda Fitzwilliams, partnering her mother and seated on Stollen's right, started. 'I don't know, Mummy. You know how cross he got when I asked about Mrs Havers.'

Mrs Havers, until arthritis fully claimed her, had been Mrs Eyre's cleaning lady.

'Really, Belinda! That is not the same thing.'

Stollen was swift to put an end to any disagreement. 'Mrs Fitzwilliams is quite right,' he soothed. 'Andrew, whom I have had the pleasure of meeting on several occasions through our mutual friend Ghazi El-Tarek, must be inundated with such requests. He is a very lucky man to have such a protective wife.'

A little put out at finding her daughter so praised, Mrs Eyre dealt the cards. Soon after, Stollen and his partner won the rubber in four hearts.

'Why on earth didn't you trump Nico's ace, Belinda? We could have got him down.'

'No we couldn't, Mummy. He always had more trumps than us.'

Sensing another row brewing, Stollen made his excuses. 'I am afraid, ladies, I have to leave. I have been invited to Westminster to listen to Prime Minister's Questions from the distinguished visitors bench. I hope we have the opportunity to play again soon.'

A few moments later, with a cheerful wave to his MI5 minders, he was whisked away in his official car. Settling into his seat, he was able to reflect he had made contact with his unsuspecting target – Belinda Fitzwilliams – with considerable ease.

Twenty minutes later his car drew up at the traffic lights in Parliament Square.

'Nico!' exclaimed a jocular voice, banging on his window.

Seeing the Defence Secretary George Hillary – to whom he had been introduced at the races by Ghazi El-Tarek – Stollen threw open his door.

'Not going in the same direction I hope! Can't have damn Ruskies taking over Westminster.'

'Indeed I am, George. Are you getting in, or shall I walk with you?'

The Secretary of State chose the former option. 'Might as well confirm the ruddy Americans' worst suspicions,' he said, climbing in. 'I was only telling Fitzwilliams the other day, they must think me a "sympathiser" given the amount of time I spend with you. Can I help it if you appear to be keeping the racing industry in business?'

'They will think none the worse of you, I assure you. I took the precaution of hinting to the acting CIA head in London that I might defect! I told him I was favouring the Brits because of the way the US treated its last Soviet defector. As a result, the CIA are green with envy and you may mix with me with impunity!'

The politician laughed. 'And are you planning on defecting?' he asked archly, as the policemen waved their car through the gates of Parliament.

'Of course not. But if this is what it takes to go to the races unhindered, I thought it a lie worth telling. By the way, I have just left the delightful company of Andrew Fitzwilliams' wife and mother-in-law.'

George Hillary guffawed. 'I suspect, mon brave, you can spend as much time with Fitzwilliams' wife and mother-in-law as you chose! He has quite a good-looking filly in tow at the moment. Picked her up at the race-track, of course!'

Stollen grinned. 'If I may say so, the young lady you had on your arm when last we met was quite a looker too. I can't say I'd mind giving her a whirl when you've done.'

'Eyes off, M'laddie! I am sick of sharing my mistresses with you. I find 'em. You pinch 'em.'

As the two men bantered, the Chief of British Intelligence was being ushered into the august presence of the American ambassador at his embassy in Grosvenor Square. In attendance was Dr Don Crotale of the CIA. The impressive former CIA head in London had recently retired, his successor not yet announced. In the meantime, Dr Crotale was in charge.

'You wished to see me, Mr Ambassador?'

Motioning his guest to a cluster of wingback chairs, the American ambassador nodded. 'My, um, colleague here, wished me to appraise you of various developments,' he responded, almost apologetically. 'First, our interest in the Russian, Nico Stollen. While accepting the United Kingdom appears to be his first choice should he chose to defect, we believe it only proper to warn HMG we will do all we can to entice him to the United States.'

The Chief raised an eyebrow. Stollen, so far as he was aware, had no intention of defecting. Clearing his throat, he asked, 'Is there any particular reason why you believe the colonel is to defect?'

The American ambassador deferred to his colleague. Glancing at the Briton, his frank eyes seemed to be imparting a message between professionals.

'He told me so himself,' responded Dr Crotale, lowering his voice.

The ambassador stared at the ceiling. He was the sort of man who hated to see other people making fools of themselves.

'If I may say so, Colonel Stollen says a very great deal he does not always mean,' responded the Chief.

The CIA man looked at him with suspicion. He had expected the Brit to fob him off. 'Oh no? Then why, if Stollen isn't planning on defecting, would he warn me about one of your guys? A fella called Ligne, Sir Peter Ligne. The Ruskie says Moscow recruited him years ago. As a result, they know all about Fitzwilliams International.'

The Chief sighed. His eyes lifting to the side walls, the benevolent features of the President of the United States gazing down at him, he replied with a wry smile, 'If I remember rightly, Colonel Stollen mentioned a couple of your boys to us. One of the names he gave was "Dr Don Crotale".'

He flashed a not unattractive smile. 'Was there anything else, gentlemen?'

'A couple of things, I'm afraid . . .' replied the ambassador, allowing his colleague time to rearrange his features.

The Chief looked at him with polite interest.

'. . . Accepting Stollen is a prankster, the US cannot afford to take any chances. The problem is Fitzwilliams International. We would not want the Russian shooting off his mouth about it. I should say, incidentally, up until recently I had no idea the CIA was using the company as a weapons conduit.'

The ambassador stared hard at Dr Crotale. The latter shifted in his chair. The ambassador continued, 'In view of this, I am making a formal request HMG withdraw Fitzwilliams International from Iraq. The Saudis are more than capable of taking on its nuclear programme. If it became known to the Israelis, the Americans were using a private British company to . . .'

'Stitch them up with their enemies?'

'Quite. It would cause us considerable embarrassment. It is duplicitous conduct.'

The Chief looked at the ambassador non-committally. 'And that, Your Excellency, you believe, would put an end to CIA involvement in Fitzwilliams International? You will, of course, have to pension off Dr Crotale's latest conscript . . .'

The ambassador raised a quizzical eyebrow at his hapless colleague. The latter squirmed.

'. . . Didn't Dr Crotale tell you? He has just recruited a former senior diplomat from the Iraqi embassy. The man has been asked to set up a bank to work alongside the Organisation d'Investissement de l'etat du Kowait – OIK . . .'

– The Chief managed the abbreviation without smiling –

'. . . To handle the financial arrangements for weapons supply undertaken by Fitzwilliams International. In view of this, Mr Ambassador, you will forgive the United Kingdom for not pulling it out of Iraq. I am sure you would agree it would not be appropriate for the CIA to strip us of a not unprofitable enterprise while bolstering its own.'

The ambassador looked embarrassed. The CIA's conduct usually depressed him. Glowering, Dr Crotale made no comment.

At his most obliging, the Chief concluded, 'Perhaps you should know also, Mr Ambassador, we were interested in the Iraqi ourselves. We decided not to enlist him when we found out about his gambling habit. Apparently, he owes Stollen a small fortune, lost over a series of private poker games. Typical Soviet snare . . .'

– The Chief paused, a dramatic trick he always put to good use –

'. . . As a result, anything the CIA ask of him will be passed to Moscow. HMG thought it only correct to warn you.'

There was an awkward silence. Trying to salvage some loss

of face, the CIA man eventually summoned the courage to move the discussion on. 'Stollen also warned the Brits are gonna join the Continental conspiracy!'

The Chief stared at him blankly.

'He means the European Economic Community,' explained the ambassador.

'. . . Stollen said it was Moscow's most daring strike yet against the free world. A British Prime Minister – and a Conservative one at that – is jeopardising the Atlantic Alliance and doing considerable harm to NATO . . .'

'Tosh,' interrupted the Chief, flicking an imaginary piece of fluff from his unremarkable suit. 'On the one hand, America welcomes Britain's entry into Europe, a bolster, apparently, against Communism. On the other, it believes it a conspiracy against the free world. It cannot have it both ways, although it does try.'

For the first time, the CIA man looked to his ambassador for support.

'There are policy differences at home, Chief,' admitted the latter. 'It has been noted with concern, Prime Minister Heath appears to be favouring rapprochement with Eastern bloc countries. The official line is that your government's position on the European issue is causing alarm in the White House.'

'Not half as much as it is to us, old boy,' laughed the Chief. 'Be this as it may, there is no stopping the Prime Minister. Ted Heath is absolutely determined to take Britain into Europe and, as you are already aware, open up the Eastern bloc.'

'Stollen says the Ruskies are blackmailing the Prime Minister. He is a bachelor after all!' snapped Dr Crotale.

Anger flashed across the Englishman's face. 'I hope, Mr Ambassador, you will ensure Dr Crotale withdraws his comment.'

He did so.

The Chief smiled his coolest smile. 'Additionally, I hope Dr Crotale's colleagues will desist from interfering in Britain's democratic process, or, in due course, the re-election of the present Conservative government if this is the will of the British people.'

Recognising his meaning, the ambassador looked nonplused. All present knew American-paid subversives were inciting the first wave of strikes against Mr Heath's government.

By way of excuse, the ambassador murmured, 'I am told the Labour party has an unfavourable view of Europe which invites good will in some parts of Washington.'

'Don't you believe it,' responded the Briton. 'The Labour party is as divided on Europe as the Tories. The Opposition leader is just more wily at hiding it. The Party's Roman Catholics, of course, are all in favour.'

Seeing his companions' surprise, the Chief opined, 'I assumed, Dr Crotale, Colonel Stollen told you "Europe" was a Roman Catholic conspiracy manipulated by the Vatican?'

The latter shook his head.

With the air of a fellow being helpful, the Chief soothed, 'Not to worry, old chap. He will in due course. It'll probably be Father Anthony who puts him up to it.'

'Father Anthony?' repeated the CIA man.

'An Irish-Bostonian Jesuit. Surely, you have a file on him?'

Dr Crotale had not.

The ambassador looked away. The Chief was, in his way, something of a prankster himself.

'I would go carefully, if I were you. The American Catholics are a formidable lobby. You are not a Roman Catholic are you, Dr Crotale?'

CHAPTER NINETEEN

※ ❂ ※

MI6 HEADQUARTERS: The Chief telephoned Peter Ligne the moment he returned from the American embassy. A short while later, the latter sat before him. Reports, flimsies and dossiers lay heaped everywhere.

Ligne was surprised to find himself offered a drink in the middle of the day. 'Women troubles, sir?'

The Chief smiled. 'If only. No. American troubles. The Yanks are so windy about this European business they've put the CIA – who have now contracted the POUKI – on alert to de-stabilise Ted Heath. There is nothing bone fide American diplomats can do about the situation, no matter how senior or embarrassed they may be.

'The MI5 Chief, the dolt, admitted he lost control of the POUKI years ago. This bloody country isn't ours any more. Meanwhile, the US is asking questions about Fitzwilliams International.

'As a result, the Chief Whip is worried about Andrew Fitzwilliams' position. He says if anything goes wrong with the company, it could embarrass the Conservatives – and just before the election too!'

Ligne grinned. 'All in hand, sir. The minute Miro stood down from Fitzwilliams International's subsidiary, I knew we had to protect Fitzwilliams. I was thinking of bringing in Ghazi El-Tarek to run the whole show.

'HMG knows him well. He's an Iraqi. Let the Americans tell him they want Fitzwilliams International out of his own country!'

For the first time that day, the Chief thought perhaps there was some light in the world after all. 'Will you approach El-Tarek?'

Ligne shook his head. 'It would be much better if Fitzwilliams did. They are good friends.'

Accepting another whisky, he changed the subject. 'Are you aware Stollen is in the habit of knocking off George Hillary's young ladies?'

The Chief chuckled. 'Uh-huh. The MI5 Chief told me. He wanted to know what to do about it. I told him to do nothing. It seemed a shame to ruin the fun.'

Lost in thought, Philippe Palmeira replaced the receiver. He had just taken another call from an American who, as on previous occasions, had refused to give his name. Stollen had advised him it was a CIA man in London, Dr Don Crotale.

'Who was on the telephone, darling?' Suzie's voice floated upstairs.

Philippe made his way to his wife. She was in her morning-room, a marmalade cat curled in her lap. 'No one, darling, just a wrong number,' he responded, stooping to kiss her.

'It wasn't that beastly American again, was it? I do wish he would leave you alone. Surely he can take "no" for an answer?'

Her husband shook his head. In the usual run of things he never lied to her, but this time he hoped it permissible. Ever since their arrival in England, he had tried to shield her from the results of his clandestine work. Jiddu's death had left her numb with grief for months. He himself had a lingering pain in the pit of his belly.

She looked at him with anxiety. 'You haven't changed your mind, darling? You are going to tell Ligne you have decided to resign from government service?'

He smiled. 'Of course,' he reassured. 'I have already told Stollen I am giving in my notice. By this evening, I will be my own man again. It will all be over.'

She heaved a sigh of relief. Pushing her complaining cat from her lap, she walked him to the door. 'You won't be late, darling?' she fretted. 'And you won't let Ligne talk you out of it?'

'No,' he replied, stroking her cheek.

An hour later, he gave his name to the doorman at Ligne's club and made his way to the civil servant's usual table. Seeing him, Ligne put down his newspaper.

'Good to see you, dear boy. What can I get you? Gin and tonic?'

Philippe ordered lemon tea.

'Nothing stronger?'

He shook his head.

Once seated, Ligne looked at him without seeming to. He was aware his companion had tried to detach himself from HMG ever since his arrival in England – this, when Ligne needed Philippe more than ever. Human intelligence was the vital link in espionage.

Finishing his whisky, he motioned the waiter to freshen his glass as his guest's tea was served. Beside him, his paper was open on the foreign news. In the Middle East, Kissinger ignored the Palestinians, increasing Sadat of Egypt's isolation, the Lebanon exploded, and the Shah of Iran's secret police, trained in Britain, violated their country's people. Meanwhile, Arab and Persian élites in Europe led the high life, swilling champagne at the gaming tables.

Hoping to keep the conversation light, he remarked, 'You'll be glad to know, old chap, HMG has made some headway with your honour. We thought a knighthood would please Suzie. Wives like to be called "your ladyship".'

Philippe stared. How little Ligne understood his wife. Stirring his tea, he responded without preamble, 'I have decided to resign from Crown service, Peter. I have already told Stollen. Suzie and I have discussed the matter at length . . .'

Ligne masked his disappointment.

'. . . The last straw was when the CIA fellow telephoned.'

Ligne laughed. Hoping to salvage things, he replied, 'Dr Crotale, no doubt. He approached me too! He's got the wind up about Stollen. He is aware you know him best.'

'Nobody knows Stollen, except, perhaps, Laure or Father Anthony. In any case, Suzie doesn't like it. She said you would probably tell me to work for the CIA as well . . .'

'It had crossed my mind.'

'. . . In effect making me a treble. "One for each of us", was her dry comment.'

Wives, Ligne reflected, as another drink was placed in front of him, were a nuisance. A damn nuisance. 'If this helps Iraq, would that matter? If you give up, your dear father, Abdullah, Samuel, the Warlord, all of those whose defining quality was their decency will have died in vain.'

'They died in vain, anyway. Saddam Hussein offers HMG and America a market beyond dreams.'

Philippe left a few moments later. For the first time in years he felt able to breathe easily.

Arriving home in time for dinner, he found Suzie in tears. She had taken a call from Laure de Chebran who explained her husband Freddie was terminally ill. Low in spirits, Philippe and Suzie ate in silence.

Although it was the school-holidays, they did not expect Jasmine. Now aged sixteen, their daughter would not even accompany her mother on her morning ride in Richmond Park. To their sorrow, Jasmine spent most of her days out with friends, or, as frequently, Belinda Fitzwilliams.

Suzie and Philippe had been away from her for so long, they could not blame her for organising her life without them. Even when she was home, Jasmine spent most of her time in her bedroom. When she came downstairs, she barely noticed them. As for Jiddu's death – after initial grief, she no longer mentioned him.

The loud ring of the telephone disturbed the quiet. Suzie answered.

'I am at Belinda's, Mum,' a cheerful Jasmine informed her. 'We have been invited to dinner by a man called Sir Peter Ligne. I remember him from Baghdad – he was "Mr Ligne" in those days! He says he saw Daddy this afternoon. I cannot think why he is insisting I call since you were not expecting me home anyway. He's such a laugh. He told me to tell Daddy that unless Daddy does as he says, he'll ruin me!'

As an amiable Ligne came on the line, Suzie passed the phone to her husband. By the end of their brief chat, Philippe Palmeira was Ligne's employee once more. The civil servant was glad the matter had been settled before he left for the Italian Lakes.

No-one resigned from HMG.

Ever.

CHAPTER TWENTY

❋ ❋ ❋

PRINCE OF WALES DRIVE: Stollen turned left over Battersea Bridge and drove to the red brick mansion block opposite the park where many MPs had their London homes. He had slipped his minders with ease. He knew Ligne had left at the beginning of the week for Italy and would be on leave for one more. This gave him ten days to secure his target: Jasmine had inadvertently furnished Stollen with the address he needed. Parking opposite, he settled down to wait.

His patience was soon rewarded – Belinda Fitzwilliams emerged from the building not five minutes later. He had not seen her playing cards at Queens the previous afternoon and this worried him. She walked slowly, her back hunched and her face pointed at the ground.

Sprinting across the road, he exclaimed, 'Belinda! What a coincidence. What are you doing here?'

She looked up in confusion before dropping her eyes to the ground again. There was a crimson mark above her left eyebrow. 'I live here,' she replied nervously.

He tilted her chin. 'What happened?'

The stricken, unhappy woman made a big effort to smile. 'Silly me. I feel such a fool. I walked into a door.' She added, with a brave attempt at normality, 'That's why I wasn't playing bridge yesterday.'

Looking out for traffic, Stollen coaxed her towards his car.

Brought up too politely to resist, she made no attempt to thwart him.

'Now see what I have for you,' he beamed. 'A back seat full of beautiful flowers . . .'

She peered through the window. 'They're gorgeous,' she gulped, seeing stems of rich reds and bold yellows wrapped in soft tissues with exquisite care so they would not be crushed.

'All they need is someone to arrange them prettily in vases. I'll bet you were taught flower-arranging as a school-girl.'

Belinda looked at him with pathetic pleasure and long forgotten pride. 'Yes . . .'

'There you are then! Come on, just because I'm a nasty Russian, you cannot blame the flowers. It is not their fault!'

She giggled. 'I've never said you were a nasty Russian,' she replied, as Stollen opened the passenger door for her. 'My mother thinks you're wonderful!'

As she got in, he secured her seat-belt in case she changed her mind. 'And so I am!' he responded, climbing behind the wheel. 'Even Ligne says so!'

She looked at him in surprise. 'Do you mean Sir Peter Ligne?'

'Of course. We have known each other for years. I am sure he has mentioned me. He probably said something along the lines of what a scallywag I am. He knows I say the same about him!'

'Are you a scallywag?'

'Is Ligne?'

'No.'

'There's your answer. I'll give the rogue a good hiding when he gets back from Italy for besmirching my reputation!'

Reassured by what she took to be his friendship with Ligne, Belinda began to enjoy herself. 'Where are we going, Mr Stollen?' She had forgotten he was a colonel.

'Nico,' he corrected. 'And we're going to my home – as much as you can call an old bachelor's apartment a home – to put our flowers in water and find something to put on that pretty face of yours. We can't let that good-looking husband of yours, catch you . . .'

At the mention of Fitzwilliams, Belinda sank deeper into her seat. 'Andrew's not here. He left on an overseas visit this morning.'

Stollen knew this already. 'Then we'll just have to make your pretty face better for when he comes home.'

Eventually they drew up outside his apartment. Despite British government controls on where a Soviet might live, he had slipped his minders yet again and rented it with Belinda in mind.

Helping him to carry in the flowers, she was immediately at ease. Amid his shabby but fine furniture, his table-tops overflowing with books, she found pretty vases for the blossoms and arranged them to perfection.

He poured her a drink. She looked exhausted now the simple pleasure of cutting and watering the stems was over. 'I don't drink vodka,' she remarked politely, as he handed it to her.

Stollen laughed. 'Then it is just as well it is not vodka! It is arac, a speciality of Iraq. I only offer it to very special people. Come on, have one glass and then I will take you home.'

Too used to receiving orders to disobey, even if she had mind or energy to argue which she did not, she did as she was bid.

She was not aware arac was almost 90% proof and was soon profoundly drunk. Her head began to swim. She felt hot and confused.

Stollen moved swiftly to comfort her. Settling her on the sofa and plumping up the cushions behind her back, he reassured, 'You've reacted this way, because you haven't eaten. Once I've cooked supper, you'll be fine. After all, whatever would your husband say, if he . . .'

At the mention of Fitzwilliams again, Belinda began to tremble. Andrew's expression, angry and violent, swam before her eyes. She blinked. Stollen's face was now before her. He looked so kind.

'My dear, you are shaking like a leaf. Whatever is wrong?' he asked, stroking her cheek and gently outlining the flush of her bruise.

Outside, day passed to early night. Stollen switched on the lights before sitting beside her and wrapping his arms around her. Half drunk, Belinda, his guest, held on to him like a child. 'What is it, little one? You can tell me,' he soothed.

Intoxicated and distressed, she poured out her heart. Andrew Fitzwilliams was the bastard Stollen had always known him to be. Stroking her arm, he noticed the bracelet she was wearing.

'Andrew gave it to me,' she muttered, following his gaze.

He did not tell her the last time he had seen it, it had been on the wrist of Peri, the Warlord's daughter. Instead, he settled her against him more comfortably and whispered, 'Can't your parents help you get away from him?'

Belinda shook her head. 'They think Andrew is wonderful,' she gulped. 'I'm sure everything would be all right if we could have a baby but he refuses. He says he doesn't want my snivelling little brats. My mother and father think it is my fault.'

She fell asleep a short while later, the result of too much alcohol and grief. Stollen carried her to his bedroom, leaving the door ajar as he left. A few hours later, he heard her sobbing once more.

Returning, he took her in his arms again. Aware of their more intimate surroundings, she froze.

'Hush, sweet Belinda. Andrew is not back until next week.'

She tried to focus her eyes. She could not remember telling Stollen when her husband was due to return. It was a rare error on the Russian's part. To distract her, he undid the top buttons of her blouse.

Rigid with fear, she observed, 'I know what happens next. I stand up so you can beat me. Andrew makes me stand up and I fall over. I try not to. He gets so cross. Andrew . . .'

'Wrong. I kiss you.'

She shook her head. 'You can't kiss me. Andrew says no-one can kiss me. I am diseased you see. Andrew got into trouble with the whips because of me. He said I should have gone to the clinic anonymously like everybody else.

'Then he wouldn't have got into trouble. But I went to the doctor instead. I didn't know, you see, I was diseased. Andrew didn't tell me about my disease . . .'

Soon she was crying again, her sobs coming out in deep gulps. 'I'm sorry I got Andrew into trouble with the whips. I didn't mean to. I didn't know I shouldn't go to the doctor. I didn't know I was diseased . . .

'That's why Andrew won't make babies with me. He says my

babies will be diseased. I didn't know I was diseased. Andrew didn't tell me,' she repeated over and over again.

Raw anger swept across Stollen's face. 'Let no-one tell you, my pretty Belinda, you are diseased,' he corrected. 'No-one.'

He rang his embassy the following morning while she showered. 'Operation "broken petal" on target,' he reported.

'We know! You ought to see the photographs,' laughed a colleague. 'They're good. Thanks for turning on the lights.'

Stollen winced. There were times when he found his job distasteful. A few moments later, Belinda ate the breakfast he had prepared. It was as if she had not eaten in days.

'What did you give me to drink last night?'

He told her.

'That was a low trick.'

Stollen sighed. 'Yes, my dear. I specialise in them.'

'Am I in trouble?'

'Any woman who is consistently abused by her husband is in trouble.'

Belinda Fitzwilliams shrugged.

'Leave the bastard, Belinda,' he urged.

Her eyes swimming with tears, she responded, 'Are you married? Do you have a pretty little wife and children in Russia?'

He shook his head. In his profession, the truth came as easily as lying. 'I told you yesterday when I invited you to my bachelor squalor, I am not married,' he reminded.

'I don't remember much about yesterday.' Puckering her forehead, she continued, 'I suppose you are such a good lover because you are a bachelor. When men become husbands they do not need to be good lovers, do they? They can do what they like.'

Stollen stared in amazement. 'That's why you allow your husband to abuse you, my dear?' Tilting her chin, he repeated, 'Dump Fitzwilliams, Belinda, he's a bastard.'

'And you are not?' Without waiting for an answer, she continued, 'Andrew says the Americans believe you are going to defect. Are you? And wouldn't that make you a traitor?'

Stollen smiled. 'I don't know. And yes, it would.'

She held his eyes. 'I don't think you would much like being a traitor. You know the difference between right and wrong. Andrew doesn't. This is why I don't think anything is his fault. He cannot help the way he is. You can. Being a traitor is not correct. It is about betrayal . . .'

Stollen stopped her with a kiss. She had an uncanny way of stating the truth which discomforted him. He liked this vulnerable young woman. It made him despise Andrew Fitzwilliams all the more.

'You mean, my pretty, you do not want me to defect or see me again?' he joked.

Belinda Fitzwilliams' eyes widened. 'You mean you would like to see me again?'

'Of course.'

Pleasure, and then regret, flooded her face. 'Thank you, Nico, for saying that. It is kind of you. But I can't. I don't know how I can have been such a fool – after all, Peter Ligne did warn me. You're a Communist. What on earth would Mummy say?'

'"Mummy" is a bitch. When you dump Fitzwilliams, make sure you dump your mother at the same time. Then you can see me!'

Belinda giggled. 'You do think a lot of yourself, Nico.'

'Yes, my dear.' Kissing the nape of her neck, he played deftly to her sympathies. 'Why can't I see you – is it because I am too old? Is that it?'

'What?! Of course not. I've told you, Nico. It's because you are a Communist.'

He refused to take 'no' for an answer. 'Would it make any difference if I did ask HMG for asylum? If I said it was because a beautiful politician's wife was going to divorce her husband and marry an ancient like me? I could ask Ligne, if you prefer.'

'Nico, I absolutely FORBID you to say anything to Peter Ligne!' she screamed with laughter. 'And you are not ancient!'

'If you say so, my darling. However, I do want to marry you.'

She looked at him in amazement. 'How can you possibly want to marry me? We've only just met. Properly that is.'

'Rather improperly, actually.' His hand felt his way underneath her bathrobe. 'And, to answer your question, I want to marry you because I know everything I need to know. You do not cheat at cards for one thing. Now then . . .'

– his eyes teased –

'. . . Do I speak to HMG or not?'

'You're nuts. Absolutely nuts. You mean it!'

'Guilty as charged. What's it to be? My future is in your beautiful hands.'

'Nico, I am MARRIED and a Roman Catholic. I have only been married for three years. What do I do about Andrew?'

Stollen gave a theatrical sigh. Scooping her into his arms, he carried her back to bed. 'Roman Catholicism is an attitude of mind, my dear. As for Fitzwilliams, what about him?'

Making a show of enjoying her body, he continued, 'Women! I'll never understand them. Why should you care what happens to that bastard? He will probably meet someone else anyway.'

She stared into his face, love pouring from her eyes. 'He does not need to. He will marry Jasmine Palmeira when she is old enough – his only problem is how he gets rid of me! He adores Jasmine. He always has. You know her, don't you?'

Lying down beside her, his head propped on his elbow, he replied, 'Of course.'

'Peter Ligne warns me all the time about Jasmine! He said you groomed her to marry Andrew. You need not have bothered – it will happen anyway. Meantime, Jasmine is sweet and protects me from Andrew as best she can. She's gone back to school now. Andrew never hurts me when she's around.'

He kissed her – a long, lingering caress. 'There you are then – Fitzwilliams is sorted! If, however, our relationship worries you so much, I will definitely ask Ligne for help and tell him about our future plans . . .'

'Nico, we have NO future plans,' she interrupted, falling deeper in love even as she contradicted him.

'. . . That way, we cannot be accused of doing anything underhand. Moreover, the Americans will at long last recognise I am serious about wanting to remain in the West.'

'The Americans? You want to tell the Americans, now?' asked Belinda, torn between exasperation and amusement. 'That could damage Andrew's career. I don't want that. Whatever he has done to me, he has worked hard at his job. He loves it and does it well. It would be wrong for me, or you, to damage . . .'

He kissed her nose. 'As I say, I will never understand women. All right, my pretty, I will not wreck Fitzwilliams' career if you do not want me to. On one condition . . .'

She looked at him in surprise.

'. . . You divorce him.'

CHAPTER TWENTY ONE

MI6 HEADQUARTERS: A few days after the start of his affair with Belinda Fitzwilliams, Stollen wrote to Peter Ligne. The civil servant saw his missive on his return from holiday. Stollen informed him that in addition to his recent liaison, he was applying for a right of residence to remain in the United Kingdom. In a postscript he added he hoped Ligne had had a good holiday.

As it happens, Ligne had not. Dialling the Chief, he thundered, 'Stollen's gone from sharing George Hillary's tarts to swiping Fitzwilliams' wife. I warned the fool something like this could happen.'

The Chief could scarcely believe what he was hearing. 'What bloody timing! The Heath government is in enough trouble as it is. Do you think we ought to tell Fitzwilliams?'

Ligne demurred. He was still annoyed with the politician for the deal the latter had done behind his back with Ghazi El-Tarek. Now, Stollen blamed Ligne and Fitzwilliams for the deaths of the Iraqi freemasons which had followed. The fact Fitzwilliams had ceded the moral high ground to the Russian persisted in irritating him.

'I am not sure it is our function to inform husbands they are being cuckolded, sir. Too labour intensive!'

'What about the Chief Whip?'

Again, Ligne thought not. 'Best keep it to ourselves for the moment. However, call the Americans, Chief, and tell them we know all about the affair. Let them think it's a honey-trap: Fitzwilliams has laid down his wife for his country, sort of thing. They're bound to believe it.'

The Chief frowned. 'So long as we do not. There is something very odd going on. It is staring us in the face but I cannot see it.'

Ligne made no reply. He had never informed his superior Stollen had determined to destroy the Fitzwilliams' marriage from the outset and saw no reason to do so now. After all, Stollen's plan to substitute Jasmine Palmeira for Belinda could be turned to advantage.

With the knowledge of the British intelligence services, Stollen's affair with the wife of a British politician was allowed to prosper. Needless to say, the press got wind of it. However, as in the early stages of the Profumo business, journalists were disinclined to report the rumour for fear of a libel action.

'My mother's sick again, darling. She's in East Berlin. You don't mind if I go and see her, do you?' Stollen called out.

'Of course not,' replied Belinda stepping from his shower and wrapping herself in a towel. 'Tell her I hope she gets better quickly and I look forward to meeting her after Christmas.'

He pulled her to him. 'As she does you. Now then, my Belle-Linda, as dismal as the Eastern section is, what shall I bring you?'

Belinda Fitzwilliams laughed. She had all but moved into Stollen's apartment and had not thought about her husband in months. The general election hoving into view preoccupied him, as it did every other politician. As for her parents – she never saw them.

'Something naughty,' she teased.

'Then I'd best bring myself.'

He nuzzled the back of her neck. 'Will you be seeing your lawyers while I'm away?'

'Yes, darling,' she reassured. 'I will suggest they write to Andrew and ask him to pop into their office for a chat. I don't want them to be specific in writing because of gossip. Not until after the general election, anyway. Hopefully the Home Office will have granted your right of residence by then. You have applied, darling, haven't you?'

She did not wait for an answer. She had never been so happy. Turning around, wrapping her arms about his neck, she pattered on, 'Which reminds me. Jasmine said your last mistress was George Hillary's – Andrew told her. Was she? And did you want to marry her as well?'

'Uh-huh,' smiled Stollen. 'And no, I didn't. As for George, I am told he is smitten by a beautiful lobbyist at the moment!'

Belinda laughed. She loved to hear him talk. He seemed to know everybody, and, unlike Andrew, liked to share his impressions with her. Andrew only yielded his thoughts to Jasmine.

She stared into his eyes. 'Jasmine's worried about me. She says Peter Ligne is right and you are a rogue! When shall we get married, Nico and prove them all wrong? It will . . .'

He stopped her with a kiss. 'Let's get that ruddy divorce first, shall we?'

Belinda nodded. 'But when we have, then we can marry, can't we? And have babies? Lots and lots of them?'

Stollen's jaw tightened. 'You will make a lovely mother,' he responded truthfully.

The American ambassador frowned. Dr Crotale had asked to see him. The prospect appalled and depressed him.

He made his way out of his embassy and around to the annex on the left. Two marines stood guard. Arriving at Dr Crotale's inner sanctum, he found the CIA man pouring himself a drink. He had a machine which made perfect balls of ice.

The ambassador declined a whisky. Crotale looked on top of the world. Once the diplomat was seated, he explained the British had advised him of Stollen's affair with Belinda Fitzwilliams.

Jabbing the air with quick victorious punches, Crotale concluded, '. . . So the Ruskie's defi-nite-ly defecting!'

He leaned forward, fixing his eyes on the ambassador's face so the latter had no chance of escape. 'Of course, I called Stollen. He informed me Belinda Fitzwilliams is petitioning her husband for a divorce. He's worried this will make things difficult for them to stay in Britain. I said we'd be happy to have them!

'And, I'm glad to say, Mr Ambassador, he's biting. I mean really biting – he liked the big bucks I offered! The Brits are so poor they could never compete. Now, Stollen's even given me a blow by blow account of his affairs with the Defence Secretary's various mistresses . . .'

Looking unusually glum, the ambassador stared at his colleague. 'I fail to understand why the latter should preface a defection.'

The CIA man grinned. 'On its own, I grant, it does not. But Stollen has also confirmed our suspicions Fitzwilliams International has extended into the Eastern bloc via its West German holding company. As a result, money is passing to the West and being funnelled into the London insurance market – no questions asked! There's more foreign money – and POUKI funds, come to that – sloshing around Lloyd's of London than . . .'

'Fascinating though this is, what is the CIA's interest in Fitzwilliams International these days? I assume the Agency has not pulled out of it.'

The ice in Dr Crotale's drink put a damp frost around the outside of his glass. Of course the Agency had not pulled out of Fitzwilliams International. Why should it? It was handling contracts passed directly from the Department of Defence in Washington and no questions asked. Not even when Ghazi El-Tarek had taken over the company.

'I will assume that is a "yes",' the ambassador's brusque voice cut into his thoughts. ' . . . So, what plans do the CIA have for Fitzwilliams International in future? It is, after all, British.'

The CIA man swallowed. The diplomat's hostility always put him on the defensive. 'These have not been finalised, sir. I have referred the matter upwards.'

The ambassador raised an eyebrow.

Clearing his throat, Dr Crotale continued, 'I believe our long-term goal should be to take over Fitzwilliams

International. I think this could be achievable. Its present chief executive, Ghazi El-Tarek, is likely to be complaisant given he's in a weak position. The Agency has asked the Home Office to continue to block El-Tarek's application for British nationality and it is agreeable.

'Stollen's affair with the wife of the owner of Fitzwilliams International can only work in our favour.'

The ambassador scrutinised his immaculately polished finger-nails. Buffing them, he remarked, 'In my opinion, you are so blinkered by the supposed coup of swiping Stollen from underneath the Brits' noses, you cannot see he is playing you as a cat toys with a mouse.'

Scarcely bothering to conceal his contempt, he rose. 'I shall ask for an immediate meeting with the Secretary of State and President in Washington.'

CHAPTER TWENTY TWO
❈ ❈ ❈

WASHINGTON DC: The President of the United States drummed his fingers on the heavy wooden desk of the Oval Office. Not even the prominently displayed photograph of his beloved wife and daughters seemed to calm him. As for the immaculately decorated Christmas tree taking up one corner of the room – he had not even noticed it.

Beset by scandal summarised in one word – 'Watergate' – and fighting to save his presidency, he had now been drawn into an argument between his ambassador in London and the CIA. The Agency's recently confirmed head of London station, Dr Don Crotale and his envoy would be with him shortly.

The President sighed. Usually, his Secretary of State would be in attendance but the latter had been called away on yet another overseas visit. As a result, he had to receive his visitors alone. This displeased him. He was suspicious of the CIA. Equally, he was suspicious of his ambassador, not least because the President believed himself to have the better grasp of international affairs.

Across the ocean, Vietnam sapped his people's confidence, American support for Israel strained long friendship with the Saudis, Europe organised itself into a 'Community' – scarcely disguising its contempt for NATO – South America grew closer to Communism and China experimented in space.

Meanwhile, closer to home were troubles with students. And dominating everything – EVERYTHING – was 'Watergate'. Part, or so the President believed, of a vast international Communist conspiracy against the United States.

'The Papal nuncio on the line for you, Mr President.'

The President picked up the phone. The White House trod warily with the Vatican. Its astronomers had recently relocated their star-gazing from Castel Gandolfo in Italy to Tucson, Arizona. This was a double-edged sword. Catholicism's international influence was seen as a bulwark against Communism. For the same reason, any hostility with the White House could similarly be telegraphed worldwide.

The President had been personally suspicious of the Vatican ever since the West German Chancellor had asked it to act as its mediator with the Russians. The Oval Office had taken this as a personal affront. The United States was jeopardising its relationship with Britain by focusing on West Germany. Now its Chancellor was trying to do deals with Russia behind America's back.

The President frowned. The United States maintained peace on the continent of Europe – when it had no real significance to America – and this was the way it was treated.

The mellow voice of the Papal nuncio interrupted his thoughts. 'We understand, Mr President, you are meeting with Father Anthony this afternoon?'

'That's right, er . . . sir . . .'

– The President had momentarily forgotten how to address a Papal nuncio –

'. . . My ambassador in London recommended it.'

The cleric cut to the chase. 'We are told you asked to see Father Anthony because you wish to discuss Colonel Nico Stollen with him. An excellent choice. The Father and Stollen go back many years.'

The last vestiges of the President's minimal good humour evaporated. He had reservations about priests friendly with Communists. The South American experience had taught the White House that.

'What does Father Anthony say are Stollen's intentions in London?' he asked in his brisk manner.

'Mayhem. Destabilisation of the United Kingdom. If I may say so, Mr President, the CIA are Stollen's dupe.'

'You think so?' queried the President. While he had no opinion of the CIA, he took no pleasure in hearing it rubbished by others. Effortlessly maintaining his self-possession, he continued, 'Father Anthony's allegiance is in no doubt? He is an American first?'

'No, Mr President. Father Anthony is an American Jesuit first . . .'

The President could scarcely disguise his irritation.

'. . . If it is any help, he is known for his independence of mind. Sometimes, I think he needs to be more careful. You are probably aware the last priest to be excommunicated was an American.'

The President was not. He found his temper rising. It was the nuncio's emphasis on the word 'American' that annoyed him.

They disconnected a few moments later. The man had made his point. While the Vatican had agreed Father Anthony's visit, he could be denied at any time.

The President glanced over the notes the CIA had prepared for him. *Father Anthony*, he read with no particular enthusiasm, *has known Col. Nico Stollen since the early sixties . . . It is unclear where the priest stands on what is believed to be a Roman Catholic conspiracy against the United States – the formation of a European Union. However, he is widely recognised to be a patriot.*

. . . Some regard the 'European issue' as a bulwark against Communism. Others, most particularly in view of the French politician Francois Mitterand's support of same, see it as an extension of the Communist plot against the free world . . .

Here there was a note to the effect Francois Mitterand was a former Communist now making his second attempt on the French presidency. The Frenchman's friendship with Colonel Stollen was remarked upon. In a different section, the CIA stated the colonel had claimed a Briton working for MI6 – Sir Peter Ligne – was a Soviet agent.

'The US Ambassador to Britain, Mr President.'

Rising, the President did up the top button of his jacket. His ambassador was soon followed by Dr Crotale. Father Anthony, he was advised, would join them shortly.

The President looked at the two men through heavy-lidded eyes. 'Perhaps you guys would like to explain what is going on. From my notes here, I see our favourite Ruskie appears to be claiming that one of MI6's fellas, Sir Peter Ligne, is working for the Soviets . . .'

The CIA man puffed out his chest. 'Quite a significant discovery, wouldn't you say, sir?'

The President turned to his ambassador. 'So, what's your problem?'

The diplomat returned the President's gaze evenly. 'Perhaps, Mr President, Dr Crotale here could explain how Stollen first came to the CIA's attention – by ruining the reputation of an excellent American political officer in Iraq some years ago. You may then understand my reservations in accepting Stollen's word the Brit is a traitor.'

The President looked to Dr Crotale for an explanation. Five minutes later, the latter finished speaking.

'WHAT D'YA MEAN THE FUCKING RUSSIAN IS SHARING A MISTRESS WITH THE BRITISH DEFENCE SECRETARY AND THE BRITS KNOW IT?!' exploded the President. 'And which MP's wife did you say the Ruskie was poking?'

It was the ambassador who responded. 'The wife of Andrew Fitzwilliams, sir. Her husband is the owner of Fitzwilliams International – the company the Agency is hoping to take from the Brits.'

The CIA man looked aghast. It had not been his intention to appraise the President of the latter. He swallowed hard.

'Stollen assures us, Mr President, that . . .'

'BUT STOLLEN IS A FUCKING RUSSIAN WHO FUCKED UP ONE OF OUR DIPLOMATS IN IRAQ!'

The CIA man sucked in his cheeks again. 'The Agency appreciates this, Mr President,' he responded, a thin line of perspiration decorating his top lip. 'In view of this, we are doing nothing precipitous. We have devised a plan to keep a check on Stollen's information . . .'

'And what might that be?'

The President made no attempt to hide his sarcasm. He had

[*217*]

too many problems of his own to be dealing with such trivialities.

'Interns working for the CIA, sir. The first batch – Brits call interns, research assistants – are arriving at Westminster as we speak. The Brits won't suspect a thing and even if they do, will not be able to tell the difference between a researcher working for the CIA and one who is not! The agents are being provided "free" – which is to say, the American taxpayer is picking up the tab. This way we can keep an eye out for developments on the "European issue", as well as see if they square with what Stollen is telling us. The agents will stick around until after the British general election.'

'Why the fuck should I be interested in the goddam Brits' general election? The Brits are nobodies. Nobodies. It's the fucking goddam Commie conspiracy against the United States I care about. And what you are paid to care about.

'Why d'you think I've spent so long kissing those goddam Chinese arses? Because that's where our country's future lies, that's why. The future lies in China.

'They're Commies too, but they hate the Ruskies as much as we do. And what's the CIA doing . . .'

'If I may interrupt, Mr President,' intervened the ambassador, doing just that. 'Accepting your disinterest in Europe, I am sure you would agree the CIA's attempts to distort the British vote – due to the European issue – is entirely reprehensible. Additionally, of course, if Britain's present Conservative government ever finds out the strikes crippling their country have been instigated by ourselves . . .'

The ambassador's voice faded.

The President's response was thick with contempt. 'The Brits won't find out. I've already told you. The fucking British are nobodies. Like the rest of Europe. Except the bloody French. They're screwing up NATO. Screwing NATO!

'Some people even say the French Commie Francois Mitterand may get in. And what do the fucking Germans do because we are not moving fast enough on the reunification of West and East Germany? Go behind our backs to the Vatican to do deals with the fucking Soviets. After all we have done for the fucking West Germans . . .'

'This is why, Mr President, we have to keep an eye on the Brits,' intervened Dr Crotale with a panicky display of boldness. 'After all, as you say, it seems the West Germans have been less than straightforward. The Agency believes the continental conspiracy against the United States is being manipulated from London.'

He had the President's undivided attention for the first time.

'Why the fuck didn't you say so? The US is threatened? What d'ya doing about it?'

Dr Crotale took a deep breath. 'As I said, we are sending interns to Westminster, Mr President. We have attached Agent Betsy Meredith to Andrew Fitzwilliams' private office. She has the appropriate social background so should get on with him. The Ruskie – Stollen – will report any developments he comes across to her.'

'What happens if this Fitzwilliams guy doesn't want an American intern?'

For the first time, the CIA man relaxed. 'Agent Meredith, sir, has impeccable credentials. Great tits!'

The President laughed. 'Sure Fitzwilliams is not a faggot? They all seem to be over there.'

'No, sir, our checks have been pretty thorough. We know all the faggots in Westminster. By the time we've finished, we'll know more about the British Parliament than even their fucking whips. WHIPS! The Brits run on sex. Kink-ee. Whole damn lot of them.'

'Who the fuck are the whips?' asked the President, raising his eyes to the ceiling.

'Internal Westminster spies,' responded the CIA man with aplomb, the light of victory now in his eyes. He had won the President over and knew it. The ambassador was routed.

'So, what's with the priest?'

Dr Crotale swallowed hard. 'The Ambassador here, wanted you to meet him, sir. We have, of course, warned him Father Anthony is working for the Vatican.'

'He would be, seeing he's a Jesuit,' came the diplomat's languid response.

The two men stared at each other. Dr Crotale was the first to give way. To pursue this line, he knew, would not be a good career move. After all, some of the top dogs in the CIA were Ivy League Roman Catholics. The ambassador had probably been at college with most of them.

'Father Anthony, Mr President.'

The priest's tall figure was shown into the room. It smelled of frozen sunlight, leather and polish. Outside, was a crisp winter's day he had been reluctant to leave.

'Good morning, Cardinal, good of you to come,' said the President, rising to greet him.

'I am not a cardinal, Mr President.'

'Well, soon to be, I guess – certainly if the White House has anything to do with it.'

Smiling, Father Anthony accepted the President's hand. 'I hope not, sir. I have long made it clear to Rome this is not my wish.'

The President looked non-plussed. Men who did not strive to attain the highest office always confused him. He invariably thought they were sissies or commies. Probably both.

Once seated, Father Anthony gazed at the President with polite expectation. The latter waved him towards the ambassador. Father Anthony had met the diplomat at an Italian embassy cocktail party in London.

'I wanted you to brief the President, Father, on Colonel Stollen,' explained the envoy.

'Yeah. Would you say the guy was trustworthy?' interrupted the CIA man. He was up against the American class system – and knew it. The Jesuit and ambassador were different. But the same.

Father Anthony took his time before replying. The President looked beyond him. A huge array of staff Christmas presents wrapped in bright shiny paper were clustered on the carpet beneath the Oval Office tree. He wondered how long they had been there.

'I would say Stollen was as trustworthy as anyone else involved in espionage,' Father Anthony was saying.

The President smiled. Insulting the CIA without seeming to, was quite an achievement. Even for the Vatican. The priest was good. Very good.

'And would you say Colonel Stollen was likely to defect?'

Looking at the ambassador in amazement, Father Anthony replied, 'About as likely as you, I'd say.'

'Quite.'

'One of the biggest problems we have with Stollen is he often tells the truth,' continued the Jesuit. 'He uses veracity as a weapon. The best I can say is that he is not a hypocrite.'

It was the President's turn to pitch in. 'He's claiming a Brit called Sir Peter Ligne is working for Moscow. Reckon its true?'

Father Anthony considered the question. 'It could be. On the other hand, it is worth remembering that discrediting diplomats is Stollen's job. Moreover, Stollen hates Ligne. The Brit is one of the men Stollen holds responsible for the massacre of the freemasons of Iraq.'

'Nah!' interrupted Dr Crotale. 'Stollen told me about that. He's a professional. He wouldn't have a grudge against Ligne just because some old Arabs died. Ligne's got to be working for the Russians.'

'And one Jew,' corrected Father Anthony. '*Some old Arabs and one Jew.*'

The President raised an eyebrow. He admired accuracy in other people.

'Two girls died as well, Mr President,' continued Father Anthony.

'Girls? What do you mean girls died? How old?'

'Much the same age as your daughters.'

The President flushed. The most powerful man of the western world – for the moment at least – could bond with the lowliest if he was father to a daughter. Getting a grip on himself, he snapped, 'Who were they?'

'A beautiful child called Leah Solomon. She wanted to be a vet. And Peri, an American-educated Kurd. She was a civil engineer, wife and mother.'

The President looked down at his hands. 'Stollen knew the kids?'

Father Anthony nodded. 'He watched them grow up. Not so long ago, he collected their broken bodies from an Iraqi prison.'

The President looked across his desk to the picture of his wife and children. They had been his ballast. He knew they would remain so, even though the worst was yet to come.

'Stollen hates the owner of Fitzwilliams International, Andrew Fitzwilliams, for the same reason he hates Ligne,' added Father Anthony.

'That's why Stollen is poking Fitzwilliams' wife!?' interjected Dr Crotale.

Ignoring him, the President queried, 'What happened?'

Father Anthony did not dissemble. 'Andrew Fitzwilliams sold guns to a man called Ghazi El-Tarek, the son of one of the Iraqi freemasons.'

'Fitzwilliams International's new chief executive?'

He signalled his assent. He was impressed by the President's easy command of the facts. 'The guns were duff,' he continued. 'El-Tarek sold them on to the French. The latter shipped them to Iraq.'

'So Ghazi El-Tarek was responsible ?'

'He had no idea what the French would do. Ligne and Fitzwilliams did. They acted with clinical precision. They –

not El-Tarek – set off a chain reaction which led to the deaths.'

Opening his briefcase, Father Anthony took out a black and white snapshot and passed it to the President. Glancing at it, the latter motioned him to continue.

'Fitzwilliams' crime was the greater. Initially, the young women escaped. Peri made it to London and embarrassed Fitzwilliams. She was deported. Fitzwilliams destroyed her because he could. Little Leah, on the other hand, with quiet heroism, opted to return to her family. She destroyed herself to be with them.'

The President studied the photograph. Andrew Fitzwilliams was pictured with his wife Belinda at the races. A teenager in a pretty hat stood between them, laughing into the camera. Belinda seemed faded next to her vitality.

'Who's the youngster?'

'Ligne and Fitzwilliams' nemesis . . .'

Nemesis was something the President understood.

'. . . Her name is Jasmine Palmeira. She is sixteen years old. Stollen trained her to fall in love with Andrew Fitzwilliams. He succeeded.'

'A sleeper?'

The President was well aware the Soviets 'grew' people for years.

'Yes. This is why Stollen is having an affair with Fitzwilliams' wife. He will avenge the dead by destroying Fitzwilliams.'

The nuances were lost on Dr Crotale. 'Fitzwilliams is spoken of as Cabinet material. The only drawback appears to be his wife Belinda. She hasn't measured up. So Stollen's done the guy a favour! Fashions in wives are always changing.'

In Dr Crotale's world, last year's wife would not do indefinitely. The President looked at him in contempt. Shifting his gaze, he unfolded his brilliant mind and sliced to the heart of the matter.

'This is not about the murdered freemasons, Father, is it? It's the dead girls that have got to the Russian. Stollen will fucking kill Ligne and Fitzwilliams. Good luck to him. This President will not stand in his way.'

The meeting broke up a short while later. Father Anthony was the first to leave. The President insisted on walking him to the door.

Once out of earshot of the others, he asked, 'Will you hear my confession, Father?'

The priest shook his head.

'I hoped for forgiveness . . .'

'God's mercy, Mr President, always forgives. I think, however, you do not really want forgiveness, for you do not believe there is anything to forgive.'

The President laughed, extending his hand.

Father Anthony shook it warmly. 'If I may say so, Mr President, we have one thing in common,' he observed. 'We love our country. Merry Christmas, sir.'

CHAPTER TWENTY THREE
❊ ❊ ❊

LONDON: Leaving the Inns of Court, an attractive young woman picked her way along the rubbish-strewn pavements. It was not yet Christmas but all around her, beset by one strike after another, London fell apart. The Middle Eastern oil exporters had given a startling demonstration of the efficiency of economic sanctions and Britain teetered on the edge of chaos.

Vivienne Solomon slipped into the Strand. Now aged twenty-one, she was an eye-catching pupil-barrister. Her mother had died after a short illness the previous year and the sale of their former home had enabled Vivienne to fund her pupillage and purchase a modest place to live.

She continued as a volunteer with the Concert of Rights when time allowed and kept in touch with the El-Tarek family: Ghazi was her final link with Samuel Solomon, her murdered uncle, and cousins. Leah's death in particular, haunted her. Her only comfort was her mother had not known of Leah's suffering.

A network of close friends did not replace her dead loved ones but provided a canopy of support. Vivienne was particularly close to two old pals from the Concert – Jimmy Richards and Bobby Lomax.

Vivienne grinned. Who was she kidding? Months could pass before she ran into Bobby. She could not even mention his name to the El-Tareks without Ghazi getting cross. He remembered Bobby from their day out at the Chantilly racecourse and lamented the fact Vivienne remained transfixed by him, missing his devil-may-care courage and willingness to venture where it might be safer not to tread.

Much to her amusement, the POUKI's inefficient recording of Bobby's name as 'Lomack' rather than 'Lomax' – meaning Bobby could not be traced or blacklisted – meant he was now pursuing what he hoped would be a lucrative career in the City.

Stepping over yet more rubbish, Vivienne hurried on. She had long accepted she did not figure in Bobby's future. Instead, she was rushing to meet Jimmy Richards.

Dear Jimmy, she thought, crossing the road. Always so loyal. His father had been the Home Office civil servant responsible for visas who had turned down her mother.

She and Jimmy were listening to Opposition Leader Harold Wilson's speech at Westminster Hall that evening and had arranged to have a drink at the St Stephen's Tavern beforehand. Arriving at the pub on time, she looked around for him. He had warned her he could be late since, not yet decided on a career, he was employed as a casual labourer on the new underground extension.

Working many feet below the City surface, he found conditions dire. The air was heavy with dust and other men's sweat. As the recession deepened, some of the contractors cut more and more corners. Jimmy Richards pulled at heavy steel rods without protective gloves. The day before, a man had lost an arm.

He flew into the pub a quarter of an hour after Vivienne.

Going straight to the bar, he turned around and caught her eye. Their friendship had no romantic quality but this did not stop him from admiring what he saw. Seeing she already had a drink, he ordered a quick half for himself.

Soon, they made their way to the political venue. Countless others streamed in alongside them. The meeting started late. Eventually, the Opposition Leader arrived. The crowd greeted him with rapture. He called for hush.

Speaking at length, his words poured out of him. Technology was the key to the future and would bring a new dynamism to the people of the United Kingdom. Patriotism, hope and a deep sense of justice characterised his every sentiment.

'And Europe,' he thundered, shirking the issue while appearing not to, 'Is your choice. The People's. I will make it your choice. A referendum is the democratic way ahead.'

Harold Wilson – the best political con-man Britain has every produced, as one esteemed political consultant observed – was mesmerising. By the end of the evening, Jimmy Richards was hooked: he had found his vocation. He wished to serve the public in parliament as a Labour MP.

Stollen dialled Belinda Fitzwilliams. 'Nico!' she exclaimed, hearing his voice. 'When are you coming home? How is your mother? You seem to have been away for ages! I have some wonderful news, darling. I went to the doctor this morning . . .'

'Tell me later, Pretty One . . .' he cut her off. 'I am only phoning to say I will stay away a little while yet. My mother's health is so much worse. Moreover, it is perhaps more prudent in view of the likely general election. You're the one who wants to protect your husband, after all.'

'I know, darling, it's all my fault. It's such a nuisance because I hate being separated from you. I am sorry about your mother. As for Andrew, thank you for being understanding. I do not want to jeopardise his chance of success. As it is, things look bleak for the Tories. I know I don't owe Andrew anything but his political ambitions mean everything to him. I am so happy, I want everybody else to be happy too.'

Stollen promised to call her soon. He already knew she was expecting his child. He could hear the delight in her voice.

CIA agent Betsy Meredith scrutinised Stollen out of a pair of wide brown eyes. These were balanced in a pretty face, framed by natural blond curls, atop a graceful figure. They had arranged to meet at the Hampton Court maze.

'How are you enjoying London?' asked the Russian conversationally.

'Who says I am enjoying it?'

Stollen laughed. Dr Crotale had informed him Betsy Meredith, Andrew Fitzwilliams' new research assistant, would be his CIA handler for the foreseeable future and this was their first meeting. They strolled towards the river, Hampton Court Palace behind them. In front, wild geese screamed as they skimmed across the water.

'So, you're the Agency's great hope? Planning on defecting, I'm told.'

'You do not believe me sincere?'

Betsy grinned. 'I just take orders, Colonel. I do not make them. But, for the record, I could never think of betraying my country, and do not understand those who do. You included.'

Stollen sighed. 'Would you understand me better if I said I love my country too – which is why I want America to assist?'

'No. I'd say you just wanted the good life for yourself and your lady-friend Belinda.'

He looked taken-aback. 'You talk as if you do not want me to defect.'

They had doubled-back now. The ticket office and tourist shop were on the left.

Betsy shrugged. 'Listen buddy, you want to defect – defect. What you do to your people is your business. What you do to mine, is my business. You hurt my country and I'll nail your balls to the hammer and sickle personally!'

Stollen gave a mock grimace. Automatically taking her arm, to which she made no objection, he guided her back to the Palace and towards the tea-room. Before going in, they stopped at the tourist shop selling postcards, guide-books and china mugs. Finding a biography of Elizabeth 1, Betsy commented, 'I admire that dame. I think she was very American.'

Stollen treasured the comment and used it to great effect with his British friends. They met repeatedly after that. As the days rolled on, something akin to friendship even developed.

Betsy's research assistant duties fascinated Stollen and she was happy to pass on her impressions. It was only then he realised what a good agent she was. Swept away on a tide of her natural openness, he almost overlooked the ease with which she got his measure.

He learned she had been in the CIA for a couple of years, having opted for a more adventurous life. Her social background was impeccable – something, he felt sure, that did not endear her to her immediate superior.

She seduced him in her small flat just off Knightsbridge about ten days after their first meeting. Dripping from a rainstorm, she pulled off her earrings, kicked away her shoes and smiled her invitation the minute they walked in the door. Standing in her hallway, he chuckled, 'This part of your duties too?'

'Could be.'

Over the coming weeks, their lovemaking was relaxed, free of inhibition or sentimentality. One day, rolling onto her back so he could caress her breasts, she murmured, 'I mentioned your name to a couple of lobbyists – one of them is dating Defence Secretary George Hillary at the moment – hanging around Westminster. Now that Parliament is on the point of rising, they do not know what to do with themselves.'

He raised an eyebrow. 'What did you mention me for?'

She grinned. 'I wanted to see if there were any rumours about your affair with Belinda Fitzwilliams.'

'And are there?'

'Uh-huh. But the press is petrified about being sued for libel. This – as well as the fact the lobby correspondents like you and Andrew Fitzwilliams – means everyone is keeping quiet. Apparently, you got to know all the hacks at the Derby. The only thing I am not certain about is whether you or Ghazi El-Tarek did the bankrolling . . .'

'Does it matter?'

'Not really.'

She stared into his eyes. 'I'm baffled, Nico. I don't know what your game is. Crotale said something about you using Belinda Fitzwilliams as part of a personal grudge against her husband.'

He kissed her lips. 'My game is greed.'

She shook her head. 'No. That's not it. What bothers me is why you are pretending it is.'

Throwing him away and wrapping the sheet around her lithe body, she walked into the bathroom and turned on the shower. Stollen lit a cigarette. He had not seen Belinda Fitzwilliams for weeks. He closed his eyes. He did not want to think about Belinda.

A few minutes later, Betsy Meredith murmured, 'Penny for them buddy?'

She stood before him naked, her wet hair in a towel. Stubbing out, he pulled her to him.

'I was thinking about Fitzwilliams. I meet him tomorrow,' he replied, rubbing her dry.

'I know. I work for the guy.'

Stollen laughed. 'Is that why you invited yourself into my bed?'

She threw him away with good humour. 'The last time I looked, this was my bed. Why are you seeing Fitzwilliams?'

He allowed her to run him a bath. When it was ready, it was full of bubbles. 'I'm after some of his money,' he replied, sinking into its warm froth.

'So you're a blackmailer! The Agency sure has found itself a swell guy.'

'I didn't ask you to like my morals.'

'I don't buddy. I don't.'

Splashing him, she added with a grin, 'Fitzwilliams already knows about your affair with his wife.'

'I should hope so.'

'He's pleased. He says he likes you!'

'He does.'

'And he's happy for Belinda that she's pregnant. However, he's pissed off with a guy called Sir Peter Ligne for not telling him about the affair.'

'How did Fitzwilliams find out?'

'A scheming little bitch called Jasmine told him.'

She left him to it. A few moments later, he heard the hum of her hairdryer.

'What's Fitzwilliams' wife like?' she shouted above the noise.

'Sweet.'

'SWEET?'

'Uh-huh.'

'So what you doing in my bed if she's sweet, she's having your baby and you're going to marry her?'

'Pretty much the same thing I was doing in your bed. Belinda told me to stay away for a while. She is adamant nothing must jeopardise Fitzwilliams' chance of re-election. That's why I say she's sweet.'

Betsy, partially clothed now, stuck her head around the door. 'Let me get this right. You're going to blackmail Fitzwilliams about your affair with his wife which he already knows about and you call her SWEET?'

Her head disappeared again.

'She is.'

'I'd say stupid.'

'That too.'

'You're a shit. A real shit. Know that?'

He hauled himself out of the water. 'If the CIA didn't like what I was doing, it could always have put a stop to it. The Agency and the Brits always knew about my liaison with Andrew Fitzwilliams' wife.'

She slipped on her jeans. 'The only thing the Agency's interested in, is how mad the Brits are going to be when they find out you've defected to us. If you're taking some stuck-up MP's wife with you, so much the better.'

She looked at him with straightforward appreciation as, naked apart from a strategically placed towel around his loins, he rejoined her.

Tugging the covering away, she remarked, 'Great bod, Ruskie!' Kissing him, she added, 'The Agency will kill you if you're double crossing them.'

'You a killer too?'

'Maybe.'

He left the apartment half an hour later.

'What's the rush?'

'A welcome-back-after-the-Michaelmas term party,' he replied, putting on his jacket.

'For that manipulative kid I mentioned earlier, Jasmine?'

'That's the one.'

She watched him slide into the stream of Christmas shoppers along Knightsbridge from her window. He turned around once, before crossing the road. She blew him a kiss as he got into a taxi opposite the Brompton Oratory.

A few moments later, she dialled her superior, Dr Crotale. 'He's gone, Don. I'm just not sure about the guy. He says he's planning on blackmailing Fitzwilliams.'

The CIA chief laughed. He liked. He really liked. That would wipe the smile off those fucking Brits. He brushed her reservations aside and rang off. Two minutes later, she dialled her ambassador.

It was against the rules – for the most part, every effort went into distancing the embassy from the CIA – but she considered it important. He was surprised by her call but happy to take it. He had known her grandfather. 'What can I do for you, my dear?'

Apologising for disturbing him, she ventured, 'I wanted to talk to you about Colonel Stollen, sir. I think the Agency is making a big mistake.'

Having heard her out, the ambassador soon shared her concerns, telephoning the Oval Office the minute they disconnected. He was relieved but unsurprised that despite ever greater worries over 'Watergate', the President remained on top of his brief.

'It looks like the Agency has cocked up, Mr President.'

'Anything the White House can do to help?'

'My guess is, it is too late but I thought it best to keep you informed. If Agent Meredith is correct – and I think she is – we are about to be hit by a whirlwind.'

CHAPTER TWENTY FOUR

✷ ✹ ✷

Stollen watched the streets of London flash by from the back of his taxi. Suzie Palmeira had reminded him about Jasmine's home-coming the previous week. 'Do come, Nico,' she had urged. 'You know how much she likes to see you.'

What she had actually meant was that if Jasmine knew he was invited, there was a possibility she might stay home herself. He sighed. Belinda Fitzwilliams had said Jasmine was sweet. Betsy Meredith, on the other hand, had called her a bitch.

The last time he had seen the school-girl had been earlier in the year at the Chelsea Flower Show. She had been with her father at the Masonic display. Standing where he could not be seen, he had watched Peter Ligne approach – all spies went to the Flower Show.

Ignoring Philippe, the civil servant had greeted Jasmine with what appeared to be unconcealed delight. She had hailed him with an equal display of enthusiasm, without, it would seem, noticing the snub to her parent. Another surprise had been her choice of banter.

'Go on, Sir Peter, you can tell me the truth,' Stollen had heard her tease. 'Did my tortoise come all the way from England in your briefcase, or did it come from Kurdistan?'

'It came from Kurdistan,' her father snapped, as if she had broached the subject for no other reason than to cause trouble. 'I've told you so before. Amu Abdullah brought it back from the north.'

'Oh, yes.'

Holding Ligne's eye, she motioned the garden behind. 'Do you like lemon trees, Sir Peter? Hussein and Uncle Nico once sent me a cutting from the Garden of Lemon Trees in Baghdad. Do you remember Hussein? He was Jiddu's driver.'

Ligne fled.

Arriving at the Palmeira household in Richmond, Stollen was surprised to see the front door open and a huge family row in progress. Jasmine was sitting on her school-trunk, her tuck-box at her feet, in her parents' spacious hall.

'. . . But why can't Andrew come to dinner? Stollen's not family, and he's invited,' she was saying.

'Uncle Nico, to you, madam,' corrected Suzie.

'Hey! What about a big hug for your favourite Russian uncle?' boomed Stollen, hoping his entrance might prove a welcome distraction.

Standing up, Jasmine smiled at him in an all too fleeting manner.

'Andrew has a wife, Jasmine . . .'

'So what? Belinda doesn't mind. She's having an affair with Uncle Nico here AND she's pregnant! Ask him yourself if you don't believe me.'

Suzie was scandalised. 'How dare you make up such wicked lies.'

'I'm not,' responded Jasmine hotly. 'Belinda told me ages ago. She swore me to secrecy. I was not to tell you or Andrew until she told me I could, so I didn't. She says Uncle Nico is going to marry her.'

Suzie looked at Stollen in disbelief. 'Is this true, Nico?'

He avoided her gaze. Instead, turning to Jasmine, he remarked, 'Whether it is or not, my business is not your business, young lady.' Catching hold of her hand, he continued, 'What are you doing, my dear, pretending to be a friend to Belinda?'

'I never pretend anything, Uncle Nico. I have helped Belinda. Andrew always behaved like a pig to her.'

Staring at him in a knowing way, she continued, 'You always wanted me to marry Andrew, didn't you? Well, one day I will. Why is it only wrong when I know what you are doing?'

For the first time in his life, Stollen was speechless. His goal had been to shape Jasmine's innocence. To his horror, he found he had polluted it.

She looked at him coldly. 'I cannot tell you the number of times Father Anthony has tried to warn me about you. Even that awful man Peter Ligne – about whom Jiddu cautioned me – is always worrying me about you. He knows why you are dating Belinda – so eventually I can marry Andrew. This is why Father Anthony keeps reminding me that as a Catholic I cannot marry a divorcé.

'It is as if you are all playing the same game. Well, I am not part of it. I told Belinda exactly what was going on. She is so in love with you, she does not care. Also, she knows I love Andrew.

'He is my choice. Not because it is what you want but because it is what I want. People are always trying to tell me things about him. Mummy and Daddy. Belinda. Father Anthony. You.

'I DO NOT WANT TO KNOW. There is nothing I do not know already about Andrew. I love him. I always have done. And he loves me. He never loved Belinda.'

Stollen's expression was blank. He was faced with what he had created. 'You cannot build happiness on somebody else's unhappiness,' he replied.

'I am not a builder – certainly not of happiness. Besides, what would you know about happiness, Uncle Nico?'

Her tears came seconds later, crashing down her face in huge splashes. Gulping, she brushed them away with the back of her hand.

'Darling, do not waste your life on this man . . .' her father tried to comfort her.

She turned her back on him. Anguish disfiguring her face, she screamed, 'It is my life. I can do what I like with it. You didn't ask whether or not you should become a spy and betray people. So how can you tell me what to do? You lost all moral authority – and the right to judge or advise me – when you signed up to espionage.'

She was hysterical now.

It was Stollen's turn to try and soothe her. 'Hush, sweetheart, don't cry. Although you do not know it, your understanding is limited, your judgement still unformed . . .'

It was useless to continue. Spurning him, but kissing her mother as she passed, Jasmine fled to Andrew Fitzwilliams leaving her parents stunned and faced with the ruins of the evening.

Stollen arrived for his meeting with Andrew Fitzwilliams at the agreed time at Westminster the following day. The Palace had a sort of 'demob' feel about it. Many parliamentarians had left early to press the flesh in their constituencies during the Christmas recess.

Leading the way to the Strangers bar, Fitzwilliams teased, 'I hear you have applied for residency, Nico. Still pretending to the Americans you are defecting?'

Stollen laughed. He might dislike Fitzwilliams but had never thought him a fool. 'Regrettably they are proving to be rather less than generous.'

Turning, Fitzwilliams looked at him in surprise. 'Really? I am amazed. I assume this is the story they have concocted to allow the Brits first refusal, as it were, if you do indeed defect! Jolly good of them.'

Pushing through the swing-doors, he continued, 'So, dear boy, you've got money problems – if you take a wife, including my own, you certainly will! You must be thinking of defecting. Well I'm damned. I suppose it's impending fatherhood that's done it. Please give Belinda my best, by the way. I am thrilled for her. She has always wanted children.'

He stood aside politely to let an elderly peer pass.

'She has been an absolute brick about this election and done all she can to protect me,' he continued. 'Not a word about our up-coming divorce has got into the papers. Damn good of the old gel. Damn good. I do not deserve it. I have been an absolute swine to her. I expect you know this already . . .'

Without allowing Stollen time to reply, he went on, 'As for the rest, and if you're in a spot of bother, talk to Ligne. HMG has always got a few readies for this sort of thing. It would be a great boost to the Tory election campaign if we hooked you!

We won't say the CIA allowed us do so, you are defecting because you've fallen for somebody else's wife AND are in hock up to your eyeballs!'

Stollen gave a polite smile. 'Actually, Andrew, I am not here to talk wives. As for Ligne, I thought I would leave him to you on the basis you might not want him to be aware of your company's East German activities, which is what I do want to discuss.'

Andrew Fitzwilliams' eyes widened. 'What East German activities?'

Deciding it best to avoid the House of Commons' favourite drinking den after all, he steered Stollen towards a green leather bench on the side. Apologising for its lack of comfort but satisfied they could not be overheard, he signalled the Russian to explain.

'Fitzwilliams International East Germany is what the CIA are so interested in – why you have Betsy Meredith in your office . . .'

- Fitzwilliams nodded. All MPs presumed some of their 'free' research assistants were CIA agents. It was one of Westminster's standing jokes -

'. . . Everybody appears to be using Fitzwilliams International as a front for their own businesses. Ghazi El-Tarek tipped me off. And, of course, my East German counterparts. They are always helpful.'

Fitzwilliams was furious. 'Why didn't Ghazi tell me?'

'He supposed you already knew.'

Stollen did not add that Ghazi, to protect himself, was putting his Fitzwilliams International business through his private bankers, the Bank of Credit and Commerce International. This way, his records would be transparent. The paperwork was Ghazi's insurance policy – it proved all he did was sanctioned by the British government in agreement with the Inland Revenue. Most of the orders were funnelled through BCCI Cayman Islands. HMG had opened the account specifically to fund Fitzwilliams International's arms sales to Iraq.

Fitzwilliams held Stollen's eye. Grasping the danger of his situation but remaining calm, he asked, 'What do you want?'

Stollen grinned. 'Nothing much. A lump sum. Plus the East German operation. Cheap at the price, don't you think? After all, any association with East Germany really would ruin you prior to the election.'

Fitzwilliams threw his head back and laughed. 'I am sure we can sort something out. And, as you say, we do not need to inform Ligne.'

They shook hands.

Before leaving Parliament, Stollen popped into one of its small offices. It was up a little flight of stairs, opposite the bookstall in the corridor leading to the central lobby. Here, he handed in a heavy A4 brown envelope addressed to the Chief Whip: The tactic prevented a secretary from opening it. Marked 'personal', it contained photographs of Stollen in bed with Belinda Fitzwilliams.

Next, he made his way at a brisk pace to Grand Lodge. It had a new Grand Secretary, Sir Richard Leystan. The latter was a worthy successor to the late Sir Julian Lawrence. The Grand Secretary in-between had been an aberration.

Stollen believed the freemasons had left it too late to reclaim their honourable past. However, he accepted the present Grand Secretary was doing his best. At Stollen's request, and without disclosing its purpose, he had called a meeting at Grand Lodge. The Russian had told the Grand Secretary whom to invite, including a representative from Lloyd's of London.

On Stollen's arrival, Sir Richard Leystan personally escorted him to his private office. Philippe Palmeira stared through him. Ever since he had found out about Stollen's seduction of Belinda Fitzwilliams, he had been cool.

Stollen opened the meeting without preamble. Ambushing the man from Lloyd's, he observed, 'I hope you did not inform Sir Peter Ligne you would be meeting me.'

The Lloyd's executive looked taken aback. 'I did not know I was meeting you. Besides, Ligne is not a Brother. I was summoned here under rules of strict Masonic secrecy.'

'Indeed,' replied Stollen. 'And under what Masonic rules did you make Bro Philippe here, a Name at Lloyd's, on the authority, and for the sole benefit, of Sir Peter Ligne? In addition, how is it you have allowed Ligne to purchase properties in Bro Philippe's name?'

Philippe Palmeira looked stunned.

The Lloyd's man did his best to defend himself. 'Ligne requested I assist on the basis this was HMG's wish . . .'

Grand Secretary Sir Richard Leystan stared in disbelief. 'You are saying you have used Bro Philippe's name fraudulently?'

'NO! Not fraudulently. I was doing it for the country.'

The Grand Secretary frowned. It seemed he was faced with yet another scandal at the heart of freemasonry. He wondered if Stollen had any proof.

Guessing his thoughts, Stollen smiled. 'Everything has been recorded, Grand Secretary. Following Sir Julian Lawrence's death, I thought it unsafe to leave the annals at Grand Lodge – I could not guarantee the integrity of the Archives. A friend, Laure de Chebran, took them to France and handed them over to the Grande Loge Nationale de France in Paris. An American Jesuit, Father Anthony, arranged for duplicate sets to be held in the Vatican and the public library in New York.'

The Grand Secretary was furious. He did not trust the Americans, the French or the Vatican. He was rather old-fashioned in this way.

Ignoring his wrath, Stollen continued, 'I leave Britain tomorrow, my Brothers. You should be informed I am now sole proprietor of Fitzwilliams International's East German subsidiary. In addition, Belinda Fitzwilliams is expecting my baby.

'I have set up a trust fund for her and her child, and ask Grand Lodge act as its sole trustee.'

Grand Secretary Sir Richard Leystan looked about him. He could not grasp what Stollen was saying. In the end, he latched onto the one thing he could understand.

'Mrs Fitzwilliams is carrying your child and you are deserting her?' he spluttered.

Stollen remained silent. It was time to go. He did not say there would be mayhem in a few days. Nor that he had set Grand Lodge and the government's Chief Whip on a collision course.

He made his way to Philippe Palmeira. The latter turned away in disgust. 'You do not say farewell, my friend?'

Philippe shook his head. 'I despise you, Nico. You groomed my daughter to fall in love with Fitzwilliams and in the process destroyed another innocent young woman. I never suspected you capable of such wickedness.'

'Belinda Fitzwilliams was her husband's responsibility, not mine. As for Jasmine, I made my move while she was under age. At sixteen, she cannot marry Fitzwilliams, were he free to do so, without your consent.'

Philippe trembled with rage. 'How dare you imply I have anything to thank you for?' Calming himself, he continued, 'The person Suzie and I give thanks for, is Father Anthony. We raised Jasmine as a devout Catholic. As a result, the Father has left her in no doubt as to what will happen if she marries a divorcé. We hope spiritual fear will safe-guard her.'

Stollen shook his head in wonder.

The minute he left the building, the Grand Secretary telephoned the Chief Whip. At the very moment his call was put through, the latter was himself in a state of confusion. 'Sorry to bother you, old chap. We have just had a curious meeting with a fellow called Stollen . . .'

The Chief Whip shuddered. In front of him was Stollen's letter and the photographs of him in bed with Andrew Fitzwilliams' wife. Good God! The story was already breaking. Even Grand Lodge appeared to know about it. He could think of no other reason why its Grand Secretary would telephone.

'Everything under control, dear boy,' he assured him.

As the Grand Secretary replaced the receiver, relief was written all over his face. He and his wife were due to leave for their Christmas holiday in Cornwall that evening. If the matter had not been sorted, he would have had to delay.

That night, Stollen slept alone at the Russian embassy in Kensington Palace Gardens. He flew out of London the following morning without telephoning Belinda. After all, what could he say?

That he cared nothing for her or the child she was carrying? That his employers had wanted her to divorce Andrew Fitzwilliams to clear the way for Jasmine Palmeira and he had been their willing instrument? That he was now in business with her husband: Henceforward HMG would be in joint venture with the Russians.

Or that he had regrets, when he did not?

CHAPTER TWENTY FIVE

MI6 HEADQUARTERS: Frowning, Ligne moved to the small window of his tidy office. He could hear the sound of Jingle Bells coming from the street below. Pedestrians scurried along the pavement, their heads bowed against the December wind. Everywhere he looked, he saw people hurrying away from him.

Someone was making trouble for him. Even his old pal at Lloyd's of London had appeared not to see him at their club earlier that evening . . .

In the Chief Whip's office, the lights burned late. Present with the Chief Whip was the government's foremost law officer, the Attorney General. 'Belinda Fitzwilliams cannot possibly be allowed to drop a Soviet brat so close to an election,' the former was saying.

'And who will tell Fitzwilliams?' queried the Attorney General.

The Chief Whip shrugged. 'I doubt whether it will come as that much of a surprise, whoever tells him. We've had copies of his bank statements sent over – his bankers have been extremely helpful. These prove Fitzwilliams transferred a large sum of money to Stollen early last week. Obviously, the blackmail has begun.

'Damn decent of him to think he can pay hush money to protect the Party. Damn decent. The fellow's only in his early thirties – still a youngster. He must be scared out of his wits.'

The Attorney General raised an eyebrow. In his experience, most men paid hush money to protect themselves, not the Conservative party.

'The most important thing is to protect the Party and save Fitzwilliams' skin,' his colleague was saying. 'We will have to put a stop to the Fitzwilliams' divorce. We cannot have anything like that going on. The country will not like it. Not with a Ruskie. I have already had a word with the woman's lawyers and they quite understand the position.'

'What about the child?'

The Chief Whip flinched. He had spoken to Belinda Fitzwilliams' doctor and discovered it was technically possible to carry out an abortion, although it would be outside the time limit laid down by Statute.

The Attorney General looked even more worried. 'How do we know we are not being duped? That Stollen is not leading us one way and the Americans another? We already know the US will do anything to bring down the Conservative party because of Ted Heath's fixation with Europe, although why they expect to fare any better under a Labour government, God alone knows. The point is, we could be playing into Stollen's hands.'

'Quite,' responded the Chief Whip, his voice now mellow. 'This is why we take control of the show ourselves. We know that whatever happens, those photographs are going to get dumped all over the press . . .'

'What do you propose?' queried the Attorney General.

The Chief Whip puffed out his chest. 'We release them ourselves in advance of Stollen or the Americans. Which is to say, we get a friend in the press – a major national journalist noted for security-breach type stories – to do so. Fitzwilliams, of course, will have to resign as parliamentary private secretary but will keep his seat. As for his wife, we'll instruct Fitzwilliams to stand by her for the moment. He'll pick up the sympathy vote that way.'

The following morning, Belinda Fitzwilliams' doctor made his way to Queens Club. His wife had invited Belinda to be her bridge partner. By the time he arrived, the women had managed several rubbers. The final contract was played in three no trumps.

'I don't like no trumps,' remarked Belinda sweetly, capturing the final trick. 'They are so deceitful. The cheapest card in the pack can bring down an ace.'

They broke for refreshments a short while after. The doctor joined them. In his best bedside-manner, and as instructed by the Party, he informed Belinda the child she was carrying had a severe handicap and a termination had been recommended.

She refused. She collapsed a few minutes later. The doctor's wife had drugged her tea.

The physician aborted Belinda Fitzwilliams' baby that afternoon. The evening news announced she had had a 'breakdown' and been taken to a National Health Service hospital. Capitalising on the public relations value, government propagandists ensured Andrew Fitzwilliams was filmed rushing to his wife's bedside.

Looking calm and composed, he gave a brief press conference outside the hospital. It attracted maximum coverage. Asking Belinda be given peace and quiet, he concluded, 'Finally, I pay tribute to the National Health Service. Let no-one be in any doubt the Tories not only support the NHS, but trust it with their nearest and dearest. The NHS is safe with the Conservatives at Christmas – and at every other time of year!'

Inside the hospital, the beautiful voices of carol singers soared into the air. *Rejoice! Rejoice!* they sang. A king is born.

Andrew Fitzwilliams spent the night at his club. He did not know what else to do. Jasmine had told him Stollen had deserted Belinda.

The next day, he made his way to the Chief Whip. 'Sorry for all the bother,' he remarked, popping his head around the door.

The Chief Whip laughed. 'Don't mention it, dear boy.' Kicking a copy of the *Sporting Life* under the desk, the latter inquired, 'Dash of soda with your whisky?'

Fitzwilliams nodded.

'Now then, young man. First things first. I have to admit certain liberties have been taken. I've seen your bank statements. Stollen, I gather, is proving quite expensive, shall we say?'

Fitzwilliams flushed.

'I've embarrassed you, dear boy. Have to be brutal, I am afraid. Now then. Don't you worry about a thing. We'll take over from now on. Don't want you bankrupting yourself and not getting re-elected, do we? We're bound to lose the election so need as many Tories returned to Westminster as possible.'

Baffled, but a great deal more relieved than the Chief Whip

could possibly have known, Fitzwilliams looked at him with gratitude.

'I can't express my thanks enough, sir. I never mentioned events . . . shall we say . . . to Sir Peter Ligne. Stollen . . .'

'I should think not. The intelligence services have no jurisdiction in this House. I shall brief Ligne when I chose.'

Their meeting soon over, the senior politician walked Fitzwilliams to the door, his arm around his shoulder. 'You won't like what I do, M'boy. I assure you it is for the best. Trust me. By the way, how is dear Belinda.'

'Bearing up – because of my meeting with you, her doctor was kind enough to escort her home from the hospital this morning.'

An hour later, Fitzwilliams spoke to journalists outside his apartment block. Looking tired but in control of his emotions, he thanked the press and public for the many good wishes he and Belinda had received. Shortly after, he waved a courteous goodbye to the throng before making his way to the first floor.

His wife looked at him in mute anguish when he let himself in. She was sitting in the hallway by the telephone. Her eyes were ringed and her night-gown was untidy.

Inexplicably, her lawyers had not returned her calls. Nor had Nico. She had tried to ring him endlessly but his line at the apartment they had once shared had been disconnected.

The Russian embassy had told her he had left the country. For some bizarre reason the official she spoke to had referred to him as 'general'. He had put the phone down before she could query the mistake.

Gazing at her husband, she wondered whether he was going to beat her again. Instead, he stared through her. Sorry for her loss and not wanting to embarrass her, he went into the bedroom to pick up a change of clothing.

He would stay at his club again. There was nothing to wait around for – at his request, the press were no longer outside. He did not say goodbye.

On her own once more, Belinda tried the telephone again. Where was Nico. She hoped nothing had happened to him. That he wasn't lying injured somewhere. Why had the Russian embassy said he had left the country? Had Nico got into trouble for loving her?

She went into the bedroom. Everything matched. The yellow chairs matched the yellow pictures and the yellow carpet. The tears tumbled from her eyes.

She had to speak to Nico. She had to tell him she had lost her – their – beautiful baby. Sitting down, she fell forward on her arms and sobbed. The hospital had thrown her baby away.

The incinerator had been labelled: *Waste Products Only*.

CHAPTER TWENTY SIX
❉ ❈ ❉

A POUKI contact of the government whips passed the photographs of Belinda Fitzwilliams in the arms of her lover to a journalist that evening. The nation woke up the following morning to find them splashed all over the *Daily Lantern*. Stollen was identified as the KGB's European station head.

As the public will know, the newspaper's front page read, *Mrs Fitzwilliams recently suffered a nervous breakdown. Colonel Nico Stollen has returned to Moscow and been promoted to the rank of general.*

No mention was made of the fact Belinda Fitzwilliams had been pregnant. It was emphasised, however: *Despite the sensitivity of Mrs Fitzwilliams' husband's position as parliamentary private secretary to the Defence Secretary, General Stollen did not have access to government secrets.*

An obviously shocked Andrew Fitzwilliams resigned immediately. Next, making clear he was prepared to answer questions, he held a press conference. Ashen-faced, he announced his deep regret the embarrassment his wife's affair had caused the government. Taking full responsibility for her conduct, he said, 'Belinda has not been herself for many months.'

Speaking self-effacingly and with immense dignity, he continued, 'It is no secret, we have not been blessed with children. This private tragedy has caused . . .' he stammered, before pulling himself together again.

'. . . Belinda immense grief. Despite what I hope has been my reassurance, Belinda was devastated when she found out she could not give me . . . I should say, of course, us, . . . the child we both wanted. I have absolutely no doubt that Colonel Stollen – now General! – saw his chances and took advantage of a vulnerable young woman.

'I am certain the intention was to blackmail me through my wife, who, as you know, has suffered a nervous breakdown in consequence. I will, of course, be standing by her. I take full responsibility for what has happened and am only sorry that, due to the pressure of my parliamentary work, I have not always given Belinda the support she needed. And now, if you'll excuse me, I have to return to my wife.'

Fitzwilliams was next seen escorting Belinda from their apartment to a waiting car. He was taking her to her parents. The latter issued a statement praising their son-in-law and saying they were appalled by their daughter's behaviour. No mention was made of the fact Belinda's mother had herself been beguiled by Stollen.

That evening, Defence Secretary George Hillary gave an interview to *Panorama*. Looking straight into the camera, he declared, 'I assure the public, General Stollen had no access to my Ministry. I am deeply sorry to be losing Andrew Fitzwilliams as my parliamentary private secretary. He has given me and the Department unstinting support.'

The interviewer remained respectful throughout.

CIA Agent Betsy Meredith switched off the television. She

was relieved to be leaving Britain. 'What schmucks,' she commented as her telephone rang.

'Miss Meredith?' she heard the polite voice of her ambassador inquire.

'Sir.'

'It appears you were right about Stollen. The Brits are very sore. They think the CIA and Stollen were acting in concert. The whole thing is a mess.

'It will take years to rebuild trust. The President has ordered a clear-out of the CIA. Its new director is to be hauled before a special congressional committee this week. It is possible the Congress will strip the Agency of all its powers. I'd clear my desk if I were you.'

Betsy Meredith laughed. She dealt with every blow in a calm manner. 'I already have.'

'Good. Oh, Miss Meredith . . .'

'Sir?'

'I have recommended you to the President. Despite his all-consuming personal worries, he shares my concern about Fitzwilliams International. The company could erupt in our faces. Since you know General Stollen, the President hopes you will be willing to negotiate the purchase of Fitzwilliams International East Germany from him. You will have full diplomatic accreditation.'

'I will?'

'Uh-huh. This way the Agency will know you report directly to the White House. Your CIA superior, Dr Crotale, tried to blame you for the Stollen affair. . .'

'I'll sue the bastard!'

'Career suicide, my dear. My solution is better. You will make a good diplomat.'

Betsy left London the following afternoon. In 'departures' she read the *Daily Lantern*'s latest editorial on the Fitzwilliams Affair. It concluded: . . . *Andrew Fitzwilliams emerges from this sorry debacle with his reputation intact. The fact he is standing by his wife is to his credit. Belinda Fitzwilliams is a lucky woman.*

The least a young politician can expect from his spouse is loyalty. Let us hope Belinda Fitzwilliams' shame, for this is what it is, does not end her husband's career. The country needs such men.

Andrew Fitzwilliams arrived promptly for his second meeting with the Chief Whip in as many days. Parliament rose for the Christmas recess that afternoon. The general election had not yet been called but it could only be a matter of weeks. The prospect dominated political life.

'Good to see you again, dear boy,' said the Chief Whip with a paternal air. 'Packing as you can see. I have already accepted the other lot will win.'

He headed to the drinks cabinet. 'As for your problems,' he continued with a benign smile, 'All things considered, we have turned the matter around rather well, don't you think? The country is sympathetic. The trick is to be ahead of the others.

'We knew you were being blackmailed and the photographs were bound to surface. So we thought we'd best take control ourselves.'

Fitzwilliams' face whitened. Slowly the penny dropped. 'You . . . You . . . did all this? Leaked the photographs?'

Looking dazed, he fell back into a chair. 'Stollen was not blackmailing me about Belinda – I couldn't give a stuff about their affair,' he continued. 'I was happy for Belinda. Stollen was, after all, applying for residency here. I was at his mercy because of Fitzwilliams International's East German subsidiary about which, until he told me of it a short while ago, I knew nothing.'

The Chief Whip stared at Fitzwilliams in horror. Before he could respond, his direct line rang. It was the Masonic Grand Secretary. Sir Richard Leystan was raging. Having left with his wife for Cornwall where their cottage did not have a telephone, he had only just found out about Belinda Fitzwilliams' shaming.

'What is the meaning of these photographs? I gave Stollen my word Mrs Fitzwilliams and her child would be protected. Unless I did so, he threatened to expose the activities of Fitzwilliams International, its East German subsidiary, as well as the conduct of Sir Peter Ligne.'

Ligne laughed with genuine amusement when he heard the news. Called before the government's lawyers, he said it was the best joke he had heard in years.

1974

CHAPTER TWENTY SEVEN
❊ ❊ ❊

LONDON: Philippe Palmeira accepted Ligne's call with reluctance. The civil servant had not been allowed to see him since the present Grand Secretary had taken over at Grand Lodge.

'Sorry to bother you,' oozed Ligne, as if there had been no break in their relationship. 'I need a bit of help. London is awash with guns, I am told. Rogue members of Five like to control this trade themselves. They are blaming Stollen, or rather Fitzwilliams International East Germany.

'Their request for assistance could not have come at a better time. Ordinarily, of course, I would have nothing to do with them. My lot never does. But needs must. Their appeal gets me out of a bit of a jam: It is important I remain useful – the only reason I have not been prosecuted is to avoid a scandal. Which is where you come in. I need you to pop over to Hamburg and then into East Germany for me.'

'I would assist with pleasure, Peter,' responded Philippe coldly, 'If such activities were on HMG's behalf. But they are not, are they? It was called racketeering in the old days.'

Ligne laughed. Not unpleasantly. 'I can still have you arrested, old man. After all, Stollen is public enemy number one at the moment, and you are a fully paid up colonel in the KGB. The British do not like traitors.'

'You ordered me to be a double agent.'

[*261*]

'I know that. You know that. But who else does? Particularly since your Soviet salary has been paid into a Swiss bank account for years . . .'

'What salary? What Swiss bank account?'

Ligne chortled. Ringing off, he remarked, 'You always were a fool, Philippe.'

That afternoon an urbane, well-dressed man approached Suzie while she was shopping. Putting a light hand on her arm, he murmured, 'You have such a pretty daughter, Mrs Palmeira. At boarding-school, isn't she? Expecting her home for half-term tomorrow, aren't you? Sir Peter does hope nothing happens. Such lovely legs, Jasmine has too.'

Suzie collapsed. By the end of the day, Philippe Palmeira was Ligne's employee once more.

'I knew you'd come round,' the latter purred down the telephone. 'Let's meet this afternoon at the safe flat in Dolphin Square.' As an afterthought, he added, 'Stollen was the one who taught me how to control a man through his child.'

Philippe Palmeira arrived punctually a couple of hours later. Ligne revelled in his victory. Making a great show of getting Philippe a drink, he queried, 'Water or soda? Don't let me drown it.'

Philippe declined.

'No? Oh well, to business. You're off to Hamburg first, to help those naughty lads in Five, after which I need you to negotiate the buy-back of Fitzwilliams International East Germany on HMG's behalf.

'You can pop into East Berlin and see Stollen for me. Must keep up appearances! The Americans are always so impressed by our ability to send spies across the border. It's touching really.

'As for Stollen, it was such a relief to discover he was in business too. He always seemed to occupy the moral high ground before.'

'NO!'

Ligne raised an eyebrow. A few moments later, he left the room. Philippe looked around him. The apartment was drab, functional and entirely devoid of personality. Anxious to get home to Suzie who was waiting for Jasmine, he tried to open the door. It refused to open.

'Are you stuck?' shouted a cheerful female voice from the corridor outside. 'Hang on a minute, sir.'

Philippe stood back as the lock turned.

'Hello,' beamed the young woman. She was perhaps thirty. She wore a severely tailored short jacket and skirt which set off her admirable figure. Giving him a cherubic smile, she added, 'I do apologise, sir. Sir Peter's orders . . .'

With that, she threw herself at him, pushing him back into the apartment and on to a sofa in the small living room. As her body locked on to his, a camera flashed, capturing the moment. Seconds later, he was alone again.

He tried the door. It would not budge. He tried Suzie. The line had been disconnected.

On the table, he noticed a small envelope. Opening it, he found a clutch of photographs. They were of Suzie washing herself.

He was still there at 22.00 hrs. Suzie, he knew, would be sick with worry. Eventually, Ligne returned.

'Ah! There you are. I hope you've had time to reconsider. After all, if we can photograph your wife, we can just as easily take snaps of your daughter.

'And very charming they will be too. Goodness knows where they might end up. There is such a market for this sort of thing. It would be difficult guaranteeing Jasmine's safety. Such weirdos on the streets, aren't there?'

'Please let me go home. I want my wife!'

'Dear, dear. You are upset. You will feel differently in Hamburg. A bit of rough will do you good. Not the sort of thing one can ask of one's lady, is it? Besides, judging by the pictures, Suzie really is beginning to show her age. Now then, here's your passport.'

Philippe took it woodenly. Glancing at it, he protested, 'But this is false!'

'What of it?'

'I am known. How can I travel on false papers? I will be caught as a spy immediately.'

'Possibly, old boy. Especially in the Eastern section. What one might call an occupational hazard.'

At his most helpful, the civil servant continued, 'I'm sure you will wish to ring Suzie to tell her you're going away for a few days. Hurry up or you'll miss the last flight! There's a car waiting downstairs. Either call her or . . .'

The line had been reconnected. Philippe quickly dialled his wife. Trying to keep the panic out of his voice, he informed her something had come up and he was leaving for Hamburg that night.

Suzie was hysterical. Jasmine had not returned home. Her

mother had found pornography on her pillow, alongside her teddy and night-gown.

Philippe looked at Ligne in fury. 'Where is my daughter?'

'She will be with Suzie as soon as you are airborne,' soothed the latter.

He accompanied Philippe to Heathrow, conversing with good cheer all the while. 'I am sorry, you know. I really didn't want things to end like this.'

Philippe stared out of the window. Once arrived at their destination, he got out of the car before his tormentor could complete his adieu. Fifteen minutes later, he was in the departure lounge waiting for his flight to be called.

'Is this free?' asked a pleasant voice in his ear.

Philippe looked up. A polite young man sat down beside him. 'Sir Peter says you will be kind enough to take this small package over to Hamburg for us. You'll be contacted once you are there. Meantime, I understand he is having dinner with your wife and daughter tomorrow . . .'

Philippe took the 'package' without a word. The rest of his trip was uneventful. Arriving at his destination, he made his way to his hotel and telephoned Suzie. She seemed calmer but had still not heard from Jasmine. In the early hours of the morning, he heard the deafening bell of his bedside telephone. He answered it at once. He had not slept. It was Ligne.

'Anything to report?'

'What's happened to my daughter?' screamed Philippe.

'Jasmine is fine,' assured Ligne. 'A school-friend invited her for half-term. I intercepted her letter informing her mother of her plans. I have always found the POUKI in the post office to be helpful. Now then, what do you have to report? Did the MI5 lads contact you at the airport?'

'Yes. I was asked to carry a "package" though customs. I am still waiting for it to be collected.'

Ligne laughed. 'Open it.'

Philippe did as he was bid. He had already guessed what it contained.

'Drugs?' queried Ligne. 'I thought they were coming in to Britain, not going out! Well. Well. Each to his own.'

CHAPTER TWENTY EIGHT

❊ ❊ ❊

HAMBURG, WEST GERMANY: The route out of Hamburg that Stollen had given his former CIA handler Betsy Meredith was more circuitous than strictly necessary but she took it anyway. From the centre of the modern town, she passed the huge Blohm and Voss shipyards. Some twenty minutes later, she found the Russian leaning over the parapet of a low bridge which spanned a pretty stream.

Drawing up, Stollen waved cheerfully as she parked. 'Shall I sell Fitzwilliams International East Germany to the Brits or will you take it off my hands?'

Getting out of the car, Betsy laughed. 'We'll buy it,' she replied without hesitation.

Kissing her hand with typical Russian gallantry, he continued, 'What about the rest of the company? I know its chief executive Ghazi El-Tarek quite well.'

'Offering to broker a deal, Nico?'

Laughing, he took her keys and locking the motor for her, led her down the embankment. At the bottom, underneath the bridge, he had laid out a picnic.

'Poor old Ghazi,' he declared, his arm around her waist. 'He cannot understand why, after all these years, his British nationality has still not come through. I said you would get the Americans to advise the Home Office to lift the ban on him.'

She raised an eyebrow. Ignoring her lofty expression, he kissed her full on the lips. She made no objection.

'I do like kissing American diplomats,' he murmured.

'Kiss a lot of them, do you, Nico?'

Pulling away, she considered him with frank eyes. 'Langley misses you, General . . .'

– Langley was the CIA's headquarters –

'. . . It does not know what is going on in Moscow. What really worries it, is the fact some of the new generation of "Stollens" may be inexperienced and edgy. The CIA felt safer when you were the devil with whom it had to deal.'

Accepting the compliment, Stollen responded, 'Your lot are edgy?! Not half as much as Moscow is. It finds as many of your colleagues as unknown as you are finding ours . . .'

He settled her on a red tartan rug and sat down beside her. Opening and pouring the wine, he teased, 'I hear every important CIA station in the world has to have a lawyer attached to it these days.'

'Something like that.'

Raising his glass, he proclaimed, 'To you my dear. How is life treating you? Or is that classified?'

Betsy grinned. 'It's good, Nico. I have left the CIA and join the new President's private office in January.'

Stollen was genuinely pleased. 'Your talents would never have been recognised in the Agency. The mysoginism in both our services is ingrained. There will have to be a cultural sea-change before either improve.'

She nodded, accepting the salmon sandwiches he produced. Taking a generous mouthful of one, and, dictated by good manners, having allowed sufficient time for pleasantries, she got to the point. 'How much do you want for Fitzwilliams International East Germany, Nico?'

Releasing a ripe cheese from its wrapping, Stollen shrugged. 'Money has never interested me. It represents the West's values, not mine.'

'Yours are duping innocents like Belinda Fitzwilliams, I guess.'

Stollen winced. Now slicing some cured ham, he pronounced, 'Spying is about assessing vulnerability, you know that. What I did to Belinda was necessary but I am sorry for it. There will be no serenity in my memories.'

Betsy nodded. 'You serve a bankrupt system, Nico. How do you stand it?'

Getting up to stretch his legs, he replied, 'I have never needed to believe in it.'

Considering his remark, she mused, 'That's the difference between us. I believe in mine. So do the Brits.'

'Bullshit,' snorted Stollen. 'Sir Peter Ligne doesn't believe in the system. He participated only because he was above it. Given what he has done, the British would have prosecuted anybody else . . .'

He offered her his hand. She allowed him to pull her up. Now standing nose-to-nose, she looked at him reflectively. They were much the same height.

'You loved Britain once, didn't you?' she observed.

Stollen nodded. 'A long time ago, I saw much to admire. I could even put up with creeps like Ligne. Then, one day, I heard that an honourable old soldier – the Masonic Grand

Secretary Sir Julian Lawrence – had "died".

'All he ever did was serve his country. He believed in public and international good. The instant I realised his death, and that of his driver who perished with him, would not be investigated, Britain became everything I despise – a bully. This was confirmed when Belinda Fitzwilliams' living child was murdered in her belly.'

It was getting late. The sun had climbed higher in the sky and the day was warm and bright. Betsy bent down and topped up their glasses. 'You dragged me out here to discuss the price of Fitzwilliams International East Germany,' she prompted.

Stollen laughed. 'No I didn't. I dragged you out here because I wanted a day in the country in the company of an intelligent, good looking woman.'

'How long have you got?'

'The night.'

'What happens tomorrow?'

'I have a rendez-vous with my past in the Eastern section.'

Putting down her drink, she loosened his tie. 'You're toying with us, Nico. You don't want to sell your company at all, do you?'

'Does it matter?'

'Not much, no.'

Philippe Palmeira made his way to West Berlin and through Checkpoint Charlie. There was no traffic. As he walked to the Eastern side, a car drew up beside him. Stollen was behind the wheel. Switching off the engine, the latter asked, 'How much are the British offering for Fitzwilliams International East Germany?'

Philippe shrugged. 'I was unaware, Nico, you had gone into business,' he confined himself to saying.

'I have not. I merely present myself in a way the West can understand. Get in, my Brother.'

Doing as he was bid, Philippe climbed into the passenger seat. He did not know where they were headed nor did he care. He was exhausted. The Russian started up the motor again.

Pulling out, Stollen explained, 'My superiors ordered the sale of Fitzwilliams International East Germany, just as they ordered its acquisition. Only by offering it to the market can we know how much it is worth and, more importantly, who is most compromised. The Americans, for sure. Our mutual colleague Ligne, who sent you out as negotiator, too.'

Philippe shook his head. He had always believed himself to be a Crown servant. Now, nothing was clear any more.

About five minutes later, he noticed they were by a dismal concrete building. A guard with a sleeping dog at his feet, lit a cigarette. A man on a bicycle slid through the dark.

Parking, Stollen commented, 'I insisted on meeting in the Eastern section because it is safer. Doubtless Ligne pretended this was his idea. We have problems, my friend.'

Philippe turned towards him. In the dark, he could just make out his profile. 'We are no longer friends, Nico. Whatever we once had, you destroyed – including the memory of my father. If he had meant anything to you, you would have protected my daughter.'

'I protect no-one, Philippe: I do my job.' Extinguishing the headlights, he continued, 'Jasmine is Andrew Fitzwilliams' heir.

That's our problem . . .'

Philippe stared at him aghast.

'. . . Fitzwilliams changed his will years ago as a joke to annoy Ligne. Just in case Ligne ever thought of pushing him under a bus. He told me so himself.'

'Does Jasmine know?'

'Ligne told her. It was not without amusement value.'

Philippe shook his head. 'One of my father's murderers has left his wealth to my daughter. I cannot trust my own child not to . . .'

'That is a father's tragedy. Whereas me, I can trust Jasmine. This is my tragedy. She still writes to Jiddu's driver Hussein, you know, and tells him all her news . . .'

'And what news would that be?'

Stollen lit a cigarette. 'That she will marry Fitzwilliams as soon as she is old enough to do so without your consent.'

Allowing Philippe time for his words to sink in, Stollen continued, 'Meantime, she is pressing Fitzwilliams to have his marriage to Belinda annulled. Were she to succeed, Jasmine would have outsmarted Father Anthony. If it is any comfort, I take no pleasure in any of this.'

Tears welled up in Philippe's eyes. 'As a small girl, her grandfather taught her to pick her way through right and wrong. Now . . .'

'You cannot blame Jasmine. When you sent her to England, Fitzwilliams was kind to her. She wasn't even familiar with the British weather. In one of the first letters she wrote to me, she complained English trees were "funny' because they had no leaves. She knew nothing about Autumn. Nobody told her about the coming of the spring.'

'And you could not, Nico?'

'I train children. I am not their comforter. All Jasmine had to anchor herself was Fitzwilliams. I encouraged her in this. Now, every time she twirls Laure's umbrella Fitzwilliams stole from Peri, its perfume chokes me.'

Philippe gripped his arm. 'I beg you Nico, to help my daughter. If you do not, I will forfeit all I cherish. Suzie will forgive me everything. But not if Jasmine is lost.'

Stollen made no reply. Instead, he started up the car. Recognising the rebuff, Philippe asked flatly, 'Time for business, Nico?'

The Russian shook his head. 'Tell Ligne I will sell the East German company as and when I chose. All I am doing at the moment is feeling my way.'

'Then why am I here?'

Switching on the headlights again and pulling out, Stollen responded, 'Ligne assumed I would hand you over to Moscow – and you would be "disappeared". Since Jasmine is Fitzwilliams heir, Ligne needs control of her – as I do. This is impossible with you around.'

'Such treachery? I did not expect this from you, nor from Ligne whom, many years ago, I considered a friend.'

'Do not insult me. I am not the same as Ligne. At least have the grace to recognise I have never been interested in treachery for its sake.'

'And that makes you the better man?'

Stollen made no reply.

'Ligne is mad, Nico.'

'Perhaps.'

Philippe bowed his head. 'Not a day goes by when I do not beg Suzie's forgiveness for what I have done. She always hated Ligne. As for Jasmine. What have you done?'

Stollen's face was a mask. 'Spying is an awkward business for a family man. This is why Ligne and I are so good at it. We are untroubled by conscience and can prey on amateurs.'

'I did not know until it was too late, I was an amateur.'

'All fathers are amateurs. To succeed in espionage a man must care nothing for his vulnerabilities. This is why professionals are wary of mothers – where their child is concerned, women are invincible. Ligne and I target fathers because they are not.'

Philippe wept beside him. 'If this is the truth, I failed from the beginning.'

'Wasting energy on what is done is never productive, my friend. Such bitterness will destroy you.'

'Only Suzie has that power.'

The rain was coming down hard now. Stollen manoeuvred the vehicle along the potted road. 'Do you still wear the masonic ring your father gave you?' he asked suddenly.

'No. I wear the ring you gave me.'

Stollen nodded, as if reaching a decision. Lighting another of his eternal cigarettes, he commented, 'It is the same. I am my Brother's shadow.'

Philippe breathed in relief. Certain of Stollen's meaning, he murmured, 'Thank you, Nico. May God bless you . . .'

The smoke from the Russian's tobacco spiralled in the darkness.

' . . . I thought you told my father other people's tragedies meant nothing to you?'

Stollen shrugged. Flicking his ash out of the window, he replied, 'They don't. But I have never liked bullies. Contrary to what you believe, Ligne is not mad – he is a bully.'

Taking his eye off the road, he looked at Philippe. 'Tell Suzie not to worry about Jasmine. She is what the past created. This is my responsibility. I accept it. Tell her mother I will put things right.'

They fell silent. It was long passed midnight. Philippe had no idea where they were.

'Why did you never marry Nico?'

'I knew I would betray a wife.'

'That's not what Father Anthony says.'

'Father Anthony? What would he know? Whenever he stares into my face, he sees himself. I am what he might have been. For this reason, he pretends I am better than I am.'

He stopped the car. When Philippe looked out of the window again, he saw they were at the checkpoint once more. Stollen had returned him to the West.

'Go my friend, go. Go with God.'

Philippe walked into West Germany his own man. Stollen had handed him his passport. The wind was rising as he hurried deeper into the Western section.

He telephoned Suzie the minute he could. She cried with relief. Two seconds later, Father Anthony came on the line.

'Ghazi fetched your passport – following Stollen's instructions, he took it to the Russian embassy in London. His colleagues forwarded it in the diplomatic bag. Come home safely, my dear. Do not worry about Suzie and Jasmine. I am with them.'

1980

CHAPTER TWENTY NINE

❊ ❊ ❊

Two Autumns after the Conservatives swept back into office under Mrs Thatcher, Andrew Fitzwilliams' rehabilitation was complete and the press reported that he would be attending party conference with his wife Belinda. TV crewmen, reporters and photographers milled around in jeans, sweatshirts and zipped jackets to photograph the couple as they arrived on the Brighton seafront.

Getting out of a taxi, a solicitous looking Fitzwilliams escorted Belinda to their hotel. All remarked on how lucky she was he had stood by her. She seemed middle aged next to his glowing vigour.

As a thousand pairs of eyes stared, only Belinda Fitzwilliams knew she had begged her husband to take Jasmine to conference instead. He had refused. The cameras whirred as Belinda walked beside him.

She made an effort to keep smiling. Knowing they would soon be in the privacy of their hotel bedroom, she kept going for Andrew's sake. He had been so kind. He had even helped her chose her dresses.

One he had selected had been cut too low for her. Belinda had protested but, not wanting to cross him, had given way. 'Pack it. You can wear it on the platform. It will be a knock-out,' he had assured. She had done as she was told.

Once in their room overlooking the sea, he poured her a

glass of champagne. 'It will settle your nerves,' he encouraged.

Belinda tried hard to refuse. The hospital had made clear she must not drink alcohol. Fitzwilliams laughed.

'Don't be daft, old thing. They don't mean champagne.'

She took it gratefully. He was being so obliging. She must not annoy him.

Taking a shower, he left the open bottle beside her. The television was on. George Hillary – now Sir George – was being interviewed.

He had been re-appointed Secretary of State for Defence. He was smiling broadly. 'I can say without hesitation one of the great joys for me this party conference will be seeing Andrew and Belinda Fitzwilliams on the platform. Mind, I expect Andrew to be much more that my PPS this time around!'

Mesmerised by the screen, Belinda helped herself to another drink. As George Hillary droned on, she refilled her glass. When her husband returned, she told him she had knocked over the bottle. That's why it was empty.

He laughed. 'Silly billy,' he said, kissing her and opening another. He held her eye. 'You haven't dressed my pretty. Put the knock-out on.'

She got up unsteadily. Eventually she was ready. He zipped her up, nuzzling the back of her neck. Turning around, she wondered if he was going to hurt her. However, he was smiling. A few moments later he escorted her to conference.

The room hushed as Belinda climbed the stairs on to the main platform. The massed banks of press photographers trained their lenses on her. She stumbled and fell, her fleshless breasts exposed by her unsuitable dress. The cameras whirred as she collapsed. The newspapers had their photographs for the following day's editions.

'Don't worry darling,' everyone heard Fitzwilliams comfort her. 'You'll feel better in the morning.'

He carried her from the hall. Once out of view, he handed her to Party attendants. They took Belinda to the first aid room. Fitzwilliams followed close behind, running into the wife of his constituency chairman on the way.

Taking her outstretched hand, he lamented, 'I don't know where Belinda got the alcohol from. Champagne apparently. I watched her like a hawk.'

The older woman was immediately sympathetic. 'Don't blame yourself, dear. Everybody knows you have done all you can and more.'

He threw her a grateful look. As Belinda was settled on a makeshift bed, he stooped to pull the covers over her. Rising, he asked, 'I don't suppose you could do me a big favour, could you?'

'Of course, dear.'

'You couldn't ring Jasmine and see if she can come and sit with Belinda? She's with her parents.'

The lady was only too happy to oblige. 'Consider it done. Darling Jasmine. I do not know what the constituency would do without her.'

Fitzwilliams flushed with gratitude. 'Thank you,' he breathed. Looking lost, he continued, 'In the meantime, what should I do? Should I stay with Belinda or go back on the platform?'

She looked at him with a maternal air. A shock of blond hair had fallen forward on his eyes. He was thirty-nine years old.

'There's only one thing to do,' she said firmly. 'You go back on the platform. Where you belong. I'll stay with Belinda until Jasmine arrives.'

Thus relieved of his responsibilities, Andrew Fitzwilliams returned to the main hall. Deliberately hesitating outside the door, he was soon spotted by George Hillary who gestured with enthusiasm. Andrew Fitzwilliams mounted the platform to wild cheers. One hour later, it was announced he had been appointed a junior minister in George Hillary's department.

Jasmine joined his constituency chairman and wife for dinner later that evening. Now aged twenty-three, she charmed them effortlessly. Regaling them with the story of her first meeting with Fitzwilliams, she said with a flourish as he arrived, '. . . and then Andrew swept me off my feet on the banks of the Tigris!'

Her eyes sparkled as he kissed her.

The meal soon over, the chairman's lady looked knowingly at her husband. A little while later, they withdrew. They were delighted with the couple's news: Fitzwilliams had told them there had been changes at the Vatican and it was now possible his marriage to Belinda could be annulled.

'It means we can be married in church,' confided a delighted Jasmine.

She and Fitzwilliams made a good-looking pair as they strolled along the Brighton seafront. It was a perfect night. As they stood to watch the water, she snuggled up to him. It seemed so right for them to be together. Seeing her chilly, he took off his jacket and placed it on her shoulders.

Admiring the view, she mused, 'The nurse told me Belinda

probably had about two bottles of champagne. Belinda said, of all things, YOU gave her the alcohol.'

'She said what!?'

Quickly soothing him, Jasmine responded, 'Belinda must have been rambling. The medic mentioned alcoholics always lie.'

Fitzwilliams sighed and held her closer. There were fairy lights all along the front.

'My grandfather used to drink. He was always getting tiddly. Daddy and Uncle Nico told me you and Sir Peter Ligne were responsible for his death . . .'

Fitzwilliams' arms tightened about her. 'Does it still bother you, darling?'

Jasmine nodded. 'Apart from Jiddu, I miss Leah the most. The last time I saw her, she wasn't speaking to me – I had ridden a pony when I shouldn't have and the stable-boy had been beaten in consequence. Even today I wish she could know how sorry I was.'

Fitzwilliams turned her around. Tilting her chin, he kissed her.

'I always knew we would have to have this conversation one day. I dreaded it,' he breathed. 'Now it has arrived, it is a relief. Stollen is not wrong in what he says. I sold some weapons to Ghazi. My job was to get the best deal for the country. It all went wrong when the French got wind of it.

'At the time, the anonymity of the victims made their murder seem less bad. It was all so . . . casual. And then I found out your grandfather had been caught up in it all. I am . . . so . . . sorry. I could not face telling you. I just hoped when the time came, you would understand.'

'And what about Peri? My father said you and Sir Peter Ligne were responsible for her deportation?'

Fitzwilliams' eyes filled with tears. 'The Home Office made a dreadful mistake. It believed Peri to be a Communist. She was, after all, the daughter of a Kurdish Warlord and living in Prague. Since the Russians were in the ascendant in Iraq, it saw no reason not to deport her to Baghdad. Following its advice, Peter Ligne and I agreed.'

Jasmine held his eye. The long drawn out consequences of those dreadful days were only now explained. That night they slept together for the first time.

CHAPTER THIRTY

✳ ✺ ✳

LONDON, 1982: Father Anthony settled into his taxi as the streets passed before his eyes in a blur. The Pope was visiting the city soon and Father Anthony had been sent to review some of the advance arrangements. Meanwhile, the Masonic Grand Secretary Sir Richard Leystan had invited him to attend a meeting at Grand Lodge.

This, Father Anthony had been informed, was at General Stollen's request, precipitated by Jasmine's headlong dash into marriage with Andrew Fitzwilliams. The annulment of Fitzwilliams' first union to Belinda had been all but finalised.

The news did not surprise Father Anthony. In a way, he had been expecting it ever since Jasmine confided Fitzwilliams sometimes attended the celebration of the Mass in Latin. Bishops could allow the Tridentine rite, but only on condition it was deemed a sign of 'affection' for the old traditions not a criticism of the updated liturgy in local languages.

Bro Nico has requested his superiors in Moscow abort their interest in Jasmine Palmeira, the Grand Secretary had written. *He has admitted Moscow hoped Andrew Fitzwilliams would be their man in Downing Street one day. Therefore, their sacrifice is immense.*

Father Anthony sighed. Stollen had 'grown' Jasmine as a future Prime Minister's wife for so long it would be almost impossible to unscramble its effects now. This, no doubt, was the reason the Russian had also dropped him a note.

The Masonic Grand Secretary Sir Richard Leystan will act as soon as he has consulted everyone, Stollen had scrawled. *As I believe you are already aware, Jasmine's relationship with Fitzwilliams is now dictating the pace.*

Please attend the meeting arranged at Grand Lodge. Philippe Palmeira, who no longer enjoys the best of health, is beside himself with worry about his daughter's intentions and begs his Brothers do all they can to protect her. I am accountable in this matter.

Father Anthony stretched his legs. He was exhausted. Before leaving Rome he had visited the US embassy on the Via Veneto. His Holiness had asked him to go.

Ever since the hostage crisis in Iran, the Russians had believed America was preparing for outright nuclear war. They had asked the Pope to defuse the situation and Father Anthony was one of those he had sent to talk in soothing words.

The taxi stopped at the traffic lights. Opposite was the Brompton Oratory, one of the most beautiful places of Catholic worship in the world. The driver sped off a few moments later, heading for Piccadilly Circus.

'Almost there, Father,' he murmured, now cruising towards Trafalgar Square. Turning right into the Strand and left into Covent Garden a couple of blocks up, he brought the vehicle to a halt outside Grand Lodge's discreet side entrance.

'No charge, Guv – I'm a Brother myself. By all accounts, there's quite a meeting going on. All the cabbies are talking about it – haven't had to drop off so many here in years!'

A few moments later, Father Anthony was ushered into a large ornate room. Blinking with tiredness, he looked around him. The country's senior masons were all present. Clad in dinner jackets and bow ties, carrying regalia cases, they had entered the building quietly, or so they believed, some quarter of an hour before him.

Putting his weariness to one side, the American Jesuit smiled as the Grand Secretary performed the introductions. Given the warmth of his reception, he was grateful his hosts were unaware the previous evening he had described them as amateurs to the Vatican External Affairs minister.

Their names and faces blurred. Father Anthony saw only the country's guardians called to address the past. The private secretary to the latest chief whip acknowledged him with great courtesy, as did several of the provincial Grand Masters. The latest Grand Chaplain was similarly cordial.

The outgoing senior executives of Lloyd's of London were in attendance – all Fitzwilliams International contracts had been insured by the market. They avoided their Brothers' eyes – having denied fraud in the City for so long, they could not feel comfortable with themselves now. (The Grand Secretary had included them as a warning. He did not want Grand Lodge involved in anything pertaining to Fitzwilliams International or Lloyd's, in case it was suspected there had been a Masonic conspiracy to switch Brothers on to favoured syndicates.)

Ghazi El-Tarek and Miro stood in the shadows. The latter was now chairman of Douglas Miro International.

The Grand Secretary cleared his throat. 'We are gathered, Brothers, so final decisions regarding Andrew Fitzwilliams may be agreed. We cannot act against him unless we resolve to do similar to Sir Peter Ligne, who, as you know, is not of our fraternity. I have invited Father Anthony to be with us because he has other information which may be useful.'

Next, he brought the freemasons up-to-date on Fitzwilliams International's activities. 'A fraud inquiry into the company, as well as the involvement of Andrew Fitzwilliams and Sir Peter Ligne, has been set in motion. Bro Ghazi El-Tarek has agreed to remain Fitzwilliam International's titular head until it can be dismantled. He has indicated he would be happier if an official body supervised his role.

'Accordingly, he is to become a member of the British Board of Infrastructure. I have ensured the block on his nationality papers – clearing the way for his BBI nomination – has been lifted. Bro Nico Stollen asked his former CIA handler Betsy Meredith, now in the President's private office, to assist from the US end and she has been most helpful. In the event of any criminal prosecutions arising from Fitzwilliams International's commercial activities, Bro Ghazi has been granted immunity.

'Grand Lodge is uncertain as to whether or not HMG or the United States will continue to use Fitzwilliams International once charges have been brought against various public servants. We accept there might be resistance from both governments were the company to disappear completely.'

Clearing his throat, he continued, 'I am pleased to say that Bro Nico – initiated into this Brotherhood by my esteemed predecessor the late Sir Julian Lawrence – has devised a brilliant plan. For understandable reasons, he cannot be here to explain it. At his request, I have invited Father Anthony in his place.'

The latter frowned. Father Anthony was present as an observer, not as Stollen's stand-in. He took out his rosary and drew comfort from its feel.

'Bro Nico asked I remind the Father, and I quote, "if I delivered Jasmine Palmeira, he baptised her".'

'I am not in danger of forgetting.'

Time was moving on.

'Stollen has commissioned an advertising company to produce a brochure of sale for Fitzwilliams International East Germany. All its details, registered office, personnel . . .'

'Personnel?' queried Ghazi.

'Stollen has described Sir Peter Ligne as a "consultant".'

Seeing where Stollen was headed, a wide smile creased Ghazi's face. 'He will never get away with it!'

The Grand Secretary laughed. 'I think he just might. He has learned what a journalist may not publish in a newspaper, may be inserted into a marketing prospectus and circulated freely to interested bidders. He made a joke about capitalism having its virtues! His glossy brochure spares nothing. Not even that Fitzwilliams International East Germany is a joint venture between the KGB and HMG. The company logo is a tortoise.'

'A tortoise?' queried the man from Lloyd's.

The Grand Secretary nodded. 'I do not understand the relevance either. However, Bro Nico was most insistent. He said it will mean nothing to us but everything to Sir Peter Ligne.'

Father Anthony caught his eye. 'I can explain its significance, Sir Richard. A long time ago, Ligne destroyed an old man's pleasure by passing off the gift of a tortoise to his grand-

[*289*]

daughter as his own. Stollen has never forgiven him that petty deed. The child was Jasmine Palmeira, the old man her grandfather: Stollen's dear friend Jiddu, the late Worshipful Master of the Baghdad Masonic Lodge.'

Thanking him for his contribution, the Grand Secretary pressed on. 'We must settle Ligne and Fitzwilliams' future today,' he murmured. 'I am assured Ligne's arrest is imminent. Things are less straightforward with Fitzwilliams. He is, after all, a junior minister. Moreover, Jasmine hardly leaves his side . . .

'The issue, gentlemen, is whether we really want to "withdraw" Fitzwilliams. Please forgive the euphemism. As a minister, he is proving himself a success.'

It was Miro's turn to signal he wished to speak. The Grand Secretary gave way with good grace. Apologising for the interruption, the former observed, 'Some of you may know I first met Fitzwilliams when he was in his early twenties – we spent a couple of weeks together in Iraq. At the time, he showed much promise.

'To my regret, and no doubt because of the malign influence of Sir Peter Ligne, Fitzwilliams did not develop well. Soon, he became responsible for heinous deeds.

'Government responsibilities saved him. He was a very able minister during the Falklands war. Today, he has helped secure large contracts for British companies which would otherwise have gone elsewhere. He acts fairly, challenging the stranglehold of the mighty while raising awareness of the specialist skills of the smaller. In addition, he is the only member of the government warning about the sophistication of the Asia Pacific region. In short, Fitzwilliams is outstanding.

'I do not wish to influence you either way, my Brothers. Nor do I forget Fitzwilliams' wickedness. I thought, however, it correct to point out what he has made of himself.'

The Grand Secretary nodded. 'Fitzwilliams has shown himself capable of redemption. I am told this is due to Jasmine. He is deliriously happy. Reform is possible.'

Father Anthony coughed. He would speak his mind and leave. He had heard enough.

'You are right. Fitzwilliams is happy. To my regret, Rome has accepted his claim his marriage to Belinda Fitzwilliams "never truly existed in the first place". Why? Because by Fitzwilliams' own admission, he never "showed due discretion" during it. His annulment will be granted shortly. People can get the Church to do just about anything today. I do not see Fitzwilliams' redemption. I see a man who has been lucky.'

He was pleased to find himself supported by the Grand Chaplain. A vote – carried unanimously – was taken a short while later. Father Anthony sighed. He accepted its consequences. The past would soon been over.

The Grand Chaplain led the prayers. A few moments later he and Father Anthony left together. 'May Almighty God forgive us,' they murmured as they parted.

As soon as the clerics had gone, an awkward silence filled the room. The Grand Secretary looked about him. 'When would be the best time to arrange "things"?' he queried.

He had no need to be specific.

Ghazi El-Tarek responded. 'Bro Nico suggested he hold his retirement party in London – Moscow is all for it. Were it to go ahead, then could be appropriate . . .'

– Here, he mentioned General Stollen had wanted to retire years ago but his employers had requested he stay on –

'... Bro Nico suggests he flies in for the occasion. He hopes Grand Lodge will look after the guest-list. He is assured *le tout Londres* will attend. The room will be top-heavy with political and executive celebrities. If everybody is at the same party, everybody has an alibi ...'

An insistent ringing interrupted their deliberations. The Grand Secretary frowned: He had left strict instructions they were not to be disturbed. Answering the telephone brusquely, he listened for a few moments before replacing the receiver.

'We will have to act against the clock, gentlemen,' he remarked with a grim expression.

'Who has set the clock ticking?' asked Ghazi.

'Belinda Fitzwilliams. She committed suicide earlier this evening.'

She was thirty three years old.

CHAPTER THIRTY ONE

❋ ✻ ❋

Andrew Fitzwilliams found Belinda's body in what had once been their yellow bedroom. He was genuinely shattered by her death. She left no note. Throughout the following week, the newspapers covered her suicide with a restrained kindness they had not shown her in life.

Jasmine, meanwhile, requested Father Anthony visit her widower. 'Please come, Father. Andrew needs you. Please hear his confession.'

The priest reluctantly agreed to see Fitzwilliams in the apartment that had once been called the marital home. Jasmine opened the door to him. A few moments later, he was on his own with the politician. He looked at Fitzwilliams with interest.

He saw the same boyish face, ravaged by grief, but still, unmistakably the young man's face he had seen in Iraq all those years ago. The same thick blond hair. The same winning smile.

'Jasmine tells me you wish me to hear your confession, Mr Fitzwilliams.'

The latter nodded. They were seated in a spacious and tidy sitting-room. It had no identity. Taking a deep breath, Fitzwilliams described his feelings for Belinda.

'May God forgive me, I wanted to end our marriage. It was a sham. I wanted it annulled – but I did not want it to end like this.'

He put his head in his hands. 'Jasmine says I destroyed Belinda. She is right. She believed an annulment would set Belinda free. It is the one thing Jasmine got wrong. Belinda wanted to set herself free. She yearned for her dead child.

'I have asked Jasmine to marry me. I have never made any secret of the fact I love her. To my delight, she has accepted. Her mother and father are against the alliance.'

He tried hard not to second-guess his companion's response. When it came, it was cold but factual.

'Jasmine is an adult. She does not need parental permission. I do not see your problem.'

Fitzwilliams accepted this was the best he could hope for. 'There is none. I merely wished to ask whether you had any objection to our marriage?'

Father Anthony stared into his face. He saw nothing in his eyes. He got up. He felt polluted. 'Following your wife's suicide, there is nothing to prevent you re-marrying.'

Seeing himself out, Father Anthony did not warn Fitzwilliams his future was yesterday. As he left, Jasmine came running up. 'You have seen him, Father?'

'Yes, my child. Now I can talk to you.'

'I have nothing to say.'

'No? Not even about Belinda? You used her ill. Since when have you grown so wicked?'

Jasmine flushed. 'I did not know she would do what she did.'

Putting his hand on her shoulder, Father Anthony continued softly, 'You undermined Belinda and stole her husband's love which he declared before God.'

She pulled away. 'No! I stole nothing. I protected Belinda as much as I could. Andrew always loved me. You think us wicked. Then maybe we deserve each other. I do not know. I only know that what I am doing is right. I told Uncle Nico . . .'

The priest shook his head. He had always believed in God's unconditional love and grace to all sinners but Jasmine's relationship with Andrew Fitzwilliams appalled him. 'Where is your conscience? You are breaking your parents' hearts. Your father is not well. The murder of your grandfather . . .'

'I do not wish to speak of murder, Father. As for my parents, I am grown up now. Shortly I will be married. I have made my decision. They must respect it.'

He tried a different tack. 'And what child, shall I write in my diary?'

– The suddenness of the question threw her –

' . . . One of its happiest entries is devoted to the day I invited you and Leah Solomon to my observatory in Baghdad so you could watch the heavens.'

Uncertain as to what was coming, she stared at him awkwardly.

'You looked for the furthest star because this was the most difficult to see. Fitzwilliams, my dear, is not the furthest star. He is . . .'

'The brightest in the galaxy.'

He tried to dissuade her a final time. 'Marriage is not a piece of paper, Jasmine. It is the carpenter Joseph placing Mary on a donkey so she does not tire. It is Mary bathing his feet when they are torn by stones. Is this what the sacred union means to you?'

'How dare you even doubt me!'

Seeing her mind made up, he turned away and made his way on to the landing. As he walked down the stairs, she called after him.

'Will you perform the ceremony, Father?'

'No.'

Belinda's funeral took place one week after her death. The bells tolled mournfully as Andrew Fitzwilliams took his place in church. It was only when he saw Jasmine, accompanied by her mother, he almost broke down. He led the future Mrs Fitzwilliams to her place at the front.

Suzie retreated to the back. On entering, she had seen an old friend, partially hidden in the shadows. 'I don't think you should be here,' she said, keeping her voice low as she led Stollen outside.

Once in the open air, she faced him. 'Do you mock Belinda, Nico, even in death, by coming to her funeral?'

'I have never mocked her, Suzie. By God believe me. Do not blame me for her death. A husband is responsible for a sweet and innocent bride. Not me. I did my job, this is all.'

'You cannot comfort yourself so easily. You should not be here. Besides, someone might recognise you.'

Stollen recoiled. To be recognised as a ladies man was one thing. To be remarked as such on the day of a mistress' funeral was something else.

'I wanted to pay my respects. No more than this. I shall ensure no-one sees me. I cannot pretend I cared for Belinda. I tried to do my best by her when I left the country. I thought I left her in safe hands.'

'Left her? She was expecting your baby, Nico.'

Stollen shrugged. 'I did not want the child. But I made arrangements for the care of both.'

He bowed his head. When he looked up, Suzie had gone. As she re-entered the church, the congregation was singing *All Things Bright and Beautiful, All Creatures Great and Small*.

He felt, rather than saw, Miro approach. He had asked the Grand Secretary to arrange the meeting. Belinda Fitzwilliams' funeral seemed as good a venue as any. He recognised the man's disapproval at once. It did not perturb him.

'You wished to speak with me, General?'

Stollen nodded. Opening his briefcase, he took out a large manila envelope. Inside were about twenty prints compromising most of the British establishment. Handing them over, he remarked, 'The KGB cannot use them. If they ever needed to, they could make further copies.'

Miro flicked through them. 'You have been busy,' he commented, holding up a photograph of Stollen with various well known Britons in barely clad female company. Another showed him in bed with a bunny girl and a respected politician. Others were of Sir Peter Ligne on holiday in Italy.

'Good grief. The whole of British society would collapse if these came out.'

Stollen shrugged. 'I have done my job. The KGB call me the Seducer.'

Miro put the pictures away. 'What do you want me to do

with them? The Grand Secretary asked I give you any assistance you require'

Stollen inclined his head. Shutting the leather portfolio, he responded, 'Please see the images of Sir Peter Ligne are given to Andrew Fitzwilliams. You can tell Fitzwilliams I gave them to you. This will set the future in motion.'

Sir Peter Ligne arrived at Andrew Fitzwilliams' home promptly at 16.00 hrs. Following Belinda's death, the minister was still on compassionate leave. Mounting the stairs, Ligne's face settled into a frown.

He had heard rumours about Stollen's retirement party. Grand Lodge, apparently, was handling the guest list. And he, Ligne, had not been invited. Silent fury swept through him.

Stollen was calling it the 'Spies Party'. Philippe Palmeira, he mused, had given a similar celebration on the banks of the Tigris seventeen years earlier. It had represented the start of his career. It seemed that Stollen's entertainment might signify its collapse.

Ligne found stairs difficult these days. They always left him out of breath. His mind raced.

He was snubbed everywhere he went. Conversations ended when he walked into rooms. Stollen's brochure announcing the sale of Fitzwilliams International East Germany was circulating.

It boasted: *Along with several high ranking American officials, senior British civil servant Sir Peter Ligne is one of our consultants.*

The game was up – and he knew it.

He clenched his jaw in fury. Stollen was forcing everybody's hands. HMG's. The Americans. The latter would stop at nothing now to purchase the company.

Ligne froze. The Americans had not been told he had been unable to persuade HMG to purchase it. HMG had left the race.

HMG was not going to bid for the damn thing. It was too expensive he had been told. A Treasury memo had said so that morning. It blamed the government's new 'cost efficiency unit'. In reality, Ligne knew it was the Masonic Grand Secretary's doing.

He shuddered. He was up against a Masonic conspiracy. The Treasury was as good as saying that he, Ligne, was being dumped. Abandoned. To the Americans.

And only he and the Americans knew what HMG did not. What Fitzwilliams International – East and West – really traded. And with whom. And Stollen, of course. Stollen knew.

Now, the Russian's brochure was circulating, its glossy 'tortoise' logo mocking them all. Hence Ligne's meeting with Andrew Fitzwilliams. Fitzwilliams, after all, owed him.

Ligne's lips curled. He had no doubt Jasmine would be with Fitzwilliams. Belinda had quickly become a memory.

Ligne needed Jasmine. She would secure Fitzwilliams for him. After all, wasn't this Stollen's game too?

Stollen. Even the thought of the Russian filled him with fury. Reaching the first landing, he felt on edge. Sick even. Perhaps it was the pressure in his head. He rapped on the door.

Fitzwilliams opened it a few moments later and led him to

his study. It had a king-sized desk. Stacked high were heavy files and sheets of embossed stationary of a dozen different subsidiaries of Fitzwilliams International. Fitzwilliams' ministerial red box was on the floor. The atmosphere – unlike in Belinda's day – was welcoming and lived-in.

Emerging from a pretty galley kitchen on the right, Jasmine greeted Ligne with affection. 'Find yourself a tiny corner, Sir Peter. I am trying to organise Andrew!'

The smile he offered in return was no more than a polite twisting of his lips. Oblivious, his laughing host pulled Jasmine to him and motioned Ligne to a seat.

'Stollen telephoned,' Fitzwilliams remarked, once his guest was seated. 'He said he was not inviting you to his leaving party, Peter, in case he compromises you! God the man's a scream. I assume you know his latest wheeze. The cheeky bugger's offered to sell Fitzwilliams International East Germany back to me. I get first refusal. Everybody, apparently, is bidding for it . . .'

Everybody, thought Ligne, apart from HMG. He wished Fitzwilliams would offer him a drink.

'He's boasting about the company's new logo. Jasmine says it is in her honour.'

Jasmine giggled. 'Have you seen it, Sir Peter? It is a tortoise.'

He accomplished a sickly grin.

'Andrew says his former researcher Betsy Meredith – apparently she used to work for the CIA – is negotiating to buy the whole of Fitzwilliams International on America's behalf. I got in touch with Uncle Nico and he confirmed it. He also said Betsy knows something we don't but wouldn't tell me what! You wouldn't know what Stollen is hiding, would you, Sir Peter?'

He managed a faint chuckle. 'Worried about your inheritance, young woman?'

She dimpled prettily. 'Nope. Just about to secure it. All Andrew and I have to do now is set a date. Uncle Nico has agreed to provide the caviar for our wedding breakfast. We've already had our first present. It's from Hussein, my grandfather's old driver.'

He looked at her dazedly. She went on and on in her bright merry voice. Next, she leaned over Fitzwilliams' desk and took a small parcel from the top drawer. 'Have a look at Hussein's gift, Sir Peter. Isn't it beautiful?'

He had no option but to pretend an interest. Out of a box, she lifted a carved wooden ornament. It was in the shape of a tortoise.

Ligne blanched. It was the logo Stollen had chosen for Fitzwilliams International East Germany. Painted on its shell were the holy emblems of the three living religions of the Tigris-Euphrates valley. Rising above it, picked out in diamonds, was the Masonic symbol that allowed the land of the three faiths to mingle as Brothers in the country they had shared.

'Hussein says the jewels belonged to my grandmother,' explained Jasmine with the blithe eagerness of the young.

Grateful to see Fitzwilliams at long last bearing down on them with alcohol, Ligne agreed the gift was beautiful.

'I know it's a bit early, Peter, but will you drink to us?' asked Fitzwilliams.

A few moments later they toasted each other with chilled champagne.

'Uncle Nico gave me my first taste,' Jasmine was happy to confide.

Feeling uncomfortable, Ligne raised his glass to the couple. Despite their politeness, they hardly seemed to notice him. His jaw clenched.

How dare they be happy? Particularly Fitzwilliams. How he loathed him. He wondered how long he had known that. The man had it all. Position. Status. Money. Maybe even Downing Street one day – the prohibition against Roman Catholics could not last forever. Good looks. Jasmine.

Jasmine protected by Stollen, that is. Ligne had no doubt the tortoise logo was Stollen's warning. Jasmine was untouchable.

Happiness. Fitzwilliams had it all. It was time to call in favours.

'So Peter, what can we do for you?'

Ligne cleared his throat. 'Its um, delicate . . .'

Taking the hint, Jasmine was quick to offer to leave.

'Certainly not,' replied Fitzwilliams, reaching for her hand. 'I have no secrets from my future wife. What is the problem?'

Ligne shrugged with seeming good-nature. 'I wouldn't really call it that, old chap. It is just that I wanted to have a word about you buying Fitzwilliams International East Germany from Stollen. After all, the Chief Whip cannot be best pleased your name . . .'

'He's not bothered. The brochure hardly mentions me. Given the press has been threatened with D Notices, I cannot see there will be much publicity either. Moreover, the prospectus is mostly about you.

'You have been naughty! Apparently, the Americans had

their suspicions you were a Commie. Stollen told them so years ago. It came as a relief to find out you were merely a crook!'

Ligne reached across and refilled his champagne flute. 'I don't care what Stollen has been saying. I am ordering you to get that company. I want it!'

Fitzwilliams looked at him in amazement. 'Well go ahead and bid for it, old boy. But don't expect me to have anything to do with it. It has no assets. Stollen would be the first to say so.'

Ligne tipped his drink down his throat. 'Stollen?! You have spoken to Stollen?'

Bewildered, Fitzwilliams and Jasmine exchanged glances. 'Yes, of course. I told you so earlier. As I said, Nico's invited me to his retirement party. In fact, I am giving the "farewell" speech.'

Ligne felt ill. His face went red. The room began to whirl.

He could feel anger rising inside him. Anger against Fitzwilliams for being happy. Anger against Jasmine for being the source of his happiness. Anger against Stollen who was the source of his unhappiness.

'Get me that company . . .' he screamed.

Fitzwilliams looked at him in disbelief. He had never known Ligne to be anything other than in control before.

'. . . You owe it.'

Fitzwilliams' jaw dropped. Jasmine watched the two men in increasing astonishment. Embarrassed, she murmured, 'Are you sure you don't want me to go, darling? I need to call my mother . . .'

Ligne's eyes rolled. Suzie. Jasmine was going to speak to Suzie.

Suzie had always loathed him. It was a plot. Everybody was trying to destroy him. Well, he would not allow them to. He would do the destroying.

'While you're on to her,' he remarked, his voice suddenly as sweet as treacle, 'Do ask whether your father is going to Stollen's party too. He worked for the KGB for long enough. You wouldn't want to shame Minister Fitzwilliams here, with your father's long friendship with the Soviet general who cuckolded Andrew with Belinda, would you?'

Visibly hurt, Jasmine replied, 'Andrew knows my family have been friends with General Stollen for decades. As for my father, he's a double. Uncle Nico told me years ago.'

Ligne could feel his temper rising once more. Nico again? He had to destroy Jasmine. This would destroy Nico.

He removed some photographs from his wallet and handed them over. They were of her father clinched in the embrace of a young woman. They had been taken under duress prior to Philippe Palmeira's visit to Hamburg. Jasmine did not know this. She crumpled.

A furious Fitzwilliams snatched them from her and tore them up. 'They're fake, darling. Your father would never betray your mother, you know that. Stollen warned me Peter could try something like this . . .'

Ligne laughed nastily. 'Stollen warned you?'

Fitzwilliams stared at him coldly. 'He sent me these,' he responded. 'Perhaps you would like to take a look. I told you about them, darling. They're pictures of Peter on holiday in the Italian lakes. They go back years. Apparently Peter's lover stood him up on one occasion . . .'

'SHUT UP!' Ligne's scream was like a wounded animal. 'How did you find out? Laure? The darling. She was always so indiscreet. We were in LOVE. Are in love. NO! Not Laure. It is the French security services who have done this. Mitterand even. He was always jealous of my relationship with Laure. I told Laure that Mitterand was not to be trusted.'

Jasmine shone on her wedding day. It was her twenty-fifth birthday. 'Maybe she is Andrew's salvation and he hers,' Suzie whispered to Philippe. 'When she takes her vows before God, she places herself in God's hands. We must respect her marriage.'

The day was brilliant and the air tingled with excitement. The church was decorated with lemon trees. As Jasmine kissed her parents with Fitzwilliams at her side, Suzie noticed a bracelet on her daughter's wrist. Following her mother's gaze, the latter explained, 'Andrew gave it to me. It was Belinda's. He said she would have wanted me to wear it.'

Suzie turned away. She had recognised it immediately as the piece of jewellery the Warlord had given Peri when, many years ago, she had made him a grandfather.

Jasmine pretended not to notice her mother's distress. She and Fitzwilliams had a plane to catch. They were honeymooning in the Caribbean.

Once arrived at their destination, they enchanted all who met them with their vivacity and delight in each other. On their return, their happiness was complete. Aged forty-one, Andrew Fitzwilliams had leapfrogged his colleagues. He was now Secretary of State for Defence.

The new government wanted to promote those who dazzled. Fitzwilliams, with his young wife at his side, did just that. Stollen had placed Jasmine at the heart of the British establishment, at the very moment it meant nothing to him.

That night, as she slept in her husband's arms, her grandfather's driver Hussein died. Grand Lodge's obituary read: *Quietly in his sleep, Hussein, head gardener, Garden of Lemon Trees, Baghdad. Devoted Muslim and friend of the late Worshipful Master Jiddu Palmeira.*

Stollen telephoned Jasmine with the news the following morning. She went immediately to her parents, meeting him on the doorstep.

'Suzie does not want your father to be told of Hussein's death. It would distress him too much,' he advised. 'Father Anthony is arranging a memorial Mass. He has asked the Imam of London's permission.

'Meantime, since your father is too ill to come to my party tomorrow, I am visiting him. Your mother has told me he will not see another winter.'

Taking her hand, he led her into the drawing-room where Suzie was waiting, before making his way to Philippe Palmeira's study. The latter was propped up with cushions and blankets in a deep armchair.

'You have come to say good-bye, my dear Nico?'

Philippe had long accepted that whatever Stollen had done in the past, in recent times he had tried to put things right. 'Help yourself to coffee,' he continued. 'Suzie and I are worried about you. What life do you have after the KGB?'

Stollen grinned. 'I shall have fun spending my money. One

of Socialism's benefits is the purchasing power of its pensions. You should have been a KGB general yourself!'

Philippe shook his head. 'I would rather have been a subaltern in my Queen's army, Nico, than a general in yours.'

Stollen looked momentarily hurt. Settling himself opposite his host and stirring his drink, he observed, 'Both armies serve an honourable people. Moreover, one of those armies – mine – saved Europe at the time of the last war. It is something the West forgets.'

Philippe apologised.

All too soon, Suzie came in, anxious her husband did not tire. Allowing Stollen to carry him to his bedroom, Philippe kissed him when they parted. They knew they would not meet again. Later that evening, Jasmine found Hussein's wedding present, the little jewelled tortoise, stolen from her dressing-table.

The last strains of the opera faded. Sir Peter Ligne clasped his hands together in ecstasy before looking with longing at his beloved. They always met in Italy at this time of year – there had only been one occasion when their dates had not coincided.

His sweetheart seemed oblivious to his scrutiny. Ligne did not mind. He was relieved in a way, conscious he looked worn. He was still handsome but his skin appeared tired, his eyes jaded.

He sighed. He had to mention the photographs Fitzwilliams had shown him but had put it off, not wanting to ruin the magic of the evening. He was certain now it was Francois Mitterand who had caused the trouble.

The house-lights went on. He and his companion filed out

of the opera house. Earlier, they had walked from the Piazza del Duomo to the Gallery Victor Emmanuel with its passages lined with restaurants and shops. Now they retraced their steps.

'Thank you, darling,' he said softly. 'A night-cap, perhaps?'

'I don't think so, Peter. It is no longer appropriate.'

Ligne stared, amazed at the harshness of the voice. Its cool precision went through him like a knife.

'Not appropriate? What an astonishing choice of words,' he replied, slipping his hand through his lover's arm. The latter shrugged but made no objection.

'Not appropriate perhaps because you have found out about the pictures. I am sorry, my dear. It was always a risk. I assume it is Mitterand who has done the dirty. Do not worry darling. He cannot hurt you. He cannot hurt us.'

Turning towards him, the light illuminating the beautiful dark eyes he knew so well, Ligne brought his face close to the lips he loved to kiss. 'Say something, darling,' he whispered.

His companion stepped away from him. 'No Peter, not appropriate because I do not deem it to be. I only agreed to this meeting to say farewell. It seemed bad manners not to. I have no more use for you.'

Hurt and surprise flooded Ligne's face. 'What are you saying, darling? You have just been rattled by those snaps. Forget them. Now I am retiring, we will be able to see so much more of each other. We love each other. You told me so . . .'

Stollen looked at him in disgust.

'. . . You told me the day we sat together on Laure's chaise longue when I made such a fool of myself. D'you remember the way you flirted with her to tease me? I have never forgotten the way you looked at me . . .'

'I flirted with Laure because I love her. I always have done.'

Ligne laughed with reckless derision. Nico always teased him. This is why he had commenced his affair with that silly hussy Belinda Fitzwilliams on the day he was due to join Ligne in Italy.

He rocked backwards and forwards. The bint had meant nothing to Nico. Unlike Laure. Laure had always been a threat.

'. . . And then, do you remember Laure's face when she stumbled upon us here? Laugh. I'll say. Her expression was so comical.'

'She did not stumble. Mitterand told her where she would find us in Italy. And I told him so he would tell her. Moreover, Mitterand did not give the photographs to Andrew Fitzwilliams. I did.'

'NO!' Ligne reeled as if he had been punched. 'You do not know what you are saying, darling. This is just one more of your little games. You do not love Laure. You love me. You have always loved me . . .'

Stollen shook his arm away. 'I buggered you. It signified nothing. I was doing my job.'

'No!' Ligne's features contracted and suddenly he was crying. He looked so pathetic it was almost comical.

'You do not know what you are saying,' he blubbered. His face was haggard, his eyelids swollen. 'You love me. This is why you gave the photographs to Fitzwilliams. You wanted to proclaim our love. Come, Nico, slap me. Slap me. You will enjoy that. You always do.'

Stollen looked as if he wanted to retch. He left Ligne sobbing in the moonlight. He did not turn around.

CHAPTER THIRTY TWO

The Masonic Grand Secretary Sir Richard Leystan was speaking on a secure line with Britain's intelligence chief. The latter was a newish appointment. He appeared up to speed.

'And what about Andrew Fitzwilliams?' the senior freemason was asking. 'It is essential we move fast. We do not want Jasmine Fitzwilliams falling pregnant and her husband leaving a fatherless child.'

The intelligence chief's urbane voice could not have been more reassuring. 'Everything under control, Grand Secretary. Fitzwilliams will be interviewed tomorrow. We wanted Ligne out of the way first – he was arrested this morning on his return from Italy. In view of Fitzwilliams' cabinet responsibilities, we thought it inappropriate to act sooner.'

The intelligence chief attended Secretary of State Fitzwilliams at his ministry the following afternoon. It seemed more discreet to do things this way around. Having dismissed his officials, Fitzwilliams suspected nothing until the ambush was sprung.

Once on their own, the intelligence chief explained the reason for his visit in a helpful manner. ' . . . Peter Ligne is in custody. He is co-operating fully and has made full disclosure regarding Fitzwilliams International. He has said that you, Secretary of State . . .'

'I know nothing about Fitzwilliams International,' interrupted the politician. He had prepared the conversation in his head for years. Jasmine had ensured he was word perfect.

'Sir Peter Ligne took part of the company off me when I was twenty-four: The British Board of Infrastructure managed the rest of it. After that, Dr Douglas Miro, now of Douglas Miro International, ran one of its subsidiaries. Subsequently, the arms dealer Ghazi El-Tarek was put in charge of the whole caboodle. Miro and El-Tarek were appointed by the intelligence services, as, of course, was Sir Peter.'

The intelligence chief sighed. Fitzwilliams, apparently, would not go down without a fight. Moreover, he was right in what he said.

'You are not making things any easier for yourself, Mr Secretary. HMG is prepared to handle things with discretion. All it asks is . . .'

'I fall upon my sword?'

'. . . You submit your resignation to the government and, in due course, stand down from Parliament.'

Fitzwilliams laughed. 'And if I refuse?'

The intelligence chief shrugged. 'We will have no alternative but to use Sir Peter Ligne's evidence against you.'

'In which case,' smiled Fitzwilliams, almost giving the impression of a man enjoying himself, 'You won't mind if I circulate his photo collection, will you? Of course, you will have to weigh up whether my resignation is as important as the reputation of your service.'

Opening his briefcase, he retrieved a clutch of black and white prints and handed them over. The intelligence chief took them without comment. They were of Ligne in Stollen's arms.

Andrew Fitzwilliams escorted the civil servant to the door a few moments later. The minister's position was unassailable, the latter conceded. Fitzwilliams made his farewells with fastidious courtesy, opining he hoped he would see the intelligence chief at General Stollen's retirement party that evening. A short while later, he changed into black tie and dialled his wife.

'Darling, are you sure you won't come along to Nico's "do"? You know how much he would love to see you.'

Jasmine giggled. 'Quite sure, husband! Away! I am not attending one more boring cocktail party with you!'

Fitzwilliams laughed. 'I did not think my charms would fade so quickly!'

'I said goodbye to Nico at my parents,' she reminded him. 'The gathering will pretty much be a men-only do anyway – apart from a sprinkling of ex-mistresses!'

The couple disconnected a few moments after. One hour later, Andrew Fitzwilliams presented himself at Stollen's celebration: The venue was the Goring, the oldest and most distinguished private hotel in London.

Everybody who was anybody was present. The establishment had been shut to all non-invitees. Champagne was served in the terrace bar overlooking the gardens.

In the far corner of the room, Fitzwilliams saw Stollen and the new American ambassador. Also in attendance was the latest CIA station head. Stollen waved, motioning Fitzwilliams to join them.

Fitzwilliams looked at the American diplomat with interest but steered clear – at the behest of the Pentagon, the envoy had protested the defence cuts Fitzwilliams had instigated. It worried that, as a result, France and West Germany could get together to form a European army at NATO's expense. Signalling to Stollen they would catch up later, Fitzwilliams joined the Italian delegation instead – his host had a long history with Italy.

Meanwhile, the American ambassador chatted amiably with Stollen. A waiter brought them chilled drinks and he insisted on transferring a glass to the Russian rather than let him help himself. The CIA chief looked on, uneasy.

Sadat of Egypt had been murdered and there had been assaults on the US President and Pope. The President suspected the Communists to be responsible for the attacks on world leaders, anxious, apparently, about the growing friendship between the Oval Office and Holy See. Some counter measures had been put in place. There were rumours these included the creation of the Social Democrat Party in Britain.

Noticing Fitzwilliams, the CIA man glowered. He had heard that Defence Secretary Fitzwilliams was Stollen's principal guest and would lead the tributes after the dinner. A cabinet minister who enabled a Communist to circulate freely in the bosom of capitalism – particularly one taking an independent line on defence matters – was always alarming.

Sensing his disapproval, Fitzwilliams chuckled. He did not blame the American for being confused. Any British politician whose policies conflicted with Washington was deemed to be suspect. Especially one comfortable in the company of a Soviet spy.

Not that the American ambassador seemed in any hurry to detach himself from one. 'Betsy Meredith sends her best regards, General. She is going great guns in the White House,' he was saying.

Stollen looked genuinely pleased.

Making an oblique reference to the last time the Russian had left the country, the diplomat continued, 'So, you leave tomorrow, General. Planning on any mayhem before you go?'

Stollen grinned. Putting on a great show of looking at his wristwatch, he teased, 'I suppose it would only take twelve hours to destabilise Sterling and rattle the markets, Ambassador. I guess I still have time!'

'I do hope you desist.'

Both men laughed. Stollen was fond of Americans. However, he considered the Soviets superior because they knew how to 'grow' people. The Americans liked to show results too quickly to do the same.

This was one reason why he regarded the Brits as Moscow's twin. Sometimes, they even 'grew' people together – as he and Ligne had proved. Stollen sighed. He had promised Grand Lodge and Jasmine's father he would finish things swiftly.

Across the room, Miro and the Grand Secretary watched with anxiety. Stollen had already briefed them as to what he would say to the Americans. The only question remaining was whether they would bite.

Having been duped by Stollen once, they were not likely to be taken in a second time. On the other hand, and as Stollen had pointed out, many seasoned CIA professionals had been withdrawn. Stollen might, just might, swing it: Particularly if he gave the Americans what they wanted.

'And how, General Stollen, would you manage to rattle the markets?' asked the US envoy in his beautiful accent, modulated to suit his audience.

'I would create a scandal, Mr Ambassador. How else?'

'Such as?'

Stollen feigned concentration. 'Nothing very complicated. One say, involving this country's most dazzling minister. A young man who embodies the whole spirit of the Thatcher age . . .'

He took some photographs from his wallet and passed them over. Seeing them, the ambassador whitened, before handing them to his colleague. They looked at Stollen with incredulity.

It was time for him to move on. Waving a beautifully manicured hand in their direction, he remarked, 'Goodbye, gentlemen. I recommend the mole working for the Brits in the Russian embassy at the moment. Now there's a defector worth poaching.'

The two Americans looked dumbfounded. Wiping his brow, the CIA man queried, 'How do you know the Brits have a mole?'

'Because one of the Soviet moles in the CIA told me. I was in France at the time. Monsieur Mitterand laughed . . . like a drain, is the expression, I believe.'

With that he was gone.

The American ambassador checked the pictures a second time. 'Where is Stollen now?' he asked his colleague.

'Behind you. With the Defence Secretary.'

'Do they look affectionate?'

'Yup. Stollen's got his hand on his shoulder.'

The ambassador shuddered. The snaps showed Stollen in bed with Andrew Fitzwilliams. If the Soviet wanted a scandal, this one was a beauty.

So. Stollen had had Fitzwilliams' first wife, Belinda. AND Fitzwilliams.

Only Stollen and Grand Lodge knew the images were fake. 'They'll fall for it,' Stollen had assured Miro and the Grand Secretary. 'The Americans are suspicious of the way Fitzwilliams is handling his defence portfolio and want to get rid of him. They think all British former public schoolboys are closet homosexuals: I have just played to their prejudices.'

Fitzwilliams was placed on Stollen's right at the dinner. He gave one of the most amusing speeches of the evening. When he left, Stollen embraced him with true affection.

Fitzwilliams made his farewells shortly before midnight and arrived home in his official car about twenty minutes later – he and Jasmine had declined to move into a government residence. Dismissing his driver, Fitzwilliams was surprised to find Ghazi El-Tarek with his wife.

'There you are, I was looking for you,' he said with good-humour. 'Why were you not at Nico's party? He was asking after you. He tells me you have decided to vote Conservative for the rest of your life on the basis the Tories are offering such favourable terms to foreign businessmen!'

Ghazi laughed. 'I had to collect Father Anthony from the airport. He gets offended if I do not drive myself. His flight from Paris was delayed. As a result, I missed Nico's celebration. So did Father Anthony. He's furious.'

'Is he here?' queried the politician with obvious delight. He had long hoped for a thaw in relations with the priest.

'Yes, darling,' interrupted Jasmine, reaching to kiss him. 'He is on the telephone to my mother at the moment. My father has found out about Hussein's death and is inconsolable. Ghazi thought it would be a good idea if I went home with Father Anthony. You don't mind, do you?'

Fitzwilliams raised her chin. 'Of course I don't.'

As he was kissing her, the telephone rang. Lifting one eyebrow, he picked up the receiver. It was almost 01.00 hrs. The American embassy was on the line.

'Sorry to trouble you so late, Secretary of State,' a cool voice intoned. 'The Ambassador thought you ought to be aware that, following General Stollen's party, there are some prints circulating which may interest you. We will, of course, inform HMG officially later this morning they have come into our possession. In the meantime, we thought it a courtesy to . . .'

'What prints?'

The American told him. Fitzwilliams laughed when he finished speaking. 'They're fakes! But do not worry about it. I'll come and have a look at them now. Be with you in about half an hour, say? At the embassy?'

'What was all that about, darling?' asked Jasmine.

Fitzwilliams pulled her to him. 'A silly departing prank of Stollen's. The Americans have bought into it because they are desperate to see the back of me!'

'But why go to the embassy now, darling? Can't it wait until the morning?'

Fitzwilliams sighed. She was not wrong. 'Because it is easier to tell VIP Yanks when they are being twits outside of office hours!'

'Then I'll go with you.'

He shook his head. This was one of Stollen's games in which he did not want her involved. He kissed her tenderly.

She left with Father Anthony and Ghazi El-Tarek soon after. Ghazi was the last to say good-bye. Fitzwilliams drove himself. Five minutes later, his car exploded into flames.

The newspapers screamed: *SECRETARY OF STATE: TRAGIC ACCIDENT.*

Increasingly fragile, coming to terms with grief, Jasmine declared her husband had been assassinated. The police refused to take her seriously. Patronised, caught up in a whirl of condolences, she collapsed.

Through her shock, she began to glimpse a pattern emerge. Whenever she condemned the authorities or spoke to the press about the last hours of her husband's life, his commercial dealings were exposed in the following morning's newspapers. She wept bitter tears.

In a vain attempt to rescue his reputation posthumously, Jasmine emphasised that, in accordance with cabinet rules, Fitzwilliams had divested himself of all his business interests the minute he became a minister. In addition, she stressed the appropriate parties had always been fully aware of what his 'interests' had been. (Two essential facts, she rightly pointed out, the media omitted.)

Then came the reading of the will. As Jasmine had always known, she was her husband's heir. Fitzwilliams International belonged to her. Visibly distressed, she made clear she did not want the company.

Within minutes, a transfer document was being waved under her nose. She signed it, subsequently making over to charity all moneys owed to herself. It was only much later, she realised the documentation ought not to have been ready in advance. And certainly not in Ghazi El-Tarek's name.

She had a nervous breakdown shortly after Fitzwilliams' funeral. Two months later, her father's life drew to its close. Suzie was with Philippe when he died. He kissed her and slipped away.

1992

CHAPTER THIRTY THREE
❄ ✦ ❄

PUTNEY, LONDON: A fine-featured, cerebral looking man in his early forties studied his newspaper. *Concert of Rights Goes International!* read the headline. The article – mildly scathing – gave a brief history of the organisation, explaining its genesis and how it had now broadened its remit to include miscarriages of justice overseas.

... In addition to its London headquarters, read the piece, *the Concert has opened offices in Brussels and New York. British alumni include Vivienne Solomon who became a QC earlier this year, City analyst Bobby Lomax, as well as Labour politician Jim Richards MP.*

There followed a quote from the MP who was now checking it for accuracy. The hacks, Jim Richards decided – it was years since he had been called Jimmy – had done a fairly good job.

He was in his 'office', which is to say the little bedroom of the tiny top floor apartment he used when his parliamentary duties required him to stay in London. It was in a terrace of four flat-fronted Edwardian houses with a strip of walled garden at the back running down to the Thames. He could see Putney Bridge from his kitchen window.

Some of the houses had been turned into a clutch of one roomed flats. Jim Richards' was one of them. An MP's salary did not purchase much in the way of property in the capital, and, unlike so many other politicians, he had neither private

[*323*]

nor commercial income. (He had been offered the latter but declined.)

Setting aside the newspaper, Jim Richards moved towards the landing. He hoped, almost unconsciously, to catch a glimpse of the girl who had just left him, as she turned out of the building and made her way towards the main road. Missing her, he went back inside, refusing to admit, even to himself, the impact Andrew Fitzwilliams' widow always had on him. Whenever he saw or spoke to Jasmine Fitzwilliams, she disturbed him. He yearned to run his hand through her flowing page-boy hairstyle.

At thirty-five, Jasmine was less poised than in the heady days of her marriage. However, there was a foreignness about her Jim Richards found appealing. Although her mental health remained less than robust, he had been surprised to find her better informed than he had ever suspected. She was even funny in a self-deprecating sort of way.

The politician's widow had sought him out following an article he had written on why Parliament needed an intelligence services oversight committee. Inviting herself to the House of Commons to discuss it, they had met in the central lobby the following week. Removing her coat – revealing a beautiful neck – Jasmine had happily allowed herself to be escorted to tea.

As she passed, every head had turned in her direction. It had soon been the talk of Westminster that Jasmine Fitzwilliams was in the building for the first time since her husband's death – and on the arm of one of the Opposition's rising stars. Once seated, Jim Richards had been conscious of her scent every time she leaned a little closer to hear what he had to say.

'Hi! The main door was open. I did knock.'

Seeing Vivienne Solomon, Jim Richards grinned. 'You will be appalled to know I am sinking deeper into love for Jasmine Fitzwilliams!' he greeted her. 'I am guilty of that which I deplore in other people. Falling for her because she gives me ample time to talk about myself.'

Vivienne laughed. At forty, two years younger than Jim, she was a good-looking woman. Disinterested in fashion and uncertain where her lipstick might be found, she was one of the sexiest females he knew.

Dropping her briefcase on the floor and surveying the small, masculine room with wry amusement, she inquired, 'The fragile Jasmine has been here – again – in this crummy hole?'

He shot her a rueful glance as she stepped over his tattered Olivetti portable in its case on the floor. Seeing the open newspaper beside it, she enthused, 'Good news about the Concert! Do you remember how tiny it was when you, Bobby Lomax and I got thumped by those POUKI brutes for working for it?!'

Her companion nodded.

Now flopping into the only available seat, she looked around her with mock disdain. A modern computer screen took up most of Jim Richards' desk. Upon every available surface could be found *Hansards*, *Order Papers* and select committee reports. A line of unwashed coffee-mugs toppled precariously along a bookshelf.

'Jasmine puzzles me,' Vivienne mused. 'On the one hand, you say she allows you to talk about yourself . . .'

'And on the other?'

'... Ghazi El-Tarek told me she is so self-absorbed, she has no interest in other people.'

Jim Richards was never a fool to himself. Perching on the corner of a wobbly table, he responded, 'Jasmine is assuming Neil Kinnock will win the election – after which she thinks I will be in a position to press for an inquiry into how her husband died. I guess she thinks showing an interest in me in advance of this, is a price worth paying.'

Frowning, he continued, 'Can you remember what reason the police gave for not pursuing the Fitzwilliams investigation?'

'The truth. That Jasmine had no proof of what she said happened.'

He made his way into his tiny kitchen to put the kettle on. Vivienne's eyes followed him. He looked tired.

'Jasmine's not for you, old thing. She'll break your heart,' she murmured.

Hunting for the sugar, Jim Richards laughed. Returning with chipped cups of scalding hot tea, he bantered, 'Possibly. But no more or less than Bobby Lomax breaks yours! How is he?'

He had never found tiptoeing around the relationship of his two oldest friends easy. However, on this occasion he invoked it willingly in order to steer Vivienne off the subject of Jasmine.

Seeing the ruse, but allowing him to get away with it, she replied with her usual pragmatism, 'Busy being successful . . .'

- It was no secret she continued to love Bobby Lomax, while he had never allowed her to pretend this was returned -

'... Which means he is permanently in debt! However, I am proud of him. He is trying to do his bit for those duped by

Lloyd's of London. He's still fearless of the powerful. Which is another way of saying he's a fool.'

Jim Richards nodded. Even he conceded Bobby Lomax had turned into a better man than he had ever imagined. He was one of the few City insiders trying to warn investors they were being fleeced.

'Dump Bobby anyway, Viv. He's no good for you.'

'He is not mine to dump,' she replied dryly. 'Bobby has been faithful to a lot of women.'

'Including Jasmine Fitzwilliams?'

Her mouth dropped open. For all her insouciance, Vivienne cared deeply about whom Bobby Lomax was dating.

He put his arm around her shoulders. 'Sorry, Viv. I did not know how to tell you. It doesn't bother me whom Jasmine sees. But I know how much Bobby means to you.'

She shrugged. 'How did they meet?'

'I bumped into him in the central lobby a couple of weeks ago. He was there to discuss the latest developments in Lloyd's. Jasmine was with me. And that was that. The attraction was instant.'

Vivienne shook her head. 'No, Jim, something else must be going on. Jasmine's mother says she remains obsessed by her late husband.'

A senior man at Lloyd's of London frowned. Names on loss-making syndicates were organising themselves, and, along with others, City analyst Bobby Lomax had drawn attention to the fact it was alleged the Conservative party was bailing out one or two supporters. Angry at Lomax's campaign to highlight the rumoured favouritism, the Lloyd's official swivelled in his chair and dialled the POUKI Secretary to the Chief Whip.

He was relieved to discover the man was equally up to speed. With a general election looming, it was his job to make sure the Conservatives were returned to power: Bobby Lomax's input into one of the support groups set up on behalf of the duped Lloyd's Names could threaten this.

It amazed both men how Lomax had ever got a job in the City in the first place. His POUKI records should have prevented it. All students who supported the Concert of Rights in the early years of its existence had POUKI files.

Now, they agreed, Bobby Lomax had taken another step too far. They disconnected a few moments later having determined the way forward. Unbeknown to Bobby Lomax, his city career would be over within hours.

Relieved the matter had been so quickly settled, the POUKI man flicked through a copy of a glossy magazine on his desk again. Its lead article celebrated Lomax's growing friendship with Mrs Jasmine Fitzwilliams. Under the heading: *Jasmine and Bobby: Official!* several column inches had been devoted to the couple.

Mr Bobby Lomax, the POUKI Secretary read for about the tenth time, *is a controversial City figure who has done a great deal to draw attention to the plight of the Lloyd's Names.*

Mrs Fitzwilliams is, of course, the widow of Andrew Fitzwilliams, the former Secretary of State for Defence. She has been a stranger to society ever since her husband's tragic death.

Mr Bobby Lomax is credited with encouraging her return to public view, first noticed when she accompanied him to a drinks party on the terrace of the House of Commons this summer. She has consistently called for an independent inquiry into the accident that claimed her husband's life.

The POUKI man drummed his fingers on the desk. Damn. Damn and double damn. If Lomax and Jasmine Fitzwilliams were not dealt with soonest, everything could come undone at different ends. The celebrity press was offering the pair profile – oxygen to their separate agendas.

As arranged, his colleague from Lloyd's dialled Bobby Lomax's employer later that afternoon. The man did not give his name but said a large slice of government business could come his way if Lomax were to be 'relieved' of his responsibilities. (He and the POUKI Secretary had agreed that if Bobby Lomax lost his job, his status would disappear, taking with it Jasmine Fitzwilliams' new found renown.)

'Delighted to be of service,' remarked Bobby's employer.

Aged forty-three, Bobby Lomax was made redundant in good conscience. His country demanded it. His loss of employment was buried in what was called 'down-sizing'.

Like countless others in the City, Bobby was given no time to clear his desk. In a daze, he handed back his company credit cards. In a daze, he asked for time to claim his expenses. In a daze, he walked the streets.

At 19.00 hrs, he arrived promptly at the Palmeira household. It was Jasmine's birthday and he was taking her for dinner with Vivienne Solomon and Jim Richards.

He waited for her in her mother's drawing-room. A large

marmalade cat, the latest in a long line, snoozed on the terrace outside. Suzie joined him moments later.

She had not welcomed his relationship with her daughter. On the other hand, she admitted he was amusing company. This, she acknowledged, was good for Jasmine.

Greeting him with a smile, she informed him with surprised good-humour it was not Jasmine's birthday. She did not add, but could have done, Jasmine never celebrated the occasion because it was also her wedding anniversary. Jasmine herself arrived before Bobby could answer.

Blowing her mother a kiss, she instructed her not to wait up. Half an hour later, they joined Vivienne Solomon and Jim Richards in the restaurant Bobby had booked. He entertained them as if he did not have a care in the world. They drank champagne all night.

Vivienne watched him with undisguised concern. She always knew when he was putting on an act. Ignoring her, he got progressively drunk. Eventually, his head sank down into his chest and he fell asleep.

Jasmine smiled. 'It's your birthday, Vivienne, isn't it?'

She nodded. It was the first time in as many years as she could recall, Bobby had remembered. In a manner of speaking.

She took him home. Half weeping, half in control, he told her he had not paid his mortgage in months. She listened in silence, making no judgement of him.

Money troubles, she knew, were seldom sudden. They accumulated assiduously over quite long periods. This was the disastrous situation in which Bobby found himself.

He was distraught. As she saw the raw and shocking detail

of his pain, Vivienne soothed him as best she could. He was enraged, frightened, bewildered and indignant.

The following day, he threw himself out of her apartment to fetch the newspapers so he could read the job pages. After this, he fixed up dozens of interviews and went from one executive search company to another. Whizzing around the place, he left no space for reflective work which meant he had no time to come to terms with what had happened. He was overwhelmed one moment by lingering, consuming anger and the next by deep depression.

As days became weeks, he lashed out at Vivienne constantly. Vitriol, abuse, rage poured off him like a constantly replenishing stream of venom. While he ate her food and accepted her money, he loathed everything about her. Their relationship was based on no more than his need for survival.

And she knew it.

CHAPTER THIRTY FOUR

�֎ ✺ ✖

The POUKI Secretary dialled Sir Peter Ligne. The latter had never been prosecuted. It would have caused a scandal at Whitehall's heart – as well as kept the death of Andrew Fitzwilliams in the public eye. All these years on, the POUKI called upon Ligne to assist whenever his 'posh' skills could be an advantage. This was one of those occasions.

Unbeknown to the still jobless Bobby Lomax, some of the Lloyd's Names were poised to offer him a job – the lifeline he needed. Recognising this would re-launch Bobby's public persona, the POUKI Secretary was anxious to get rid of him for good. Hitherto, the official had been successful in blocking even the possibility of his employment elsewhere.

The POUKI knew they would not be so lucky with a few of the Lloyd's Names. The latter had had their suspicions as to why Lomax had lost his job in the first place and, so they believed, had wised up to POUKI tricks. As a result, the POUKI Secretary had been asked to come up with a different ruse, this time guaranteeing Bobby left the country. Which was where Sir Peter Ligne came in.

As requested, Ligne contacted Bobby Lomax at Vivienne Solomon's the following day. Introducing himself as 'a friend of HMG's', he invited the former City man to his club. Bobby agreed with alacrity albeit little optimism. He had had too many disappointments to get his hopes up. He assumed on the eve of the general election, he was being called in to discuss Lloyd's again. The only dignity he had left was that he would never sell out the Names he had tried to assist.

One hour later, he found himself sitting in a corner of Ligne's club eating tea and muffins. He never knew about the job offer that came from some of the Lloyd's Names because it never arrived. As Ligne had observed many times before, the POUKI in the post office could be most efficient.

It did not take Bobby long to realise his meeting with Ligne had nothing to do with the Names. Following a leisurely warm-up – they swapped opinions on the progress of the general election campaign, agreeing Neil Kinnock would win – his host remarked, 'I understand, old boy, you might be interested in employment?'

Bobby tried hard not to look too keen. His heart, he knew, was pounding. 'I've got a couple of irons in the fire, at the moment, sir,' he lied. 'But I am always interested in talking other things through. What exactly did you have in mind?'

'Serving your country.'

Bobby gawped. Like so many of the unemployed, he had felt irrelevant, without identity or purpose, for so long it took a few moments for Ligne's words to sink in. Incredulous, he replied, 'In what way? That is to say, it would be an honour.'

Ligne scrutinised him with ostentatious regard, as if weighing him up. In that short time, understanding swept across Bobby's face.

'I'm hazarding a wild guess, sir, but do you mean in a clandestine capacity? I read in the press only the other day, the intelligence services were seeking to broaden their recruitment base.'

Ligne smiled, apparently delighted with Bobby's perspicacity. 'Good lad!'

Innocents, particularly desperate ones, were easily hooked. 'If you agree, you will not be able to discuss your work with anyone.'

'I understand, sir. What do you want me to do?'

Ligne told him.

'. . . The "dirty" money HMG is chasing is generated by Fitzwilliams International overseas. The company ought to have been closed down years ago but never was. A man called Ghazi El-Tarek wheedled his way into Mrs Fitzwilliams' affections and she passed the firm to him after her husband died.'

Bobby nodded. Jasmine had mentioned Ghazi El-Tarek. He had met him years before with Vivienne Solomon, when they had spent a day at the Chantilly racecourse with the El-Tarek family.

Passing him a briefing note, Ligne continued, 'What bothers HMG is that Fitzwilliams International seems to have moved into new territory. For this reason, it needs someone it can trust to go to Johannesburg . . .'

Skimming the document, Bobby raised a quizzical eyebrow.

'. . . HMG knows that with the help of officially appointed NATO suppliers in Canada, America and Germany, sanction busting firms have supplied armaments and chemicals for decades – via Fitzwilliams International – to, of all places, Iraq . . .'

Here, he added with a wry smile – a nod at Bobby's specific expertise – all the contracts had been insured at Lloyd's.

'. . . It appears the shipments go through South Africa. NATO is riddled with corruption.'

Bobby was fascinated. 'Do the Americans know?'

Ligne inclined his head. 'A Soviet spy, a man called General Stollen, told them. The general hit the headlines over a decade back following his seduction of Andrew Fitzwilliams' first wife, Belinda. He is also well known to Mrs Jasmine Fitzwilliams and her mother, with whom I understand you are acquainted.'

Bobby nodded.

Signalling the waiter to freshen the teapot, Ligne continued, 'Stollen used to visit the Italian Lakes with his real sweetheart. The latter was not aware he was running their affair as a cover while he checked up on NATO shipments from Italy!'

'What a bastard.'

'My thoughts exactly.'

Later that day, a cheerful Bobby Lomax boarded his flight to South Africa. Before leaving for the airport he left Vivienne Solomon a brief message telling her he had gone abroad on business. *Call you tonight from my hotel. See you when I get back. Thanks for everything*, he signed off in his usual breezy manner.

Vivienne smiled when she read it. She had watched Bobby suffer a thousand indignities as he looked for work and was relieved something had turned up. Accepting he would leave her the minute he was back on his feet, did not change anything. She loved him unconditionally.

She gave up waiting for his call at midnight and went to bed. Shortly after 02.00 hrs, she was disturbed by the telephone. Only half awake, she answered.

Ten days after the general election returning the Thatcher government to power, Bobby Lomax was found dead in the boot of a car in Johannesburg. Lying on his chest was General Nico Stollen's prospectus – complete with tortoise logo – of Fitzwilliams International East Germany.

Later that day, Vivienne flew out to South Africa to identify Bobby's body and bring it back for burial. Jim Richards MP accompanied her. Everyone but her was astonished by the laudatory obituaries and profiles that were written on him.

At his funeral, she paid tribute to Bobby's dignity and stoicism which was typical of his perverse combination of pride and courage, stubbornness and determination. She spoke of his wit, intelligence and the extent of his bounding optimism, mercurial energies and achievements. Few were surprised when she put her London apartment on the market and moved out of the capital.

Jasmine Fitzwilliams was too distraught to go to the service. Instead, she went to see Jim Richards MP prior to its start. He did not know how to calm her. She was claiming Bobby's death was directly connected to that of her husband's ten years before.

The press seemed to be on her side for once. *JASMINE* screamed billboards up and down the country. *BOBBY MURDERED. WAS ANDREW?*

POUKI officials – and various others – were dismayed. The slaying of Bobby Lomax had not been in the scheme of things. They genuinely did not know who had killed him.

Meanwhile, a bewildered Suzie tried to comfort her daughter. The latter, choking back her tears, wept, 'You don't understand. Bobby and I meant nothing to each other. If he cared for anybody, which he probably didn't, it was Vivienne. All Bobby and I were doing was using each other for different ends. And now he is dead.'

As soon as she could, Suzie telephoned Ghazi El-Tarek. He had problems of his own – the Bank of Credit and Commerce International had collapsed, taking a chunk of his fortune with it. However, as he said, everything was relative. Hearing her anxieties, he recommended they talk things through with the Masonic Grand Secretary Sir Richard Leystan.

One hour later, they slipped into Grand Lodge. The Grand Secretary saw them at once. 'You are here because of what Jasmine has been saying?' he murmured.

Suzie nodded. 'Bobby Lomax's death has knocked her sideways. Unless we stop her, she could force everything to blow up like a lit firecracker in a tinderbox,' she warned.

Fitzwilliams International unravelled as a result of the investigation into Bobby Lomax's murder. First, Customs and Excise moved against the company's proprietor Ghazi El-Tarek. Charges included the fact Fitzwilliams International had broken the arms embargo imposed on Iraq two years earlier, following Saddam Hussein's illegal invasion of Kuwait.

Ghazi was relaxed about things, not least because Grand Secretary Sir Richard Leystan, as well as Miro – knighted in the New Years Honours and now president of the British Board of Infrastructure – had made sworn statements absolving him of any misconduct associated with the firm. Their unequivocal joint statement declared Ghazi El-Tarek had 'purchased' Fitzwilliams International from Mrs Fitzwilliams after her husband's death at the request of HMG, had done so with taxpayers' money, and had remained in situ because the authorities had not known how to close it down. Supporting evidence included the fact that although Fitzwilliams International had been placed on a US Treasury sanctions black list, Ghazi El-Tarek had not.

It was to no avail. A law unto themselves, Customs and Excise charged Ghazi with fraud, expecting him to plead guilty. As a softening up exercise, it organised for a newspaper to run one of its longest profiles to date on a private individual. Ghazi El-Tarek was condemned for his arms-dealing, the large political donations he made, and the huge number of MPs, peers, civil servants and journalists he bankrolled or entertained.

With the exception of the Grand Secretary, Miro and Suzie Palmeira, Ghazi's 'friends' dropped away like flies. He was hurt, baffled and bewildered by the extent of the vilification. Unaccustomed to impotence, he ordered his solicitors to issue an immediate denial facing down the branch of the British executive which expected him to sink without trace. Their statement concluded: . . . *All Mr El-Tarek's activities have been at the behest of HMG and supervised by the British Board of Infrastructure.*

The media was prevented from publishing or broadcasting the Notice on the basis it contravened the Official Secrets Act. Unable to defend himself, Ghazi became public enemy number one. Wild rumours began to circulate about Fitzwilliams International.

The tortoise logo from the brochure found on Bobby Lomax's body turned up everywhere, a sort of media graffiti for corruption and murder. Although it was not said, it was implicit: Ghazi El-Tarek was either responsible for Bobby Lomax's death or knew who was. In addition, the public were reminded Ghazi had been the last person to see his one time business partner, Andrew Fitzwilliams, alive. Which is to say, he was being implicated in not one suspicious demise, but two.

At the height of Ghazi's battle to clear his name, Father Anthony crossed the Atlantic and visited Jasmine at her mother's request. Arriving at Suzie's comfortable home, he greeted the politician's widow with affection.

'You look tired child, although I am glad to see you have put on a little weight. It suits you.'

'Perhaps it is because I am pregnant, Father,' responded Jasmine. Leading the way into the garden, she added, 'I am not going to keep the baby.'

The priest reeled in disbelief. 'Whatever do you mean, my dear?'

'Exactly that.'

Terrible understanding dawned on his face. 'You are sure you want to have the infant adopted?' he asked, wilfully misunderstanding.

'I am going to have an abortion.'

Tears filled Father Anthony's eyes but he listened without accusation or condemnation. Jasmine had gone, she told him, to see Jim Richards MP on the morning of Bobby Lomax's funeral. They had ended up in bed together.

Their coupling had meant very little to either of them. Afterwards, Jim Richards had called her a taxi to take her home, while he escorted Vivienne to Bobby's vigil. One month after, Jasmine had discovered she was pregnant.

'So you are expecting a Christmas new-born,' remarked Father Anthony softly. As a child in Baghdad, he had lifted her on Christmas Night so she could see the Baby Jesus in his cradle.

Jasmine looked away. 'What difference does this make?'

It was the ultimate betrayal.

'Only you can know the answer to that.'

Jasmine and Jim Richards MP's daughter was born on Christmas Day.

CHAPTER THIRTY FIVE
✹ ✸ ✹

Customs and Excise soon recognised two things: Ghazi El-Tarek would never plead guilty; and, unless he did so, its case against him would not stick. Seeing its officers struggling, the POUKI tipped them off about Sir Peter Ligne's existence. As a result, they gleefully concluded they had a star witness – it would be Ligne's word against El-Tarek. Legal action proceeded accordingly.

On the eve of Ghazi's trial, Ligne read and re-read his notes. He had been rehearsed by Customs and Excise lawyers a thousand times. Now he was on his own again.

Ligne was tired, a shell of his former self. The irony of his situation did not escape him. He reached for the whisky. So. He was HMG's star witness against Ghazi El-Tarek.

He laughed. Ever since Andrew Fitzwilliams' death, Ligne had known he was on borrowed time. That Andrew Fitzwilliams' killer would come for him too. The only reason he had been spared thus far, Ligne had worked out long ago, had been because he could be useful to Ghazi.

After all, Ligne was the only person who could corroborate the evidence. And now here he was, the prosecution's sole witness against Ghazi. He had explained all this to Customs officials but they had not been listening. They did not take the threat to his life seriously.

Ligne gibbered and chattered. He appalled himself. This did

not stop him from topping up his glass again. He drank his whisky so quickly these days he no longer had time to admire its aroma or golden colour.

He used to love to watch it in the glass before tipping it down his throat. Now he merely drank. The same thoughts swirled around his brain.

If he was to go into court against Ghazi El-Tarek, Andrew Fitzwilliams' killer had no reason to keep him alive. In fact, he had been told so. Why else would a small jewelled tortoise have arrived in the post?'

He took another gulp of whisky. He had seen that damn tortoise before. It had been the day Jasmine and Andrew Fitzwilliams had told him they were getting married.

Jasmine. She had loved that tortoise. Just as she had loved Fitzwilliams. This had not protected Fitzwilliams. Fitzwilliams was dead. Jasmine could not save him.

He helped himself to another drink. Nico Stollen wanted Jasmine to marry Fitzwilliams. Stollen had expected Fitzwilliams to become Prime Minister. Well, she had married Fitzwilliams. Clever Nico.

Ligne screwed up his face. The priest refused to marry Jasmine and Fitzwilliams. What was the priest's name? Nico's friend. An American. Father Anthony. That's right. The American Jesuit had loved those fucking freemasons in Baghdad, those fucking Arabs and Jews. Had the fucking priest killed Fitzwilliams because of those fucking wogs?

Ligne slumped in his chair. On the floor beside him, on its brown paper wrapping, sat the tortoise. His mind was tortured by who had sent it. His head flopped on to his chest.

Nico Stollen sent the tortoise. No. Father Anthony did. Nico was a freemason. Maybe the freemasons sent the tortoise? Who else died? The Kurdish peasant, Peri. The daughter of the fucking Kurdish Warlord. Who loved that peasant sufficiently to murder Fitzwilliams? And the child. Leah. Samuel Solomon's youngest. She had been murdered too. Who had loved the fucking Jewish child so much Fitzwilliams had to die?

The tortoise was stolen just before Jasmine and Fitzwilliams married. Now, here it was again: Teasing, its pretty jewels twinkling. The tortoise was also the logo for Fitzwilliams International East Germany – Nico's company.

Ligne frowned. He wished he could remember why the tortoise meant so much to Nico. Suddenly, it came to him. It was that fucking Indian! Jiddu, they had called him. Jasmine's grandfather. Jiddu had been the tortoise-man. Nico had loved Jiddu.

Ligne remembered now. He had explained all this to Customs. Customs had laughed. 'Nobody's going to kill you,' its lawyers had assured him. They despised him. After Ghazi's trial, they would have no further use for him.

Ligne shuddered. He was an embarrassment. He knew what happened to embarrassments.

He switched on the television. It flickered into life. The only light on in his apartment. Outside, the rain crashed down. It was a bleak night. He helped himself to another drink. The tortoise stared back. Ligne shut his eyes.

Sometimes, in his dreams, Nico kissed him. Nico. Beloved Nico. Naughty Nico. Always playing games with him.

Suddenly, he chuckled. It was Nico who sent the tortoise. Of course it was. It was another of Nico's games – like bedding Belinda Fitzwilliams while he waited for Ligne in Italy. He wasn't going to die after all. Nico would come and get him. Then he would not have to testify against El-Tarek.

He rose. Unsteady on his feet, he opened another bottle. Nico loved whisky. It was his favourite. He would have another drink for Nico. Nico was coming back for him.

His mind was getting cloudy. He tried to sort it out. Nico loved him. Of course Nico loved him.

He was elated. Nico would come for him. Then he wouldn't be frightened. Nico would protect him. Then he wouldn't need to wonder who had killed Fitzwilliams.

There was a knock on the door. Opening it, Ligne pulled the shadow in from outside, feeling the cashmere of his overcoat. Smelling his smell. Nico's smell.

'My darling,' he sobbed, 'My darling. I knew. I always knew you would come for me.'

Sir Peter Ligne was found hanging in his apartment the following day. A jewelled tortoise glittered in the gloom.

Ghazi El-Tarek's trial opened at the Old Bailey in 1994, two years after he had been charged. Customs and Excise officials were jubilant even before its start – the 'sudden' death of their key witness was far too fortuitous an event for El-Tarek, they decided, for a jury not to be suspicious of him. For this reason, they did not ask for a postponement.

The unspoken rumour circulating was that while on trial for fraud, Ghazi was also implicated in Bobby Lomax's killing, as well as two other curious deaths: Those of Andrew Fitzwilliams and, now, Sir Peter Ligne. Grand Lodge meanwhile condemned the government's blanket use of gagging orders and its privilege from disclosure of documents.

In her black robes, Vivienne Solomon QC looked dramatic, her fine deportment enhanced by a head of thick chestnut red hair. Nature had bestowed upon her the only colour her character would allow – she habitually dressed in dark clothes. Nevertheless, these seldom managed to disguise her sparkle. In court, they set it off to best advantage.

She stared across at the Crown's QC and was pleased to see a tall, nervy looking man. Her client, Ghazi El-Tarek, sat nearby. He had the appearance, she noted with wry amusement, of being no more than an interested spectator at his own trial. He did not appear contrite, as a litigation lobbyist had recommended, nor was he humble, as a publicist had advised.

The court filled up by degrees. Ghazi El-Tarek's case had aroused national and international interest. Suddenly, everyone hurriedly stood as the judge's small procession entered. A short while later, Ghazi El-Tarek was sworn in.

'. . . Ghazi Abdullah El-Tarek. How do you plead: Guilty or not guilty?'

'Not guilty.'

Everything now seemed a little unreal but Ghazi felt better than he had in weeks, perhaps in relief at having been able to get into action at last. The Crown's QC rose in a leisurely way. He went on to give an outline of the defendant's activities. This bore little similarity to the truth.

Four days later, Ghazi was finally in the witness box. Now familiar with the court, he appeared relaxed. A striking, immaculately dressed figure.

'Do you acknowledge, Mr El-Tarek, you were aware Fitzwilliams International traded with Iraq throughout the Gulf War?' queried his barrister, Vivienne Solomon.

'Of course. HMG gave it permission to do so.'

Vivienne offered the jury a glimpse into his world. 'Do you fund any political activities, Mr El-Tarek?'

'Some, certainly. Originally because I hoped it would assist in my acquisition of British nationality.'

'Did it?'

Ghazi chuckled. 'No'.

'You are, I understand, a major donor to the government party?'

'I have, in the past, donated to the Conservatives.'

'And this is how you met Andrew Fitzwilliams, the former proprietor of Fitzwilliams International and late Secretary of State for Defence? Is it true to say you deliberately courted him with the long term view of controlling his company?'

'Rubbish. As you are aware, all ministers of the Crown have to give up their commercial interests once they accept appointment. In view of this, Andrew asked me to take over Fitzwilliams International. And incidentally, I did not 'court' him. If anything, it was the other way around.'

'You entertained the late Mr Fitzwilliams lavishly?'

'I entertained – lavishly, as you put it – countless politicians, civil servants and journalists and did so until recently. They expected it.'

'Such entertainment, Mr El-Tarek, could be construed as an attempt to corrupt . . .'

'They required no encouragement.'

'What did you gain by socialising with Mr Fitzwilliams?'

Ghazi looked at Vivienne in astonishment. 'Fitzwilliams was attached to the Ministry of Defence – first as a lowly parliamentary private secretary, subsequently its Secretary of State! Why does any businessman socialise with politicians? I was happy to do so because of Andrew's political and executive connections. Moreover, his business interests complimented my own.'

'Did you entertain the late Sir Peter Ligne – also connected with Fitzwilliams International – too?'

Ghazi nodded. 'Civil servants in powerful positions are always useful.'

'Did you know Sir Peter Ligne worked for MI6?'

'It was common knowledge.'

'Were you surprised to learn he was to give evidence against you?'

'No. Nothing surprises me about betrayal.'

'How did you meet Sir Peter?'

'He met me. I was a student in Paris at the time.'

'He groomed you.'

'I was willing.'

Journalists in the press box noticed even the judge was listening to the exchanges between Vivienne and her client with rapt attention.

Oblivious to their scrutiny, Vivienne continued, 'Did you consider Ligne corrupt?'

'Yes.'

'Were his colleagues in British public service similarly so?'

Ghazi considered his reply. 'No. Only Ligne. The problem honourable civil servants have in Britain is that with a man like Sir Peter around, honest people are encouraged to be dishonest. Those who resist can damage their careers.'

'Did you consider Andrew Fitzwilliams a crook?'

'He became one, certainly – Ligne corrupted him. Britain's political system has always been open to venality. This has tarnished the reputation of those who behave impeccably.'

'By extrapolation, you mean espionage and government are . . .'

'Wherever your question is leading, Miss Solomon,' Ghazi cut her off with a laugh, 'Is no place for me! I am a businessman. I do not get involved in spying or politics. In my experience, those who do so, never had a business to start with . . .'

The jury was fascinated. Its members had expected Vivienne Solomon to concentrate on the fraud charges laid against her client: Dull, technical arguments. Instead, they were being treated to a comprehensive review of the inner workings of the British state.

Their collective gasp was audible when she took them all – including her client – with her next surprise. 'You hated Ligne and Fitzwilliams, didn't you, Mr El-Tarek?'

'Of course I did!' replied Ghazi, years of disgust crashing out of him. 'Because of them, two lovely young girls – Leah and Peri – died in a palace of the damned called Abu Ghraib. Nobody will have heard of it. It is one of Saddam Hussein's filthy hellholes. One day, Inshallah, it will be destroyed. However, none of this has anything to do with my case.'

At this point, Vivienne stopped the court proceedings and asked that its record state the 'Leah' to whom Ghazi El-Tarek had referred, had been her first cousin, Leah Solomon.

Turning once more to her client, she admonished, 'I think, Mr El-Tarek, you should let me decide what is or is not relevant to your defence. Now then, perhaps you would tell us about Peri. Why did she die?'

Accepting the reproof, Ghazi replied, 'She had documentary evidence about Fitzwilliams International's conduct. For this reason, Ligne and Fitzwilliams had her deported – they blamed the Home Office.'

'This does not mean they can be held responsible for her death.'

Momentarily, Ghazi lost his self control again. His face reddening, he retorted, 'So far as I am concerned, they murdered Peri as surely as if their soiled hands snapped her beautiful neck. They knowingly sent her to her doom because Fitzwilliams International was not a prize they wished to lose.'

Vivienne Solomon gave him a few moments to compose himself.

'Are you aware, Mr El-Tarek that Mrs Jasmine Fitzwilliams, widow of Andrew Fitzwilliams, claims that Sir Douglas Miro, former chief executive of a Fitzwilliams International subsidiary, had a tendre for Peri whom you say Ligne and Andrew Fitzwilliams had deported?'

Ghazi El-Tarek smiled. 'Yet again, Miss Solomon, I cannot see how this is relevant to my circumstances, nor the crime of which I am accused.'

The Crown's QC and the judge appeared to agree. Vivienne Solomon however assured them her questions were germane to Fitzwilliams International.

'Please answer the question, Mr El-Tarek.'

Annoyed, Ghazi responded, 'Sir Douglas Miro is sixty-seven years old. In the course of a long life, Jasmine Fitzwilliams – whom I have known since she was a child – cannot possibly know for whom Sir Douglas has, or has not, had a tendre as you put it.'

'Are you aware of an interview Laure de Chebran gave to a celebrity magazine last month, in which she mentions Sir Douglas Miro and Peri?'

Puzzled, Ghazi shook his head. Retrieving it from her briefcase, Vivienne Solomon read aloud to the court: *Princesse Laure de Chebran admits Sir Douglas Miro loved the Warlord's daughter Peri. She recalled that Colonel Nico Stollen – subsequently promoted to general – had first pointed this out while watching Miro dance with the young woman in Baghdad.*

Princesse Laure said, 'In those days, Iraq was a wonderful circus of diplomatic and private parties. My late husband Freddie de Chebran christened Miro "L'Ecossais Noir". The "Black Scot". Miro was magnificent – he so dark, Peri so fair.

'Freddie said they did justice to the beauty of the night. As for Peri, all she ever dreamed about was developing the north of Iraq into a ski resort so the children of Abraham could whiz down the mountains together. Kurdistan was so beautiful. It had wonderful wild streams and pure mountain air. It was a long time ago.

'... After her father was murdered, Peri visited Britain to raise the issue of Fitzwilliams International with the British govern-

ment. She hoped to set Miro free from the company. This act of kindness led to her death: I do not believe Miro ever forgave Sir Peter Ligne or Andrew Fitzwilliams for their part in this.'

Princesse Laure is to marry Sir Douglas Miro in the spring.

'Was Sir Douglas Miro in love with Peri, Mr El-Tarek?'

Ghazi consistently refused to answer the question, as Vivienne knew he would. She noted with satisfaction the jury were on his side now – the five women approved his discretion, the men empathised for the same reason. Suddenly, he was no longer a 'foreign businessman', an 'Arab', an 'Iraqi', or a 'Muslim', but a man doing his best to protect the reputations of those unable to defend themselves.

Accepting the judge would not allow her indefinite licence, Vivienne continued, 'Following Secretary of State Andrew Fitzwilliams' death, did you not think it odd that Jasmine Fitzwilliams, despite being her husband's sole heir, waived all claim to his company in your favour?'

Ghazi looked embarrassed. 'This was not my business. HMG organised Fitzwilliams International's purchase.'

'You paid the market price for it?'

'No. The taxpayer did.'

'Since that time, Mr El-Tarek, all Fitzwilliams International's contracts have been with government?'

'Yes. The contracts were always negotiated by British or American public servants.'

'And what about its East European subsidiary?'

'So far as I am aware, this is in the hands of East European public servants. I should say, however, I had absolutely no idea of any NATO connection until Bobby Lomax's tragic death.'

'How is it, Mr El-Tarek, you have no proof of what you claim to be a long association with government?'

Ghazi took the question in his stride. 'When Douglas Miro "ran" the Fitzwilliams International subsidiary, the only person with any corroborating paperwork was Peri. When I took over the whole shooting-match, Sir Peter Ligne cautioned me to keep no documentation. As a government company, Fitzwilliams International did not need to submit audited accounts to the Inland Revenue. The only records that existed were those pertaining to the Fitzwilliams International account at the Bank of Credit and Commerce International. The latter has since gone bust expunging the data in the process.'

'BCCI was encouraged to handle Fitzwilliams International?'

'Certainly. The company was looked after by a special BCCI office which had a trading arm in Geneva. This in turn had a Bahamian subsidiary with offices just outside the gates of the exclusive Lyford Cay complex.'

Vivienne raised an expressive eyebrow. 'And this special office was known to HMG?'

Ghazi shook his head. 'Not necessarily. Parts of HMG know one thing, other parts another. I would say BCCI's "special" office was known to parts of HMG. Not to HMG as a whole.'

'Do you think General Nico Stollen is to blame for the corruption uncovered at Fitzwilliams International?'

'No. Nico is first and foremost a Soviet spy. He is retired now, of course. His sole aim was to destabilise the West. He behaved with the utmost propriety in all matters financial and had no interest in money.'

'Did the Russian Mafia get involved in Fitzwilliams International as is claimed?'

'You will have to ask General Stollen.'

'Do you believe General Stollen was manipulating Fitzwilliams International and in consequence you and others, such as the Americans?'

'He was certainly closely involved with the East German subsidiary. The Americans played straight into his hands. He never manipulated me: I was a willing party.'

'Did he murder Andrew Fitzwilliams?'

The judge was furious with the question and prevented Ghazi El-Tarek from answering. The Crown's QC, milking the moment for all it was worth, similarly made strong objection but overplayed his hand. Vivienne stood her ground maintaining the case against her client should have been stopped – the judge privately agreed – and Ghazi El-Tarek not subjected to a well-orchestrated character assassination via media in the meantime.

'My client is on trial for fraud,' she said with crisp authority. 'The Crown has seen to it he is also in essence accused of murder. If the Crown wanted to avoid sensitive subjects, it should not have subliminally used them against Mr El-Tarek in the first place by means of off-the-record press briefings.'

The judge grudgingly dismissed the Crown's objections but put Vivienne Solomon on notice she behave herself. This did not stop her from repeating her question.

'I asked, Mr El-Tarek, whether General Stollen murdered Andrew Fitzwilliams?'

'You will have to ask the General.'

'And what about Sir Douglas Miro whom we discussed at some length earlier?'

Ghazi was outraged by the suggestion. Accepting he would not answer, Vivienne allowed his peers a final glimpse into his character. 'What, Mr El-Tarek, would you say was your greatest vice?'

'My greed.'

'Your greatest virtue?'

'My lack of hypocrisy. HMG has that monopoly.'

'You are known to be a generous donor to British charities.'

Ghazi looked momentarily confused. 'It is easy for a rich man to be generous,' he replied.

The Masonic Grand Secretary Sir Richard Leystan was Vivienne Solomon's penultimate witness. On being sworn in, she presented him with an obviously heavy tome. 'For the benefit of the Crown, Grand Secretary, would you kindly identify what I have handed you.'

His clear authoritative voice rang out. 'The first volume of the duplicate archives of Royal Arch. Each page has been authenticated, witnessed and date stamped . . .'

- The judge threw out the Crown's submission the files endangered national security -

'. . . It concerns the freemasons of Iraq.'

'You say duplicate archives. What happened to the originals?'

'They were sent out of the country some years ago. They have now been restored to Grand Lodge. They cannot be used in Mr El-Tarek's defence because their contents are covered by the Official Secrets Act. Those you have were provided by kind permission of the Grande Loge Nationale de France.'

The judge peered at the Grand Secretary in apparent amazement. 'Am I to take it, Sir Richard, British and French freemasons are co-operating?'

The Grand Secretary laughed. 'This is certainly a possibility, Your Worship. A more likely explanation could be that the French would be more than delighted if our intelligence services were embarrassed. Sometimes opposing interests coalesce.'

The archives proved beyond any doubt, the activities of Fitzwilliams International had been known of and approved for decades.

'Would you cast your mind back, Grand Secretary, to the weeks preceding Andrew Fitzwilliams' death,' continued Vivienne Solomon.

The judge frowned.

'... According to your archived records, you held a meeting at Grand Lodge. Some of the country's leading freemasons were present. The written account suggests Andrew Fitzwilliams' future, and that of his company, were decided on this occasion.'

The Grand Secretary bowed his head. 'It was,' he admitted, as if, even today, he found it incredible, 'Like a madhatter's tea-party. Everything about that discussion was mad.'

'And it was at this ... tea party ...' continued Vivienne, 'That it was decided Ghazi El-Tarek would purchase Fitzwilliams

International on behalf of HMG after Andrew Fitzwilliams' death?'

'Yes.'

Vivienne knew she had to keep the Grand Secretary in the witness-box until lunch. She could not bring in her final witness until the jury had had a break. Risking the judge's wrath a final time, she manufactured another question.

'Are you aware, Sir Richard, Mrs Jasmine Fitzwilliams has long maintained that at the time of her husband's death, her evidence was blocked by a Masonic conspiracy?'

'Yes.'

'Was it?'

The Grand Secretary's expression was impossible to read. 'At the time of Andrew Fitzwilliams' death, Mrs Fitzwilliams was in a highly emotional state. The police who investigated . . .'

Looking at her wristwatch surreptitiously, Vivienne interrupted, 'They were freemasons?'

- It was well-known the freemasons were deeply entrenched in Britain's police force -

The Grand Secretary signalled his assent. '. . .Took this into account, when they heard her evidence. Mrs Fitzwilliams was interviewed on no less than three occasions. Following this, the police took the view that what she had to say could not be supported nor did it materially alter the circumstances or history of events.'

Shortly thereafter, he admitted Grand Lodge had been responsible for ensuring Jasmine Fitzwilliams' understanding of the last hours of her husband's life had not been covered in the national press. This, he claimed, was for Mrs Fitzwilliams' 'sole benefit'.

Vivienne Solomon posed her final query. 'Are many journalists freemasons, Sir Richard?'

'Yes.'

The court rose for lunch moments later. As always, Vivienne's timing was impeccable.

CHAPTER THIRTY SIX

❋ ❀ ❋

O LD BAILEY, LONDON: It was the eighth day of Ghazi El-Tarek's trial. Vivienne Solomon called her final witness. She had no way of knowing how the jury would react nor what conclusions it would draw. However, its members had had a decent break and were following the case with evident attention. They looked at Vivienne with interest as a tall, well built man made his way through the courtroom, smiling at her as he passed.

It was widely expected to be General Nico Stollen. Ghazi El-Tarek was the first to realise it was not. He stared at Vivienne in astonishment. The man seemed oblivious to the stir he was causing. Shortly after, he was sworn in.

'Would you please give the court your full name.'

'Robert James Lomax. Known as Bobby.'

A ripple went around the courtroom. The Crown Prosecutor looked at his colleagues in disbelief. Lomax? Bobby Lomax was alive?

As soon as the lawyer had pulled himself together, he raised an objection. The judge dismissed it. The 'ambush' – and Bobby Lomax's appearance in court was certainly this – was a legitimate part of a criminal trial. For the time being at least.

'Your address, Mr Lomax?'

Bobby gave it in a crisp clear voice. 'Courtenay Square, Sussex.'

Vivienne Solomon coughed. 'If I may interrupt, My Lord. I would like it known the address Mr Lomax has given is also my own.'

The judge raised an eyebrow. Vivienne Solomon looked embarrassed. A huge grin spread across Bobby's face. Despite – or maybe because of – the circumstances, her discomfit delighted him. He made no attempt to conceal his affection.

Ghazi El-Tarek chuckled. Only Bobby Lomax could have the nerve to flirt with Vivienne Solomon in court. Or anywhere else come to that.

The couple's eyes locked. In the two years they had lived together, they had come to understand each other on a deep level and what they had established worked. A few minutes later, Bobby began his evidence.

He explained he specialised in financial services and pursuant to this had been sent to South Africa by the late Sir Peter Ligne. Following a brief interruption from the judge wishing to clarify a technical issue, he continued, '. . . Once arrived in Jo'burg, I followed the insurances. Wherever I looked, I found evidence of Fitzwilliams International's corruption. Its stuff was being shipped everywhere. Iraq. Iran. Serbia.

'In addition, everyone, it seemed, was using the company. The Brits. The Americans. The Indians. Even the Chinese. No wonder it could not be shut down. It was surreal. An organisation that did not exist could not be closed because so many were involved.

'By the time I rumbled the NATO connection, I was really worried. I had no official status and felt immensely vulnerable. The Americans, I discovered, had been covering up the NATO scam for years.'

'What, in particular, was the NATO scam?'

Bobby took a deep breath. 'The Mafia on the one hand.'

'And on the other?'

'High explosives, rocket launchers, hand grenades designed to maim and kill, high powered machine guns ...'

'And these armaments came from NATO and were supplied to Iraq via Fitzwilliams International?'

'Not everything went to Iraq.'

'You are referring to the supplies that were diverted to the countries of the former Yugoslavia?'

Bobby stared straight ahead. 'Yes. I am also saying Fitzwilliams International was exceptionally well placed to meet any foreseeable requirements of most terrorist groups, including the IRA.'

'The IRA, Mr Lomax?' repeated Vivienne Solomon, for emphasis.

Bobby nodded. 'This is the NATO scam the Americans have been trying to hide. While most IRA weapons came from Eastern Europe and Arab leaders such as Colonel Gaddafi of Libya, some have been from NATO countries...'

He paused. '... Which is to say, Fitzwilliams International, along with a few renegade American and British public servants, have been supplying the IRA for decades. Fitzwilliams International's ledger for its NATO accounts was held by a subsidiary office of BCCI.'

'And what happened after you discovered all this, Mr Lomax?'

'I was very, very frightened. I was alone in a foreign country. However, when I got back to my hotel room, I was astonished to find General Stollen there. And even more amazed when he told me the Masonic Grand Secretary, Sir Richard Leystan – who gave evidence earlier today – had sent him.'

'Did you trust General Stollen?'

'Not in the beginning, no. Sir Peter Ligne had mentioned him in disparaging terms.'

'Why did you change your mind?'

Bobby laughed. 'Stollen told me to telephone you! He knew you were the only person I trusted.'

Smiling, Vivienne turned to the judge. 'The record should state, My Lord, that for many years, and with the assistance of the freemasons of Grand Lodge, Nico Stollen funded – which is to say, with KGB money – the Concert of Rights when it was a small, local charity. I am associated with this organisation.'

She continued, 'How did the Masonic Grand Secretary know you were in trouble, Mr Lomax?'

'Stollen told him. He had requested the Russian embassy in London keep an eye on me when my friendship with Mrs Jasmine Fitzwilliams became public. The man still tailing me knew Sir Peter Ligne had put me on a flight to South Africa and contacted General Stollen. The latter telephoned the Grand Secretary immediately . . .'

He took a sip of water. ' . . . At his request, the General flew out to South Africa to be with me.'

'From where?'

'Moscow. The Grand Secretary believed Stollen to be the best man to extricate me from the circumstances in which I found myself. I will always be profoundly grateful to him and the Masonic fraternity who made such protection possible.'

'Did General Stollen know Fitzwilliams International was supplying weapons to the IRA?'

'Yes. He had taunted the Americans about it for decades.'

'What happened next?'

'Stollen took me to the airport and told me to head for home on the false papers he had provided . . .'

– The Court recorder again inserted Miss Solomon's address –

' . . . In addition, he gave me a letter with what he called my "instructions" which I was not to open until I landed. I did as he asked. It was only when I arrived at Heathrow I realised what he had done.'

'Which was what?'

Bobby took a deep breath. 'General Stollen had taken his own life, placing my passport in his pocket.'

'Nico Stollen is dead?'

'Yes.'

'What were his instructions?'

Bobby looked at her neutrally. 'You and Jim Richards MP were to identify "my" body.'

The judge looked at Vivienne askance. 'Does your witness mean, Miss Solomon, you and Mr Richards knowingly identified General Stollen's body as that of Bobby Lomax?'

'Yes,' replied Vivienne without dissembling. 'For this reason, Mr Richards will stand down from Parliament at the next election in a few months time. I am similarly resigning from the bar after my present commitments have completed.'

'How contrite of you.'

The judge leaned forwards, his curiosity getting the better of him. 'Am I expected to believe, Moscow did not notice one of its generals was missing?' he queried.

For the first time, Vivienne hesitated. 'Nico Stollen was retired, My Lord. Given the break-up of the Soviet state, he believed it would be easy for him to slip away.'

'You know this or are guessing?'

'It is what he told Father Anthony. The Father was the only person General Stollen telephoned to say "adieu". The dismemberment and attendant corruption of the Soviet Union depressed him and he was pleased to go. He wanted it reconstituted.

'In the meantime, he could not bear the the fact countless Soviet citizens were living in poverty – he was trying to help as many as he could. Because of this, he was in some difficulty himself and too proud to ask his friends in the West for financial help.'

'Would they have assisted?'

'Assuredly.'

Shaking his head, the judge motioned Vivienne to continue.

Holding Bobby's eye, she queried, 'And Stollen's other instructions, Mr Lomax?'

'These concerned Sir Peter Ligne. General Stollen believed it would be only a matter of time before Ghazi El-Tarek was charged with the Fitzwilliams International conspiracy and that, in consequence, Sir Peter Ligne would be forced to testify against him.

'In view of this, Stollen asked that I remain hidden until Ghazi's trial, whenever it happened. The General was anxious about my safety – Peri's death many years before was due to the fact she could embarrass people about Fitzwilliams International.

'Given the embarrassment my own evidence could cause the British and American governments, Stollen did not trust the authorities to guarantee my security. He told me to reveal myself to Peter Ligne on the trial's eve.'

'Why?'

'He hoped I could persuade Ligne not to give evidence against Ghazi.'

'And did you see Peter Ligne?'

'Yes.'

'When?'

'On the evening he died. It was as if he had been expecting me. Or rather, Stollen. I was wearing Stollen's overcoat. He pulled me inside to embrace me. Once he realised I was not Stollen, he collapsed. "If you are alive", he wept, "It must mean Nico is dead".

'I confirmed this. Ligne went to pieces. Literally to pieces. His disintegration was complete when I told him the General had taken his own life to save mine. "NO! NO!" he screamed. "Nico would not die for you. He would only die for me". It was only then that Ligne truly accepted Stollen had never loved him. It destroyed him.

'I left about half-an-hour later. Stollen's trick, I knew, had worked. There was no way Ligne would be in a fit mental state to give evidence the following day. I did not realise he intended to take his own life but it did not surprise me.'

'You are sure it was suicide and not murder?'

'Quite sure.'

'Do you know anything about the jewelled tortoise found beside Sir Peter Ligne's body?'

'Yes. Stollen told me to post a small parcel to Ligne to arrive before Ghazi's trial. He gave it to me when I left South Africa. I did as I was instructed.

'I did not know its significance until Ligne showed it to me. He was distraught. The tortoise belonged to Mrs Jasmine Fitzwilliams. Stollen expressed the wish that one day it be returned to her. This has since been done. Jasmine had its jewels auctioned for charity.'

'Was it Stollen who stole the tortoise from Mrs Fitzwilliams in the first place?'

'I believe so, yes. Certainly, this is what Mrs Fitzwilliams herself suspected for many years.'

'Did General Stollen speak to you in detail about Andrew Fitzwilliams death?'

Bobby hesitated. 'Yes,' he replied, a few moments later. 'In addition, he gave me a letter and notebook.

'He asked me to pass the former to Father Anthony, the latter to his one-time CIA handler Betsy Meredith, now Congresswoman Betsy Meredith. He explained that before Miss Meredith went into politics, she served with the CIA, followed by a stint in the then President's private office. She was well briefed on Fitzwilliams International.'

'What did Stollen's letter and notebook say?'

'As requested, I did not read them.'

'Did he give you anything else?'

Bobby smiled. 'His silver cigarette case. He asked me to give it to Father Anthony. Stollen said he had spent his life trying to tempt him to take up smoking again!'

Laughter rippled around the court. Vivienne pressed on.

'Did General Stollen make any comment about Mrs Fitzwilliams' claims?'

'He said she was telling the truth.'

'Did he implicate Ghazi El-Tarek in Andrew Fitzwilliams' death?'

'Certainly not.'

'What did Stollen say about the charges he believed would be levelled against Ghazi El-Tarek?'

'That he expected better from the British. Stollen did not like bullies and thought this was what the British had become.'

General Nico Stollen was a posthumous hero the minute Bobby Lomax left the witness box. Come the early evening news, he was being referred to as 'James Bondski'. With tacit agreement, the British press made no mention of Stollen's previous infamy, including the part he had played in the destruction of Belinda Fitzwilliams' life.

Father Anthony accepted questions about him on the steps of the Old Bailey. Flanked by Grand Secretary Sir Richard Leystan and Vivienne Solomon QC, he described the Russian as 'the Quick-Silver of the world'.

' . . . Above all else, Nico despised corruption. He was as appalled by the nomenklatura of the former Soviet empire seizing its assets, as he was by venality in Britain or America. The only thing Nico got wrong was his belief he could slip away. He could not . . .'

Grasping for the right words, and looking faintly embarrassed when he had discovered them, Father Anthony continued, 'Nico's friends loved him dearly. I did not realise I was one of them until he died.'

Responding to further media queries, the American Jesuit willingly conceded Stollen had been responsible for terrible deeds. He continued, 'However, Nico also tried to put things right. I do not mourn him, because he did not mourn himself. Nevertheless, not a day passes when I do not miss him.'

Turning around, he saw Bobby Lomax waiting for Vivienne. 'Stollen did not want you to pray for him, you know,' commented Bobby quietly. 'He said it would be a gross violation of his privacy.'

Father Anthony nodded.

Later that night, General Stollen's body was flown to Moscow. Come the weekend, he was given a state funeral. The Soviet people whom he had served with the utmost loyalty lined the streets.

Miro escorted Laure de Chebran and Suzie. Ghazi El-Tarek – allowed to leave Britain on a forty-eight hour pass – walked with Jasmine and Congresswoman Betsy Meredith. Bobby comforted Vivienne: There were two red roses – for her cousin Leah and Peri – on the general's coffin.

Father Anthony declined to walk behind the hearse – it was drawn by a gun carriage. Instead, in a quiet corner of a Moscow park, he planted a lemon tree. Here, he buried Stollen's cigarette case – it was still full of his favourite brand.

The priest chuckled. As Stollen had himself said, even now, at the very end, he had tried to put temptation in his way.

Removing one of Stollen's Sobranie's, he patted the soil around the plant to keep it warm. At Stollen's request, he did not pray for him. Instead, he commended him to Our Lord – a neat American trick which he thought would amuse Stollen's spirit.

Lighting the cigarette, Father Anthony watched its smoke spiral into the air. Taking pleasure in its smell for a final time, he paid his last respects. When it had finished burning, he rubbed the ashes of Stollen's tobacco into the earth.

Ghazi El-Tarek joined him as darkness fell. Turning in the direction of Mecca, he prayed for the men Stollen had loved – Abdullah, Jiddu, Samuel, the Warlord, as well as a British public servant, Grand Secretary Sir Julian Lawrence.

In sombre mood, he and Father Anthony returned to the rest of the funeral party. Stollen's absence left them all feeling bereft. Later that night, Father Anthony accompanied Stollen's body on its final journey.

Bobby, Vivienne, the Congresswoman, Jasmine, Miro, Laure and Suzie stood in the Moscow rain to watch them leave. Stollen's former colleagues formed the honour-guard. Those in uniform saluted as the coffin was loaded on to the private jet Ghazi had chartered.

It arrived at its destination as the sun came up. The beautiful Mediterranean sea shimmered in the dawn. Soon, the plane swung inland. As it flew over the holy Mount of Olives, it dipped its wings. Stollen had asked Father Anthony to take him home. A secular man, he was a Jewish prince returning to the land of his fathers.

As Stollen had wished, no prayers were said. However, the stonemasons of Grand Lodge carved his headstone. Its inscription read:

STOLLEN
SINNER, BROTHER, FRIEND

CHAPTER THIRTY SEVEN

※ ✤ ※

While Father Anthony led the mourners at Stollen's funeral, the judge presiding over Ghazi El-Tarek's trial retired for the weekend. He took with him the Fitzwilliams International file. Once the court proceedings were over, he would have to decide whether or not to instruct the police to re-open their investigation into Andrew Fitzwilliams' death.

The issue was sensitive in view of the fact an intelligence services oversight committee was to be established in the Autumn. In anticipation of this, Sir Douglas Miro had been raised to the peerage. He had divested himself of his commercial interests – including the sale of Douglas Miro International – to become its founding chairman. To the consternation of some, Jasmine Fitzwilliams had already intimated she would encourage the new committee to look into her husband's case.

The judge flicked through the dossier with interest. It contained a mix of old press cuttings and annotated intelligence reports. Andrew Fitzwilliams had been the golden boy of British politics.

Rumours about the circumstances of his accident had circulated the minute it had been discovered he died when his car's fuel line, joining the tank to the engine, ignited. (A design fault, the judge understood, which had since been corrected.) A hand-written note dated June 1982 was attached to a brief report praising Ghazi El-Tarek's discreet handling of

Fitzwilliams International following the 'event'. *Much appreciated by HMG*, the scrawl read.

A further note indicated Ghazi El-Tarek had again been helpful. Jasmine Fitzwilliams was described as 'distraught' at the time. An article, out of chronological order, headed: *Minister's Widow Leads Mourners,* came next.

Mrs Fitzwilliams, the journalist had written twelve years before, *was escorted into church by Father Anthony who had flown from his home in the United States. Behind them were Mrs Fitzwilliams' parents, Mr and Mrs Philippe Palmeira, and Mr and Mrs Ghazi El-Tarek. Flanking them were two senior Masonic officers.*

The church was decorated with lemon trees cultivated by Sir Douglas Miro at his home in the Highlands. Sir Douglas, president of the British Board of Infrastructure, was accompanied by Madame La Princesse Laure de Chebran, widow of His Excellency Freddie de Chebran, the former French ambassador to Iraq and Czechoslovakia. General Nico Stollen, representing the Russian ambassador, also attended.

Father Anthony's funeral address was attached. '*May the love of Christ*', it read, '*victorious over sin and death, grant everyone the courage of forgiveness and reconciliation without which there can be no solutions worthy of man.*

'*... But what of the man who did not know there was anything to forgive and became king?*

'*Pray for him all the more ...*'

Next in the file came a series of photographs. The judge looked at them with interest. Several were of Jasmine Fitzwilliams and Bobby Lomax. Others showed the

Fitzwilliams' on their wedding day, the Fitzwilliams' with the El-Tarek family, and Andrew Fitzwilliams with Ghazi El-Tarek and several dignitaries from Lloyd's of London. Another showed Nico Stollen flirting with Laure de Chebran.

The penultimate item in the file was an undated note from the then British intelligence chief. It stated: *It is to be hoped with the upcoming first anniversary of the Prince of Wales' marriage to the former Lady Diana Spencer, the press and public will lose interest in the Fitzwilliams case. Active steps to discredit Mrs Jasmine Fitzwilliams are in hand.*

Finally, there was a brief note dated a month ago to the effect no obituary of Sir Peter Ligne would be authorised.

The judge sighed. It was dark outside and raining hard. Reaching for the telephone, he dialled the Masonic Grand Secretary Sir Richard Leystan. They chatted briefly. The senior freemason had been expecting his call.

'I have no doubt, Judge, one of my predecessors – Sir Julian Lawrence – and his driver were murdered by the POUKI.'

'What year?'

'1968.'

Considering the issue, the judge finally remarked, 'It is a long time ago, Sir Richard. Can anything really be served by asking the police to open an inquiry?'

'Sir Julian's driver was blamed. It would be nice for the family to know he was innocent.'

'In my experience, his loved ones will know this already.'

The Grand Secretary coughed. 'There is another matter, My Lord: Belinda Fitzwilliams and her aborted child. The doctor concerned . . .'

Anticipating him, the judge interrupted, 'At this late stage, it would be impossible to prosecute, Sir Richard. You must know this. There is not enough evidence.'

Closing the matter with detached humility, the judge asked the Grand Secretary to visit him at his earliest convenience. He wished to examine Sir Richard further on the Masonic Archives to which he had provided testimony in court. The Grand Secretary was with him some half an hour later.

Reminding him he was still under oath, the judge remarked, 'I understand the common denominator in the Fitzwilliams-Ligne affair is the fate of the Iraqi freemasons, in particular the deaths of Jiddu Palmeira, Samuel Solomon, Abdullah El-Tarek and a Kurdish tribal leader known as the Warlord?'

The Grand Secretary shook his head. 'No Judge,' he corrected. 'The common denominator is that Jiddu Palmeira and Samuel Solomon wanted papers.'

'Papers, Sir Richard?'

'Yes. Papers. Men wanting travel documents for their children so they could send them to safety. We must never forget that at the time – to protect their families – Jiddu and Samuel had joined the Communist party in Baghdad. Meanwhile, because he was Jewish, Samuel had been forced to carry yellow identity documents.

'The assistance Grand Lodge tried to give the men was one of my fraternity's finest hours. Regrettably, we – by which I mean the then Grand Secretary Sir Julian Lawrence, and through no fault of his own – failed. Similarly, we must remember that Abdullah El-Tarek, Ghazi's father, and the Kurd known as the Warlord, both of whom were Muslim, grieved at what was happening to their Iraqi Christian and Jewish Brothers.'

He removed three black and white snaps from his wallet.

'You had better put these with the file, Judge. Father Anthony gave them to me – he explained whom everybody was. He found them in Stollen's cigarette case.'

In one, two little girls were pictured running towards the camera, holding hands. Another showed a striking blond. The third caught a large happy group, including the young woman and the children pictured previously.

'The old man with the outstretched arms is Jasmine Fitzwilliams' grandfather, Jiddu Palmeira. His late wife was half Iraqi, half Kurdish and a Roman Catholic. Jiddu himself was an Indian Catholic. Out of this mix came Jasmine – who has an English mother.

'Seated beside Jiddu, opposite Jasmine, is Abdullah El-Tarek, a Sunni veterinary surgeon. His wife was a Shia. The little girl next to Jasmine is Leah, Vivienne Solomon's cousin.

'The beauty on the right is Peri, a Kurd – the Warlord's daughter. Next to her, is Leah's father Samuel Solomon. As you know, the Solomon family was Jewish. All of them, in their own way, represented what Iraq was. A unity of many people.'

Sighing heavily, the judge turned the photograph over. On the back Stollen had written, *Jiddu and friends, Baghdad race course, 1965.*

The trial of Ghazi El-Tarek collapsed on the Monday after Nico Stollen's funeral. The police considered charging Bobby

Lomax and Vivienne Solomon QC with wasting their time – as a sitting MP, Jim Richards could not be prosecuted. In view of the 'mitigating circumstances', they did not pursue the case. Customs and Excise came to the same conclusion.

Jasmine Fitzwilliams' delight at Ghazi's acquittal did not stop her from again calling for an inquiry into her husband's last hours. Following consultation with the police, the authorities refused. The judge met her in his chambers to tell her of their decision.

'Everybody, my dear, believes General Stollen to have been responsible for whatever happened to Secretary of State Fitzwilliams. HMG considers it best to leave things there . . .'

'Andrew was ASSASINATED!'

His Worship looked embarrassed. Staring at a spot above Jasmine's head, he continued, '. . . Perhaps I should also say, HMG has asked me to advise you that anything pertaining to the matter falls within the scope of the Official Secrets Act.'

Jasmine Fitzwilliams had been gagged.

2002

CHAPTER THIRTY EIGHT
✳ ❈ ✳

Suzie Palmeira sat alone with her thoughts in her drawing-room. At seventy, her white waved hair cut to perfection, she remained a head-turner. It was eight years since Ghazi's prosecution: He had quickly resumed the hurly-burly of his life again. Her only grandchild, Philippa – Jasmine and Jim Richards' daughter – was now ten years old.

Jasmine had gone to collect the girl from school. Suzie smiled. She knew that on the way home, mother and daughter would stop off at the vet. Suzie's latest cat had had a minor operation and on the return car journey required the soothing ministrations of a doting school-girl.

The family court had given Suzie custody of Philippa, in the full knowledge she would allow both parents, as well as the paternal grandparents, just and equal access. Suzie had been the one to register the baby's birth.

Under the mother's details, she had written 'Jasmine Palmeira', airbrushing the Fitzwilliams surname. She had noted Jim Richards as the father with his proud and happy consent. It being a private matter, she had also arranged for a court order preventing the press from identifying him.

Today, the man Suzie regarded as her son-in-law in all but name, was one of Parliament's most distinguished servants: With the agreement of all sides, the House of Commons had refused to accept Jim Richards' resignation in 1992. He had been re-elected in the 1992 general election and doubled his majority in 1997 when his own party, New Labour, swept to power.

The clock in the hallway chimed the quarter hour. Suzie sighed. The guest whom she was expecting – the *Times of India*'s London correspondent – had already telephoned twice to apologise for running late. He was stuck in traffic.

She had been quick to reassure him not to worry. It would be some time before Jasmine and her grand-daughter arrived home. He could still be in and out without bumping into them on the doorstep.

Whiling away the time, she reached for Stollen's textbook *Children & Spies*, published posthumously the previous week. Having gone to the top of Amazon Books within days of publication, it had caused quite a stir. Leafing through it in a desultory manner, she mused that her visitor's lateness came as an inadvertent relief. Undermining her daughter – which was what their meeting was about – was not a circumstance to which Suzie looked forward.

As a counter to Jasmine, she had met the journalist for the first time at Grand Lodge the previous day. Here, she had showed him the model of the tortoise decorating Stollen's book jacket. Now, she had invited him to select a few photographs of Jasmine enjoying herself.

It was the best she could come up with to weaken the latter's case – finally accepting she would be consistently thwarted, Jasmine had short-circuited the status quo by seemingly changing her agenda and championing another: The need for a public inquiry into the involvement of children in espionage.

This, she hoped, would unravel into the Fitzwilliams affair. Miro and Jim Richards MP had alerted Suzie to the fact the intelligence services oversight committee could not hold off her daughter for much longer.

It was essential, they said, for Suzie to act. Accepting the inevitable, and unbeknown to Jasmine, she had consented to the publication of Stollen's book. In addition, she had agreed to speak to the press. Finally – and only just in time – Downing Street had announced that Miro and Jim Richards MP would chair a Special Hearing on *Children & Spies*.

Jasmine had been dismayed. Bursting into her mother's bedroom the night before, she had demanded, 'Why are you doing this?'

Cautioning her to lower her voice so as not to waken Philippa, Suzie had made no reply. Instead, she had glanced at a black and white image by her bedside. It was one of her most treasured possessions – a picture of herself with Jasmine's father in the 1960s. Philippe, handsome, dark, foreign, in white tails. Suzie, a pretty English girl in a chiffon ballgown.

Lifting it from the table beside her, she stared at the portrait, a single tear rolling down her cheek. Bowing her head, she traced the outline of Philippe's face with her finger. Only he could know the depth of her anguish.

Everything for which Suzie had striven was beginning to unravel. She could not understand why Jasmine persisted in her desire to achieve justice for Fitzwilliams, when she had been blessed with a happy, healthy child whose future had no connection with him. Suzie ached for her daughter and the years she had lost.

Her only comfort was that Philippe was dead. Jasmine's marriage had turned everything he stood for on its head. He had not known how to save her.

Seeing her mother so distressed, Jasmine's face softened. Now aged forty-five, she was taller than Suzie and had Philippe's black hair and brown eyes. Her expression took Suzie's breath away. She looked so much like her father.

Patting the counterpane, she motioned her to sit down. Requiring no further invitation, Jasmine slipped on to the bed, tucking her legs beneath her. Together, the two women studied the photo.

'It was taken at the "Spies Party" your father and I gave for Peter Ligne in Baghdad in 1965 – the night you met Andrew. The photographer caught Daddy and me at the beginning of the evening. We were so happy. The world was different then,' Suzie murmured.

She touched her daughter's hair. How Philippe would have loved to see her as a mother herself. He had missed so much: Jasmine's delight in Philippa; the joy of watching a grandchild stroke a marmalade kitten now grown into a matronly cat.

Suzie sighed. Not a day went by when she did not miss Philippe and the life they had shared. For all its tragedy, it was the dancing she remembered most. Long ago, she and her husband had kicked up their heels to the beat of the Tango on the banks of the Tigris.

Sometimes, the music had been provided by the Masonic orchestra. As often, it had wafted along the river passed the back gardens of other peoples' lives. Suzie could still hear the melodies.

'I would like to take Philippa to Iraq one day – when these unforgivable sanctions have been lifted,' she remarked.

Jasmine raised her mother's fingers to her lips. 'There are so many other wonderful places you can take her, Mummy. Does it have to be Iraq?'

'Of course, darling. How else will she understand you?'

Jasmine laughed. Kissing Suzie goodnight, she commented, 'In which case, I hope you get your wish, old thing. Sadly, the news from Baghdad seems pretty bleak. Some are even saying the British and Americans could invade.'

'Of course they won't, darling,' Suzie reassured, switching off the bedside light. 'The Iraqis are desperate for change but the British and Americans know this is not the way. We would never jeopardise so many lives.'

CHAPTER THIRTY NINE
❈ ❈ ❈

It was a beautiful day. Suzie would much rather be outside. However, playing for high stakes, she displayed no impatience. The government had announced that its Special Hearing into *Children & Spies* would begin the following morning. In the meantime, she had invited those closest to the case, home for afternoon tea.

Philippa was away, staying with her paternal grandparents. Jasmine was polite but distant. Vivienne Solomon – who arrived early – did all she could to pretend not to notice the tension between mother and daughter.

As Jasmine hovered outside the large, arched doors of Suzie's drawing-room, a prosperous looking Bobby Lomax slipped in. Greeting her and Suzie with affection, he went swiftly to Vivienne. Somewhat to her surprise, she had ceased to be a convenience to him.

Instead, she and Bobby continued to live sweetly together. Their relationship was hideously complex. Nonetheless, theirs was a true love story.

Miro and Laure de Chebran's union was of a different type and bore witness to the joy of happiness found late in life. They turned up with Jim Richards MP. Jasmine accepted the politician's presence with the coldness he had long come to expect. From their body language, few would have known they had once shared a bed, far less that their brief coupling had resulted in an adored child.

Suzie, however, welcomed her grand-daughter's father with undisguised pleasure. Ignoring Jasmine's froideur, she motioned Jim Richards to sit beside her. A spy's widow, Laure later recounted to Miro, was always in control of her environment and Suzie was no exception.

Jasmine's eye swept the room. Sunlight flooded in, catching the transparent crystals of its central chandelier. Filtered by the sun, beautiful pinks, blues and greens bounced off the walls. Ignoring Laure de Chebran and Jim Richards, she stared long and hard at Miro. He returned her gaze evenly. His hair, streaked with silver, retained some of its one-time vigour.

'We might as well stop pretending. We all know the Special Hearing tomorrow is designed to prevent discussion of Andrew. He was groomed for politics. In the end, it got him killed,' she said accusingly.

As she spoke, it was as if Suzie froze. Jasmine had a distinct impression of her mother's hand, now petrified in mid-air, reaching towards her, seemingly begging her to leave the past alone.

Jasmine turned away. It was Jim Richards who comforted her parent. For a single moment, he had a vision of Suzie as Philippe Palmeira would have seen his bride. The idea came out of nowhere and vanished as quickly. However, it left him with an instinctive recognition of her life as it once was.

'You have upset your mother, Jasmine,' he rebuked. 'The Fitzwilliams-Ligne affair was about a lucrative industry of fear. It was about negligence, cover-up, fearful intimidation and worse, as well as commercial impropriety. The players, however, are dead. It is best to leave things there.'

'Best? Best for whom?'

'Best for me, darling,' replied Suzie, her eyes filling with tears. Clutched in her hand was the image from her bedside table. Philippe's brilliant smile gazed out. 'Do not destroy my memory of your father.'

Ignoring her, Jasmine snapped. 'I was talking to you, Miro.'

'Indeed you were. However, I am not the Special Hearing's chairman. If you wish to alter its remit, you will have to take the matter up with Jim.'

'Jim did not know Andrew. You did.' Her cool linen dress was slightly creased. A delicate shade of peach, it showed off her exotic skin tone to perfection. 'You hated him.'

Miro did not insult Jasmine's intelligence by denying what she already knew. Instead, he gently pointed out in his soft Scottish burr that many people had disliked her husband, and he had been one of them.

'I saw his potential and admired what he could have been. Accepting Andrew's wickedness, I believed his redemption possible.'

Before they could pursue the matter, Father Anthony arrived with Ghazi El-Tarek.

'We were discussing Andrew's murder, Father . . .'

– Those who knew Jasmine well, could see her hysteria rising –

' . . . You will not have forgotten you refused to marry us.'

Turning to his companion, she continued, 'Last, as usual, Ghazi. A bit like the night Andrew died.'

Ghazi kissed her but made no reply. Suzie, with Vivienne Solomon's assistance, fussed around offering tea and cake. Father Anthony, meanwhile, poured himself a glass of Madeira.

Seeing Jasmine's eyes now upon him, he took out his rosary. Raising his glass, he pronounced, 'Nico Stollen groomed you to marry Andrew Fitzwilliams, my dear. This does not mean your alliance stands scrutiny. I drink to that.'

When it came, the confession of Andrew Fitzwilliams' killer was undramatic. Father Anthony looked composed. Ghazi El-Tarek embarrassed. Suzie anguished.

As for Andrew Fitzwilliams' widow, tears crashed down her face. She could not bring herself to look her mother in the eye. Turning away from her, she murmured, 'You always knew I did it, didn't you?'

Father Anthony was the first to respond. Putting his hand on Jasmine's shoulder, he replied, 'Jiddu always said you were the best little car mechanic in the world.'

Jasmine shuddered. Words tumbled out of her. She spoke at first in halting gulps and then in an incoherent torrent of emotions.

'I loved Andrew and never saw his badness. But I recognised it. Other people's lives meant nothing to him. I knew the parasol he gave me had been lent to Peri – I remember Laure twirling it on the race-course in Baghdad – and that the bracelet I wore on my wedding day was Peri's too. It was as if it burned my skin . . .

'I kept on hoping Andrew would show remorse for what he had done but he never did. This is why I wanted his first marriage annulled – so he could take the Sacraments. I hoped he would confess. If he had, everything would have been different.

'You see, he adored me and I ached for love of him . . . Even as a school-girl I knew him better than anyone else. When he explained at party conference what had happened to Jiddu, the Warlord, Ghazi's father and Uncle Samuel he seemed . . . so innocent. He was innocent. He had no concept of what he had done. How could he when he never had the benefit – as I did – of someone like Jiddu's old friend Hussein to teach him right from wrong?'

Turning to her mother, she continued, 'Daddy always knew what I was planning, didn't he?'

Suzie was beside her in an instant. Wiping away her tears, she soothed, 'You told us yourself, darling. We always understood why the annulment of Andrew's marriage meant so much to you. You said it was your life and you could do what you liked with it. This is why Hussein sent you the tortoise as your wedding gift. To tell you to do nothing. To let the past heal . . .'

Leading Jasmine to the sofa, she continued, ' . . . But of course, there was no healing. When your father met Nico in East Berlin, he begged him to prevent you from destroying yourself. It was like living on a time-bomb.

'Stollen agreed and asked Grand Lodge to help. The freemasons did all they could to prevent you from killing Andrew. They hoped if he was arrested in time . . .'

Jasmine buried her face in her mother's shoulder. 'I would have let the freemasons act if I had had any certainty they would confront Andrew with his real crimes. But this was not what they intended. I do not think they even remembered Jiddu's name or what a lovely person he was. They were making decisions on my behalf solely because Uncle Nico had agreed to abort his plans!

'Had this not been the case, Grand Lodge would have done nothing. How dare its members make this choice? I could have accepted all the happiness Andrew offered and they would have been agreeable. I did not want to be as wicked as him . . .'

Huge sobs shook her body. '. . . Then, after I killed him, I wanted to confess but nobody would let me. The minute the police told me Andrew was dead, I told them what I had done. But the freemasons had got to them first. They denied me the right to declare Andrew's guilt by denying my own.'

Father Anthony sat down beside her. Taking her from Suzie, he commented, 'All the police did was deprive you of your vanity, Jasmine. You wanted the world to see you as you saw yourself.'

She tried to pull away from him but he refused to let her go. 'You have to speak in terms of vanity, Father, because you cannot accept that what I wanted was revenge – for Jiddu and the others. Have you forgotten with whom I played beside the motor-cars while Hussein watched over us? It was Leah.

'She was my friend. But because she was from Iraq and Jewish, she did not mean anything to Andrew. She has no memorial. Nor does Peri. Nobody really cares about the fate of a Muslim girl.

'Andrew had to be punished. Once he was dead, I felt only nothingness. I loved him so much. I only understood the wrong I had done, when I realised retribution does not give identity to the dead.'

'It seldom does. I have always believed God punishes the guilty in a currency they understand. For those of us who are left, we can chose to forgive, although I admit I cannot. Instead, I strive for understanding.'

Shaking herself free, Jasmine searched for Jim Richards. He gazed at her out of candid eyes. 'How can you look at me? I killed Andrew. Moreover, I loved him. I did not love you.'

'I had a choice, and this was freely made,' he replied. He would have liked to add, but did not, the daughter Jasmine had given him was his joy. In his mind, the mother was indivisible from the child.

Father Anthony coughed. 'You should take a look at Stollen's letter, Jasmine. He gave it to Bobby in South Africa.'

She took it from him without a word. Stollen's strong handwriting covered the page. *Wish Laure and Miro joy for me, they are well suited. She will take him shopping and he will pay the bill!*

Jasmine read on. *I have left instructions with my embassy in London to provide the champagne for the Miro-de Chebran wedding breakfast. The ambassador will escort Suzie. He appreciates a beautiful woman. Moreover, he knows the correct way to kiss a lady's hand – a dying art in the new Russia! My country's diplomacy will be all the poorer without it.*

There was much more in the same vein. At the end, Stollen had added a postscript. *By the way, tell Jasmine she is a lousy mechanic! Luckily I was around to complete the job she started.*

Jasmine stared. She studied Stollen's words again and again. Uncertain as to their meaning, she looked around the room.

Taking the letter from her, Father Anthony explained, 'You did not kill Andrew Fitzwilliams, my dear. You tried, there is no doubt about that. But you failed. Stollen killed him.'

As Jasmine crumpled into Jim Richards' arms, the priest looked across at Suzie. Stollen did not always tell the truth. They both knew that.

Suzie bowed her head. Only a mother recognises the burden of guilt a spy's child carries. Betrayal is an uneasy upbringing.

'God bless Stollen, for the gift of a daughter,' she whispered.

She was wearing a soft lilac dress, not unlike the one she had worn when she danced with Philippe on the veranda of their home on the Tigris. The house where Jasmine had met Fitzwilliams, Jiddu had hated Ligne, and Philippe nonetheless had been recruited into the service of the Crown. Where Leah Solomon and her sisters had whirled to the sound of the bagpipes, Abdullah El-Tarek had danced with Ghazi's mother, and Peri the Warlord's daughter had entranced Miro.

Father Anthony sighed. So many were betrayed. All the joyous communities of Iraq smashed by the greed, corruption, ignorance and inhumanity of guilty men.

Out of the corner of his eye, he saw Jim Richards lead Jasmine into the garden. Sometimes, he mused, the reward for constancy was love. Perhaps the same could one day be true of the politician.

Meantime, Laure and Miro carried the empty tea plates into the kitchen. The others, declining to stay on, got ready to leave. Helping Vivienne with her coat, Ghazi remarked, 'Suzie made the mistake of forgetting Jasmine's twin identities.'

Hearing him, Suzie was visibly hurt. 'I always recognised Jasmine's Eastern blood!' she corrected.

Ghazi smiled. 'It is Jasmine's English blood you overlooked. Her belief justice must be done, comes from you. She is a daughter of England. She always was.'

Father Anthony chuckled. It was not often that Suzie was

caught out. Taking her hand, he led her away. Her guests were intimates. They could see themselves out.

Returning to the drawing-room, he heard Laure instructing Miro, 'Enough Dubonnet to add colour, chérie. The rest gin.'

It was the cocktail hour.

Alone with Bobby and Vivienne, Ghazi looked at his former defence counsel out of shrewd eyes. 'Did Stollen write *Children & Spies* because he believed Jasmine would indeed one day stand trial for Fitzwilliams' murder?'

'He asked about her legal position, certainly.'

'He was worried she would be convicted?'

All the goodness of Samuel Solomon's soul shone out of his niece's eyes. 'He fretted the police would not believe his written confession. Therefore, he prepared the manual. As a result, and if the worse came to the worse and Jasmine was charged, he hoped I could argue he had manipulated her from childhood.'

'Did he really write *Children & Spies* in the 1960s?'

Vivienne laughed. 'He wrote it – in English – in a couple of hours in Bobby's hotel room in South Africa in 1992. At Stollen's request, Bobby sent it to Congresswoman Betsy Meredith for whom he retained an abiding respect. He asked her to keep it safe for Jasmine.'

'And what if Jasmine hadn't needed it?'

Vivienne shrugged. 'Stollen still wanted *Children & Spies* published. He hoped to prevent other intelligence officers from grooming young people for espionage. Unlike Sir Peter Ligne, he accepted a child had to be allowed to find its own identity.'

'Do the Soviets know the book is a fraud?'

'Of course.'

'The British and Americans?'

'Certainly. Chivalry has no nationality.'

The Special Hearing concluded the day after it opened. In a private note to the Prime Minister, Lord Miro wrote: *Suzie Palmeira wishes me to pass on her thanks to your civil servants for the assistance they have given. Similarly, she asks that her gratitude be conveyed to their Russian colleagues. She has been overwhelmed by the humanity of all in this private affair.*

. . . With the active encouragement of British and Russian officials, the profits from General Stollen's textbook Children & Spies *will be donated to charities caring for young victims of armed conflict. Father Anthony, who has returned to his home in America, has agreed to oversee this from Boston.*

. . . Meantime, soundings have been taken from government law officers. They are of the opinion further investigation into Andrew Fitzwilliams' death would not be in the public interest. It is accepted the Secretary of State was murdered.

Reporting restrictions remained in place.